DEMONS AND DISORDER

CHRONICLES OF THE DAWNBLADE BOOK 6

ANDREW CLAYDON

ANDREW CLAYDON

Demons and Disorder

By Andrew Claydon

Just because you're chosen, doesn't mean you want to be.

A city built for peace is on the edge of chaos.
A murderer stalks the streets of Babylon, and with each kill, the civil unrest rises. How long will it be until the tipping point is reached and violence erupts in the streets?
Is there any hope for the poor citizens of this once-great city?
Perhaps.
Because true to form, Nicolas Percival Carnegie and his companions are about to walk right through the city gates and into a world of trouble. Tracking the demon Koth and Nicolas's kidnapped people, the group quickly find themselves deputised by the City Watch to aid in the hunt for this elusive killer.
Dodging demons, assassins, and the usual general villainy he somehow gravitates towards—or vice versa—Nicolas must restore order to this beleaguered city before it's too late.
A daunting task for someone who can barely keep his own life in order.

Dedicated to Izzy, who has *sassy queen* down to a fine art.
And to Beba Andric...super fan extraordinaire.

And, of course, to everyone who loves a good adventure.

'The city of Babylon is a fascinating place. A true mixture of architecture and culture, with each street giving some new wonder for tourists to enjoy. Built on a noble precept, the fostering of peace and understanding between the many and varied races of Etherius, it still boggles this author's mind that there are those who decry it to this day. Apparently – if you follow their dubious logic – creating a city to demonstrate the principle that 'look, we can all get along' is naïve, dangerous and doomed to failure. To them I would say this one thing...go there. If you do not come away from your visit understanding what an amazing world Etherius is, then perhaps you, good sirs, are part of the problem.'

Etherius, A Travellers Guide – Dieter Von Ostric

Yarringsburg
Nalbina
Ivilar
Narus
Sarus
Babylon

CHAPTER 1

S hift wrinkled their nose in distaste. 'Auron, where in the Underworld have you brought us?'

'Exactly where I said I was going to,' the spirit replied curtly.

Ahead of them, sat in the middle of a swamp from which steam rose, creating a haze in the air, was a shack. The building had an ominous quality to it that had been carefully, and purposefully, cultivated. The single path leading to it was lined with ferns that had gone brown with neglect. Braziers placed at regular intervals down the track burned with small fires, the smoke making the path itself look misty. Though *eerie* was probably a better term for it. Last, but by no means least, were the pair of statues standing silent guard on either side of the beginning of the path. Their faces, chiselled into demonic visages, made Nicolas shudder. His last encounter with a demon had not gone well.

And yet, somehow, I'm here seeking a second one.

'So this is the place then?' he asked, more for reassurance than anything else. Nicolas tried to ignore the niggling urge to turn in the opposite direction, start walking, and not stop.

There isn't any walking away now...if there ever was.

'This is the place.' There was a clear unease in Auron, and it had built the closer they'd gotten. Drifting smoke from the path, carried by a gentle night-time breeze, mingled with the spirit's aura, expanding it in a way that was just plain creepy.

'This is *exactly* where a witch would live,' Garaz snarled as he glared at the shack, eliciting a sigh from Shift. Their journey here had been marked by Garaz being extremely vocal regarding his displeasure about coming here, and his dislike of witches in general.

At least he's talking again.

'Off you go then,' Shift said, gesturing ahead. 'The shack's right there. Don't tell me you're unnerved by a bit of smoke and some dead plants?'

Not as much as the statues.

Their fanged faces didn't exactly scream *welcome*. In fact, they screamed *die*. But, again, he did have to go in.

Does it have to be first, though?

He looked into his companion's green eyes and gave a forced smile. 'I don't suppose you'd care to lead the way?'

Shift sucked their teeth and glanced at the path. 'This is your quest. I think it's only right you go first.'

Thought so.

'This is ridiculous.' Garaz sighed. 'It is just a pathway. We will walk down it and knock on the door. Then a low, craven witch will answer and we will try to have an intelligent conversation with it.'

'Why do you not move then?' Silva asked flatly, at the orc's side. If it had been anyone else asking the question, Nicolas was sure they would've been smirking. Sometimes, he didn't think Silva was capable of showing emotion. Although, occasionally, something would slip out.

The large orc looked affronted, making an odd guffawing sound. Yet he didn't move.

'Perhaps,' Auron began slowly, 'I didn't think this through in its entirety.'

'What?' Nicolas couldn't control the annoyance in his voice, which was understandable, given the circumstances.

The group were tracking down the people of Hablock, taken by the Maestro's forces. Their previous leads—Alric Tavish, Oleg Hobranth and the faun Fo—were all dead.

May Sha'then have a thoroughly enjoyable time with all three of them.

Right now, their best bet would be to track down the aforementioned dark lord's—or whatever he was—servant, the demon Koth, which was something Auron had assured them could be done here. Once they found the creature, they could defeat it—somehow—and save his people whilst avenging his...

Nicolas closed his eyes for a moment, ensuring that he could still remember his parents' faces. Ever since the news of their deaths, he constantly tested his memory, to ensure they would never fade.

If Fo was even telling the truth.

Right now, he couldn't second-guess it. With the others' help, he was handling his grief as best he could. But he needed to focus on those he could still save, not dwell on those he'd lost.

'You said there was a witch here who could help us track down Koth,' he said quietly but firmly, already annoyed that Auron had refused to answer follow-up questions about this *witch* of his when asked. 'It took us days to get here, and now you aren't so sure? Were you wrong?'

That got the right reaction: Auron visibly bristling. If he knew anything about the spirit, it was that he didn't like having his honour challenged.

The hero cradled his reputation like a mother lovingly holding her new-born baby. If he knew anything about Auron, it was that he liked a good story.

With a deep breath—that had no actual breath because Auron was dead—the spirit visibly calmed and grinned at him broadly.

I did not *ask for a story.*

'So this one time,' Auron began with smug gusto, 'I was tracking a local warlord. I say *warlord* only because that's how he self-referred. He had ten guys, if that.' The spirit shook his head and chuckled. 'I've fought bigger gangs of highwaymen. Anyway, I hear he's planning to raid a village and I work out his most likely line of approach is through this rocky canyon. I set myself in ambush, ready to strike like a coiled snake.' Auron's dramatic pose suddenly relaxed. 'Unfortunately, that was exactly the moment the flesh-eating goblins that lived in the cave I was hiding in front of felt peckish and came out to play. From there, things got...tricky.'

'Your point?' Nicolas asked flatly.

Auron shrugged. 'Not every idea I have is a good one.'

Oh. Perhaps he isn't as precious about his honour as I thought.

'We both know you're stalling,' Nicolas replied. 'So answer me this: Is this place the best chance for us to track down Koth?'

What followed was the long silence of someone who really didn't want to answer a question.

'Yes,' Auron said finally. And a little petulantly.

'Great.' Taking a deep breath, Nicolas began to stride toward the arch, keeping his eyes froward and off the monstrous statues with the vehemency of someone walking past a pair of gorgons.

'Hold up.' The urgency in Auron's voice made him stop.

'What?'

Nicolas didn't think he'd ever seen Auron look sheepish before. 'So, this place belongs to a witch, I told you that much.' Exactly that much, and not a single piece of information more, no matter how anyone had pressed. 'But she's very...temperamental. I just want to make sure we consider *every* possibility before we go in.'

'Before *you* go in,' Garaz corrected gruffly. 'As I have stated before, I shall not set foot inside such a craven creature's lair.'

Oh, for Deities' sake. Again?

Judging by Silva's eyeroll, the warrior was mentally recounting the number of times the orc had said that in the past week too.

'I don't get the issue,' Nicolas asked. 'Witches and wizards are basically the same, right?'

It was as if Nicolas could physically see Garaz's high horse ride up and the orc mount it. His green-skinned companion was literally shaking with outrage, making a cluster of *humph* noises before he finally found some words. 'They most certainly are *not*,' Garaz said with vigor. 'Wizards, both male, female, and other, are venerable and wise users of magic. Witches are craven little folk, who live in places like *that* and use magic as if plying a trade. Do *not* put us in the same category with them. *Ever.*'

Here we go again.

First Auron didn't like being called a ghost because it was too common, and now Garaz was refusing to be put in the same sentence as the word *witch.*

'I'm sorry,' Nicolas said. 'I didn't realise the term was offensive to you. I always thought they were the same, but I was wrong.'

Garaz seemed to calm a little to this, or at least he stopped *humph*-ing. Somehow, it was nice to see him outraged again. Since the death of his brother Shagraz, the orc hadn't been the same, but he finally appeared to be coming out the other side of his grief. That was something Nicolas was working hard on himself. Some days he was more successful than others.

'I suppose it depends *witch* way you look at it,' Shift quipped, earning a glare from Garaz.

'Are we going in, or are we going to stand here inhaling these fumes all night?' Silva asked testily.

Auron had insisted they come at night. Apparently, this was the only time the place was open. At least the fires were keeping the chill at bay. Though Nicolas did yearn for a nice comfy bed. The group were camping out again. There was a tavern nearby, but after a journey up Yarringsburg's famed Ale Trail, the group didn't want to see another tavern again for a long time. They'd been well and truly burned on that experience...and poisoned, and punched, and stabbed.

'I, for one, would like to go in,' Nicolas offered.

'Now, kid,' Auron interjected. 'This one time—'

'You're still stalling,' Nicolas cut in. 'And I'm going.'

It was where the answers were, after all. Wishing he felt as confident as he was trying to seem, he continued toward the archway, until a flicker of something caught his eye, and he stopped dead.

Those statues did not just move.

Nervously, he eyed them. Each had a leering demonic face that seemed to be looking right at him. He shook his head. Of course they hadn't moved. Ridiculous. He took another step forward—

—and immediately jumped back. That time, they'd definitely moved.

His sword was in his hand even before the things stood, rising to a very imposing height with a grinding of rock, small pebbles falling from their bodies.

'*Auron of Tellmark shall not pass,*' they said as one, their eyes glowing yellow.

Nicolas looked around at the even-more-sheepish spirit. 'What did you do?'

Auron's mouth opened and closed several times before he shrugged. Nicolas was pretty sure he could guess if he tried, but he didn't care to.

'A better question: how do they know Auron is even here?' Garaz said, keeping his eyes firmly on the monsters.

The best question: how do we get past them?

CHAPTER 2

S tone ground as the monsters both stepped toward each other, using their literally rock-hard bodies to completely block the entrance they were guarding. Nicolas was suddenly very aware of how ahead of the others he was. And the fact that he was going to have to try and get past these things, no matter what.

Bugger.

In the vain hope that diplomacy was the answer, he lowered his sword—dropping it would be lunacy—and cleared his throat. 'Um...hello. My name is Nicolas Percival Carnegie, and I was hoping to go in...there.' Talking to statues was...a little odd, sure, but still less strange than talking to a chicken. 'If Auron stays out, may the rest of us enter? Please?'

The statues regarded him silently. For a moment, he thought they might've gone dormant again, but then they answered as one, in deep, rumbling voices. '*Auron of Tellmark shall not pass. Companions of Auron of Tellmark shall not pass.*'

'When you said the witch was *temperamental,* I think you may've understated it slightly,' Shift said behind him. 'What you meant was that you pissed her off enough that she'd have attack statues to keep you away from her.'

'I didn't do anything,' Auron snapped. 'Besides, I don't like to live in the past.'

'Oh, you most certainly do,' Shift disagreed with vehemence.

Nicolas stared at the slight gap between the two monsters' legs. He could just make out the shadow of the shack, the place where the answers lay.

I didn't come all this way to leave at the first sign of trouble. Even if it is a bloody huge sign.

Hoping to avoid fighting the statues if at all possible,—Nicolas decided to take one last stab at diplomacy. 'You see, we need to get in to see the witch. Our business is urgent and...and...'

As the statues stepped forward, Nicolas took and involuntary step back. Their arms came up from their sides and stone grated as their fingers flexed. A fight was getting more imminent by the second.

'Auron of Tellmark shall not pass. Companions of Auron of Tellmark shall not pass.'

'Yes, you said,' he muttered, backing away as the pair advanced. Apparently, it was no longer enough just to block the entrance. Now, the monsters had to chase them away completely. Or maybe kill them.

Nicolas looked at his sword, the *Dawnblade*, then up at the creatures.

How do I get past these things?

'Auron of Tellmark shall—'

'Shut up,' Nicolas interrupted, before sighing and returning to his companions, all of whom had their weapons ready. Raising his eyebrows, he looked at Auron. 'Any sage wisdom?'

The spirit pursed his lips as he stared at the statues, who'd halted their advance. It seemed Nicolas's backing away had given the impression that they would all just leave now. The statues had that very wrong. They weren't going anywhere, except into that shack.

Which had better be worth it.

'Generally,' Auron began, 'things like this have some sort of animation charm. It'll be in a hard-to-reach place, maybe concealed. Find it and remove it. Then those things are just rocks.'

As simple as that, eh?

Staring at the statues, he narrowed his eyes, trying to think of the most difficult place to put a charm.

Maybe on the upper back?

'Okay,' Nicolas said with a firm nod. 'Garaz and Silva, keep the statues occupied. Shift and I will circle them and try to get at the charms and take them off.' Frowning, Nicolas turned to look at his companions. They were all staring at him strangely. 'Because I think the charms will be on their backs,' he clarified.

'We aren't looking at you because of that,' Shift said with a half-smile.

'Why then?'

'It's a good plan.' Auron grinned. 'Nice and easy.'

Nothing about fighting two giant stone monsters screamed *easy*. In fact, the creatures looked anything but. Yet if Nicolas had learnt anything in his short adventuring career, it was that needs must.

And I'm going in that bloody shack. Rock monsters or no rock monsters.

'Off we go then,' he muttered in the exact tone an inspiring leader wouldn't use.

Taking a deep breath, he split to the left, circling the monsters, as Shift did the same on the right, and Garaz and Silva whooped and hollered to keep their attention. At first it didn't work, the statues beginning to turn toward Nicolas and Shift. Then Garaz and Silva began throwing rocks, charging forwards then retreating again when the monsters attacked.

Still, just because the creatures were made of stone didn't make them stupid. Though the others were doing a good job of keeping them occupied, the monsters still lashed out with long stone arms when Nicolas and Shift got too close. Jumping back, Nicolas watched in agonizingly slow motion as a boulder sized fist passed by his face close enough that he could see every minor indentation in the stone. The gust of wind resulting from the swipe tussled his hair.

How are big rock monsters so damned fahhhhh...

Jumping aside, the same fist that had nearly taken his head off crunched into the ground where he'd been stood, causing tremors which reverberated out from the fierce impact. As the stone monster pulled it's fist out of the hole it had made in the earth, pieces of mud and grass clung to it's gritty knuckles. It could've quite easily been Nicolas's blood and innards.

'Garaz, you're supposed to keep them busy,' he shouted as the monster pulled his arm back and swung, forcing Nicolas to throw himself to the floor.

'We are doing our best,' the orc shouted back as two fireballs struck the stone creature on the side of its shoulder. The statue didn't appear to give the slightest of shits.

'Garaz, go for the eyes.' The way Auron was walking around with his hands behind his back like some tourist when the others were fighting for their lives—because of him—was pretty damned frustrating.

Stepping back, the orc circled his staff in front of him, chanting. Soon a large fireball had formed. Thrusting his staff forward, he launched it at the nearest monster's head. It struck the beast between the eyes, exploding in a flash of yellows and oranges, just as its hand was about to scoop Nicolas from the ground and crush him to death. Breathing a heartfelt sigh of relief, he watched the hand retract as the creature stumbled backwards a few steps, the ground shaking slightly with each movement.

Get up Nicolas.

Pushing himself off of the ground, he stopped in surprise as he saw a familiar hand being offered to help him up. 'Don't you have your own statue to deal with?'

Shift gave a single snort. 'Nick, getting to hard-to-reach places to steal things is my specialty.'

He followed their nodding head to the inert pile of rocks by the statue he'd been attempting to take down.

'Close your mouth. It ruins your handsomeness,' Shift said with a wink, punctuating their victory by throwing the small charm they held in their other hand into the air and catching it.

How did they do…? Wait. Handsome?

His companion took his hand, which he'd left hovering near theirs, and hauled him up. Suddenly, they were nearly nose to nose.

'Would you like me to take care of the other one for you?' Shift asked with a tantalising glint in their green eyes.

'No, I can do it.' He gave them a half-smile. 'I can't let you destroy them both. I'll never hear the end of it.'

'But you like it when I have an excuse to talk to you.' The tantalising glint became a mischievous one.

I certainly do.

'Any time this evening,' Silva shouted as she dodged a swipe from a giant rock hand.

'Oh, sorry,' he called sheepishly. 'Garaz, can you—'

'I already am,' the orc interrupted, sending a second large fireball right at the remaining creature's eyes. The effect was the same, and this time Nicolas used the opportunity.

Running behind the monster, he mounted the statue's leg. Of course, it vehemently tried to shake him off, leading to some extreme nausea, but it couldn't concentrate on him alone when his other companions were doing their best to get its attention. As the others baited the creature, he scrambled up it's hips and onto it's back. The monster let out an annoyed roar which caused him to wince as it stabbed at his ears.

Getting a solid handhold, he instantly spied the glowing yellow orb in the monster's upper back, between what passed for shoulder blades. Climbing up the rough stone hurt his hands, but he was thankful it wasn't smooth, or there would be no handholds and he would slip right off of the thing. Moving as quickly as he could, he ducked and dodged as the monster tried to grab him and fling him off. Fortunately, Nicolas was in that hard-to-reach area where itches normally appeared just to piss you off.

Securing his arm around the monster's neck as it flailed violently, he drew a knife from his belt and set to work digging the gem—or whatever it was—out. Frantically, he chipped away at the annoying glowing stone that was making it try to kill them, until it finally came loose and fell from the creature's back.

Aarrrrgggghhh.

The mini mountain he was perched on became an avalanche of rocks tumbling to the ground, and he kicked himself clear, managing to land on the grass and not a pile of stones. Rolling slightly until he came to a halt looking up at the starlit sky and take count of all the bumps and bruises that were nagging for his attention right now.

Aarrgggghhhh.

His eyes caught movement—the monster's head tumbling toward him. Quickly, he splayed his legs, and with a heavy *whump,* the head hit the floor, inches from his groin. His lip trembled for a moment as he visualized what could have just happened, then he let out a very justified sigh of relief.

'That was close.' Shift smirked, offering him a hand again. 'But at least we're even. One monster apiece.'

'You'll have to find something else to tease me about,' he said as he let them pull him up, his voice slightly shaky from the near-miss.

The smirk deepened. 'That won't take long.'

'Well done, folks,' Auron said, nodding at the defeated stone monsters.

'Shut up,' Nicolas snapped. 'That was your fault.'

'Hey, I should be getting sympathy after that stone giant bullshit,' Auron remarked, staring at the rubble and shaking his head. 'I can't believe she would think they were enough to keep *me* out. I'm offended.'

'Maybe she didn't,' Silva said. 'Who knows what else could be waiting for us?'

As one, the group shared a look of trepidation. She made a very good point.

Only one way to find out.

This wasn't getting any saner while they waited, so Nicolas led the way up the path. Coming to a halt just before the steps leading to the deck surrounding the shack, he studied every detail, hoping to discern a possible trap before it was sprung. All he could see, though, were strings hanging from the porch with what appeared to be odd-looking stones attached to them.

Maybe they're potatoes?

'Look at that.' He narrowed his eyes. 'They have faces painted on them.'

Reaching up, he held one. It turned out the faces weren't painted on. They'd been crafted somehow, and in impressive detail. It even had lips that opened.

'Those are shrunken heads,' Garaz noted dryly.

With a yelp, Nicolas let go of the head, rubbing his hand furiously on his jacket as it swung lazily before him. Maybe this wasn't such a good idea, after all? 'Perhaps we should—'

His choice was taken away when Silva knocked heavily on the door three times.

'We can sneak off before she answers,' Shift said, noting his concerned look.

Knock on a witch's door and flee before she answered?

Yeah, that'd end well.

Again, his choice was taken away from him. Behind the door, heavy-sounding locks were drawn back, before it was pulled open with a creak that seemed to last an eternity. He winced as the high-pitched noise assaulted his ear drums.

A figure emerged from within with a masterful flourish of her cloak. 'Noble travellers, welcome to Xedora's Emporium of Magic and Wonder,' she declared. 'Here, you shall find answers to the mysteries of the universe. You will unlock potential you never knew you had. You will... Oh. It's *you*.' Her whole demeanour changed as she set eyes on Auron. The friendly expression vanished as her lips curled in disgust. 'You made it past the statues then? What in the Underworld do *you* want?'

Nicolas could already feel his head shrinking.

CHAPTER 3

Nicolas had expected hostility, but he hadn't expected the second-hand awkwardness that gripped him as the ebony-skinned witch glared at Auron with disdain.

'Hello, Xedora,' Auron said sheepishly. 'You can see me then?'

'More's the pity,' the witch replied, before pointing an accusing finger at the spirit. 'And do not try your dubious charms on me. Dead or not, they shall not work.'

Auron pursed his lips in annoyance. 'As if I would with *you*.'

Xedora closed her cloak around her in very much the same way Garaz did when he was in the presence of something distasteful—just as the orc was doing right now, as a matter of fact. The gold trinkets adorning the edges of her purple-trimmed cloak tinkled as she did.

Now, Nicolas would be the first to admit he wasn't very worldly—if he managed to say it before Shift did—but this wasn't what he'd been expecting of a witch. The popular image was usually some withered old hag with black stumpy teeth, more than a couple of warts, and a penchant for cursing people and eating children. Not the proud-looking woman standing before them. Her large bushy hair was interspersed with streaks of white. Her cloak looked to be made of a finer material than anything he was ever likely to wear. Her teeth – bared in a snarl – were strong and white.

Ideal for eating children maybe? Garaz said witches do that, amongst all the other accusations he threw around on the way here.

'Hello, I'm Nicolas Percival Carnegie,' he found himself saying, partly to break the tension and partly so they could get this over with and leave. 'We've travelled a long way to get here because Auron said that you, being a powerful witch, could hel—'

'*Witch?*' Xedora scoffed as Nicolas internally shrank back from the dark eyes that regarded him from beneath a furrowed brow. 'Is that what *he* told you I was?'

What's the right answer here?

'Umm...'

'Never mind,' Xedora said with a dismissive wave of her hand. 'Of course that's what he said.' A cold gaze was turned on Auron. 'When he isn't boasting, he's missing the obvious, such as the fact that I am not a witch. Also the fact that when someone's enchanted statues deny you entry, you should not go knocking on that person's door.' Xedora stopped suddenly, frowning, before craning her neck to look past the group. 'How did you get past the statues anyway?'

I don't want to be the one to tell her they're rubble at the bottom of her path.

'They are rubble at the bottom of your path,' Silva said bluntly as Nicolas tensed, waiting to be turned into a frog or something.

Xedora gave Auron a filthy glare, tutting loudly. 'Never mind. I'll rebuild them. Perhaps next time, you will take heed of their commands.'

'Thank you for that, by the way,' the spirit remarked testily. 'Having enchanted statues that attack me on sight? Very nice. Very mature of you.'

The witch—or not—made the same kind of offended noises Garaz did when he was upset. 'Like I need a lesson in maturity from *you*,' she spat back as the chances of them all getting turned into frogs increased.

Maybe I'll have a more peaceful life. Relaxing on a lily pad, eating flie—
Actually, never mind.

'Out of interest, if you aren't a witch, how can you see him?' Trust Shift to poke someone when they were annoyed, though the question appeared genuine.

'Despite what your *companion* told you,' the woman said, 'I am not a witch. I'm a seer. My gaze penetrates the veil of life and death, allowing me to see and converse with the dead.' Her eyes flicked toward Auron. 'A gift I'm currently rueing.'

Nicolas needed to try to take control of this situation. 'Look, I'm sorry if our coming here has upset you—'

'What upsets me,' Xedora cut in, 'is that none of you can take guard statues as a hint. But as you are here...' The seer waved her hand at him impatiently

So you cut me off then gesture for me to continue. Okay then.

Taking a calming breath, he picked up his train of thought. '...but we need assistance, and our companion here told us you would be able to help.'

Xedora folded her arms tersely and looked exactly the way you'd expect someone about to refuse you help to look.

'And you can *pay* for this assistance?' she said finally.

'We can,' Nicolas confirmed.

Xedora held out her fingerless-gloved hand. 'Because you're with *him*, I'll need to see it first.'

'Which window did you jump out of after you bedded her?' Shift whispered.

'Hush,' Auron snapped irritably.

Probably one of the back ones.

Nicolas took a couple of coins from his pouch and held them up. Xedora took one and bit into it. Then she checked it against the light at frustrating length before handing it back. 'Fine,' she relented. 'You can come in.'

'What *did* you do?' Nicolas whispered as they followed her inside.

'Nothing,' Auron hissed back.

Sure. People enchant statues to repel you for no reason at all.

Expecting a sordid shack with a centrepiece of a bubbling cauldron, surrounded by cobwebbed tables, with maybe some fresh skulls used as decorative ornaments, Nicolas was surprised to find the inside of Xedora's shack more like a store. Racks lined the room, the shelves filled with bottles of coloured potions, powders and some very strange-looking ingredients. Tables in the centre of the room were covered with amulets, trinkets and other curios, each neatly tagged and priced.

Of course it wouldn't be like a witch's hut. She isn't a witch.

He needed to keep that at the forefront of his mind, lest he slip up again and annoy his host. Who knew what else Xedora had to unleash upon them?

Speak of avoiding her ire...

'Keep your hands to yourself,' he whispered.

Shift's head bobbed indignantly. 'I think I'm quite capable of refraining from touching you, Nicolas Percival Carnegie.'

Great, now I've flushed.

'I didn't mean that,' he said, quickly catching his stammer before it unleashed itself. 'I meant don't steal anything.'

'I know,' his companion replied dryly. 'But as you insulted me, I get to make you go red-faced, you giant tomato.'

At least we're on good terms again.

After an errant, and apparently accidental, kiss their relationship had been strained. But now things seemed to be warming again, and he couldn't deny that he was happy about it. He just tried not to let it show too much and give Shift the satisfaction. Though judging by how easily they always seemed to read him, it was likely they already knew.

Stopping in the middle of the shop, Xedora stared aggressively at Auron with her arms folded for a moment before she addressed the others. 'I am currently with a customer in the back,' she declared. 'Wait here 'til I'm done.'

With that, the woman disappeared through a beaded curtain at the far end of the room, the beads tinkling gently when disturbed.

There's another room? This place doesn't look that big from the outside.

As soon as Xedora vanished, Nicolas and his companions turned to Auron as one.

'Did you bed her?' Shift asked quietly but angrily, pointing in the direction Xedora had gone.

In life, Auron had been legendary for vanquishing every villain and slaying every monster that crossed his path. Unfortunately, he'd also had a habit of bedding any woman who looked in his general direction.

'What?' The spirit scoffed. 'No.'

'Did you though?' Nicolas asked.

'I said *no*,' Auron protested. 'And you two can stop looking at me like that,' he added, pointing to Garaz and Silva.

'She is angry at you about something,' Silva stated simply. 'You do not enchant statues to attack people over a minor slight.'

Silva knew a thing or two about wanting to attack Auron. She'd been the one to kill him, after all. Though the reason for their deadly feud was still a mystery to Nicolas.

'I didn't do anything,' the spirit protested passionately. 'I swear.'

He was clearly holding something back, but as much as Auron liked to brag about his adventures, when he didn't want to talk, he wasn't going to talk. Best to let the matter lie for now. At least they were in.

Shift shrugged. 'Fine, keep your secrets. I'm going to have a look round.'

'As Nicolas said, keep your hands to yourself,' Garaz cautioned, keeping *his* arms firmly inside his cloak. The orc eyed everything around him with distaste. 'She may claim not to be a witch, but this place has a distinctly *witch* feel to it.'

Does it?

Shift made a big show of keeping their arms high in the air, fingers splayed as they inspected the shelving. As if that would stop them stealing if the mood took them. Silva guarded the door, and Garaz stood beside her like a pouty child at a play. Auron was seemingly content to glare at the beaded curtain, his jaw set in indignation.

Idly, Nicolas perused the shelves himself, a stack of items whose labels read *Dragon's Toenails* catching his eye. They were about the length of his arm and curved. At a glance, they looked like toenails. Making sure no one was looking, he touched one. Its surface was smooth, certainly nail-like.

Are dragons real?

Some said they were once, but there'd been no record of a dragon sighting in over a century—save for a cow-dragon, of course. But that didn't mean they weren't real. The elves had been gone longer, packing up and leaving nearly a thousand years ago. Yet there was clear evidence they'd existed. Many of the cities of Ivilar, the First Kingdom of Man, were apparently elvish cities that had been resettled, or maybe gifted when their previous occupants left.

'Nick, come here.'

He turned, and Shift was waving him over. There was a mischievous glint in their green eyes so this would end with him being the butt of some jest or other, yet he went anyway.

I just can't stay away.

When he reached Shift, his companion presented a bottle of brown powder to him. The glint was getting bigger. Steeling himself, he examined the label.

Xedora's Erectile Enhancement Enchantment
Put the 'Steel' back in your sword!

'I thought this might be a wise purchase for you.'

Damned if he didn't find Shift's self-satisfied smirk adorable.

Just friends.

'It'll take you some serious wooing before you ever find out if I need it,' he replied with a smirk of his own.

Shift nodded approvingly, holding his gaze in a way that made him feel lighter. 'Well, well, Mr Carnegie,' they said with a mock bow. 'It looks like you're getting better at this.'

'Good teachers help,' he remarked glibly.

Settling back into their normal repartee was pleasing. Comfortable. Since he'd come back from the dead, so much of his life had been turned upside down. At least he still had this, even if the phrase *just friends* struck him round the head with a spiked mace every single time he thought it.

Still. Better that than nothing.

As Shift turned to the rest of the contents of the shelf, slightly raised voices caught Nicolas's attention. They were coming from behind the curtain. Despite his every sense telling him not to peek, he found himself inching closer to the beaded curtain. Then he found his hand parting it slowly and silently, just enough that he could, indeed, peek.

Nicolas's eyes widened.

CHAPTER 4

This new room was decorated with thin, hanging silk drapes, making it appear as if the room was surrounded by mist—undoubtedly a purposeful effect. The light was dim, but there was another light source in the middle of the room, one Nicolas was trying very hard not to look at directly. Most of the room was taken up by a large table upon which sat a crystal ball in a holder shaped like a skeletal hand. On one side of the table, Xedora, in a large, almost throne-like chair, steepled her fingers as if in deep thought. Across from the witch...*seer*...was a middle-aged village woman with an expectant look on her face. The third person in the room, and the other source of light, was what bothered Nicolas.

'If she thinks I'm moving on, she's got another thing coming,' the ghost of the disgruntled man snapped. 'I'm still her husband. I don't care if I'm dead.'

Now that Nicolas was paying attention to the ghost—an average-looking fellow with a slightly squat nose—he couldn't pretend he wasn't seeing it. Though he had plenty of experience with the undead, mostly in being attacked by every variation imaginable, this was the first time he'd seen a ghost who wasn't Auron.

Except...that's not true, is it?

During their deadly jaunt down the Ale Trail, where they'd been attacked in, outside, or in the general vicinity of every tavern they'd passed, he'd caught glimpses of what he thought were ghosts a couple of times. He'd put it down to stress, or the faun Ro messing with his mind. Yet there was no denying the gentleman stood clear as day before him. The ghost's aura was reddening, just as Auron's did when anger gripped him.

'And you can tell this bloody whore that I know she's been seeing Dar Atkins,' the ghost ranted. 'How do I know that? Because I've been watching them.'

'And you say your husband's been dead for nearly three years now?' Xedora asked the woman calmly, as if someone wasn't shouting at her.

'Yes,' the woman said. 'He was a good man, but I always told him that drinking and bad night vision was a poor combination. Then he...' She cast her eyes down. Her grief was still clear.

Xedora looked at the ghost and raised an eyebrow.

'Stupid place to leave a cliff,' the man grumbled, before returning to his ranting. 'Do you think I enjoy watching her? I don't want to be here like...*this*. But I can't leave. Why? Because instead of being the chaste widow, she's opening her legs to anyone who gives her a kind word three years on. It's an outrage. And Dar...he ain't good enough, not by a long shot.'

Xedora watched the display dispassionately. When she was satisfied the ghost had finished his diatribe, though it looked to Nicolas that he had plenty more in him, the seer gave the woman a warm smile. 'He says you've mourned long enough. Now it's time to move on. Truly, he just wants you to be happy.'

'I bloody well did *not*,' the ghost snapped.

'He understands that although he is gone, you are not. You still have a life to live,' Xedora continued, unperturbed. 'You have mourned. Do not feel guilty about building a new life for yourself...

'She bloody should,' the ghost grumbled.

'...because it doesn't mean you value the old one any less. It's time to go out and see what life can give you.'

'I saw what Dar bloody Atkins gave her the other night. Do you think I enjoyed watching that?'

'Sometimes moving on is difficult.' Nicolas got the impression Xedora was speaking more to the ghost than the woman now. 'Or to watch others moving on. But when you cling to the past, especially a past with no future, you only cause pain for yourself. You wither and become lesser for it. There is a time to let go and see what the future has in store. Only then will you find peace.'

'But it feels like a betrayal,' the woman said softly. 'I've begun seeing someone. It's new, but I think it could be something. I just—'

The seer held up her hand. 'I know your husband only wants what's best for you. No man will ever be him, but that doesn't mean another can't make you happy.'

The ghost's demeanour changed, his shoulders sagging as the wind went out of his sails. The red in his aura slowly receded until the spectral figure was light again. 'I'm being an ass, aren't I?'

'It's time for you both to move on.' Xedora gave another warm smile. 'There will be no more random pots falling from the shelf or doors slamming, because he understands that you deserve to be happy. You are still alive, so grab that life and make the most of it. But never forget what you had.'

The woman looked around until Xedora pointed her in the direction of her husband. Her eyes were streaked with tears. 'Thank you.' Her voice was hoarse. 'I'll always love you, you big drunken oaf.'

'And I'll always love you, buttercup,' he replied with a half-smile. 'Go be happy.'

The ghost met the Seer's eyes and nodded thankfully, before he transformed to shimmering light, which dissipated with a few twinkles.

I hope the Eternal Forest awaits you.

Nicolas blinked to clear his watering eyes. The woman had her head in a handkerchief, collecting herself. His intuition made his head turn, and Xedora was looking right at him.

Shit.

Quickly, he backed away, letting the curtain shut.

'You all right?' Auron asked, taking his attention away from an amulet on the table and looking him over. 'You've gone pale. Are your eyes watering?'

'No. And I'm fine,' he replied, a little too quickly, judging by Auron's raised eyebrow. 'Just...this is a weird place, isn't it?'

Further questions were cut off by the woman appearing through the beads before leaving the shack.

'Looks like a happy customer,' Shift commented.

'Hopefully,' Nicolas muttered.

A gentle tinkling announced Xedora walking through the curtain again. 'I will see you now.' She was clearly not happy about it.

As the seer disappeared, the companions followed her. Now he was in the room properly, there was an unnameable quality in the air. A sensation of power, but not an overt one. As if it were only on the edges of his perception.

Let's try to get this off on the right foot.

He extended his hand. 'As I said before, I'm Nicolas Pe—'

The seer held up a silencing hand. 'When you're with *him*, I don't care.' Then she looked past him as he retracted his hand. 'Auron of Tellmark.' Xedora scoffed, shaking her head as she sat leisurely back into her chair. 'Trust you to keep hanging around here after you die instead of buggering off to the afterlife.'

'I wasn't given a choice in the matter,' the spirit grumbled, more to himself than anyone else.

'Oh, you want to go?' Xedora smiled coolly. 'Then take care of your unfinished business.'

Auron was starting to get his back up now. 'If I knew what it was—'

'You were murdered, correct?' the seer cut him off snappily. 'Then go find your killer.'

'She's stood there.' The spirit snorted, nodding toward Silva.

The warrior appeared stoic, but Nicolas noted the subtle unease in her bearing.

Xedora's brow furrowed. 'She's travelling *with* you?'

Auron let out a sigh. 'She's trying to redeem herself and—'

'You know what? I don't care,' the seer said with a shake of her head, making her bushy hair bounce in a way that reminded Nicolas of his mother. 'It's the same as always. Auron and drama walking hand-in-hand. I imagine your unfinished business would be more complicated than regular folks' anyway. Deities forbid anything common happens to the mighty *Dawnblade*.'

Auron's aura flashed red. 'You have some nerve, *witch*. You have no right to be angry at me, but I have every right to be mad at you after what you did,' he declared, pointing an angry finger at Xedora.

'Oh, is that what you believe?' the seer scoffed, sitting bolt upright in her chair.

'I didn't do anything,' the spirit enunciated slowly through gritted teeth. *By the Deities.*

'Can we please just get to our business?' Nicolas was trying his best not to shout, but Shift's smirk suggested he was at least raising his voice slightly.

'Mind your tone with me,' Xedora said, her brow darkening. 'I don't know what business you think I can help you with, but if it's anything to with Auron, the erectile enchanter is clearly marked and pri—'

'We need help finding a demon.'

Xedora's wide-open mouth looked almost comical. 'You what?'

CHAPTER 5

S lowly, Xedora closed her mouth. Frowning, the seer opened and closed it again several times, as if trying to find the right words. In the end, she settled on, 'You *what*?'

The fact that the question stunned her into a brief stupor didn't bode well.

Still, if you don't ask, you don't get.

'We're hunting a demon, and we need help tracking it down. We came to you because we were told you were one of the people who could do it,' he elaborated, purposefully leaving Auron's name out of it, now that they'd finally got the seer's attention off whatever issue she had with him.

'That's not a simple, or sane, request to make,' Xedora said slowly. 'One generally doesn't go looking for demons, because one generally wouldn't like what would happen when one found it.'

'The creature we seek stole everyone from Nicolas's village and...' Silva trailed off, thankfully sparing Nicolas having to hear about his parents' fate again, '...much more besides.'

'If it took them, they're already dead.'

Nicolas hadn't even realised he'd slammed his fist on the table until he registered the others' shocked looks. But he was unperturbed. 'They're alive. I mean to find them, and I need your help. Please.'

Xedora appraised him with a long look, before her eyes softened slightly. 'You are a passionate young man with a noble cause. Even if a demon *had* been in our realm, Au— *he* knows they don't manifest here for long. The demon possesses a human host and burns the body out within a few days, forcing them to return to their dark home.' The seer paused before she spoke next, likely knowing how he'd react to her words. 'The creature you seek is likely long gone.'

'This one may be different,' Auron said. 'What the kid described was...unusual.'

'This wasn't some puppet,' Nicolas said solemnly, trying to ignore the pain in his palm as his fists clenched at the memory of Koth. 'This was almost a melding of man and demon. The demon mutated the host and turned it into something worse. They were one.'

Nicolas couldn't help but briefly wonder who the poor soul Koth inhabited had once been. Were they still in there, doomed to watch as the demon used their body for evil? He had been possessed one – thankfully brief – time, and he hadn't cared for it.

'You saw this?' Xedora asked Auron, her mouth down turning the instant she looked at the spirit.

'No.' Auron's honesty was annoying, but what came next was almost endearing. 'The kid isn't worldly, and prone to bouts of massive overexaggeration, but not about this. I believe he saw what he saw. And it took his people. Men, women and children. Please help him.'

'I understand the stakes,' the seer retorted harshly. 'I just do not think this demon will still be around...and then there's the other consideration. But...I will try.'

Thank the Deities. I thought I'd have to get Silva to beat it out of her.

Nicolas didn't mean it, but sometimes it was nice to mouth off mentally. Though he was curious what *the other consideration* was.

Rising, Xedora picked up her crystal ball and took it to a shelf Nicolas hadn't noticed at the back of the room. When she returned, she held a parchment. Unfurling it on the table revealed a map of Etherius. Nicolas's eyes instantly drifted to Yarringsburg and a single point on it.

Home...or what was home.

In his mind, he traced his journey so far. Sarus, Merida, the damnable Ale Trail. Considering the size of the world, he'd only seen a small portion of it, and most of that had involved too much buttock-clenching fear to properly take in the sights.

Before him was set out the world of Etherius. There were kingdoms and cities with climates of all types. Koth could be anywhere, but he prayed it wouldn't be far north, where the map became a bleak wasteland. The home of the orcs. No features had been drawn on it, most likely because no cartographer crazy enough to go and map it had come back alive. To the south of the kingdoms of man lay a vast and varied topography, from huge mountain ranges to wide-open plains.

'The Wildlands,' he whispered, leaning in to inspect it more closely.

'You do realise that is a generic term given to a land that consists of many and varied peoples?' Garaz chided softly. 'It is the equivalent of calling the Nine Kingdoms *human land*.' Finally taking his hands out of his cloak, the orc began to point to various areas of interest on the map. 'The Kascat Pridelands, The Dwarven Freeholds. The Ser—'

'Be a tour guide on your own time,' Xedora interrupted. A glint in her eye suggested enjoyment at goading the orc, whose distaste for being here was as clear as the giant statues they'd recently felled. 'I will try to find your demon then you can take your ghost and leave.'

'I'm not a ghost,' Auron replied through gritted teeth.

Xedora looked the spirit up and down with great theatricality. 'Well, you do a damned fine impression of one.'

From her cloak, Xedora produced a small stick with an arrow on the end. A chill ran down Nicolas's spine at the sight of it, and the urge to snatch it and snap it, before it caused too much trouble, was very real

Is there someone who sells these stupid all-purpose sticks? Great for seers, and for choosing inept village boys to go and get killed.

If Nicolas ever found such a vendor, he would have some very strong words for them.

'Now for the *other consideration* I mentioned,' Xedora said, eyeing the map with pursed lips, her free hand – which was shaking slightly – hovering above the stick. 'Etherius is a huge place. Just this continent alone has millions of people upon it. A single demon is a hay-coloured needle in a haystack. Even *if* the creature is still here, and I successfully attune the stick, the chances that I'll be able to pinpo—'

The seer cried out in shock as the stick yanked itself from her hand and threw itself at the table, sticking into it with an audible *thunk*. For a moment, Nicolas was worried Xedora would soil herself, just as the Oracle had, but apparently, his fears were unfounded. Or her bowel control was infinitely better than the cranky old man's.

Which is more likely, thinking on it.

Xedora's eyes widened as she stared at the stick stuck in her table, which still shook from the vibration of the impact. The point on which it stuck appeared to be a city.

'I...I have not seen this before.' Her voice betrayed her fear. 'That shouldn't be possible. For the stick to jump like that...the demonic energy must be immense. I...I...'

'*Babylon*,' Silva said as she leant forward and studied the map.

'Nick, I know you aren't very *worldly*,' Shift said with faux seriousness. 'but you know Babylon, right?' They raised an equally inquisitive and sarcastic eyebrow.

'Yes,' he answered dryly.

'The city built to foster peace between the peoples of Etherius?'

'Yes.'

'Where all races come together in harmony?'

'*Yes.*'

'A city built on diplomacy and reason that—'

'Bloody *yes*, all right,' he snapped. 'I've heard of Babylon. Everyone has heard of Babylon. *Deities.*'

Their work done, Shift gave him a wide grin. 'Just checking.'

I don't know what annoys me more: their antics or how endearing I find them.

'This is no time for jesting.' Xedora was clearly a woman who wasn't fazed easily, so to see her so disconcerted was worrying. 'I shouldn't have been able to find anything, but the demonic energy radiating from this place drew the stick in like a flaming beacon. Whatever is there is very powerful and very dangerous.'

All eyes turned to the stick as with a final small shiver—just like the one Nicolas was feeling—it stilled, pointing them towards a demon.

I just pray it isn't a coincidence.

'Whatever is there must be destroyed,' the seer said gravely. 'I hope you are up to the task, because I hate to think of the kind of evil it will perpetrate if left unchecked.'

'Maybe you fancy coming with us and getting involved in events for once, instead of just watching them unfold,' Auron goaded. The last part of the sentence seemed especially pointed.

'No, thank you,' Xedora said flatly.

'We had best go,' Silva said. 'It will be a long journey, and we need to plan accordingly, mapping our route and sourcing supplies—'

'And sleeping,' Shift said.

It was a good thing other people were looking at the practical, because his mind was consumed with the image of Koth and questions about how to defeat the creature that he had absolutely no answers to, just a vague hope that something would turn up.

Maybe he has a weak spot, like the statues we faced outside?

Or maybe Auron had a tale that would impart a somehow useful lesson, though he was sure the spirit would've shared it by now. The fact that Auron appeared equally flummoxed as to what Koth was made it all the worse.

If it's going to be a long journey, I'd best make use of my training time.

Taking coins from his pouch, he passed them to Xedora. 'Thank you.'

For a moment, their hands brushed, and the seer gave him an odd look but said nothing.

'I'd say it's been a pleasure,' Auron said, giving Xedora a theatrical and completely insincere bow, 'but it hasn't. I hope I never see you again, witch.'

'And I hope when your unfinished business is completed, you end up in the Underworld, with Sha'then using your genitals as target practice for Etherius's most-skilled knife thrower.'

The spirit gave Xedora a heartfelt middle finger then turned to leave.

'Let's go, folks,' the spirit declared with gusto. 'It's adventure time.'

CHAPTER 6

The morning air was cool, but Nicolas was hot and sweaty. Keeping his eyes on Silva, he circled the clearing, just as she did. Only occasionally did he register that the sword was in his hand. That was a good thing. Silva and Auron both kept telling him to treat it like an extension of himself.

Plus, I'm getting used to the weight.

Carefully, he scrutinised the warrior, looking for an opening. He knew Silva wouldn't give him one, and if she did, it would be a trap. The warrior, as usual, was stony faced, looking as if she meant to tear him apart.

There was a time when that was true.

With half an idea, and one he wasn't entirely sure about, he charged Silva. Just before he reached his sparring partner, he faked a stumble. Silva bought it, lowering her guard in annoyance, surely about to reprimand him for his poor footwork. Stepping his stumbling foot across the other, he spun, swinging the sword. Silva jumped back, bringing her blade up to block the attack, just.

'Well played,' the warrior grunted as she moved.

He wasn't about to let the momentum go now that he had it for once. Drawing the *Dawn Blade* back, he thrust forward. Silva parried the blow, which he turned into a downward strike. Again blocked. Nicolas let go of his mind, allowing his instincts to do the work for him. Blades clashed again and again as the pair moved about the clearing. It didn't take long for Silva to nullify his advantage, coming in with attacks of her own. But the fight was more to and fro than usual.

Silva parried one of his downward strikes, flicking his blade away. This time, his stumble forward was real, and he cursed himself. Already, he could see Silva's sword coming around to turn into a thrust at his gut. He couldn't stop it, his sword in no position to block, and he couldn't jump aside in any way he hadn't seen her counter a thousand times before.

Instead, he let go of the *Dawn Blade*. The weight pulling him forward gone, he slid back a step, grabbing Silva's wrist and striking her arm between the bicep and triceps with his knuckle. The warrior's sword hand opened, and she dropped her blade. Turning in, Nicolas grabbed her arm and threw Silva over him to the floor.

His moment of elated triumph was short-lived as the warrior spun her leg around, sweeping his own out from under him. Crashing to the ground, Nicolas cried out as Silva was suddenly atop him, knee on his chest and knife at his throat.

'Do you yield?' He was sure there was an uncharacteristic smugness in Silva's voice.

'I don't think I have a choice,' he said, looking at the knife pressed to his skin.

'Sensible.' Silva rose, sheathed her knife, and offered him her hand, pulling Nicolas to his feet. 'Inventive counter,' the warrior said with a smile.

'It didn't work.' He shrugged.

'Not on me, but there are many on whom it would.' The warrior stared at him for a moment. 'You are getting better each day. One day, you will surpass me.'

Nicolas let out a laugh that rang around the clearing. 'Even I don't have the imagination to see that.'

'Because your *imagination* never lets you see positive outcomes,' the warrior chided.

'No,' he said glibly. 'I'll always need you as my protector.'

'No, you won't.' Silva's sternness surprised him. 'You are improving at a greater rate every day, more so than you believe.' Her eyes softened a little. 'Progress is hard to see when it is daily and gradual, but you are making it.'

'Really?' he scoffed. 'Because I think you're forgetting how badly I came off in the fight with Tavish.' It hadn't even been the wounds he could see, which were plenty. He'd had a bad reaction when Garaz had used his healing magic, the damage being worse than was obvious.

I was dragged on a horse...and my thigh was gashed open, arm nearly broken by a flail, chest cut with a sword and stabbed in the hip...

The ghosts of some of the wounds still lingered. The scars certainly did.

'And yet six months ago, you would have died instantly in one-on-one combat with anyone.'

He couldn't argue that point. Now that he thought about it, he had come a long way. Maybe he should try being...proud of himself.

First time for everything.

'You've come a long way too,' he said with a smile.

'Oh?'

'Six months ago, you would've kicked Xedora's door in, pinned her to the table, and demanded she help us.' He smiled. 'You didn't even threaten to kick her in the face once.'

'It did not mean I did not want to.' Silva smirking was odd. 'Fighting those statues was an annoyance.' Her eyes became distant for a moment. 'It seems we are both walking the right path to better ourselves.'

He didn't know exactly how much Silva had to atone for, and he didn't want to know. Attacking him, he could forgive. Anything more he learned could only mar his relationship with his companion. Maybe he was being naïve, but he'd come to trust Silva and wanted nothing to shake that.

'I will find out how well I am succeeding when I eventually die in battle.'

Nicolas's jaw dropped. It was partly because of what Silva had said, and partly due to the casual way she'd said it.

'What do you mean? You're going to die?' His voice had become shrill, but he didn't care.

'That's...not what I said,' Silva replied with a frown.

'Is this a suicidal last stand thing again?' he snapped.

'No.' Silva shook her head with a chuckle. 'I have learnt my lesson about that. I simply meant that we get into a lot of fights, and I tend to throw myself into the forefront of them. Statistically, I will die in battle sooner rather than later.'

'Nope,' he said, shaking his head vehemently. 'I won't have it.'

'Nicolas, you cannot just—'

'I said *I won't have it*,' he interrupted. 'I told you no glorious, heroic deaths, and that you needed to walk the proper path to redemption. You're doing that, so I forbid you to die.'

'This is not a *glorious, heroic death*, as you put it. I am just speaking of odds. We get in a lot of fights, and at some point, I will die. You cannot just say *no* to death.'

'Yes, you can.' He shrugged. 'I did. I died, went to the Underworld, and came back.' It was poor logic but the only logic he had.

'That was a lot more complex than you make it sound,' Silva replied with a raised eyebrow. 'I am a warrior. Warriors die.'

What part of 'no' is she having the issue with? 'Yes, but you're better than anyone we've met.'

'So far.'

'But—'

Silva put a hand on his shoulder. 'Let's stop this talk about my fate and focus on yours. My task is to make sure you are better than anyone we will meet, and you are getting closer every day.' Stepping back, she brought her sword up. 'Guard position.'

Nicolas would've been content to stand there arguing until Silva got that silly notion out of her head, but she was right, he did need to train. So he'd just have to make sure he was good enough to protect her when the time came.

I'm not losing anyone else.

For a moment, before sparring recommenced, Silva's face softened. 'I appreciate that you care. Thank you.'

He was so surprised by the display of emotion that Nicolas dropped his guard. Silva made him pay for it two seconds later.

****

'Four weeks?' he said as he checked the saddlebag on his horse.

'The distance between here and Babylon hasn't changed since the last time you said that, kid.' Auron smirked.

'About ten minutes ago.' Shift sighed laboriously.

Though Nicolas was no longer the stay-at-home village boy he had been, he was hardly well-travelled, and four weeks to get to one place seemed like an eternity. Who knew what havoc the demon could wreak in that time...or if it would even still be there when they turned up?

'We will progress South, into the kingdom of Nalbina,' Silva said, map in hand. 'We can then break east toward the city. Fortunately, Nalbina has plenty of towns we can stop at for provisions and shelter. We may need furs before reaching Babylon. Winter will be beginning soon, and we need to be ready to battle the elements.'

Nalbina will be the fourth kingdom I've visited. I should start getting souvenirs.

The city of Babylon was built near the borders of Nalbina, Ivilar—the First Kingdom of Man—and the edge of the Wildlands. Apparently, it was aligned with no kingdom but a neutral state of its own, run by a council and an elected governor. Made sense when it was devised to bring people together.

'What's Nalbina like?' he asked.

'It is a warmer climate, so winter will not touch us as quickly as anywhere more northern, but beyond that, pretty much the same as any other kingdom,' Silva explained. 'Some of the flora and fauna are different. For some reason, there are sandy plains. Some say it is because of a wizard's spell in times gone by.'

Sand. Yuck. Reminds me of that desert island.

'They have these water worms there... Giant things with big mandibles' Auron said, clicking his fingers. 'So, this one time I was bathing, and one grabbed me around the leg, yanking me under. Of course, I'm buck-ass nude and... Kid, where are you going?'

Nicolas stopped in his tracks. 'I need to relieve myself.' He tried to sound as casual as possible.

'But I'm telling a story.'

'Sorry, but we're going in a bit, and it's a long journey. I—'

His second attempt to leave was stopped abruptly by an arm encircling his.

'Can it not wait? Auron's telling a story.' Shift, the owner of said arm asked. Leaning in, they dropped their voice to a whisper. 'If you think you're running off while we have to stay and listen to this, you are sadly mistaken.'

'Sorry, weak bladder,' he said with a sheepish grin. He gave his trapped arm a tentative tug. It didn't move.

'I don't care how much bigger your arm's getting,' Shift hissed in his ear. 'You're going nowhere.'

My arm's getting bigger?

There was a strange moment. As he stared into Shift's eyes, he could feel his heart pounding against the inside of his chest like a debt collector banging on the door of someone who owed them a lot of coin. Shift's eyes widened and for a moment he was sure he caught a hint of red in their cheeks. Suddenly the grip of his arm loosened.

'Nature's calling,' he said with an awkward cough as he carefully un-picked Shift's fingers from his arm. He tried to ignore the heat he was feeling in his palm as he touched their skin.

He was actually starting to feel a little guilty about leaving them to suffer Auron's tale. But the spirit had lost him at *buck ass nude*. And all the lying about needing to pee had actually made him really need to go.

As he was finally freed, Shift took their hand back, stroking their palm slightly as they looked away. Nicolas frowned as he realised that he already missed having their arm on his.

'Back in a minute,' he said as he began to leave again.

'Your loss.' Auron shrugged. 'Anyway, Shift, Silva...I'm under the water, thrashing around, my stuff...'

Just before he disappeared around the corner, he glanced back. Shift's lips were curled in distaste as the spirit continued his story. They saw him looking and pointed at him before slowly running their finger across their throat.

That's more like it.

Making his way through the bushes, he finally found somewhere quiet to urinate. As he unbuttoned his breeches, the back of his neck tingled. Yes, Nicolas was a paranoid man, but he'd also been attacked before whilst going for a forest pee, so he knew it for a warning. He wrapped his hand around the hilt of his sword then, turning quickly, drew it and confronted the person sneaking up on him.

'You.'

CHAPTER 7

'**M**e.' Xedora glanced at the sword with the exact level of disinterest someone with a blade pointed at them shouldn't have had. 'You can put that away.'

His gaze flitted between the sword and the seer. Sheathing his blade when he caught someone sneaking up on him didn't seem the most logical move.

'Not yet,' he said warily. 'Not until I know why you're here.'

'Just to talk,' she replied, holding up her hands.

Her cloak and gown were hues of earthy browns and greens, ideal for sneaking up on someone in the forest, a fact that wasn't lost on Nicolas. Nor was her ability to animate giant stone monsters and do who knew what other kinds of magic. His eyes flitted to the trees nearby, just in case one was about to clobber him.

The sword stays out for now.

'Very well,' he said, doing her the courtesy of lowering the blade. Seemed polite if he wasn't going to sheath it completely. 'The others are—'

'I want to talk to you.'

The blade rose again. She *had* meant to sneak up on him. What did that mean?

'Why?' his tone was half cautious, half nervous. He was more than a little concerned he was about to end up on her hate list with Auron.

The seer looked away as she seemed to ponder this. 'Honestly, I'm not sure,' she answered finally. 'Once you left, I was happy to be rid of you. Yet my curiosity got the better of me, and I knew I had to come and see you before you left. Because I have a question that intrigues me.'

After a protracted pause, Nicolas circled the tip of his blade to encourage the seer to speak. Keeping it, obviously, pointing in her general direction.

'You saw the ghost, didn't you?' Xedora said, narrowing her eyes. 'Do not lie to me.'

Blinking a few times, Nicolas found himself sheathing the *Dawn Blade*. 'Yes.'

The seer approached, and suddenly Nicolas was very aware that his breeches were undone and he didn't have a sword in his hand.

Completely invading his personal space, Xedora studied him carefully. 'Fascinating,' she said, staring into his eyes. 'You are no seer, yet you saw.'

'I see Auron all the time. So do the others.' He shrugged, poorly faking nonchalance.

Xedora shook her head. 'Do not try to fast talk me, boy.' She scoffed. 'You are all soul bonded to Auron, your fates intertwined due to your shared quest. The other one was different. You should not have seen him.'

'I...'

The seer smiled slowly. 'And it isn't the first time. I suspect you have an idea why.'

His eyes widened and his stomach dropped. The idea wasn't one he wished to entertain.

'Tell me.'

'I...' He took a deep breath. 'I died. My soul went to the Underworld, but Auron saved me and Sha'then returned my soul to my body. Ever since then I've...seen things. Ghosts. Glimpses, really. Maybe it's getting worse?'

Xedora closed her eyes and raised her arms, letting her hands hover on either side of his head. There was a tingling sensation in his temples. 'Yes,' she said. 'I can see it clearly now. Your soul has been to the Underworld and back. But you cannot travel both ways without death clinging to you, leaving its mark. That is why you can see that which no mortal – save one like myself – should.'

'Will there be other effects?'

The seer made several frowning motions, probably the same ones Nicolas made when grappling with a particularly stubborn turd. 'I...cannot say.'

Bugger. That'll give my mind something nice and juicy to worry about.

'Am I alive?' Internally he winced as he awaited an answer.

'Mostly. But there will always be a connection between you and the land of the dead.'

'Am I a zombie?'

Xedora laughed. 'Do you smell like one, silly boy? No, the change in you is subtler than that. You are no undead creature. You are just...'

'Just what?'

The uncertainty in his mind suddenly boiled over, and the desperate urge to understand took hold. In that moment, he reached out and grabbed Xedora's hands, as if he were worried that she may leave before telling him what he needed to know. As they touched, both Nicolas and Xedora's bodies shook as if struck by lightning. Suddenly, he was unable to let go as he watched the seers' gaze become glassy, as if her mind was now somewhere far away – or she was extremely drunk and about to black out.

'*When the time comes, you must let them in.*' Her voice was a dreamy whisper. '*You must let them all in.*'

Whatever force bound the pair together, now pushed Nicolas away from the seer. Stumbling, he backed against the tree, his heart pounding like a running giant's footsteps. 'W...what?'

Xedora blinked several times, the glaze receding. 'I said you were no undead creature. You are alive...just different. Pay attention,' she snapped.

Nicolas frowned, his mouth half open.

The relief that she'd said he was alive was overshadowed by whatever had just occurred. Clearly, Xedora had no memory of it, which was frustrating, because he really wanted to know what that meant.

'My curiosity is satisfied,' the seer said with a nod. 'I could not let you leave without knowing.'

'Before you go, I have one more question...'

The seer nodded for him to continue.

He really wanted to ask who, exactly, he was supposed to let in, but since the answer would be something like, '*What are you talking about?*' he asked, instead, 'Why didn't you tell that woman what her husband really said?'

Xedora gave him a half-smile. 'Because he was angry and upset. He needed healing to move on, not the venting of his anger.' That sounded reasonable enough. 'Besides, what woman wants to be called a whore?'

Xedora had obviously never met Gornak. He called everyone a whore. Well, whoreson. Close enough.

'One more thing.' Judging by the glare the seer gave him, he was treading on thin ice. 'Why are you so upset with Auron?'

'Mind your business.'

And with a waft of her cloak, she left Nicolas alone to ponder the very strange occurrence.

****

Nicolas?

Hearing his name made him detach himself from his thoughts. He couldn't deny that he was pleased about that. His mind had sent him running in circles trying to understand what had happened, and he was still none the wiser. Turning, he began to smile at Garaz, until he saw the look of concern on the orc's face.

'Are you okay?' his companion asked.

Good question. No idea.

'I'm fine.'

'You were leant against the tree frowning,' the orc said. 'I called to you three times. You should be more aware. We have many enemies.'

'I know. Sorry.' He gave an approximation of a warm smile. 'Just in my head. Let's go back to camp.'

'You may wish to do up your breeches first,' Garaz said with a raised eyebrow.

Nicolas was about to ask the orc what he meant when he realised what he'd originally come here to actually do. Apparently Xedora had chased away his need to pee along with his peace of mind.

With a sheepish grin, he followed the orc's suggestion. Mentally, he chided himself. Garaz was right; they had many enemies. And here he was, stood in the forest daydreaming with his breeches open like a fool.

As he re-dressed himself, his mind couldn't help but drift back to what Xedora had said. That he was different. She'd made it seem like he had a foot in both worlds now. Life and death.

'Are you sure you are well?' Garaz was searching his face.

'Yes...' He paused for a moment. 'Can I ask a question?'

'Of course.' The orc smiled. 'I am not Shift. You will get a sensible answer.'

Nicolas couldn't help but chuckle. 'After my fight with Tavish, what happened exactly?'

Garaz stroked his chin thoughtfully. 'I surmise you wish something more specific than *we won*.' The orc's yellow eyes searched his. 'You mean when I was healing you?'

He nodded.

'You were very badly hurt.' *That much I remember.* 'I had believed your wounds all on external, but when I began my healing magic, your body convulsed. I believe I aggravated some internal damage I had not foreseen.'

'Thank you.'

Garaz's large hand rested on his shoulder. It was accompanied by a warm smile. 'But you are better now.'

I'm not sure.

What Xedora had said had spooked him, he couldn't deny that. It should've been easy to put it down to the ravings of a mad witch—not that he'd say that out loud—but he'd seen the ghosts, and the reaction to Garaz's healing magic... Once, when they'd been fighting vampires, Garaz had grabbed one of the creatures by the face and using his healing magic to melt said face. Apparently, healing magic had an opposite effect on the undead. So that would mean...

'I'm fine.' As Garaz frowned, Nicolas chided himself. His companion hadn't asked. And why was he trying to deny it? He had a very nasty habit of keeping things to himself, only for it to cause something to go horribly wrong down the line.

Time to prove you're learning your lessons.

'Actually, I'm not fine.' With a deep breath, he filled Garaz in on the strange conversation with the seer, and what he'd been seeing.

'And you believe because my healing magic hurt you, that you are therefore an undead creature?'

'That pretty much sums it up, yes,' he admitted sourly.

Garaz stroked his beard as he thought. 'Then we must conduct a test. Sorry.'

What kind of t... Did he just say sorry?

Before Nicolas could react, the orc drew a small knife from his cloak and cut Nicolas's arm. 'Ow,' he cried, cradling his arm tenderly. 'What in the Underworld, Garaz?'

Taking his arm, Garaz examined it. The cut was small, disproportionate to Nicolas's cry, which had been more from the surprise of it, really. The cut was only an inch, but a trickle of blood ran from it. The orc chanted under his breath, and one of his hands began to glow with the white light that signalled some healing was on the way. Gently, Garaz laid his hand over the cut.

'Oww.' Nicolas winced as pricks of heat stabbed at his arm. 'Dammit, Garaz.'

'That hurts?' the orc enquired.

'I think you can surmise that by me going *oww*,' he snapped back testily.

Garaz frowned at him and shook his head. Within a second, he took the hand away and dispelled his magic. The cut was gone.

'Interesting,' the orc said, examining his arm closely. 'The cut has healed, but there is some slight discoloration of the skin. Please describe how it hurt.'

'It stung. Burned.' Nicolas shrugged.

The orc let go of his arm, and Nicolas went back to cradling it tenderly, interspersed with blowing on it for good measure.

'It would appear you have a somewhat unique reaction to my healing magic,' Garaz mused. 'Whilst it does heal your wound, it also causes you damage. When I used strong healing magic on you after the fight with Tavish, it triggered your convulsions, yet you healed. I only used a small amount of my magic just then, which lessened reaction, though it still occurred.'

'And that means...?'

'For the meantime, we had best use my power on you as little as possible, lest it hurt you further.' Garaz's eyebrows rose as Nicolas stared at him in horror. 'Do not worry, I can still brew herbal healing remedies and potions. As they are generally slower acting, it should mute any ill effects the healing properties may have on you. But you will not heal as quickly as with my magic.'

No access to healing magic...the number of times I get badly hurt?

Fantastic.

CHAPTER 8

Auron let out a loud huff. Turning in the saddle of his ethereal steed Mare, he glared at Shift. 'For the last time, will you stop it?'

'I'm not doing anything.' Shift's face suggested otherwise.

'I can feel your eyes on me,' the spirit snapped. 'I told you to leave it alone. It's been four days.'

A very long four days. Adventuring was turning out to be eighty percent getting to places, ten percent figuring out who the villains were, and ten percent actually fighting them. (The percentages of breech-wetting fear, barely surviving, and nervously recovering had their own system of measurement.) Of course, the side effect of long-distance travel with a group was running out of things to talk about. Even Auron's stories had been less numerous than usual. There was the beautiful rolling hills and forests of Yarringsburg to marvel at, but that only worked as a distraction for so long then it was back to idle chat about where to camp, finding good food sources and the like—which was necessary as they were avoiding taverns like the plague. Though Nicolas found quiet comfort in this routine, it being the first time in a long while his life had had consistency. But Shift bored easily. And when they did, it was usually made someone else's problem. In this case, Auron's. The spirit had refused to give up the reason Xedora hated him so much.

Shift doesn't give up easily either.

'Apologies,' Shift said insincerely, with a broad grin. 'I did not receive the raven informing me that looking in your general direction had been forbidden. But I will rectify this breach of protocol forthwith.' The shapeshifter made a big production of looking in every other direction.

Auron's white eyes turned to Nicolas with a glare.

'Do something,' the spirit growled through gritted teeth.

Me? What makes him think I have any influence over Shift's antics?

'Tactically, it would be wise to know what you did, so that we may prepare for a similar situation in the future, should it arise.'

'Shut up, Silva,' Auron snapped, Mare casting an annoyed glance at her rider as he did. 'We aren't going to be in a situation where we're attacked by giant statues again. Ever. Things like that don't repeat themselves.'

'I was transported to a strange place against my will twice,' Nicolas said thoughtfully. 'Once to a desert island, and once to the Underworld. How many people get transported to strange places *once* in their life, never mind twice?'

'Kid, I asked for help. That was not it.'

'Sorry.' Nicolas shrugged.

'For the last time,' the spirit said with exasperation, rubbing his hand over his face, '*I didn't do anything.*'

'That would appear to be highly unlikely.' Garaz's head bobbed from side to side, as if weighing up various scenarios. 'One does not curse statues to attack someone with no basis for a grievance against them.'

Mare whinnied in annoyance as Auron let out a scream. Pulling on his mount's reins, the spirit halted her. The others slowly brought their own steeds to a stop. Nicolas found his interest piqued. Of all the stories Auron had forced on him, it would be nice to hear one he'd actually asked for.

'Fine,' the spirit said with a set jaw. 'You know what I did? *Nothing.* I actually did...nothing.'

'Come on,' Shift said with a derisive snort.

'I didn't. And don't interrupt,' Auron snarled. 'I met Xedora because she'd prophesied that a local lord was going to die. She said it would be at the hands of *a man who lived to serve.* Half the time that prophecy stuff is a load of nonsense, but the lord was riled up, so he hired me. I went to visit Xedora hoping to get her to elaborate a little on this would-be killer, possibly with his name, description, and address. When I met Xedora, I made some...shall we say, *overtures.* She's a very proud and attractive woman, and I'm only human.' *A very horny example of one, but still a human.* 'At first, I got her heart skipping a beat or two with my never fail combination of handsomeness, roguishness and heroic tales.' Auron let out a big sigh. 'But she is a seer. She *saw* how things would go between us and didn't care for it.'

Shift's nose wrinkled in confusion. 'Is that it?' they asked. 'Why were you so precious about telling us that?'

The spirit rolled his eyes and bit his lip. 'Because what she did next was pretty embarrassing. She put a curse on me.'

'A curse?'

Trust Garaz's ears to prick up about magical stuff.

'Yes,' Auron replied gruffly. 'She cursed...' The spirit coughed awkwardly then pointedly looked down. Shift let out a single hearty laugh as Garaz's lips curled in distaste. 'She said she was *'giving the women of Etherius the holiday they so desperately deserved.'* Auron repeated the last part in a very petulant tone. 'It took me a whole bloody month to find someone to remove it. And in that time, I was held captive by a group of warrior women looking for a prime specimen to breed their next generation with. They didn't believe in clothes, and they had these...muscles...' Auron set his jaw angrily and shook his head. 'When they found out, I was laughed out of their camp. They called me the *Man without Manhood*.'

Nicolas's mouth formed an O as he considered what he'd just been told then he burst out laughing. Doubling over in the saddle, clutching his ribs, tears rolling down his cheeks. His laughter was echoed by Shift, and his gaze turned to them. After a few seconds, his laughter petered out as he stared at the shapeshifter, unaware of even the scenery around them. There was just Shift.

Just friends.

'By the Deities, I needed that,' Shift said with a couple of last guffaws, wiping the tears from their eyes with their sleeve.

'I have some questions about this curse.' Garaz looked conflicted about asking them, but as usual, his curiosity won out.

'Well, you can shove them right up your ass,' Auron declared, wide eyed. 'I've said as much as I will on the matter.' The spirit's head tilted toward Shift. 'Happy?'

'Bloody ecstatic.' They smirked, catching Nicolas's gaze, their green eyes glinting.

Thank the Deities I didn't do that dreamy sigh out loud.

Just friends, Nicolas...

Just friends!

****

Nicolas turned in his saddle, looking back the way they had come and counted his blessings. The border crossing in Nalbina had been nice and smooth. Considering they didn't get smooth very often, he wanted to appreciate it to its fullest. And they'd managed to avoid the kingdom of Sarus, and its very unwelcoming citizens, completely.

'This place doesn't look any different to Yarringsburg,' he mused as he took in the sights around him.

'That's because we've only just crossed the border,' Shift said with a shake of their head. 'The topography doesn't just suddenly change the second you enter a new kingdom. Once we get properly into Nalbina, you'll notice the difference. More sand, for one thing.'

'There appears to be a trading post ahead,' Silva called back. 'We had best stock up on supplies.' The warrior then rattled off a list of everything they'd eaten over the past few days, which therefore needed replacing. Impressive. Silva was quite thorough.

'Has she been watching us all eat this whole time?' Shift whispered conspiratorially to him.

Less impressive. More unnerving.

Still, a break from the saddle was most welcome, as was knowing there would be meals on the journey. He still couldn't quite get used to not having his meals at set times. This *we'll eat when we stop* malarkey was way too wishy-washy for his liking. But he had no say in the matter, so he didn't grumble aloud. His stomach did once or twice, though.

The trading post, Wanderer's Wares, was an odd type of building. Made of old wood and almost squat looking, it stretched back quite far, yet only had one floor. There was nothing outstanding about it, but it probably didn't need to be flashy on a main trade route like this. And judging by the horses tied up outside, it had plenty of custom. The group approached the hitching post and dismounted, Silva giving each of them specific items to procure.

'And whatever we pick up, we pay for,' the warrior finished pointedly, talking to one specific member of the group.

'Please credit me with a little self-control.' Shift snorted as the group approached the shop.

Nicolas was walking directly behind Shift, so he clearly saw the sleight of hand that made the purse go from the belt of the man leaving the shop into Shift's pocket. Suddenly, the shapeshifter came to a halt and abruptly turned. Nicolas nearly didn't stop in time and ended up very close to them.

'Impressed?'

He stared into their green eyes, letting the moment linger a little too long. 'Umm, yes.'

Shift leaned in close. A warmth grew between them which Nicolas was sure only he could feel. It took considerable willpower not to tilt his head and pucker his lips. Suddenly, he felt he was sweating profusely. His companion got so close to his ear, their breath tickled his earlobe.

By the Deities...

'You tell Silva you saw that, and you'll be waking up with a giant spider in your bed. Got it?' the shapeshifter whispered, before turning and walking into the shop, leaving Nicolas swaying on the spot for a moment, before following.

The man behind the counter was busy when they entered the store, but he still found time to give them a hearty wave. It was quite endearing. The store itself was well-stocked with pretty much anything anyone could need.

He was just passing the weapons when he heard raised voices.

'Brother, then I took my spear, gave it a nice run up, and launched that beast. *Thunk.* Right in the guy's back. That's what happens when you try to run.'

'The poster said *dead or alive*, brother,' another deep voice added.

Peering around the racks, he saw three burly men in leather armour checking out swords. One was picking up various blades and swishing them through the air whilst the others stood aside, arms folded. From their rugged nature, it was clear they were well travelled.

'Damn right, brother,' the first one boomed. 'And do I want this guy tryna run off again?'

'Nobody wants that, brother.' The man with the sword chuckled. 'Easier to just carry the dead body. Am I right, brother?'

'Eurgh, bounty hunters,' Auron said, wrinkling his nose. 'If ever a group of people made me look humble...'

'Besides,' the first one continued, 'where's the fun if they come quietly? Am I right, brothers?'

The three men burst into booming laughter. A lot of back slapping occurred.

'See the symbol on their shoulder guards?' Auron asked, pointing. 'The sword and the net? That's the symbol of the Bounty Hunters Guild. A little on the nose for my liking, but they aren't subtle folk, as you can tell.'

Ever since the business on the Ale Trail, *guilds* was a dirty word to Nicolas. Billy—really the faun Ro—had done his best to stir up trouble amongst the guilds. He was dead now, but only time would tell if he'd succeeded.

'Excuse me, please.'

Nicolas turned. Behind him was an elderly woman with a basket. The woman looked at him expectantly and he realised he was blocking the walkway. Dutifully, he stepped aside. 'Sorry.'

The old lady gave her thanks and shuffled down the weapon aisle. Nicolas was sure she'd have a harder time getting the trio of bounty hunters to move than she had him. None of them looked like the gentlemanly types.

Turned out, it wasn't a problem after all. Approaching two of the men from behind, she drew two long knives from her basket and sliced the backs of their knees. The men crashed to the ground and with a flick of her wrists, the knives were embedded in their foreheads. The first man was still staring in stunned disbelief as the woman drew two more knives from her shawl and threw them into the bounty hunter's legs. Like his brothers, he collapsed to the floor, screaming.

'Shush there, deary, shush,' the old woman said.

'What is this?' the bounty hunter roared between gasps of pain. 'Do you know who we are? Do you know what'll happen?'

'You started it,' the old lady said with a titter. 'The Assassin's Guild doesn't take kindly to its members being attacked, especially by brutes like you lot.'

'What?' the man cried in confusion.

'Billy Bobknobs was a member of our Guild, and had secrets belonging to us,' the old woman explained. 'Yet you *brothers* tried to take him from us so you could learn them. And assaulted poor Alexi and Emelina. It's time to be held to account.'

'Are you crazy?' the man howled. 'We were tryna safeguard our secrets from you. We lost men in that tavern too, you stupid bit—' The man's curse became a shrill cry as the old woman kicked him in the groin.

'Language,' she said, wagging her finger. 'Consider this a warning about what happens when you cross us.'

'The Bounty Hunters Guild won't take this lying down,' Auron remarked solemnly. 'Unlike the gentleman there with knives in both legs.'

They'd hoped once the faun Ro was dead that all his mischief would peter away. They'd taken Ro's body to the nearest garrison and explained what had occurred, making the captain swear to send a message to King Eldric, who would help nip this nonsense in the bud.

It seems they didn't listen.

Nicolas froze as the old woman gathered her basket, leaving her knives where she'd put them, and walked back toward him. Reaching Nicolas, she stopped and gave him a warm smile.

'Be a good boy and tell people what you saw,' she said sweetly. 'No one crosses the Assassin's Guild and lives.'

He nodded numbly, to the background noise of cries of pain.

CHAPTER 9

That wasn't the only evidence of discord between the guilds the group heard of over the next few days. By the Deities, did travellers on the road like to gossip when there was something juicy to share, as long as Garaz kept a respectful distance. Apparently, there'd been a spate of incidents in Yarringsburg alone, and it was spreading. There was even word of a royal response soon, maybe outlawing guilds. Auron had said that this would go down like a troll at a fancy ball. Guild culture was so ingrained into the kingdoms of man, that to try to remove or outlaw it would cause massive upheaval. More so than little old ladies assassinating bounty hunters in local shops, apparently.

Though if they take up arms so quickly, maybe them being disbanded is no bad thing?

'Nick.'

Following Shift's voice, he pushed his horse through the last of the brush, quickly catching a branch before it flung back and whipped him in the face. Ducking under the branch, he urged his horse to a halt beside his companion. Only then did he notice the sheer drop in front of him. After a second of *oh crap, that's high*, accompanied by some very tight gripping of the reins, he began to appreciate the view.

They'd started early, before first light. It hadn't been their choice, but that of some Deities damned noisy birds who had no respect for travellers who needed their rest. The cawing bastards had woken everyone except Garaz. But in Shift's mind, if they were being forced to wake so early, everyone was. Garaz had a single thought on the matter when he was woken, an expletive unusual for the normally well-spoken orc. Still, being awoken by a lion roaring in your face will do that. Shift was highly amused once they changed back.

And now the sun was rising.

A golden hue covered Etherius from sky to earth as the bright orb peeked tentatively over the horizon to start a new day. Somehow, Shift had managed to position themselves right at the centre of it, so it appeared as if they were emitting a golden glow that made Nicolas swallow hard…a second before his mouth flopped open.

'Isn't it beautiful?' they asked.

Yes.

They meant the scenery, he knew that, but that wasn't what he was finding beautiful. Right there and then, he wanted to manifest the words *just friends* into something solid that he could throw over the edge of the cliff.

Actually, that isn't at the top of the list of things I want to do right now.

'You don't close your mouth soon, the wind will change, and your face will be stuck like that,' Auron remarked with a smirk. 'And once it is, you'll no longer be known as *Nick Carnage* but instead as *Gawping Nick.*'

'I'm not known as that anyway,' he replied testily.

'Some circles disagree.' The spirit shrugged.

Thank you for ruining the moment, Auron.

Instead of giving into his annoyance, Nicolas looked out at the sprawling kingdom before him. There were large valleys, forests and areas that were clearly sandy. But something else caught his eye: an unnatural shadow on the horizon. 'Is that where we're going?' he asked.

'The town of Narus,' Silva confirmed. 'We should get there late afternoon. It will be a good place to rest before the final push to Babylon.'

'I want a bed,' Shift said, cupping their hand over their eyes to view the town. 'I know we said we'd avoid taverns, but it's been days since I slept on something that wasn't ground. We're getting a bed.'

'Do you think that—'

Shift cut Garaz off with a glare. 'We are getting a bed. Or I will make all of your lives miserable.'

The orc considered this for a moment. 'Maybe I will sleep better if we have a wall between us.'

'That's settled then.' Shift grinned broadly. 'A warm bed tonight. The first in a long time.' The shapeshifter closed their eyes, tilting their chin to the sky. 'I can already feel it.'

Nicolas had no inclination to argue. A warm bed was worth whatever risk right now.

The shapeshifter was so excited they kicked their horse to a trot and traced the edge of the cliff, with the others following.

'Is it just me, or are all the buildings in the town squat?' Nicolas asked, squinting toward Narus. 'I mean, we are way off, but it doesn't look like there's anything above a single storey.'

'It's a worship thing,' Auron explained. 'The Nalbians are a pious lot. Apparently, they equate having too many levels on your house as vanity, as you're trying to get yourself closer to the Deities.'

'Really?' he said, wrinkling his nose. 'What about places like the castle then? Surely that can't be a single floor.'

'They allow extra storeys based on status,' the spirit answered. 'The higher you are up the social pecking order, the more you are allowed...within reason. Even the castle itself in the centre of the capital is like a cake that someone's sat on.'

'Though interestingly there is another side to that.' Nicolas knew Garaz well enough to know that when the orc said something was interesting, it generally was. 'There is no issue with the Nalbians building downwards.'

'Would that not get them closer to the Underworld?' Shift asked.

Garaz shrugged.

'They get quite funny if you ask them about that,' Auron interjected. 'But most homes have large underground additions. With some of their 'mansions,' most of the sprawling estate is beneath the surface.' *Whatever works for you, I suppose.* 'It's given me a lot of work in the past. They have a lot of trouble with mole folk or rat men. Underground serpents. Sometimes spiders. Generally nasty stuff that likes to live deep in the dark and doesn't care for someone putting their larder in the hole it lives in.'

****

After a good half-days travel, the wall surrounding Narus was finally in sight, and so was the promise of a warm bed. Part of Nicolas wanted to press on, though, to get to Babylon as quickly as possible. The longer they delayed, the more chance the demon would be gone by the time they arrived. All Nicolas had was the hope that it would still be there, and that it would be Koth.

And that my second battle with it will go better because I won't be alone.

He would have no idea until they fought. One thing he did know for certain, though: he would never let the demon bushwhack him with an arrow again.

Still, if Koth is gone, there are bound to be minions of the Maestro in Babylon. Probably a bloody faun, knowing my luck. I'm sure we can find someone to beat some information out of. His minions don't stay quiet for long.

'Business must be thriving here,' Shift said, nodding at the stream of travellers queuing to enter the town.

Before them stretched a long line of wagons, horses and people on foot. Nicolas assumed the wagons were laden with food and goods for the town stores to help see it through winter, when travel would be almost suicidal.

If we get to Babylon and it isn't Koth, we'll be stuck there until winter breaks.

As they got closer, it became more apparent that most of those on their way to Narus were pilgrims, dressed in simple robes, with many carrying a book of some kind. Something felt off about the pilgrims, or maybe it was in the air. Try as he might, Nicolas couldn't put his finger on what it was. The only obvious thing was that everyone approaching the city was human. It was odd, but they were in a human kingdom. He noticed Garaz cover himself in his cloak. He wanted to tell the orc not to, but whatever was in the air was telling him that it was a wise choice.

Reaching the queue, the group took their place at its end and fell into step with it. The line might've been long, but at least it was moving quickly.

'Greetings, friend,' the pilgrim beside him said with a warm smile. 'May this day be prosperous.'

The man was in his thirties and very clean-cut. Not someone who'd done much in the way of manual labour in his time. Nicolas didn't know the proper response to the greeting, so settled for, 'And yourself.'

'Niam Vell, scribe by trade.' The man offered his hand. 'At your service.'

'Nicolas Percival Carnegie.' He shook the hand.

'Are you here for the talk?' Niam asked eagerly.

There was an odd enthusiasm about the man that made Nicolas want to end the conversation quickly. 'No, we're just passing through. On our way to Babylon.'

Niam turned up his nose as if Nicolas had just let rip an earth-trembling fart. 'That place?' he scoffed. 'You don't want to go there.' The man leaned in closer. 'That place is a den of integration and degradation,' he whispered with distaste. 'Living in harmony with other races is not working out well in practice. Stuff is going on there. Dark stuff.' The man shook his head. 'Hardly surprising with those non-human folk around. If you ask me, it gives them grand ideas. That's why they keep coming into our kingdoms, causing trouble, and upsetting good, honest human folk.'

Nicolas smiled politely through the urge to vomit. Though it did raise a good question. 'What's going on there?'

Could Koth still be there?

'Don't know the specifics,' Niam said, before pointing to the gate of Narus. 'But he knows. He knows all about it.'

'Who?' *Dammit, I'm starting to get invested in this conversation.*

Niam raised the book he held and tapped the cover twice, knowingly. 'Tobias Helstrum, that's who.'

Nicolas frowned as he read the cover of the leatherbound book with gold filigree.

Eschatology of Humanity
By

Tobias Helstrum

By the Deities, they've given the man better publishing options.

The group had first become aware of Tobias Helstrum in Merida, where they'd found his hate-filled pamphlets. Apparently, Mr Helstrum had a dislike of anyone who wasn't human and suggested that those non-human folk stirred up trouble. He also appeared to have a strange foreknowledge of events. Nicolas had wondered at the time who would read such trash, but now his question was more about how many people would read it and believe the printed nonsense.

Niam opened the book to a page with the corner folded in, clearly a favourite of his. Again, he tapped the book. 'Here, you see. This tells you how depraved they are,' the man said in shock and horror. 'Did you know, centaurs do not use toilets? They just leave their droppings where they go. Disgusting and unsanitary.'

If Nicolas recalled rightly, centaurs were half man half horse. How *would* such a creature use a toilet and—

No. I'm not letting my imagination loose on that one. It'll... By the Deities, he's actually underlined bits.

'Great man, Tobias Helstrum,' Niam said with a nod. 'I can't wait to see him in person.'

Suddenly, it clicked. 'Tobias Helstrum is *here*?'

'He certainly is.' Niam beamed. 'He's giving a talk in the town square. He's going to let the truth of the world be heard. You see the red-robed people in the crowd? They're members of the Shield of Humanity. It's nice to see so many good folks stepping forward to protect us Deities-fearing humans. Hopefully, I'll have a red robe of my own soon.'

There were a disconcerting number of red robes in the crowd. Nicolas glanced back to double check that not an inch of Garaz's green skin was on show. It wasn't.

'Do you want to come?'

'Beg pardon?'

'To the talk, with me.' Niam grinned. 'Be good to get you some education before you enter that pit of inhuman creatures.'

Nicolas tried to find a way of politely saying, *I'd rather be trampled by a herd of shitting centaurs.* He was even tempted to fall from his horse and fake an injury.

'I...I can't, sorry,' he said finally. 'My companions and I need to find an inn for the night.' The hope seemed a forlorn one, with so many people entering the town. But he noticed that a large number of them were carrying their own camping equipment, so there was hope.

It was a simple excuse, but a good one. Even if it didn't work, Silva would back him up, maybe look angry and make Niam hastily find another person of interest. Trouble was, he wasn't riding beside Silva.

'You should go.' Shift grinned, reveling in the moment. 'You are quite naïve and could do with having your eyes opened to how the world really is.'

'But don't you need me for...' he began leadingly.

'Nonsense.' Shift waved his sentence away. 'Go have fun with your new friend.'

'Would you care to come, Miss?' Niam asked expectantly.

Shift's smile wavered slightly at the *Miss*, but they soon recovered themselves. 'Thank you, but no. One of us has to get the room sorted whilst Nick is away.'

'Your loss.' Niam shrugged, before slapping Nicolas on the back. 'With me then, friend. Let us teach you a thing or two about the ways of the world.'

Many things could be said about Niam, based on their very short acquaintance, but he didn't think *worldy* was one of them. And this was from him...

As his horse was led away by Niam, he looked back at his companions. Judging by the smirk on Auron's face, Shift was filling him in on what had occurred. Silva looked set to follow him, but Shift said something, and she stopped.

Thanks for that. Indeed, thanks for all of this.

'Probably a good job she didn't come,' Niam said in a whisper.

'What's that?'

'Well, you know how they are,' Niam said, rolling his open palm as if to coax an answer out of him. 'Women. Not exactly a lot prone to rational thinking. Why else would they need men?' Niam looked around before he continued, 'That and for protection from all these inhuman things running around.'

Nicolas had a very clear mental image of himself punching Niam right off his horse. Instead, he unclenched his fist and rubbed the hand Niam had shaken on his jacket. Any violence now would attract the wrong attention—attention which might suddenly become aware of the orc in their midst. And you couldn't just punch random folk for being stupid, more's the pity. Besides, his curiosity was piqued as to how many of the other pilgrims were like this fellow, and what this Helstrum actually had to say.

Still, Shift's going to pay for this one.

CHAPTER 10

The closer the pair got to the town square, the harder it was to actually approach it. The place was bloody heaving, the crowd of people ahead each jostling for a good position from which they could view the upcoming event.

I don't know why. I've read Helstrum's work. I can't imagine what he says in person is any less crap.

Nicolas cast a casual glance at Niam, who was living proof that opinions varied. They weren't even at the square and in sight of Helstrum yet, but the man was gazing ahead of him like a Deity was about to appear.

Once the group had made it into Narus, Garaz managing to slip through without anyone catching sight of his green skin, Nicolas had tried once again to lose Niam, telling him he needed to know where his companions were going so he didn't get lost later—and that he needed to hitch his horse before he went anywhere anyway. Once again, Shift had embuggered his efforts to ditch Niam, inviting him along to the tavern—though Nicolas got a measure of revenge, judging by Shift's strained smile as they listened to Niam expound on religion, politics, and women.

Nicolas had even tried to convince Silva to come with them. There was evidence Helstrum knew more about events than he ought to, but apparently, Silva would've stuck out like a sore thumb, defeating the object of gathering intelligence. Besides, she had to plan the next part of their journey, which somehow required Auron's input as well, leaving the spirit sadly unable to accompany him.

'It's a rally, kid. Even you can't get into trouble at one of those.'

Though the closer they got, the more curious Nicolas became. What sort of man wrote such things? What would he look like? Did he really have foreknowledge of events, or was the Etherius gossip network ridiculously efficient?

'Hm hmm. Right,' Nicolas said for what felt like the thousandth time.

Niam had spent the whole walk banging on about Tobias and his theories, citing specific passages like they were divine scripture, and Nicolas had mostly learned to consign his rantings to background noise. Though he had asked the odd question or two, to try to discern why Niam was so enthused by Helstrum's theories, but all he could get was that Niam had lost his home in a random earthquake that he had, somehow, attributed to a non-human.

Mind you, fauns cause plenty of trouble. But making earthquakes...

Joining the crowd was a claustrophobic's worst nightmare. For a moment, he could barely see as various coloured robes surrounded him, closing in then parting like a bizarre tide of enthusiastic fools. Getting through them took some deft footwork and the liberal application of his elbows. The sheer excitement around him, from smiling faces to waving banners, felt so out of place, considering the speaker.

Finally, they broke out into the town square, whose perimeter was surrounded by beige, flat-roofed buildings. It was hard to make out much detail amidst the sea of people, but Nicolas did see some folk hanging from the odd, angular piece of art in the square's centre. Whatever had happened to a good, old-fashioned statue? Maybe the Nalbians considered it vanity to chisel the likenesses of certain citizens?

I do not look forward to the day I come across a statue of Auron.

'Here.' Niam led him to one of the edges of the square, beside a grocer's shop. The shopkeeper glared out the window at the crowd, many of who weren't paying attention to where they were walking and knocking his produce off the barrels outside the shop window.

Finally free of the throng, Nicolas looked back the way they'd come and cursed himself. He'd had ample opportunity to lose Niam in the masses of people, but he'd been so busy trying to get through them that the thought hadn't occurred to him.

Dammit.

As his unwanted tour guide babbled on about something amazing Etherius's most famous novelist had written, Nicolas craned his neck to look over the crowd. A large stage had been set up on one side of the square, with a single podium atop it. It seemed all the people nearer the stage were wearing those crimson robes, and a squad of soldiers formed a human fence around it. Their armour was plain and functional, with cloth wrappings obscuring all but their eyes as they watched for trouble.

Nicolas jerked suddenly as the corner of a book struck his arm.

'And you see this passage here? Tobias—'

Nicolas should've been happy that Niam had stopped talking, *finally*, but it was unnerving, because the same thing had happened to the entire crowd, a hush descending on it as if some unseen will had impressed the need for silence upon them. Despite himself, Nicolas was interested in what was about to happen. Curiosity can be a strange mistress sometimes. A man could see a pair of orcs fighting in the road, but instead of turning back the other way he could be equally likely to ride by them so he could catch a glimpse of the carnage they wrought on each other, which would then be gossiped about in the nearest tavern. And Nicolas was curious about Tobias Helstrum.

The man who walked out was exactly the opposite of what Nicolas had expected. He'd pictured someone larger, more imposing…maybe breathing fire. Instead, he was an older man in a simple black tunic and wide-brimmed hat, who hobbled across the stage supported by his cane. And yet, the crowd uttered an awestruck gasp. Were they seeing something different to him? The only thing vaguely gasp-worthy about him, as far as he could see, was his escort of four red-robed men who would clearly cave your skull in with the spiked maces they carried at the slightest nod from their master. Once he arrived at the podium, the man gave his cane and his hat to the nearest follower. Even from here, Nicolas could make out the mess of burn scars that made up one side of his face. Tobias Helstrum rested on the podium, gazing out at the crowd in the manner of a dissatisfied tutor. The unmarred part of his face was lined with wrinkles and something else, more obvious than the scars.

Rage.

As the man took in the crowd before him, Nicolas found the lack of applause—or anything else from the crowd—eerie. This was the attentive silence of people ready to learn, which, considering the information they were likely about to be given, was not a good thing at all.

'It does me good to see so many here today.' Helstrum's voice was deep and resonating, carrying across the square with ease. 'To see so many ready to open their ears and eyes to the truth. You…all of you…are a credit to humanity.'

His declaration was followed by a smattering of applause and a couple of enthusiastic *whoops.*

Tobias held up a hand, and any noise vanished. 'And when I say *humanity*, I mean our people. Humans. I do not mean what we have become: people fractured into various kingdoms, giving in to base squabbles with each other over resources, petty political slights and suchlike. We are not the different peoples our kings and queens would have us believe. We share a common bond: humanity. And we need that common bond, now more than ever.' He let his words hang in the air for a moment, giving the people time to properly digest them. 'And why is that? Because we are a people under siege. But it is not a siege of armies and castles. Instead, we are being corrupted from within, by those without.' There was a smattering of jeers and boos from the crowd. 'Those who aren't like us look upon us and see our potential as one race, and it frightens them. So they work their insidious schemes to keep us apart, to make us the fearful ones.'

Deities, this is such a load of crap.

Tobias leant over the podium for a moment, as if the burden of speaking his *truth* was too much for him. 'And how do they create that fear?' he asked, his voice rising like a rumbling volcano, ready to explode. 'By chipping at the fabric of our society, by inciting war and economic issues. We have dwarves bankrupting kingdoms. Fauns making designs to start wars. Rat men tainting the wells with their filth to bring sickness to the masses. And now the Guilds are going to war with each other, incited by...yes, another inhuman.'

They're acknowledging that Billy was a faun? That's news to me.

Shaking, Helstrum slammed his fist on the podium. 'Ogres in Hoflar. Vampires in Yarringsburg... They are getting bolder every day. And what do we do? What do our rulers and lords and protectors do? *Nothing*.' Tobias put his hands to his eyes as if looking over a great distance. 'I see no heroes from the Hall of Champions riding to our rescue.'

'Filthy drunkards,' someone in the crowd shouted.

'Barely better than mercenaries,' another chimed in.

To Nicolas's horror, the crowd was in the palm of Helstrum's hand, intent on his every word. Credit where it was due, he was a skilful orator; it was just a shame he was using his skill to spit such venom.

'To survive, as a people, we can no longer rely on others. We must become bold, my friends. We must find it within ourselves to face this onslaught.' Another pause for effect. 'Even today, word has reached me of a murderer loose in the city of Babylon, a city built to promote a supposed peace between us and the nightmare creatures at our door.' *A murderer?* 'Good human folk killed. I hear tell of roving gangs haunting the streets at night, inciting violence as people cower in their homes. Let that sit with you, my friends. All this in a city made for peace.'

'They don't know the meaning of the word,' a woman shouted.

Helstrum raised the hand on the burnt side of his body, and it was practically a withered claw. He stared at his open hand intently. 'As a people, we are represented by this hand. We are open, and therefore, we are weak.' Trembling, the fingers began to move, closing slowly until the hand made a fist. Even from where he was, Nicolas could see that it must've caused Helstrum great pain. 'But once that hand comes together, it is a mighty fist. It is not us who are weak, but those who oppose us.' He slammed the fist against the table. 'I will happily make a fist if it saves us from machination...from integration...from dilution and destruction.'

Each statement was punctuated by a banging of his fist on the podium. 'I will stand up in the name of humanity. If a scarred, elderly man can stand, who else can? Who is willing to help hold the line between us and the craven hordes encircling us?' Slowly, a rhythmic beat rose around him. It was the crowd, beating their fists against their chests. It sounded disturbingly like a war drum. 'I say *no* to those who would lay us low,' Helstrum was positively screaming now. 'I say *no* to those who wish us ill. I say *no* to the inhuman menace.'

He had to look away. Nausea rose in his belly. This much hate, it was…too much. He couldn't bear it. Beside him, Niam watched Helstrum as if tempted to run up on the stage and kiss him on the mouth. With tongue.

I'm sure the guards will have some opinions on that.

He looked toward the sky—the only place free from Helstrum's damnable fan club—and a flicker of movement caught his attention. There was a shadow atop the building he was stood in front of. Squinting, he cupped his hands over his eyes. It was hard to make out detail, but a pair of antlers rose from the top of the figure's head. Its arms reached forward, and he saw something else.

A bow.

And the arrow was already notched. Quickly, he followed the archer's line of sight, though he'd already guessed the intended target. Tobias Helstrum.

Dammit.

Sure, the world would be a better place without that man in it, but he couldn't just sit back and let him get killed.

Besides, how many will die in the ensuing riot?

Whatever the archer was thinking, it would do nothing good for the relations between humans and non-humans.

The string of the bow pulled taut as Nicolas slipped a knife from his belt. There was no time to line up his shot; he just had to hope his training was paying off. Flicking his wrist back, holding the knife by the blade, he swung his arm forward and launched it. His aim wasn't great, but it did the job. The blade pinged off the wall just beside the archer's elbow, surprising him and throwing off his shot. Nicolas cringed as the bow twanged. The arrow was too fast to track, and by the time he turned his head, it was stuck in the bottom of the podium, vibrating with the force of the impact.

That'll do. Thank the Deities.

Within an instant, chaos gripped the square, people screaming and shoving each other so they could get away as quickly as possible. On stage, the red-robed men formed a human wall between Helstrum and further arrows as they escorted him away.

As he turned his attention back to the roof, the archer had vanished. There were a lot over cries of, '*It came from over there,*' but beyond that, none of Helstrum's previously engrossed followers seemed intent on doing anything about it beyond waving their hands in the air. And none of the soldiers had been positioned on that side of the square.

Looks like it's left to me then.

Ducking down the alley beside the building, Nicolas had no idea what he intended to do beyond hoping that if he kept just doing things, a favorable solution would sort of...appear.

And so it has.

Breaking into a run, he smiled as he saw the old crates almost perfectly lined up as a set of steps. Only vaguely aware that he should be concerned about how sturdy they were, Nicolas hopped on each of them until he was within reach of the edge of the roof. Grabbing it, he quickly pulled himself up onto it.

'Oi, stop.'

The archer actually obeyed, halting in his flight and swinging round in surprise. His face was definitely not human, but it was strange...off somehow. Still, Nicolas wasn't about to waste an opportune moment contemplating it, so he launched himself from his perch and onto the archer. Together, they tumbled to the surface of the roof, the bow flying from the archer's hands as they did.

There were a few moments of frantic grappling as the pair rolled across the roof. When this came to a stop, Nicolas was on top of the archer, giving him the advantage until a blow caught him in the ribs. Bringing his arm back to protect his side from further attacks gave the archer an opening. Getting his leg up between him and Nicolas, the archer planted his boot on Nicolas's chest and pushed him off.

Falling back, Nicolas scrabbled to his feet, doing so a second slower than the archer, who was ready to continue his flight. Throwing himself forward, Nicolas reached out, managing to take a handful of the archer's leaf covered cloak. Planting his feet, he yanked hard, pulling the archer to the floor with an *urk*.

Careful to circumvent the antlers, Nicolas jumped back onto the archer, pinning his neck to the ground with his forearm.

'Yield,' he demanded in between panting.

As he looked into the archer's eyes, he frowned. Something wasn't right. Was it because they didn't look like they matched his face? They were almost...

Blade.

Nicolas's hero instincts saved him. His free hand whipped out and grabbed the knife hand. Taking his forearm off of the archer's neck, he drove his knuckle into the pressure point on the bicep of the knife hand, which opened involuntarily. A moment later, the blade clattered to the ground. He wouldn't get stabbed today, but his focus on the knife also cost him. A fierce punch struck him across the jaw and he fell to the side. The archer came with him, rolling until he was now atop Nicolas. Instantly, hands were around Nicolas's throat, squeezing.

There was a time when this would have caused him to spiral into a panic. But he'd had Silva atop him plenty of times now, and whoever this was, it wasn't Silva.

Silva would be critiquing my fighting prowess whilst cutting off my air supply.

He stuck down on his attacker's—well, technically, he was the attacker in this scenario—elbow joints, collapsing him forward before driving his palm up into the archer's chin, causing a satisfying grunt of pain. And then the man's face...dislodged.

'What the...?' He held the face in his hand, staring at it dumbfoundedly.

A mask?

The distraction cost him dearly. Another fist caught him hard across the jaw, turning his world into a spinning, blurred mess, as the archer's weight lifted off him. Reeling, he managed to scramble to his feet just in time to see the figure jump off the far end of the building and vanish. He didn't catch even the slightest glimpse of his real face.

'Dammit,' he said, picking up the discarded bow and examining it side by side with the mask. 'Why would—?'

'You there!'

Nicolas wheeled round to see the first of the red-robed men climb up onto the roof via a trap door leading to the building below. He didn't look happy with Nicolas for some reason and was unslinging his mace.

As he looked from the man to the mask and bow he now held in his hands, he quickly understood what the problem was.

Oh shit.

CHAPTER 11

Putting on his most innocent look—which, of course, only served to make him look guiltier—Nicolas dropped the incredibly incriminating items he was holding. As they clattered to the floor by his feet, he raised his hands and began to back away slowly. 'No. No, no, no, no,' he said nervously. 'There's been a mistake here. A misunderstanding. I can see how this looks, but you need to understand...

That I'm babbling like a moron. Deities damn it.

The red-robed man, whose rage-contorted face did not indicate his inclination to listen to Nicolas's tale, advanced towards him, swinging his mace arm very much like someone about to cave a skull in.

'Spare me your lies, assassin,' the man spat as two of his colleagues hauled themselves up onto the roof with him. 'At least go to the Underworld like a man.'

I certainly don't want to go back ther—

The implication hit him like a stone launched from a catapult. They were going to kill him, right here on this roof. There would be no trial, no witnesses, no long walk to the hangman's noose—all of which would've given his companions ample opportunity to save him. No, there would just be him having his head turned into a pile of bloody goo by three robed maniacs.

But I can't exactly fight them. They're only up here because they think I'm an assassin. It's not their fault they've got the wrong end of the stick.

Slowly, the three men fanned out, one rhythmically slapping his mace in his hand as he did. The metal meeting the flesh of the palm sounded hard, and the robed man wasn't even putting any heft into the swing. He would be soon though. Unwilling to fight—and even more unwilling to let them turn his head to mush because of a misunderstanding—Nicolas only had one option.

With an impulsive, and very unmanly, yelp, he turned and ran. It wasn't a great option, considering he was on a roof. But he lacked Shift's ability to grow wings and fly away, so this was it. A shout of surprise was followed by pounding footsteps as the robed men pursued him. Ahead of him, the roof simply stopped. Yet beyond the gap was another roof just like it, at the same height.

I can make it.

Pouring energy and hesitant self-belief into his legs, Nicolas ran faster. The edge almost seemed to be running towards him, eager for him to fall off. He reached it sooner than he would've liked and, with three deep breaths, launched himself into the air. Naturally, time slowed, letting him luxuriate in every second of uncertainty and fear to its fullest. Then his feet hit the solid rooftop. He rolled with the impact, coming up and continuing his flight almost seamlessly. Risking a glance back, he saw the lead man make the jump. The other two let their fear get the better of them, coming to a halt. Shaking their heads, they took a small jog backwards before running and making the jump too. But at least the three were more spread out now.

The chase continued. Over one roof, then another, then another. By the third, some very inventive curses about his lineage were coming from his pursuers. The lead man was clearly the fitter of the three, as he kept up with Nicolas, showing absolutely no sign of tiring, whilst the other two lagged behind more and more, puffing and panting as indulgent living took its toll. They hadn't caught him, but how long would that last?

How many times can I jump across roofs before someone cuts me off? I'm in the open up here.

His ears pricked up as he heard a noise. A whinny. *A horse.* Angling his run so he ended up moving along the edge of the roof without slowing, he saw a pair of horses and wagon tied to a post ahead. The wagon was quite large. Easy to land on.

And jumping is better than the alternative.

Flying in the face of every survival instinct he had, Nicolas launched himself from the roof. Another few seconds-that-dragged-like-an-eternity later, he landed on the wagon with a thud, violently shaking it and causing both horses to rear up and bolt, snapping the post with their combined panic. The horses ran in the direction they had been facing when their surprise passenger dropped in, which was, naturally, right back toward the town square.

Bollocks.

He spied the reins flapping around one of the charging horse's rumps. He began to inch toward them when one of the robed men leaped into the cart in front of him. Somehow, the bloody show-off had landed on his feet, weapon at the ready. But the sudden impact made the horses rear again, jinking the wagon fiercely. The man lost his balance, stumbling forward with a cry. Waving his arms in desperation, he tripped past

Nicolas and over the side of the wagon. As he did, his robe caught on the side, and he found himself being dragged in its wake, throwing up a dust cloud as he was pulled along.

Instantly, Nicolas jumped up and went for the reins. He clambered into the driver's seat and leant forward, stretching his arm as far as it would go. His fingertips tickled the dancing reins.

Thud.

The second man had landed in the wagon. Above, Nicolas caught a glimpse of the third ahead, ready to jump too.

Some very undeveloped sense Auron might've called his burgeoning *hero instincts* told Nicolas to duck. The mace swung over his head, not leaving the sizeable hole in it the weapon bearer had intended. The next instinct that kicked in was *him or me.* Knowing he couldn't reason with his attacker so that he could grab the reins and bring the runaway wagon to a halt, Nicolas turned and threw a right hook. It caught the robed man in the jaw, sending him stumbling back and over the side of the wagon.

Sorry.

Thud.

Dammit.

He'd been boarded again. The third man swung his mace in a furious downward arc. Nicolas dodged the weapon, which turned the driver's seat into kindling. The robed man tugged but didn't dislodge his mace, whose spikes had dug into the wooden frame. Nicolas wasn't about to politely wait until he was armed and ready to try and beat him to death again. Jumping up, he pulled the man's hood over his head, before launching him from the side of the wagon.

Sorry.

'You little bastard.'

Great. Robed man number one had clambered back onto the wagon, and he had a knife.

Deities, these guys are persistent.

With a cry of rage, the man charged him, stabbing with his deadly blade. Nicolas sidestepped the knife and grabbed his attacker's head. Using his assailant's own momentum, Nicolas drove the bridge of the man's nose onto the handle of the stuck mace. Even over the din of the rumbling wagon wheels, he heard the crunch. He managed to catch the man's body as it went limp, before rolling him off the back of the wagon.

Sorry.

At least that's three attackers down. Now to stop this rampaging wagon before it—

Oh no...

The wagon broke out into the town square. People, who'd only a moment before had been milling around trying to calm themselves after the shock of the assassination attempt, began screaming and running in all directions.

Jumping forwards, he dived past the stuck mace and reached for the reins again. A lucky bump in the road made them flick upwards, and he grabbed them. Problem was, he couldn't stop here. Already, soldiers were charging toward him, spears at the ready. As much as he wanted to stop this wagon and get off—his current nausea was half due to being accused of murder and half due to the bouncing wagon—he couldn't. Instead, he snapped the reins, urging the horses to great speed, whilst doing his best to try to veer it out of the path of pedestrians. The last thing he needed was to turn some poor townsperson into a stain on the road.

Sorry. Sorry. Sorry. Sorry.

The horses, wagon and unwilling driver swerved across the square. Nicolas was so busy watching the people, that he didn't notice the statue in the town centre that he was hurtling towards. With a grunt of effort, he yanked the reins, turning the horses aside just in time. But the sudden turn caused the wagon to jump, striking the statue, which toppled, hitting the floor and breaking into thousands of pieces.

Sorry.

Three brave soldiers tried to block the road ahead of him, but once it was clear the wagon wasn't going to stop, their bravery was exhausted and they threw themselves aside. Which was a blessing, really, because he didn't want to add stampeding over the local soldiery to his growing list of crimes.

An apple struck him on the side of the head as the people's panic turned to anger, and the crowd began to lob whatever they held in his direction. Still, he didn't stop.

Passing the stage, he saw the podium with the arrow still stuck into it.

At least he'd saved a life. Even if it was Tobias Helstrum's.

Now to save my own.

The wagon burst out the other side of the square, and he drove as far from it as he could, as fast as he could.

****

Emerging from an alleyway three removed from where he'd finally dumped the wagon, Nicolas tried to control the shaking in his legs and act naturally.

Do not *draw attention to yourself.*

'Do you hear that?' a passer by remarked to the man he was walking with. 'Something must be going on in the square.'

The man listened then frowned. 'It's just those Helstrum idiots getting overzealous. For a bunch of people who dress in robes and act pious, they do make a lot of commotion.'

The news hasn't reached here yet. Good.

Trying to check he wasn't being watched, without making it look like he was checking if he was being watched, Nicolas slipped into the inn. Thankfully, it was quiet, and those who were there were too drunk to pay him any heed. Most of the patrons must've been at the Helstrum gathering.

I probably nearly ran a few of them over.

'Excuse me,' he asked the well-built man behind the bar, a former warrior judging by the old scars. 'My friends checked in recently. Fo...three people. They probably booked under the name *Shift*.' He cursed himself for nearly counting Auron, who the innkeeper wouldn't have been able to see. 'Which room are they in, please?'

'Four,' the barman said, barely looking up from his book to gesture to a corridor off the main room.

'Thank you.'

Following the corridor, his casual walk became an urgent jog once he was alone.

2...3...

He opened the door to room four, slipped inside, then quickly closed it and leaned against it, panting heavily. His companions stared at him, frozen in the middle of whatever they'd been doing when he entered. In Shift's case, it appeared they'd been making the most of finally having a comfy bed to lie on.

Shit.

'Kid?' Auron asked with a raised eyebrow.

'We...um...well...we can't stay here tonight.'

Shift sat bolt upright on the bed. 'What did you do?' they hissed.

Nicolas tried not to notice their hand holding onto the bedsheet for dear life.

No sense sugar-coating it.

'I...um...may be wanted for theft...assault, public disorder, and...attempted assassination.'

Four sets of jaws hung wide open, causing him to laugh nervously.

'But we only left you for half an hour,' Silva said in confusion.

CHAPTER 12

Night had descended on Narus, but the streets were still packed with people, the majority of them soldiers, hunting for a would-be assassin.

'The gate's still locked tight,' Auron confirmed as he walked through the door to the room. 'There were a fair few people protesting about it, until the guards got liberal with their clubs when a trader tried to muscle past them. Suddenly, they got very quiet.'

The town militia had been very quick in shutting and guarding the gate once word spread about the attack on Helstrum.

'What about the patrols?' Silva, positioned by the window, asked.

'Still sweeping the streets,' the spirit confirmed. 'They're kicking in cellar doors and searching alleyways. I think the assumption is that the assassin would've gone to ground, instead of holding up in a room he'd paid for.' Auron's mouth curved up in a slight smirk. 'Still, once they've exhausted all other options, they'll start banging on inn doors.'

'We can't stay here much longer then,' Nicolas said nervously.

'No,' Shift said through gritted teeth. 'We can't stay here at all. Because apparently some moronic malcontent tried to kill Tobias Helstrum then charged a wagon through the town square.'

'I only did half of that,' Nicolas replied weakly.

'And yet I don't get to sleep in half a bed,' the shapeshifter retorted.

'Well, they think you did all of it, kid.' Auron clearly knew something he wasn't sharing. It was kind of frustrating. 'But don't worry. We've been in tight spots before, plenty of times.'

Very reassuring from the man who can't be hung.

'We will find a way out,' Garaz said quietly at his side.

'You should be worried too,' Nicolas exclaimed. 'If they find an orc in the town, they'll stab first and ask questions later.'

'The thought had occurred that entering this town was a mistake,' the orc said with a sigh. 'But we are here now.'

'And we need to get out.' Nicolas swallowed hard. 'Any ideas? Maybe we could pretend we need to get medicine to a sick relative urgently.'

'You and thirty others at the gate.' Auron chuckled. 'If any of them actually have a sick relative, I'm a ghost.'

'B—' Nicolas cut himself off quickly as Auron's pupilless white eyes flicked to him. 'B...but there has to be another option.'

'I suggest we get out of this building unseen first,' Silva said, moving from the wall. 'I checked this place over when we arrived. There is a back door to an alleyway running behind the inn. We can use it to slip out then work on getting out of town altogether.'

With no better options, the group quickly gathered their belongings. Luckily, the corridor was quiet. The back door was locked, naturally, but that barely mattered with Shift around. It was open in seconds. Silva ducked out first then gestured that the coast was clear. Shift went next. Nicolas frowned as they hesitated briefly before stepping out into the alley. There was an odd look of surprise on their face, which quickly became one of mirth.

I could've sworn they just glanced at me.

Putting it down to paranoia, he followed them out into the alleyway. When he pressed himself to the wall, though, something caught his attention.

'What the f –'

Silva's hand clapped over his mouth. After a few moments, she took the hand away. Nicolas barely noticed. He was too busy staring at the piece of parchment stuck to the wall across from him, which was currently illuminated by Auron's aura.

I'm on...a wanted poster.

'How did they get such a good likeness?' he gasped, pulling the hood of his cloak a little tighter. 'And why am I gawping like that?'

'That's your usual expression,' Shift replied, cold as ice. 'You're doing it right now.'

Nicolas closed his mouth.

'It was most likely Helstrum's bodyguards,' Auron said thoughtfully. 'They were the only ones who would've got a good enough look at you.'

I should've hit them harder. At least enough to impair their memories.

'M-maybe I could just go and explain all this. I'm sure—'

'You've done enough already,' Shift said with a glare in his direction. 'Like costing me a warm bed.'

I'm going to be hearing about that for months.

'Well, I'm sorry,' he hissed back. 'I wasn't exactly planning on getting marked as an assassin. I was trying to save someone's life. And you weren't the only one looking forward to a warm bed, you know.'

'Ooooh,' Shift held their hands in the air. 'I humbly apologise. Knowing you're upset too makes it all better.'

'Will you two cut it out?' Auron chided sternly. 'Let's focus on finding a way out of this town before they hunt down the *Alexi in training* here.'

Shift studied the wanted poster closely. '*Two hundred gold pieces*. Someone could buy a nice room for the night with that. One with a *bed*.'

Quickly, Nicolas tore the poster from the wall, folding it and stuffing it into his belt as he glanced from side to side to ensure no one had seen him. Well, no one likely to try to cash in on the reward, anyway.

Why don't I just discard it? Screw it up or tear it to pieces and stomp it into the dirt.

But he just couldn't. Part of him was vaguely worried he was keeping it to add to some sort of adventuring scrap book in his old age.

If I live that long.

'You are not helping,' Garaz admonished the shapeshifter softly.

Shift appeared to not give two hoots. 'I could always distract the guards. I'll turn into Nick and run past the gate naked, screaming, *'I like to kill people. Everyone, look at me.'* You lot can slip out while the guards chase me.'

Nicolas narrowed his eyes. 'Why *naked*?'

'Because you cost me my first warm bed in a week.' Shift smiled evilly.

'As much as I'd enjoy that show,' Auron chuckled, 'there's no way they won't leave someone to guard the gate. These are professional soldiers, not a village lynch mob.'

'Shame.' Shift shrugged. 'I was going to make the form very unflattering.' Nicolas opened his mouth to protest, but Shift cut him off. 'First warm bed in a week.'

Dammit.

'That still leaves us with the issue of how to get out,' Garaz said.

'Don't worry,' Shift sighed with an eyeroll, 'I have, once again, come up with an idea to save the day.'

****

Nicolas rubbed the tips of his fingers anxiously as he looked up at Auron's torso. The spirit's body ended at the ceiling and the hatch to the roof, which might offer them salvation. Though really it wasn't the whole group who were in trouble.

Just me. I'm the one on the wanted posters.

'The roof is clear,' Auron confirmed as his head reappeared through the wood.

'Move,' Shift said to the spirit.

Auron descended the ladder, and Shift went up it to work on the lock with the same skill they'd used to get them into the empty house.

Nicolas was trying hard not to urge them to just use the magic key they wore around their neck that opened any lock, but he was already on the shapeshifter's bad side, and though the situation was grave, travelling with a pissed-off Shift was worse.

'We will need to be quick once we are on the roof,' Silva said, keeping an eye on the corridor around them. All it would take was an unexpected return home for them to be discovered. Then they would either have to let Silva knock out some innocent homeowner or give said homeowner the chance to become a fair bit richer.

'Funnily enough, I do have a little experience escaping places at speed,' Shift remarked coolly, taking the padlock off the hinge and throwing it to the floor. Nicolas winced at the clang. It might as well have been a war horn, summoning every soldier in the area.

'But apparently not quietly,' Silva said sternly.

Shift glanced down at the lock and appeared ready to argue. Instead, they took a breath. 'Sorry,' they said in a rare display of sincerity. 'I'm a bit distracted. My mind keeps drifting back to that *bed*.'

Sigh.

'You're sure about this idea?' Nicolas asked, his nerves overcoming his ability to hold the question back.

The shapeshifter looked him over. 'You, yes,' they confirmed. 'Garaz will be the issue.'

'Once again, I am reminded that I am the largest in the group,' the orc muttered in annoyance.

'But it's all muscle.' Shift grinned. 'And you know you're the largest, so stop being so sensitive. But the bigger the bird I turn into, the more chance I have of getting spotted. That's why you're going last.'

'That is logical.' But Garaz was clearly still aggrieved by the mention of his size.

Shift nodded to Auron, and the spirit ascended the small ladder, passing through the hatch and onto the roof.

'You're still good,' came his muffled voice through the wood.

'Time to change,' Shift said, opening the wooden hatch slightly. Before they slipped out onto the roof, they gave Nicolas a withering glare. 'No peeking.'

'What?' he stammered. 'I wouldn't.'

'Good. You lost that privilege when I lost a good night's sleep.' *I had that privilege in the first place?* 'And just so you know, you're carrying my clothes and pack.'

'Fine, yes,' he said. Their quick escape was starting to become pretty long and drawn out.

With a single fluid motion, Shift vanished through the hatch, gently easing it back into place behind them. Within a few moments, there was a scratching on the other side.

Wordlessly, Silva pushed it open, letting in the cool night air. Staring upwards, all Nicolas could see was the starry sky.

Maybe I can move to one of those? From here, they all seem a lot more peaceful.

The rungs of the ladder creaked slightly as Silva ascended. The warrior put her head and shoulders through the opening. Briefly, Nicolas caught a glimpse of talons gripping her arms before Silva was lifted into the air with a gentle beating of wings.

Bang. Bang. Bang.

Nicolas jumped, thankfully without crying out. Both he and Garaz stared toward the door of the house. After a moment, there was a second, more insistent round of banging.

'Militia. Open the door,' a voice called. 'We need to search the house.'

That's not happening.

'I don't think anyone's home,' a second voice said from beyond the door.

'Well, we still have to search it,' the first voice snapped. 'The fugitive may be hiding in there. Fugitives love empty houses.'

With a gulp, Nicolas put his hand on the hilt of the *Dawn Blade*. He didn't know why; he wasn't about to use it on innocent soldiers. Yet it was comforting. Garaz was doing something similar, his green hands wrapping more tightly around his staff.

Nicolas jumped again as Auron flew down from the roof hatch, before disappearing through the wall to the tune of a third round of knocking.

'No answer sir.'

'Fine,' the first voice huffed. 'Just kick the door in. We can— What was that?'

Nicolas gave Garaz a puzzled look at the sudden crash that came from the side of the house. The orc tilted his head and raised an eyebrow.

Of course, Auron.

'It came from the alley. Let's move.' The statement was followed by the sound of urgent footsteps moving away from them. Slowly, Nicolas let out a sigh of relief.

'You're getting better at that,' he whispered to Auron as the spirit appeared back through the wall.

'Thanks, kid. That was a big one.' The exertion was clear on the spirit's face, his aura slightly dimmed.

Glancing up, Nicolas jumped a third time. A giant eye was staring at him through the roof hatch. Even as a bird, Shift's eyes imparted their distaste at having their chance of sleeping in a bed tonight ruined. The head disappeared from the opening, and Nicolas climbed the ladder. As soon as his upper body was through the hatch, he grabbed Shift's pack and then splayed his arms.

'*Urk.*' Shift's talons grabbed his arms roughly and yanked him into the air. Apparently, he was not to have a gentle ride, no doubt in payment for costing them their bed.

Rising into the air, he fought the urge to kick his feet to find solid ground. When he looked up, the shapeshifter had taken the form of a giant black raven, which made sense, with it being night and all. Within a few flaps of Shift's wings he could see the outlines of the buildings making up the town of Narus, illuminated by the street lanterns that glowed between them, or lights in the houses themselves. And more importantly, he could see the wall of the town was directly ahead of them. Freedom was in sight. Then Shift stopped, flapping their wings gently to stay aloft. Nicolas glanced at the bird then looked down. Directly below them was a troop of soldiers standing around a fallen barrel.

'It didn't just fall on its own,' one said, holding his torch closer to inspect the object. 'Someone must've been here.'

He stared at the guards, willing them not to look up. Fate had never bowed to his will yet, but that didn't mean he wasn't going to try. His concentration was broken when he heard the fluttering of paper.

Shit.

The wanted poster had slipped from his belt. It lazily drifted down as Nicolas watched in horror, unable to do anything to try to catch it without giving himself away. Again, he tried to use his will to influence the outcome of an event: where the paper would land.

Come on. Come on.

Just before it went between the buildings, a breeze caught it, lifting it to the roof of the nearest house.

Thank the Deities.

He was about to sigh with relief when his nose twitched.

Oh no.

Smoke from the torches below was wafting lazily into the night sky and straight into Nicolas's nostrils. Instantly, his nose tickled with the promise of the loudest sneeze in all Etherius. Unable to reach his nose with a giant bird holding his arm, he tried to force his nostrils shut. Inside, the pressure was building, the tickle worsening until he was internally screaming, his eyes streaming from the smoke and exertion.

Crash.

'There,' one of the guards cried, the troop already moving away.

Bless you, Auron.

The sneeze battered against his nose, demanding to be let out as he was swung from side to side in the short flight between the roof and the wall of the town. With a gentle beating of wings, they lowered him. About halfway down the thick wall surrounding the town, Shift let go. They'd calculated the distance perfectly: not enough for him to break his ankles on the fall, but plenty enough for him to end up on his ass covered in dirt.

As soon as he hit the ground, he wrapped his arm around his nose and unleashed the demonic sneeze. The wave of relief afterwards was euphoric.

Silva's shadow stood over him. 'Are you well?'

Nicolas picked himself up and dusted himself off. 'Yes, Shift was just paying me back for the bed.'

The warrior looked up again. 'I doubt their thirst for vengeance is quenched yet.'

Naturally.

A few moments later, Shift was gently lowering Garaz to the ground beside him, their wings beating slightly harder to adjust for the orc's weight. When Garaz was down, they landed themselves, uncomfortably close to Nicolas.

Not a second later, Auron strolled smugly through the wall. 'Who's dead but still very useful?' The spirit didn't need to point to himself, but he did. 'You guys all good?'

'We are well,' Garaz confirmed quietly.

A wing butted Nicolas. Turning to Shift, he guessed they were gesturing for their clothes with their insistent beak movement. After a moment rummaging in Shift's pack, he produced their clothes. He made a big show of stopping halfway as he lowered them to the ground then dropped them the rest of the way. Bird Shift was not impressed.

Within minutes, Shift was back in their preferred form and the group were making for the ridge line in a crouched run. Concealing themselves in the nearby bushes, they watched and waited. There appeared to be no sign of pursuit, nor that anyone even knew they'd left. Good. The soldiers could wear their feet out looking for him all night if they fancied. They were away.

Without our horses. Dammit.

CHAPTER 13

Burning blisters nagged for his attention as they trudged down the road. Nicolas had assumed that, by now, his feet were used to a lot of walking; problem was, he'd been wearing the same boots for a long time, and they were wearing away to the point they were only a single level up from walking bare foot. Longingly, he glanced at Auron's boots, which were hanging from the side of his spectral steed, Mare, who Auron was able to summon at will—unlike their horses, which were now probably being sold to some trader. Whilst the spirit wasn't openly lording it over them, there was a certain mischievous smugness to his aura.

Why does it even matter to him? He wouldn't get blisters if he walked anyway.

One of the first things he needed to do when they reached Babylon was find a good shoemaker and get some decent adventuring boots. Given the state of his feet now, it would be money well spent.

Maybe the rest of my outfit should reflect my new life too?

Inwardly, he cursed the fact that he was slowly resigning himself to this malarky. He might as well get some armour and have someone etch *Nick Carnage* into it.

At least I'm not the wheezing mess I was when Auron first dragged me up that bloody mountain.

It'd been barely a quarter of the way up, really, but hyperbole suited his mood.

At least, in the two days they'd been on the road—though it felt like they'd visited Narus weeks ago—there'd been no sign of pursuit. And, according to Auron and Silva, Babylon should be coming into sight very soon.

I wonder if they're still searching the town for me? Is it still locked down?

How long would the search continue? Maybe the gate would be shut forever? Perhaps he would become a legend, the infamous vanishing assassin—albeit an incompetent one. Generations would pass down the tale of the stupid assassin who'd missed his target, rampaged through the town square, and then simply disappeared.

Hmm. If I am going to be remembered as an assassin, I'd rather not be remembered as a bungling one.

'Ow.'

'You're thinking something daft,' Shift said, retracting the fist they'd used to punch him.

He looked at them and let out a small chuckle. 'How could you possibly know that?'

Shift raised an eyebrow. 'Your face is all thoughtful but dreamy. And you aren't scrunching your eyes, so it's not you imagining a horrible fate. So what is it?'

'You know me too well.'

'I do pay attention.' They smiled back after a brief pause. 'So come on then, entertain me. I think you owe me that.'

'Well,' he could guess their reaction, but decided to open up anyway, 'I was wondering if there'd be a legend in Narus about me from now on. The assassin who vanished. You know...'

Deities, I was thinking something daft.

Shift's face went from confusion to full-on smirk. 'A local legend based on you? That's a big head you've got there, Nick. Too much time spent with Auron, methinks.'

He realised something then. Shift always called him *Nick*. And it never bothered him.

Why do I let that go when I'm so pernickety about it with everyone else?

'I guess,' he said with a smile. 'Maybe I just overestimate my importance. Must be because *you* pay so much attention to me.'

Shift scoffed. 'Oh, is that it?' they asked. 'Or maybe you'd just like me to.' They went to punch him again, but this time, he blocked the blow. 'Oooh,' Shift stopped and squared up to him. 'A challenge then, is it?'

'Apparently so.' He grinned. 'Have at me.'

A mischievous grin crossed Shift's lips. 'If you say so.'

In the middle of the road, the pair began to play fight, exchanging flimsy attempts to slap each other. Well, Nicolas's attempts were flimsy. Shift was playing to win.

'Ah-ha,' the shapeshifter gloated, pointing at him after landing a slap across the face.

He feigned shock as he rubbed his cheek.

Does the kiss come now?

He quickly shook that errant thought away. Shift came at him again, and he acted reflexively, grabbing their wrist and pulling forward. Shift stumbled forward, bumping into him. Now they were practically nose to nose.

'Um...' Nicolas had no idea what to say. But he had a very clear idea what he wanted to do.

'I yield,' Shift said, stepping back and giving him a dramatic bow. 'I have been bested.'

Things got awkward quickly.

'What was Tobias Helstrum like?'

I could kiss Garaz for the interruption.

Nicolas fell into step with the orc as he passed by. Ahead of them, Silva and Auron turned back to face the direction they were headed after watching Nicolas and Shift's antics.

Why are they both shaking their heads?

Putting it out of his mind, he reminded himself of the old figure on the podium. 'He was just a hateful old man,' Nicolas said thoughtfully. 'He had a lot of burn scars. You'd think he was unassuming, but he knew how to hold a crowd's attention. If I hadn't known better, he might've been able to pull me in with the rest.'

'Sounds accurate enough, judging by his literary works,' Garaz commented gruffly. 'It is disturbing how so much is changing for the worse. All this fighting takes its toll on you. It changes you.'

Nicolas frowned. There was a hidden meaning in the orc's words that he was missing.

'It is a shame you missed him with your arrow,' Silva commented from the front of the group.

'It wasn't *my ar—*' Best not to let himself get baited. Besides, Silva might've had a point. As much as he hated the idea of someone being killed, part of Nicolas was sure that the *greater good* of the universe might've been served if that arrow *had* been on target.

Well, my instinct was to save him. That's who I am.

There was one concept he couldn't get his head around. 'I just don't understand how people could swallow such...hatred.'

'It's like eggs,' Auron said with a shrug. *This should be good.* 'Eggs come out of a chicken's butt, yet we eat them. And why? Because we fry them, scramble them, whatever. We make them more palatable, so we don't think of the stinky hole they emerged from.'

That seemed...really oversimplified. But not entirely wrong. 'Still, all those people listening and cheering. It was terrible.'

'A lot of tragedies are occurring in the kingdoms of man of late,' Garaz said. 'The desire to find someone to blame in such instances can be strong.'

'Maybe next time, let the assassin do his job,' Shift said with a dry chuckle.

'No point crying over hatemongers who aren't dead,' Auron said breezily.

'What do you know about the *actual* assassin?' Silva asked.

'So we're sure Nick didn't do it then?' Shift asked.

Nicolas's loud *tut* appeared to only fuel their broad grin. 'There isn't much to tell.' He tried to recall any detail he could. 'The archer was on the roof. I threw off his shot then managed to get up there after him. We wrestled a bit. Turned out he was wearing an antlered mask.'

'Did you get a look at his face?' Garaz asked.

'Sorry.' He shrugged. 'I think I saw a glimpse of a beard. But that's all.'

'What type of beard?' Silva asked.

Nicolas racked his brain but couldn't bring the image to the fore. In lieu of not answering at all, he decided to give an answer he knew was stupid. 'One made of hair on the face.'

'I doubt you'll ever make a great investigator.' Shift chuckled, shaking their head.

'The mask is an interesting—' Auron pulled Mare to a halt. All the others stopped instantly, an alertness passing through the group. 'Kid,' Auron said with a smile. 'Tell me what you see.'

Nicolas studied the road ahead. There was a smattering of trees and bushes. A couple of rocks. And then just scenery.

'Etherius,' he said with a shrug.

Auron sighed. 'Use your hero instincts, kid. You must be developing some by now, even if by accident. Look again.'

Concentrating intently, Nicolas moved his eyes slowly across the scenery. Gradually, he noticed unnatural shapes. A bush bulging from the ground. A bump protruding from the side of a tree that could've been a belly.

'I...I think there's someone in the bushes.' Now he knew what he was looking for, he began to pick things out more clearly. 'I can see a belly sticking out from behind the tree there. Someone's behind that rock. Andddddddddd—'

'That'll do, kid.' The spirit almost sounded impressed. 'Point is, we have ourselves some bandits.'

'You might as well come out,' Silva bellowed, drawing her sword. 'We know you're there.'

Hesitantly, seven men emerged from the undergrowth. They all wore cloaks with twigs and leaves randomly stuck on them. From the wary glances they gave each other, being called out was not part of their plan. Their leader, a rotund bald man, soon got them in line with a liberal application of grunts and glaring, and they assembled across the road, blocking the way forward.

'Oh, Deities,' Auron said, rubbing his hand over his ethereal face. 'They don't even have bows or swords. Just clubs. I hate lazy bandits. If the best goal you can come up with in life is *'I'm gonna rob people on a road,'* at least put some effort into it. Some flair.'

I'm not about to stand here giving them a critique of their work.

Resting his large club on his shoulder, most likely to prove how at ease he was, the leader took a step forward. 'This 'ere's a toll road. You wants to pass then you gots to pay.'

'Toll road, eh?' Shift replied, nodding. 'Of course. We'll be happy to pay, once we've seen your proper badges of office and...' Shift made a big show of leaning forward and narrowing their eyes. 'I'm sorry, I don't appear to see them. Are you fellows *sure* you're kingdom-registered toll collectors?'

'Oh, you're a funny one, are you?' The big man sneered, taking his club from his shoulder and slapping it into his hand. 'I've gots some medicine for thats right 'ere.'

'That's a club.' Shift sucked their teeth. 'It has no medicinal properties,' they said slowly and loudly, enunciating every word.

An odd shade of red appeared in the man's cheeks. 'Look, love, I'm in no mood to play silly buggers.'

Did he just call Shift...

'I'm sorry,' Nicolas said, holding up his hands. 'There's been a mis-understanding. I'm sure you have the proper badges of office. I think the problem is that we can't see you clearly due to the glare of the sun reflecting off your bald head.'

Normally, Nicolas wasn't one to rile up bandits. However, he'd faced a lot worse than a group of louts with clubs, and they'd insulted Shift.

'Oi,' the leader roared with indignation, pointing his club at Nicolas. 'No bald jokes. My 'air loss is a stigma I've 'ads to live with for years. A disability, some might say. You wants to laugh at someone with a disability? That's *low*.'

Lower than robbing people on the road?

Nicolas looked to his companions, who seemed equally dumbfound-ed.

'Can I just go and kill them now?' Silva asked. Judging by her expression, this was more of a chore than anything else.

'No,' Auron said firmly. 'Kid, off you go.'

'Off I go where?'

The spirit gestured to the bandits. 'Go kick their heads in.'

CHAPTER 14

After a long pause, Auron finally realised that Nicolas was staring at him. The spirit gestured to the bandits again.

'Me? Alone?'

'Yes, kid, you, on your own,' the spirit said with a huff. 'If you can't handle some inept local bandits by yourself then I've been training you wrong.'

'This seems like more of a group effort,' he said, looking up at the spirit. 'Or something Silva might enjoy alone.'

Auron gazed back down at him levelly.

'Who's you talkin' to?' the bandit chief asked, his voice betraying a hint of uncertainty.

Nicolas held up a silencing finger. 'Why me?'

'There are some bandits blocking the road,' Auron said slowly and firmly. 'Defeat them.'

He opened his mouth to protest, but found himself thrust forward as Silva pushed him from behind.

So, I'm doing this then.

With a sigh, he approached the bandits. Maybe he didn't need to resort to violence? Auron said *defeat them*. He could do that with diplomacy as well as he could a sword. Forcing some confidence into his stride, he held out his hand as he reached the bandit leader.

'I think we've gotten off on the wrong foot,' he said with a smile. 'My name is Nicolas Percival Carnegie. I think we can negotiate some kind of agreement before things get ugly.'

'You threatenin' me?' he snarled.

Nicolas looked at his outstretched hand, just to double check there wasn't a knife in it. 'What? No. I didn't mean *before things get ugly*. I meant, before things get ugly.'

'Sounds the same to me,' one of the bandits chimed in. 'And sounds like a threat.'

'That it does.' The leader sneered.

'I don't see any fighting,' Auron called from the back.

'Shut up,' Nicolas snapped.

The bandit leader's eyes went wide with shock and offence. 'Did you just tell me to shut up?'

This is going well.

'No, sorry, I wasn't talking to you and—'

'Look,' the big man grinned maliciously, 'you wants to make a deal, 'ere are my terms. You gives us all your supplies, the orc so we's can sell 'im to 'elstrum's lot, an' the mouthy bitch so we's can 'ave our fun, then you an' the angry lookin' cow are free to go. 'ow's that sound?' He put an exclamation point on the sentence by poking Nicolas firmly in the chest and leaving his finger there.

Mouthy...

Gripping the man's finger, Nicolas twisted it upwards, causing the attached arm to turn at an awkward—and judging by the cry, painful—angle. Still holding the finger, Nicolas drove his fist into the bandit leader's nose, before following up with an uppercut that caught the man right between chins two and three. The bandit's eyes glazed over, and he gradually toppled backwards. Nicolas mentally imposed the sound of a falling tree over what he was seeing, and chuckled.

Before the leader passed out completely, he managed two final words. 'Get 'im.'

One of the bandits was quite keen to obey, charging Nicolas with club raised.

Fine.

Holding his arms up crossed in an X, Nicolas caught the incoming blow. Snatching his arms back, Nicolas took the bandit's club, promptly introducing it to its former owner's face at great speed. As the bandit collapsed, Nicolas swung the club around his head and launched it. The thick piece of wood circled through the air until it collided with the head of an oncoming attacker, who crashed to the ground in a heap.

Four left.

He was half tempted to draw his sword, but it didn't seem...fair? Sporting? He knew he was being ridiculous, but sometimes he couldn't *not* be ridiculous.

The next bandit came at him, weapon swinging. Ducking the blow, Nicolas drove his shoulder into the man's gut. Wrapping his arms around the bandit's torso, Nicolas lifted him into the air and quickly drove him spine-first onto the road. A stomp on the jaw ensured he stayed there.

Three.

Unfortunately, the last three got the bright idea to charge him as one.

Oh crap.

Side stepping to the left of the oncoming attackers, he tripped the nearest one and sending him sprawling to the dirt. Blocking the next incoming blow, he struck the point in the arm where bicep and triceps met. The bandit's hand opened automatically, and he dropped his club. But he was nowhere near done. His other fist caught Nicolas right on the cheek, sending him staggering to the side. Grabbing his collar, the man spun him around and punched him in the stomach, doubling him over. It took some reserve Nicolas didn't even know he had to not only keep the man between himself and the third armed attacker, but to get his guard up and block the next strike. With a cry, he struck the man twice in the face before driving a headbutt into his nose.

Crunch.

Shoving hard, even though he was dizzy from his last attack, Nicolas pushed the bandit into the armed one. Managing to seize his moment, Nicolas rolled forward, grabbing a discarded club and cracking the attacker in the side of the knee with it. The man crumpled as Nicolas rose and smacked him across the head with the weapon. Vaguely aware that the man he'd tripped had gotten up, Nicolas swung wildly, striking him in the jaw and sending him back to the ground from whence he'd come.

'Got...them...' he said between puffs and pants.

'Kid...'

A hand grabbed him and wheeled him around. The bandit leader, his nose a bloody mess and his eyes blackened, punched Nicolas in the gut twice, before striking him across the cheek with a vicious backhand. Nicolas fell to his knees, coughing a glob of blood onto the ground.

'C'mon then,' the bandit leader snarled. 'Get up an' get some more.'

Wiping his chin on his sleeve, Nicolas rose.

'Let's see 'ow good you fight when you don't sucker punch me,' the bandit leader bellowed.

If you insist.

With an angry shout, he punched the leader in the stomach as hard as he could. After the first punch he threw another, and another...and then a couple more. Despite a nauseating sloshing sound from the man's belly, nothing else happened.

'Too much meat for those puny fists to 'andle,' the bald man said, looking down at him with a smirk as he patted his stomach. He raised his club.

Meat? Okay, then.

Dropping down to one knee abruptly, he swung his fist in an upward arc until it connected with the point between the man's legs. Now he reacted, his legs collapsing inwards as he fell to his knees, his entire head a shade of bright red, his eyes crossing as he panted for breath. Nicolas grabbed his discarded club and hit him with it.

'Everything Silva and I have taught you, and *that's* what you go for?' Auron commented, shaking his head. 'In fact, that's your go-to quite a lot. It's strange.'

'Oh, I'm sorry,' he replied sarcastically as he nursed his sore gut. 'Is he not down?'

The spirit scrunched his face up. 'Well, yeah. But just stop touching people there. You have balls yourself. You should be more sympathetic.'

'Kid, go and beat that guy up.' 'Oh no, not like that. What you did is wrong.' 'Doesn't matter he's down, it's like you like touching people there.' For Deities' sake.

Both Garaz and Shift were chuckling openly. The slight look of strain around Silva's mouth suggested she was barely suppressing her laughter.

'Seven bandits defeated,' he declared, raising his arms in victory though he was swaying slightly on the spot.

A noise caught his attention. Most of the bandits were rising, some still groaning in pain. He drew the *Dawn Blade. Rising* soon became *fleeing.*

Why did they attack a group of people armed with swords when they only had clubs anyway?

'Didn't feel like drawing your sword before now, kid?' Auron asked.

Sheathing the blade, he turned to the spirit. 'It didn't seem...fair.'

Auron put his fingers to the bridge of his nose and sighed. The motion was more annoying since the spirit couldn't breathe so it was all for show. 'You still have a lot to learn.' Auron looked up as the last of the bandits disappeared. 'But you're getting better, I suppose.'

Praise indeed.

'Though you really do need to learn to stop introducing yourself to the bad guys,' the spirit continued.

A sudden jab of pain stabbed at his gut, and he winced. Carefully, he sat down, trying to keep his breathing even, despite the pain. 'Garaz,' he said, waving the orc over.

Maybe he can have a look at my blisters whilst he's at it?

Shift was the first to him. 'Are you okay?' they asked quickly.

He nodded and gave a fake smile.

'Good,' the shapeshifter said with a nod. 'Because I'm pretty sure you just defended my honour again, so I'm going to need to give you *another* stern talking to.'

'That was sloppy,' Silva chided—and thankfully interrupted—as her head appeared over him. 'You shouldn't let yourself get hit so many times.'

'I wasn't *trying* to get hit,' he protested weakly, tentatively touching his sore cheek. 'And there were seven of them.'

'Still,' Auron added, making Nicolas squint as his bright form came into view. 'A lot of work to do.'

'Don't listen to them.' Shift smiled. 'You did all right against seven guys.'

Did they just...compliment me?

He suddenly felt oddly warm.

'No,' Silva corrected. '*Do* listen to us, because we're the ones training you.'

'Can you all step away so I can get to work?' Garaz asked testily.

That'd be nice.

The orc looked him over, prodding areas and asking, *'Does that hurt?'* until he finally found a point where Nicolas would go *ow*.

'There is nothing serious,' Garaz said finally as he rose. 'Just some bruising. I will not risk my healing magic, for obvious reasons.' Reaching into his cloak, he produced and unstopped a small bottle before offering it to Nicolas. 'This should help ease the pain.'

Ease? If he used his magic, it'd be gone by now.

Except it wouldn't, because he was some strange half-dead thing, or whatever Xedora had said.

'...death clinging to you, leaving its mark.'

Nicolas barely noticed the foul taste of the potion as he drank it. He was too focused on the Seer's words, and the possible implications.

CHAPTER 15

*F*inally.

Ahead of them, the city dominated the view. Much of it was obscured by the great wall surrounding it, but a rock face rose from the city's centre, allowing Nicolas to view the castle atop it, made up of three adjoining buildings with curved roofs. It almost looked like someone had put three giant pepper pots together, though the one in the centre was bigger than the others. As impressive as it was, another sight entirely was causing his jaw to hang open.

'Close your mouth, darling,' Shift said with a faux-seductive voice.

'But...but...it's in the sky.' Once again, he found himself looking around to see if any of his companions shared his surprise. They did not.

Above the city, toward the southern end of it, was an island. Suspended in the sky. At this angle, he couldn't make out much detail, save for the jagged rocks beneath it and something glowing at the centre of its underside. A vast chain ran from the island to the ground.

'It's floating,' he said with a furrowed brow. 'In the sky. How's it doing that?'

'That's an island town of the aviar,' Auron explained. 'The bird folk.'

'I know who the aviar are,' he replied testily. 'I just didn't realise they lived...in those.'

'Where else would bird folk live?' Shift asked with mirth.

'I don't know. A big nest in a tree?' he snapped back.

'They do not care for being on the ground unless necessary,' Silva explained. 'So their towns and cities float.'

But floating ground is still ground...I'll never understand Etherius.

Auron chuckled. 'I heard a tale once that a kascat pride insulted an aviar flock. Some stupid honour thing. But the aviar were livid, enough that they took one of their towns and parked it right over the offending kascat settlement. They had no sun for a month until they apologised, and the birds finally buggered off.' The spirit smirked. 'I heard every statue in the town was covered in droppings once they left.'

That's...an odd image.

'But...how does it float?' Nicolas asked, still eyeing the city. Common sense told him something that big should not be in the sky, and half of him was waiting for it to fall.

'Magic,' Garaz answered. 'The aviar keep that a closely guarded secret.'

'I'd rather know,' he muttered nervously. 'If I can understand how it stays up, I might not worry so much about it coming down whilst I'm in the city.'

'Sometimes I forget how sheltered you were before we met,' Auron said sincerely.

He just wasn't going to look at the giant floating rock in the sky then he couldn't get nervous about it.

In theory.

When he forced his gaze down to the city itself, something caught his eye. 'Is it just me or does all the architecture look a little...mishmash?' What little he could see of it beyond the outer wall, anyway.

'Not just you, kid,' Auron said. 'There was never an intention to build a city here. Originally, the citadel was built after the Pioneer Wars to promote peace and harmony. That led to trade, which made this place a hub. Soon enough, all sorts of races were settling here, building shops and homes. And so, the place grew organically and quite oddly.'

Which means there's going to be a lot in there I've never seen before. Best work on controlling my facial expressions lest I end up accidentally offending someone.

'Don't worry,' Shift whispered in his ear. 'If you do something to make a fool of yourself, I'll intervene. Once I've had my laugh, of course.'

He turned to his companion and stared at the shapeshifter for a moment. 'How do you know me so well?'

Shift did something as unexpected as the floating city. They flushed.

'So it's not part of Nalbina then?' he asked quickly, beginning to redden too.

'No,' Auron confirmed. 'It stands as an independent city state. No one kingdom or people rule it. That's the only way it can work as a place of diplomacy for all. They say over twenty-two races, including the various kingdoms of man, gathered to set the first stone in place. That stone had *'With this first stone, we build not only a citadel but a new world,'* carved into it.'

'I've never taken you as a historian,' Silva said with thinly veiled suspicion.

'So this one time...' *I know that smug look. Here comes a sex story.* 'I travelled to the Great Library of Tarnia. A witch had barricaded herself in the forbidden section, which these bloody places always have for some reason. I took care of it with ease then stayed for a few days. The head librarian...well, even under those frumpy robes you could tell she was worth wooing. Had this real stern-but-beautiful look to her. However, she preferred smart to charming, so I ended up doing some reading to aid my seduction of her.'

'Did it work?' Shift asked.

'No.' Auron chuckled. 'She was too smart for that, and I'd only skimmed the books I'd bothered to pick up. She started quoting specific times and dates, tripping me up in lies. Though she thought I was *'sweet for trying."*

Damn, that's twice in recent memory I've learnt about Auron's failure with women. Thank the Deities he's teaching me fighting and not the art of seduction.

'Babylon's like the enchanted forests then?' Nicolas asked thoughtfully. 'As in being protected or sacred ground.'

'It is similar, yes,' Garaz answered. 'When the elves left the world we know a thousand years ago, they decreed that the enchanted forests were *sacred ground*, as you say, and must be left alone lest the spirit of Etherius herself be damaged. They left the rest of us—well, you, as the orcs were the ones who drove them to near extinction and vice versa—as caretakers of the world. Same with Babylon. It is its own entity, not beholden to the other kingdoms or their armies.'

'Tell *them* that,' Silva suggested as she looked back to the west, her eyes narrowed.

Following the warrior's gaze, Nicolas saw a dark blot on the horizon. He cupped his hands over his eyes, as if that would magically magnify what he was seeing.

Are those...tents, maybe?

'What is it?' he asked once he'd given up trying to work it out.

'It's an army camp,' Auron answered, pursing his lips. 'Though they aren't dug in, so they don't plan on staying there long, especially with the cold starting to set in. Armies don't move in winter. That would lead to said army freezing to death.' The spirit's eyes narrowed. 'Unless they plan on being in the city sometime very soon.'

'That would be considered an act of war,' Garaz said, aghast.

'That it would, big guy,' Auron replied. 'And yet, there they sit.'

'What are they waiting for?' Shift asked. 'If it were me, I'd be keen to get on with our task, rather than sat on my ass in the cold.'

Nicolas raised his eyebrow at the shapeshifter.

'What?' Shift said defensively. 'I'm not suggesting war should hurry up and happen. I'm just saying, if I were them...'

'I don't think we'll know anything for sure until we actually go into the city.' For a moment, Nicolas couldn't believe he was the one who'd said that. The idea of entering a city with a potential besieging army just up the road wasn't something he relished.

Just shows how much I've changed, I suppose.

'Well, at least we won't be bored,' Shift said with a shrug.

'The army being there does suggest that whatever evil Xedora sensed is likely still active,' Silva noted.

'Good.' Auron smiled. 'I'd hate to have walked all this way for nothing.'

If his blistered feet could've voiced their thoughts on the spirit saying that, the language would've been very improper. But still, the idea heartened him. Whatever demon Xedora had sensed was likely still there.

Which puts me one step closer to Koth. One step closer to finding my people.

'And avenging my parents,' he whispered firmly, their faces appearing in his mind.

CHAPTER 16

Nicolas wasn't sure where to look when they joined the queue of travellers on their way to Babylon. It was certainly much more interesting to look at than the line to get into Narus. There were many and varied folk on their way to the city, such as grand serians with multicoloured plumes atop their heads being carried on litters by hulking, scaled, bodyguards and centaurs clopping along the road proudly. So much so that he had to keep reminding himself not to stare.

Sweet laughter caught his attention, and a trio of twittering nymphs wove through the crowds so fluidly and with such grace that it was almost like they were performing some kind of dance, rather than walking.

A sharp elbow jabbed him in the ribs. 'Ow.'

'Stop drooling over the nymphs,' Shift told him sternly. 'They don't parade around in nearly see-through silk garments that barely cover anything in the hope some scruffy village boy gets hot and bothered watching them.'

'Actually, that's *exactly* why they do it,' Auron corrected.

Shift let out a single, annoyed laugh. 'Well, I think we should carry ourselves into the city with a little dignity. And we won't do that if Nick's strolling along with his tongue hanging out like a soldier on payday making his way to the nearest brothel.'

'Kid, take a good look at Shift's face.' Nicolas frowned but did as he was bade. 'That right there is the exact face you were making when we were sailing with Ramerez and Shift was getting doe-eyed over him.'

'Ha.' Shift's sarcastic laugh made a couple of nearby heads turn in their direction. 'Are you suggesting that I'm jealous? Because if that's the case, you are definitely losing touch with the land of the living...*ghost*.'

'I wasn't jealous of Shift staring at Ramirez,' Nicolas put in defensively.

'Of course you were,' Silva interjected. 'Just as Shift is whilst you ogle those nymphs.'

'I wasn't bloody well *ogling* them,' he cried.

'Weren't you?' Shift asked.

'Jealous?' he retorted.

Shift made a series of offended noises.

'Perhaps we can put this lovers' quarrel on hold until we enter the city,' Garaz said calmly. 'This is neither the time nor the place.'

Auron laughed at Shift and Nicolas's wide-eyed expressions. It was unusual seeing Shift lost for words.

'Just friends,' the pair said in unison, before looking at each other awkwardly.

Were they jealous, though?

Tittering grabbed his attention. The nymphs were dancing around a dwarf who didn't look like the type who cared for sudden dances in his vicinity. Maybe that was the point?

A hand clipped him around the back of the head.

By the Deities, they are *jealous.*

The shapeshifter said nothing, just glowered in silence.

Nicolas had no idea what to do with that information. Luckily, he had another imminent distraction. Some exotic-spiced smell grabbed his nostrils, pulling his attention ahead to the entrance of the city. It promised tantalising food, and his mouth was already watering at the idea of ingesting whatever it would turn out to be.

As he looked at the city gate expectantly, though, his hunger slowly abated. They weren't here for food. They were here for a demon. He shook his head. What was wrong with him? His people needed him, and he was here making jokes and worrying about his stomach. Closing his eyes, he remembered his parents, despite the pain that came with their dear faces. Then, he pictured the people of Hablock on market day, focusing on each and every face.

The people I need to save.

The closer they got to the city gate the more impatient he became to get in and get on with what they had come here to do. His eyes flicked to the top of the gate's giant archway. In it's centre a symbol had been carved into the stone. It was a rising sun sat atop a laurel of peace. Either side of it were various sculpted figures, staring at the symbol with hope.

'As symbols go, it is a little ham-fisted for my taste,' Garaz noted, scrunching his nose up. 'But I suppose it gets the point across.'

'People do like a good symbol,' Auron mused. After a moment of silence, he suddenly turned to Nicolas. 'So, this one time...' *Sigh.* 'There was this warrior wizard in Hoflar, named Trok the Stormbringer. When he walked, he could summon rumbling storm clouds to follow in his wake. Very impressive, and very intimidating. Of course, the unsavoury element of Etherius gathered to him, thinking he had mighty powers, so he started raiding and pillaging, as they do. This legend builds up around him that he can smite towns with lightning bolts and all that.'

'Could he?' Garaz asked with interest.

'Pfft, no,' Auron scoffed. 'Turned out that thing with the clouds was all he could do. But it built him a mystique and gave his army confidence. It also gave those who opposed him a bad case of cravenness. Of course, old Trok started buying into his own legend. Decided to try marching on the capital. The king of Hoflar raises an army, including myself, and went to face him.'

'And you did...' Silva began leadingly, when the dramatic pause dragged on too long.

'I know a thing or two about showmanship, believe it or not, so I saw right through Trok. Called him out in front of his army. Told him to smite me. When said smiting wasn't forthcoming, the dupes following him suddenly realised they'd made a terrible mistake. We took the field in minutes. Having the storm clouds fade away the instant I removed Trok's head didn't help their courage either, I can tell you. Point is, symbols, even the ham-fisted ones, can be powerful. People gravitate towards them.'

'People can lose all reason with a few well-chosen words and some showmanship.' Garaz sighed.

Just like Tobias Helstrum in Narus.

Nicolas's yearning to get into Babylon was tempered wildly when he saw the checkpoints people had to pass to enter the city. To his knowledge, he was still a wanted man.

'Soldiers,' he whispered nervously, wishing he had Shift's ability to change face.

'Not really, kid,' Auron replied. 'Babylon is forbidden from having a standing army. Those men and women are the city watch.'

Bronze armour. Sashes of office. Swords...I'm not sure I see the difference.

'Don't worry.' Shift grinned. 'I'm sure the soldiers in Narus are still looking for you there. Word of *Master Assassin Nick Carnage* probably hasn't reached here yet.'

'Firstly,' he hissed, trying not to draw attention to himself, 'I am *not* an assassin. Secondly, that *isn't* my name. And thirdly...*probably?*'

'I highly doubt they will have your name, real or otherwise,' Garaz soothed.

And yet someone saw me clearly enough to draw a perfect likeness of my face.

'If they recog—'

'They won't,' Silva cut in. 'The only way they will is if you draw attention to yourself, by staring worriedly at the ground and pulling your cloak around yourself, as you are doing now.' Nicolas hadn't even realised he'd been gripping his cloak so tightly. 'Drop the cloak, stand up straight, and look up. If you do not act like you are fleeing the law, they will not assume you are.'

'Besides, kid, this is an independent state,' Auron added. 'The Nalbians have no jurisdiction here.'

'Are you all together?'

Nicolas had to control his urge to start. He hadn't even realised they were this close to the checkpoint until the kascat man of the city watch spoke. He sat at a table, parchment and quill in front of him. Judging by the downward droop of his whiskered moustache, it'd been a long day.

'Um...yes.'

'Very good,' he replied with disinterest. 'Names?'

At least no one here seemed bothered by Garaz, save a few wary glances. The orc, Shift, and Silva gave their names. Auron obviously didn't need to.

'Name?'

It was only when the man looked directly at him that he realised he hadn't answered. An impatient eyebrow was raised.

Why am I still not answering?

'Name?'

'Ni...Nick Carnage.' He tried to ignore Shift's chuckle.

'Finally,' the watchman muttered under his breath as he wrote it down. 'And the reason for your visit?'

His first instinct was to say *trader*, but they had no goods to trade. 'Came to see the sights,' he answered finally.

'You picked a poor time to come here for a tour,' the man mumbled dourly to himself as he wrote his answer down.

'We're actually looking for work for the winter too,' Shift said.

'Very good,' the man said as if he didn't care at all. 'The Sanitation Guild are always looking for workers, and there are some labouring jobs in the human district getting another silo built before the winter sets in fully.'

The man held out a piece of paper, which Nicolas took. 'That's a list of places with accommodation that have vacancies, though I've been handing them out all day, so I doubt the information is accurate anymore.'

'Thank you, officer,' Shift replied with a smile.

The man looked at them all neutrally. 'Stay out of trouble.' His eyes turned to Garaz. 'You especially. Orcs are welcome here, but your lot do have a tendency to cause mischief.'

'I understand,' the orc replied. 'You will have no trouble from me.'

'In that case, I officially welcome all of you to the city of Babylon and hope you enjoy your visit.' The tone was flat and the words rehearsed and without emotion. Still, they were in.

Passing the checkpoint, Nicolas almost started again when Shift took his arm. 'You used the name again,' they said quietly into his ear, their tone excitable.

'I panicked.'

'And yet that was your response.'

'Face it, kid,' Auron, who had evidently overheard, said. 'You're warming to it.'

'I most certainly am *not*,' he replied testily. 'Besides, we're here. Can we focus on finding Koth instead of my chosen name, please?'

'The mighty hero is all business,' Shift said with faux casualness.

'How do we go about finding the demon?' he asked, ignoring his companion's nonsense.

'It's a big city,' Auron said thoughtfully. 'So it's easy to hide. But it also means there are plenty of people to ask. Besides, kid, demons aren't generally your stealthy types.'

Nicolas cast one more glance up at the arch as they passed beneath it. What did this city built for peace have in store for them?

Chapter 17

After a long journey, they were finally in the city of Babylon, and like in the queue of travellers leading to it, Nicolas didn't know where to look first. Directly inside the city gates was a vast and bustling marketplace made up of stalls who used vibrant banners to try and stand out from each other, creating a tapestry of colours, enticing smells, and wonderful sights. There was almost so much going on that it was hard to make out any actual details. Everything was bright and busy, which made the palpable tension so unnerving. It radiated from everyone, from the smallest child to the stall holders, covering the market like a blanket of unease.

'Deities, it's warm in here.' Nicolas shrugged off his cloak as beads of sweat gathered on his temples.

'So it is,' Shift noted, doing the same. 'Must be all the people around.'

'It is odd. Unseasonable, even,' Garaz muttered, looking around.

Though Nalbina had been relatively temperate, the closer they'd gotten to the border, the cooler it had become, especially with the chill breeze that had crossed the plain on the final stretch. Kneeling, Nicolas put his cloak in his pack, his attempt to fold it neatly rendered moot as he found himself stuffing it in. After heaving it onto his back and standing, Nicolas stumbled for a second and reached out to steady himself.

'*Ow.*' Quickly, he retracted his palm, blowing on it vigorously. The skin was a little red, and the ghost of the sudden burning sensation hung around like an uninvited party guest.

'Tourists,' a blue-furred kascat muttered as he passed, shaking his head and making his whiskers bob.

Holding his hand protectively, he looked at the wall he'd tried to lean against. Along it ran a set of metal tubes with a *Do Not Touch* sign on them. Now that he'd noticed them, the pipes were everywhere, along all the walls he could see.

'Tourist.' Shift sniggered, tapping the sign.

Eyeing the brass pipes, Nicolas realised now that the heat he could feel was radiating from them.

'Fascinating,' Garaz said, as he inspected the pipes, letting his green hand hover just above them. 'These would appear to be the reason the city is not suffering the cold. I wonder if they are magic or science by design?'

'They're bloody hot,' he grumbled.

'How many times have you been punched in the face?' Silva asked with disdain. 'And you whine because your hand got a little hot?'

'You can touch them if you like and see how you fare?'

'I had best not,' the warrior replied, raising an eyebrow and tapping the sign.

'Now, come on,' Auron interrupted, holding his hands in the air. 'We all know the kid has a low pain threshold.' *That wasn't very supportive.* 'He's working on it.' *Not by choice.*

'Might need to work on his reading too.' Again, the bloody sign was tapped, making him glower at Shift.

He was about to suggest where Shift could stick the sign they loved so much, when a raised voice got his attention.

'Hey.'

Just a little way from him, the kascat who'd sighed at him was on the ground. Around him stood several human males, each perfectly mimicking each other's look of annoyance, almost as if it had been rehearsed. The most prominent was a thick-jawed fellow with long greasy hair tied back in a ponytail. He was burly and not at all friendly. 'Watch where yer goin',' he snapped, shaking his balled-up fist threateningly.

The kascat rose slowly and dusted himself off. Nicolas knew the feline race were proud; the question was, would that pride cause more problems here?

'You bumped into me,' the kascat said. There was a clear nervousness in his voice, his pride obviously battling with his flight response.

The big-jawed man feigned offence, though Nicolas could tell that was the exact response he'd been hoping for, as the man was no actor.

His fists are still balled. He wants a fight.

Slowly, purposefully, the man opened one of his hands and brought it up to his ear. 'I beg yer pardon, *furball*?'

Going by the fact the kascat hissed and extended his claws, that was quite the slight for his people.

Nicolas wasn't sure if the kascat noticed, but the man's companions, maybe goons, were fanning out slowly, ready for the inevitable pile on.

'Now, I really don' take kindly ta havin' claws flashed at me, *furball*.' The kascat hissed again, much to Big Jaw's delight. 'It's an aggressive action, ye see. And when people, or creatures, are aggressive toward me, I feel the need te defend meself.'

I bet you do.

There was a lull whilst the kascat likely measured his next words carefully. It was in that lull that Nicolas found himself standing between the kascat and the big-jawed man.

Looks like I'm getting involved in this then.

'Why don't we all just calm down a little,' he said with what he hoped was a genuine smile. Smiling at Big Jaw took serious effort.

The leader of the ruffians eyed him incredulously...a word he likely couldn't spell. 'Perhaps ye mind yer own business and let me sort this out.'

Nicolas didn't take his eyes off the man. Even he knew that'd be a huge mistake. 'I think I can guess what you mean by *sort this out.* So no, I don't think I will be minding my own business, actually.'

'Listen here, boy,' the man snarled, leaning in close enough to give Nicolas an unhealthy dose of fish breath. 'Ye need te stay out of affairs which don't concern ye. Especially affairs in which ye're outnumbered.'

'Mayhap we even those odds a little,' Shift interjected, Garaz and Silva at their side.

The man glared at Nicolas's companions, before looking at his own followers. He was clearly weighing up throwing a punch. Nicolas casually set his stance and readied himself.

'What goes on here?'

Several men of the city watch had stopped nearby and were scrutinising the scene.

Judging by the filthy look Nicolas got, Big Jaw was still torn as to whether or not he'd finish what he was starting. Finally, he took a step back, smoothing his hands over his hair. 'Nothing, officer. All's well here.'

'All is also well *elsewhere.*' If the officer's less than subtle hint wasn't enough, his hand on his baton ought to have been enough to get through to Big Jaw.

'C'mon, Kurt,' one of his followers whispered. 'Let's go.'

'This ain't over,' Kurt muttered through a fake smile, before turning and leaving with his comrades, making a petulant show of keeping his hands high to demonstrate that he was peaceful.

'Don't dally here,' the officer of the city watch said, before he and the others moved off too.

Checking to ensure that Big Jaw and his cronies intended to stay gone, Nicolas turned around and offered his hand to the kascat, who'd thankfully sheathed his claws. 'Nicolas Percival Carnegie.'

'Kanjar.' The hand was taken and shook. The kascat even threw in a small bow of thanks. 'It does my heart good to know there are still friendly humans here .'

'There are friendly humans everywhere.'

I'm not sure why I sounded so defensive, but there are.

Kanjar chuckled. 'You really are tourists, aren't you?' When the chuckle finished, the kascat's face become serious. 'I had best warn you. Too many people here are worked up about the murders. *Friendly* is a term that's slowly eroding due to fear and suspicion. Those...gentlemen are just a small example of what's happening.'

'Murders?' Silva asked.

Kanjar frowned. 'You don't know? In the last months, a spate of brutal murders has shaken this city,' Kanjar explained. 'When a human's found dead, non-humans are blamed. When a non-human's found dead, humans are blamed. Some say it's one murderer, some say it's a series of escalating revenge killings. Either way, this city's beginning to slide toward the brink of chaos. Why do you think the city watch are out in the bazaar in such force?'

Nicolas scanned the crowd, picking out the numerous bronze-armoured men amongst it. It was both comforting and disconcerting. This was a silly place for Big Jaw to start a fight.

Unless it was intentional.

There was a very inappropriate moment of elation inside Nicolas. All their journey here, he'd wondered if they'd be too late, if Koth would be gone. But they were here, and it seemed Koth was still around. The elation was immediately followed by guilt. People had died. There was no way this was a coincidence.

'I must be off on my business,' the kascat said. 'Thank you for your assistance. If I ever see you in a tavern, I will buy you a drink.'

'That's very generous of you.' Nicolas smiled.

'Not really,' Kanjar replied with a grin. 'My money's safe, human. None of your kind come to our taverns anymore.'

Waving the kascat off, Nicolas turned and saw Auron staring at him askew.

'What?' he asked.

'Just thinking, kid,' the spirit replied vaguely.

'You are getting quite brave, young Nicolas,' Garaz said. 'The boy I first met would not have thoughtlessly thrown himself into that situation.'

Well, it wasn't entirely thoughtless and...shit, I'm blushing.

'Thanks,' he mumbled. Though he was quietly proud. He'd seen something wrong and stepped in. It was...

Oh Deities. Adventuring's growing on me.

Nicolas might've stopped that incident, but there were clearly plenty more brewing. Suspicious glances were rife in the bazaar. This place was a pile of kindling, ready to catch flame and turn into a mighty blaze at any moment.

Not if I can help it.

CHAPTER 18

Moving through the bazaar was strange. Each stallholder barely acknowledged their approach, yet animatedly came to life as they passed, ferociously trying to peddle their wares as they attempted to draw his attention to various potions, fashion items, and...well, anything someone could think to sell, really.

Silva sighed as they passed the seventh trader, who wanted to explain to Nicolas how his life wouldn't be complete without the long snake he was holding up, that was, naturally, only available today and for a very reasonable price.

'You don't have to say *no thank you* to everyone we pass.' The warrior tutted.

'I can't be rude,' Nicolas gasped. 'They're making an effort to engage with me.'

'They're making an effort to take your coin.' Silva took a moment to scowl at a trader offering her perfume.

The turbaned fellow was unperturbed, explaining how Silva could smell like a summer orchard.

Braver man than me.

'My, my, young man,' an elderly goblin said as he stroked his long beard, 'what a lovely sword you have.'

'Oh, thank you.' Nicolas smiled, coming to halt. Gazing over the goblin's stall, he saw all manner of amulets and charms. 'And what a nice stall you have.'

'Have you had it long, adventurer?' the goblin asked.

'Not too...*ahhhh*.'

Grabbing him by the arm, Shift yanked him away from the stall.

'That's how they get you.' Shift tutted. 'They start a general conversation to reel you in, and the next thing you know, you're leaving wearing enough protective charms to give you a neckache.'

'You mean he really wasn't interested in my sword?'

Shift looked at him with mock sadness. 'Oh, Nick...'

He looked back. Already, the goblin was asking someone about their fine shawl. That was disgusting. He felt so used. Absentmindedly, he brushed off the hilt of the blade, lest it be tainted by the goblin's sales pitch.

'Ignore them.' Garaz smiled, cape wrapped tight around him. 'Your innocence is quite endearing.'

He really wasn't sure how to take that remark.

The group stopped as the crowd ahead of them parted urgently. A fearful-looking vendor charged past them. Nicolas had worn the *running for his life* look enough times to know it on sight. He readied himself to intervene as the man got closer, but his courage wavered slightly when he saw what was chasing the man.

'It isn't real...It's just a label...packaging...' the man puffed and panted, glancing back at intervals and letting out an unmanly yelp as he realised his pursuer was closing on him. 'It doesn't even make people stronger. It's all lies. The whole thing.'

'*Ground minotaur penis*,' roared the minotaur who was charging after him, head tilted down and horns at the ready.

Oh Deities, do I really have to jump in front of a charging minotaur?

As it turned out, he didn't. Suddenly, the minotaur fell forwards, crashing onto the ground and sending up a cloud of dust. Four members of the city watch piled onto the creature, using the rope that had caught its legs to also bind its wrists.

'Thank you, thank you a thousand times,' the vendor cried, coming to a halt and falling to his knees. 'Bless you all.'

An officer came and gripped him tightly by the collar. 'We're going to have a word about your product advertising, my good fellow. Especially the one that led to a public disturbance.'

The man was hauled off, the struggling minotaur was carried away, and the marketplace instantly became business as usual. The show was done. Time to shop.

What a strange place.

Continuing, Nicolas found himself veering off to the left as a delicious smell grabbed his nostrils and pulled him in. The store was covered in rows of sticks, upon which skewered animals were stuck. They were so well cooked he couldn't tell what they were.

Probably a good thing.

After checking the price, he pulled out some coins, handed them to the serian stallholder, and took a stick.

If I buy something from one stall, I won't feel so bad about ignoring the others.

'Are you sure about that?' Shift asked warily. 'serian food can be spicy.'

He waved them away. Nothing that smelled so delicious would hurt him. Taking a small bite, he was surprised how tender the meat was. He found himself making involuntary *mmmm* noises as he chewed and swallowed.

Then the burning began. Within moments, a thousand flaming lances were pricking at his tongue. Then his throat took on the essence of a desert floor. He found himself hacking, his vision blurring as his eyes watered. Nicolas stuck his tongue out of his mouth in an effort to cool it whilst he fumbled with his water skin. Hastily, he raised it to his lips, practically drowning himself as he desperately chugged the water, spilling more than he drank. Enough went in to quench the fire, leaving his tongue fuzzy and his throat raw. Still, he kept his mouth open, letting the fresh air circulate inside it.

'Enjoy that?' Shift asked. Garaz and Silva stood behind them smirking.

He replied with a very rude comment that didn't sound right with his wide-open mouth and raw throat.

Why must I always be humiliated in front of all my...

'What's Auron?' he asked, daring to finally close his mouth.

'I think you mean *where is Auron*,' Garaz corrected.

Great, my tongue isn't working properly. It gets me in enough trouble when it is.

'There he is...' The strange tone in Silva's voice made him immediately look round.

What's he doing?

In between the passers-by, Auron was waving at them excitedly, gesturing to something they couldn't see. Nicolas didn't want to shout over the crowd to someone no one else could see—especially when he wasn't sure he could control what actually came out of his mouth—so he looked at the spirit and shrugged.

'We're being followed,' the spirit cried, cupping his hands together so he could be heard over the background noise.

Usually, the lack of reaction to Auron talking was something he took in his stride. But no one paying attention to the shouting spirit was disconcerting.

How do I know they can see me...? I may be a gh— Oh, shut up, Nicolas.

Exchanging wary glances, the group approached.

'It's a dwarf,' Auron continued, starting to do some kind of odd pointy, waving dance. 'He thinks he's being all sneaky, but he doesn't even know I'm right here watching him watch you.' A broad grin crossed Auron's face. 'Look...' The spirit turned, stretching out his arms and waving his fingers at their stalker. '...*wooooooooo*. Nothing.'

'Isn't *woooo* something ghosts say?' Shift said to the others.

'*Shh*,' Garaz scolded. 'If he hears you call him that, he will be unbearable for hours.'

'We may get a story,' Nicolas added.

Shift mimed sealing their lips.

Those lips tho— Shut up, Nicolas.

Auron put his hands on his hips as they got closer. 'He's in that alley-way. He's just edged behind a barrel.'

Nicolas turned to Silva. 'Would you mind?'

'Not at all,' the warrior said before vanishing into the crowd.

Perhaps I should've specified she shouldn't hurt him?

Hopefully Silva was getting to the point where she didn't need telling beforehand, but at least they were close by just in case. Giving the warrior time to circle around and come at the alley from the other side, Nicolas and the others stood around and waited, so as not to give the game away.

'So, we're faking talking naturally then,' Shift asked. 'This is awkward.'

'The amount of times we talk, and now we need to pretend to, I can't think what to say.' Nicolas chuckled.

'It is odd that when the brain must do something like this, it almost rebels against it,' Garaz mused.

'You could all congratulate me for spotting someone pursuing you,' Auron suggested without a hint of modesty.

'*Ahh.*'

At the cry, the group ducked into the alleyway. By the time they got to the dwarf, Silva had him pinned to the wall. Not literally, thank the Deities. And doubly thankfully, no one else seemed to have noticed the cry.

'He's unarmed,' Silva said calmly as they approached.

At Nicolas's gesture, the warrior stepped back, using the hand on the hilt of her sword to make a very unsubtle point. The dwarf let out a big sigh of relief as he eyed Silva warily. Nicolas had cause to be wary too. His last encounter with a dwarf hadn't been a pleasant one. Though this one was very much the opposite of the well-dressed Big Boss. His apron was covered in black stains, and he wore thick gloves that looked as if they had a specific purpose other than keeping his hands warm.

The dwarf stroked his red, plaited beard as he regarded Nicolas intently. There was recognition in his eyes that made Nicolas glad Silva was on hand, even if he got no sense of threat from the dwarf.

'You were following us?' he asked.

'I was following *you*,' the dwarf replied gruffly. 'I needed to be sure you were who I suspected you to be. Are you...Nick Carnage?'

He didn't need to look to know the snort of laughter behind him had come from Shift. For once, he really couldn't be bothered correcting someone. 'Near enough,' he said with a faint sigh.

The dwarf's eyes lit up, and a wide, bright smile appeared from beneath his beard, creating crows feet at the edges of his eyes. 'Ah-ha, I knew it. Well met, lad.' The dwarf took off a glove, grabbed Nicolas's hand, and shook it vigorously. 'Durag Axetoe, pleasure to make your acquaintance.'

'Same.' He really wanted to get to the point of this. 'So what can we do for you?'

'I owe you a debt.'

'Beg pardon?'

'I owe you, Nick Carnage, a debt.' The dwarf nodded firmly. 'Well, not just me, personally, but my people.'

'Your people?' Nicolas frowned as he struggled to get his head around this. 'They owe me a debt?'

'Yes.' Durag nodded with enthusiasm. 'The dwarven people.'

All of them?

'Kid?' Auron asked quizzically.

'I've never met you before, so I can't see how you owe me anything,' Nicolas replied, very concerned as to where this conversation was going. 'And I'm certainly not owed anything by the dwarven people.'

'Modest, eh?' Durag laughed and punched him on the arm playfully. 'I like it. But I speak the truth.'

As much as Nicolas really didn't want to delve deeper into this conversation, his curiosity got the best of him. 'Because?'

Durag leaned in close, and his voice became a harsh whisper. 'Gorin Thundabrig.' The dwarf promptly spat on the ground then stepped on the pool of spit and crushed it into the earth.

Gorin Thundabrig? Who in the Underworld is...? Oh.

Nicolas had only ever met a single dwarf before now: Big Boss. The dwarf gangster had been hired by Sarus's High Chancellor to assassinate King Silus of Sarus and make it look like a robbery gone wrong using the stolen power of a deity to break into the treasure vault when the king would be there. But instead, the dwarf had decided to turn the king into a chicken to kidnap and ransom him.

Deities, these villainous plans are convoluted.

'What about him?' Casually, he put a hand on the hilt of his sword, just in case this was about revenge somehow. Who knew nowadays?

Durag thought for a moment before he spoke, his face becoming grave. 'Gorin was a stain on the honour of all our kind. A giant brown smear on the undergarments of the dwarven people.' *Eww.* 'His lust for gold took him down a dark path. Calling himself a gangster. Hurting a lot of people.' The dwarf spat again. 'But you, you took care of him and helped tear down his organisation.'

'Oooh,' Shift said with a chuckle. 'All him, was it?'

'Well, it was all of us.' It didn't feel right to Nicolas, getting all of the accolades. It had been a joint effort at best. At worst, the others had done most of the actual work whilst he'd flailed around at visions of vampires that weren't there.

'Nonsense, lad.' Durag laughed. 'I've heard the legends of your exploits.'

You have? How?

'And all dwarves owe you a great debt for taking care of that idiot. When I saw you walking through the gate, I just knew it was *you*. And as headman of the local dwarves, I wish to repay that debt on behalf of all my people.' Durag leaned in and whispered conspiratorially, 'We dwarves love our honour, but we also hate owing people, lad.'

The entire dwarf race is indebted to me?

He didn't want that. 'A thank you will be fine.'

'No, no, no,' Durag insisted, waving his hands in the air. 'I must repay our debt properly or our honour will be forever stained.'

'What can we get?' Shift asked over his shoulder.

Durag looked at them in confusion. 'I'm sorry. But I don't know who you people are.'

Nicolas glanced over his shoulder to find Shift slack-jawed. 'Oh, I see,' they scoffed petulantly. 'The followers of the mighty *Nick Carnage* don't get a mention in the tales.'

'Not surprising, really,' Auron commented. 'Do you know how many hangers-on I've had in my time? Plenty. Ever heard of any of them? No.'

'*Hangers-on?*' Shift snorted in outrage.

'Okay, so what can you do to repay your debt?' As amusing as Shift's outrage was, he didn't really want to get off track and keep this hanging over his head.

'I already know the answer to that, laddie.' The dwarf smiled then poked Nicolas in the chest pointedly. 'A mighty warrior like you should be walking around in armour, not some leather jerkin that wouldn't stop a squirrel bite.'

Furrowing his brow, he glanced down at his clothes. They were worn and tatty and...Durag was right. It wouldn't stop a squirrel.

Especially one that's half squirrel half spider.

'*Mighty warrior*, he says,' Shift muttered behind him.

'Just so happens I'm a master blacksmith, and I'd be honoured to craft you some armour,' Durag continued, looking positively giddy at the idea.

The dwarf's head kept tilting this way and that, and Nicolas soon realised the dwarf was measuring him. It wasn't the most comfortable sensation in Etherius.

Armour, though? That'd be…nice, actually.

'Thank you,' Nicolas said sheepishly. 'I mean…if you're sure. You don't have to…'

'Ah, ah,' Durag said, waving a finger. 'None of that *humble hero* nonsense. You need it. You earnt it and I won't take no for an answer.'

Despite his awkwardness at the whole situation, part of Nicolas was strangely excited to finally get some armour of his own. He'd been in a lot of fights without any real protection, so it would make a nice change to have some.

'Thank you again,' he said with a nod. 'So, do I come to your shop to get measured?'

Durag narrowed one eye and looked him up and down several times. 'No need laddie,' he grinned finally. 'I've just done it.'

'Really?' Slightly narrowed eyes and some head movements didn't seem to constitute a proper measuring system in Nicolas's mind.

Durag waved his hand dismissively. 'I can size anyone by sight.' The dwarf laughed. 'Part of the craft, laddie. Give me a few days, and it'll be done.'

'Garaz, you and I are going with him,' apparently the dwarf wasn't the only one who was giddy. Auron was practically jumping on the spot, his white eyes wide. 'I have some ideas.'

'Ideas? Like what?' he asked worriedly.

'Don't worry, lad. I have plenty of ideas up my sleeve,' the dwarf said, assuming Nicolas was talking to him.

'You guys go and check us into the nearest tavern whilst we go with the dwarf.' Auron looked like he was barely aware the others were there. 'We'll find you later.'

Nicolas looked at Garaz, and the orc shrugged.

'That's great, thank you,' Nicolas said to the dwarf. 'I look forward to trying it on. Garaz would like to come with you. He has some…ideas.'

The dwarf seemed surprised, as if he'd suddenly realised an orc stood close to him. For a moment, he eyed Garaz with a hint of distrust but finally shrugged. 'If you vouch for him, he's fine by me.'

At least Nicolas didn't need to explain that there was a spirit as well.

But there's still one thing.

'Um, Durag.' *This feels awkward.* 'I'm really grateful for what you're about to do, but you need to understand that I didn't do this alone, at all. My companions all helped take down Gorin. I shouldn't be the only one to get recognition for it.'

'Thanks for the recognition, hero,' Shift whispered.

Durag stroked his beard for a moment then shrugged. 'Then I shall whip up some chain mail undershirts or something else for them. Won't do to have your followers go without.'

Nicolas offered his companions, none of whom looked impressed at being referred to as *followers*, an apologetic smile.

'Oh, not for me,' Shift said quickly. 'If I need to change in an emergency and I'm wearing a chain mail undershirt, it could get very unpleasant for me.'

'Very well.' Durag shrugged. 'I'll give you the *something else* then. Probably the warrior woman too. She's already got some robust armour...even if it isn't dwarf-forged.'

With a prideful look, Durag bowed slightly then took his leave, Garaz and Auron following in his wake. He could already hear Garaz questioning the dwarf on the finer points of metallurgy.

'One of you meet us back here in a few hours,' Auron called as he followed.

I'm getting armour? Wow.

CHAPTER 19

Finding a tavern to stay in turned out to be a quest all of its own. Many of the human taverns shooed them away at the mere mention of the orc in their company, and the non-human taverns went silent the moment they entered. Nicolas was half tempted to find a doorway to sleep in. It was getting to the point where he hoped never to see a tavern in his life again. They'd visited so many, and at least ninety percent of them had turned out to be more trouble than they were worth.

Eventually, however, their labours were rewarded. The Minotaur's Horns sat near the edge of the human and non-human districts of the city and was more tolerant. Or, really, less picky. Business was light as a murder had occurred outside just a few nights before, so the landlord couldn't afford to turn anyone away. The way the old man had sighed laboriously and hung his head when they mentioned Garaz had been irksome. The petulant way he'd said, *'Fine, you can stay,'* had nearly pushed Nicolas into telling him to stuff both minotaur horns up his ass. But Shift had read him correctly, as usual, and told him a kick in the balls awaited him if he cost them another comfortable nights sleep.

And so here they stayed.

It was almost worth it for the landlord's cry of surprise and despair when Garaz walked in, Silva having gone to the market to collect them whilst Nicolas and Shift settled into their rooms.

'I see I am most welcome,' the orc said as he joined the others at their table, Auron in tow.

'Ignore him,' Shift said. 'He needs the money. And I'm sure you'll find amusement in making him feel uncomfortable.'

A small smile creased the edges of the orc's mouth. 'Quite.'

'So, how did it go?' Nicolas asked.

'What?' Auron asked.

'What's the new armour going to be like?'

'Mind your business, kid,' the spirit replied flatly.

'Garaz?'

'Sorry, young Nicolas.' The orc shrugged. 'But Auron swore me to secrecy.'

'Damn right I did.' Auron sniffed.

'You certainly seem eager to get it,' Silva noted.

'I... What... I was just curious.'

'Tell your face and tone of voice that.' Silva didn't smile, but he could sense her amusement. 'That was quite an expression of eagerness just then.'

What? I...suppose I was a little excited.

'You do seem to be getting into this adventuring lark. I don't know what else could make your eyes light up like that,' Shift said, coyly sipping their drink.

'I do.' Auron ran his tongue along his teeth as Shift glowered at him and Nicolas tried to work out exactly what that meant.

'So you won't tell me anything?' Nicolas asked, turning back to the original subject.

'You can keep trying to break into the unassailable fortress that is Garaz, or we can go order some food.' Apparently, Shift shared his opinion about his chances of getting Garaz to talk.

'As amusing as the landlord's face is, I do not wish to be responsible for the heart attack he has if I eat down here, so I shall take my leave.' The orc began to rise.

'I'm famished,' Nicolas said, noting the emptiness in his stomach. 'Maybe we can get some plates and come back up to Garaz's room to—'

Garaz held up a silencing hand. 'You are thoughtful as usual, Nicolas.' The orc smiled. 'But I ate on the way here and would enjoy some quiet time. This place is quite hectic, and I need to meditate.'

Need?

The idea of going and eating without their companion made a wave of guilt surge in his gut, which, coupled with the hunger, caused a tiny rumbling. 'If you're sure?'

'Of course. I just wish to be alone for a while.'

Thankfully, they'd been able to afford a room each. Once Nicolas had recovered from his encounter with the bandits, the group found that the leader had dropped a hefty purse of gold during his flight. Nicolas had been hesitant to take it, but Auron insisted it was *poetic justice*. And they *had* tried to rob him.

'You hear that, Sir Goodheart?' Shift said. 'We can go ahead and eat, guilt free.'

It's really annoying how well they know me.

'I'm going to explore the city a little,' Auron said.

'I will join you,' Silva said. 'We can begin making enquiries about these murders.'

'Great,' Auron said sourly. 'You and me alone together. What's the worst that can happen?'

'You tell too many stories, I get bored and return early,' the warrior commented.

For a second, Auron looked annoyed, but a good-humoured smile soon crossed his lips.

'Are you sure we shouldn't go and help with the enquiries?' Nicolas was already rising, ready to find this demon.

'We're just going to poke our noses around,' Auron said, gesturing for him to sit. 'The real work begins tomorrow. Enjoy a chance to rest.'

'Looks like it's just you and me for dinner then,' Nicolas said to Shift as he sat down.

'Sounds delightful, Mr Carnegie. I... What?'

Nicolas followed Shift's gaze to their companions, all of whom were staring at them with odd smirks on their faces.

'Let us be off,' Garaz said with a bow, before they all dispersed, leaving him at the table with Shift.

****

'And so...' Shift held up their finger, took a big swig of ale, placed the tankard down, and wiped their mouth with their sleeve. '...I'm there, hanging from the ceiling by a rope, and the guards decide to stop their patrol on that exact spot and have a chat. One of them was having marital problems, and by the Deities, did they discuss it at length.'

'What did you do?' Nicolas asked. 'Did you change into a bird or something and fly away.'

'That's just it. I couldn't risk changing.' Shift laughed. 'If I did, my clothes would drop on the guards, and the alarm would be raised. But all they had to do was look up, and they would've seen me.'

Nicolas took a swig of his own drink. 'So?'

'So,' Shift leaned back and grinned, 'I fell asleep.'

'You fell *asleep*?'

Shift held up their hands. 'I got bored, and I...fell asleep. When I woke up, the guards were gone. I lowered myself down, stole the jewel then slipped back out. Though my stomach was sore for days afterwards where the rope had dug in.'

'That's crazy.' He laughed.

'Better than any of Auron's stories,' Shift said, before drinking again.

The tavern around them was bustling. Apparently, though people weren't keen on staying, they were less concerned about eating and drinking there. Because that made sense. Not that he really cared anyway, he was too busy enjoying Shift's company. It was only when some raucous shouting from the corner got his attention that Nicolas finally looked out the window.

Huh. It's night time. How long have we been here?

Nicolas frowned. He would have thought himself more wary of taverns by now, considering what happened on the *Ale Trail*. Really, he should be looking around nervously, trying to discern exactly how many assassins surrounded him. But all he could focus on was Shift.

It's just nice to have a chance to relax with a friend. That's all. Just friends.

Shaking the thought away, he turned his attention to the serving maid, who had just appeared with their food: plates of meat, potatoes, and some green mushy thing he couldn't quickly identify.

How long ago was lunch? My stomach's growling.

'Hey.' Shift clicked their fingers in front of his face. 'Decided not to pay attention to me because of food?'

'Never,' he said with a cheeky half-smile. 'Just realizing how blessed I am. Good food *and* good company.'

'You doth know how to flatter, you silver-tongued demon.' Shift sniggered, before picking up their cutlery and diving in, just as he did.

'So, what do you think of the place?' Shift asked between mouthfuls. 'Babylon.'

'It's amazing, really,' he replied, the enthusiasm in his voice again surprising him. 'So many peoples and cultures in one place. It's so unique.'

'There goes the naïve village boy.' Shift smiled warmly.

Nicolas held his hands up. 'I'm learning. It's a slow process, but I'm learning.'

And I've come a long way from the village.

'You're making progress,' Shift replied with a knowing nod. 'You've actually only embarrassed yourself a couple of times since you've been here. That's good...for you.'

'Hey,' he scoffed. 'Just because you've probably been here ten times already, don't make fun of the new guy.'

'Five, actually,' Shift corrected. 'Don't get me wrong, I think it's sweet. The childlike wonder you have when seeing places for the first time is...nice.'

'Careful,' he said solemnly. 'You are skirting dangerously close to paying me a compliment.'

Shift feigned upset. 'Gasp. Why, sir, we can't have that.'

'Hang on.' Nicolas put down his fork and pretended to be worried. 'If you've been here before, you aren't wanted for any...thievery, are you?'

Shift chuckled. 'First, I'm too sly to get my face on wanted posters, unlike some.' *Touché.* 'And second, if I had, I wouldn't be wearing this.' They used their fork to indicate the face of their preferred form.

'Thank the Deities. I don't fancy having to dodge the law because of a lackadaisical shapeshifter.'

'Maybe if they come for me, you can try to assassinate them and spirit me away in a charging wagon,' they replied with a half smile.

For a moment, he was lost for words, and he had no clue why.

And why am I just staring at them?

'Well, well. Love blossoms in the strangest places.'

Oh shit, this guy.

Behind him stood Big Jaw and assorted followers—four rugged men who wouldn't have been out of place in a cell.

How does this guy have so many friends?

He offered the man a polite smile then turned back to his food, hoping he would just go away.

'It's kind of sweet, lads.' *So much for the hope he would bugger off.* 'Or it would be, if the boy here wasn't a blood traitor.'

'Beg pardon?' Shift asked cooly.

A hand rested on Nicolas's shoulder, and the sudden urge to remove it from the arm gripped him.

'Blood traitors,' the man whispered in his ear. 'People who turn on their own kind in favour of subhuman trash.'

'Thank you for your input,' Nicolas said dismissively, removing the hand. 'But I'm quite capable of deciding who is and isn't trash.' Even this idiot would surely get his meaning.

'Perhaps you should go drink in the non-human quarter with all your mates,' the man suggested. 'You can leave the fine piece of ass here.'

Nicolas rose and looked Big Jaw in the eye, despite the height difference. 'Do not talk about them like that,' he said through teeth gritted in a polite smile.

'*Them?*' the man scoffed. 'Did you hear that, lads? *Them.* Guess we have another subhuman on our hands.' He scratched his giant jaw. 'Oh yes, I think I heard *that* say something about being a shapeshifter. So maybe not so fine, after all?'

Nicolas balled up his fists.

'Nick...' There was caution in Shift's tone, most likely because it would be five on one.

'I think your sweetheart's trying to get you to back down.' Big Jaw sneered. 'Perhaps you should. You are whipped by those cats into fighting their battles for them, now you can be whipped by shapeshifters...blood traitor.'

'If I share blood with the likes of you, I think that's actually a compliment.' He smiled.

'*Nick...*'

If Shift's *urging caution, maybe I should—*

'I think your *companion* wants to leave,' Big Jaw continued. 'I think it has a point, this being an establishment for fine, honest humans, after all. Creatures like *that* aren't welcome here.'

Nicolas furrowed his brow.

'Confused?' the man asked with a chuckle.

'No,' he said slowly. 'Just trying to make my mind up...'

'Well, maybe you ought to take that piece of filth shapeshifter and go do it outsid—'

Made it.

The big ruffian went reeling back from Nicolas's uppercut. Apparently, the jaw was more for decoration than anything else. Big Jaw staggered back from the blow, tripping and crashing into a table. The nearest legs of the old wooden table buckled under the sudden impact, and it collapsed on one side, taking the man who had broken it along for the ride. As Big Jaw followed the collapsing table to the floor, the food and drink that had been on it rained down on him.

'We don't have to do this,' Nicolas said to the others in the surprised lull that followed.

The balled-up fists sported by Big Jaw's minions suggested that wasn't going to happen.

A cry from behind made him turn quickly. There were two more he hadn't noticed. Both had grabbed Shift and hauled them into the air. His companion wasn't making it easy for them, though, lashing out fiercely with their legs.

A hand grabbed his shoulder and spun him round. Nicolas instinctively ducked the arcing punch meant for his head, striking his attacker in the ribs before driving him to the ground with a vicious left-right combination. Another man came at him, and Nicolas cracked him square in the nose, which broke under the impact, decorating the man's shirt with a spray of blood as he fell back.

In his peripheral, he could see that one of the men had Shift firmly around the waist, lifting them high as they kicked his companion in the face. He knew why they weren't changing form—so no other bigots would decide to get involved in the fight—but he really wished they would.

A giant tiger in the room would finish this quite quickly.

Two hands grabbed his collar and drove him back into the nearest pillar with a painful thud. Nicolas circled his arms high and struck down on the elbow joints of the arms holding him. The grip broke, and he headbutted the attacker to make him stagger away.

Another came in, swinging wildly. Nicolas ducked and let the pillar take the punch instead. Judging by the cracking sound and the man's howling, his hand was broken. He drove up with an uppercut to send him sprawling before wading into the others.

The fight continued, and Nicolas used every limb at his disposal to keep dropping anyone who came at him. The problem was, he was in a confined space and outnumbered, and sooner or later, they'd get the best of him. It was sooner. His world flashed to black as something shattered over his head. When he doubled over, shards of glass rained to the floor from his hair, which was then yanked up hard.

'Blood traitors get what's coming to them,' Big Jaw snarled before punching him in the stomach with his meaty fist.

All the air was driven from his lungs as he fell to his knees, a handy punch to the cheek ensuring he ended up flat on the floor. Then all he could do was roll himself into a ball as the kicks and punches rained down.

Even in his dazed state, trying to block multiple attacks, he saw one of the men flung to the side with a cry before a familiar leg kicked another in the stomach. There was a flurry of fists and impacts and grunts, and then nothing.

Silva looked down at him with a raised eyebrow. 'Are you okay?'

Other than all the pain...yeah.

'I love you,' he said with a dazed grin.

The warrior smiled oddly. 'You lot have a tendency to say that.' There was an awkward pause before she spoke again. 'Same.'

Then he was hauled from the ground. 'You sort this out with the land-lord, and I'll take him to his room.' Shift slung one of his arms around their shoulder and carried him—dragged him, really—across the tavern. It was a tricky exercise, considering the floor was now littered with unconscious bodies.

CHAPTER 20

After taking a long swig of water, he felt at least a little refreshed, though he hadn't expected it to be a miracle tonic. Thankfully, he seemed to have absorbed the beating without any lasting damage.

A couple of months ago that would've laid me up for days.

There was nothing serious enough to require Garaz's ministrations. He had a few bruises and a cut on his head, which Shift was currently tending.

'Ow,' he said with a hiss.

'Grow up,' Shift said sternly, dabbing at the cut with an alcohol-soaked cloth. 'It could've been a lot worse.'

It really could've been. For a bunch of burly thugs, they were actually poor fighters. They definitely would have come off worse in the fight, if they hadn't cheated and smashed a glass over his head.

Deities praise Silva.

'It could. I think I'm okay.'

'Oh, do you?'

If Shift's tone hadn't alerted him that he'd incurred their displeasure, the set of their jaw would've. Unsure what he'd done, he offered an apologetic smile.

'Why do you insist on doing that?' Shift barked, dropping the cloth and glaring at him.

'What?' He was very aware he was on treacherous ground. The less he said, the more easily he could keep himself from getting in further trouble.

'Defending my honour,' they growled. 'What have I told you about doing that?'

'Not to,' he replied sheepishly.

'Exactly.' The shapeshifter snorted. 'And yet there you were, throwing fists at a thug who insulted me when you were clearly surrounded.' Their hands went to their hips. 'I was quite capable of destroying his self-esteem with a few well-chosen remarks, but even I know you don't start a fight when you're outnumbered *five to two*.'

'I've fought more before. What about those bandits on the road here?'

'That's different,' they snapped after a moment's thought. 'You lost control down there, and it nearly cost you. I...we could've lost you. Again.' Shift got right in his face. 'You could've been seriously hurt. And that is not acceptable. Clear?'

Shift was right, and he knew it. If the men had said those things about him, it wouldn't have bothered him. But it'd been Shift, and he...

'I'm not apologising for defending your honour,' he said, suddenly resolute.

Shift's eyes widened incredulously. 'I *beg* your pardon, Nick?'

'I'm not,' he repeated. 'He was insulting you. He deserved a smack in the jaw. I delivered it.'

'Oh, so you don't think I can defend myself?'

If he'd been on treacherous ground before, he was now in a dragon's cave with a pocket full of the creature's gold and it had just woken up.

'Not at all,' he answered instantly. 'You're one of the most capable people I know. But I'm not about to stand idly by whilst someone calls you filth. If you don't like that...well, I don't know what to say to that.'

'You're an idiot,' Shift said after a moment.

'An idiot who starts fights in bars because someone insulted you,' he said quietly. 'And I'd do it a hundred times more.'

Shift threw their hands in the air and cried out. 'I don't understand you. You're just this village boy. You go around doing this stuff that's so...*ridiculous*, but somehow you're so damn sweet at the same time. It's confounding. It's infuriating. It's...It's...'

For a second, they looked into each other's eyes. There was a loaded pause.

Grabbing his head, Shift kissed him, quickly and passionately. Within one blissful moment, it was over. Shift stepped back, breathing heavily, eyes wide and jaw slightly slack. Remembering last time, Nicolas tensed, waiting for the inevitable slap. It didn't come.

Slowly, he got up, standing in front of Shift, whose face was still locked in the dumbfounded expression.

'I...um...well...'

Before they could finish their sentence, or even make one, Nicolas kissed them, quickly and passionately. There was a second blissful moment.

He pulled back, again readying himself for a slap.

'I'm not apologising for that either,' he whispered defiantly.

Shift's green eyes looked right into his, and softened. 'Dammit, Nick...'

Within a moment, they were locked together again, arms intertwined as they kissed. And this time, it didn't stop after a second.

Whoa.

Shift's bodyweight pressed against him, and he fell back onto the bed, Shift atop him. Breaking the kiss, Shift looked down at him, chuckled, and shook their head. 'Dammit, Nick.'

They gave him a playful, soft slap on the cheek. Then the kissing resumed.

****

Don't be a dream. Don't be a dream. Don't be a dream.

Tentatively, Nicolas opened his eyes. There was light in the room, slipping between the cracks in the tatty red curtains that hung across the window. He could feel a warm body next to his, but his imagination had been known to be a powerful tool. He couldn't stay in this blissful uncertainty forever, though. Sooner or later, he'd have to look and be sure. With a deep breath, he turned over.

The smile was so sudden and intense it hurt his face a little.

It really happened.

Shift lay on the pillow beside him, eyes shut, hands beneath their head. Strands of their short auburn hair hung to the side in a way he found oddly endearing.

'I can actually hear you smiling,' they murmured sleepily, eyes still shut.

'I'm not apologising for that either.'

A limp hand reached out and playfully slapped his cheek. 'You should always apologise for waking me.'

'Depends how many times I'm in a position to do it.'

Shift's eyes shot open, and they nodded. 'Mr Carnegie's very smooth now he's a man. Even if he does have an inane grin on his face.'

He shrugged. 'I have a lot to smile about.'

They tapped his nose with their finger. 'See, ridiculous but sweet.'

Leaning in, Shift kissed him.

'Sorry about the morning breath,' they said once their lips had parted.

He held up his hands. 'I woke up next to you. I have nothing to complain about.'

Shift rolled their eyes and sighed. 'Dammit, Nick.'

Moving swiftly, they were suddenly atop him again. Kissing resumed.

An hour later, they were finally rising and getting dressed. Nicolas was still almost half sure this was some kind of dream. Or hallucination.

Maybe when I got hit over the head, I was knocked unconscious? Am I still on the tavern floor?

No, it wasn't a dream. Sudden uncertainty gripped him. If it wasn't a dream, what was it? Yesterday, they were just friends, and now...what?

'So, about, what happened...'

Shift sniggered as they pulled their boot on, shaking their head. 'I am not about to sit here and define what we are to each other.' They gave him a sideways glance. 'Well, you belong to me now. You're my property and follow me around dutifully.'

'Oh, ha, ha,' he replied indignantly, trying to ignore the part of him that kind of liked the sound of that.

They got up and walked over to him, planting a kiss on his cheek. 'We were friends. Then some other...stuff happened. Beyond that, I don't know. Let's just figure that out as we go, shall we?' Their face changed for a second, and they sat on the bed next to him. *Oh no.* 'Look, I steal things. I used to when I was fun, anyway. But that life, and being surrounded by other people in that life, makes you...guarded, let's say. When you d— went to the Underworld, I was shocked how upset I was. And since then, I've been looking at you differently and couldn't figure out why exactly, and then the tavern, and then...I...well...I...'

Seeing Shift lost for words was very unnerving. 'Like you said. Let's just figure it out as we go,' he said with a reassuring smile, rubbing their leg gently.

Shift's smile betrayed their relief. 'Okay, but you are my property now. Especially after last night...and this morning.'

He gave a faux bow. 'At your service.'

'Excellent,' Shift said, clapping their hands together. 'Your first task is to find me breakfast. It's the least you can do after helping me work up such a fierce appetite.'

He didn't even need to see his reflection to know he was blushing. Moving quickly to the door in the false hope Shift wouldn't notice, he opened it.

'*Ahhhhhhh.*'

CHAPTER 21

Nicolas stared at Silva, who turned and looked back at him with a raised eyebrow.

'Are you okay?' the warrior asked, as if her being there was perfectly normal.

'What...what are you doing here?' he asked warily. 'Were you stood in front of the door?'

'Of course,' the warrior said casually. 'I have been here all night.'

'What? Why?' And why had his voice suddenly gotten so shrill?

The warrior's scrunched-up face suggested it was a stupid question. 'I was guarding the door in case those idiots returned seeking vengeance.'

'All night?'

'Yes.' Silva frowned at him, most likely wondering why he was having such difficulty with the concept.

There was something he wanted to ask, and he knew he would have no peace of mind until he did. 'You weren't...listening, were you?'

'No,' Silva answered flatly.

Thank the Deit—

'But I couldn't help but hear.'

He felt himself pale as the floor threatened to fall out from under him. 'You...you...you...'

My mouth is flapping, isn't it?

'You need some breakfast,' Shift suggested, taking his arm and leading him into the hallway. The whole time he kept Silva's gaze, his mouth still flapping.

Silva returned his gaze formally before her jaw set, and she uttered a single word. *'Yippee?'*

Suddenly, the corridor shrank then began to sway. His mouth stopped flapping, but only because it was now stuck open.

She heard that?

Looking to Shift for support, he found their face bright red and lips pressed tightly together as they tried to contain their laughter. A single tear escaped their eye. 'I'm sorry,' they said finally. 'But I was surprised when you...shouted it.'

Kill me. Koth, come and send me back to the bloody Underworld.

'Please don't tell Auron,' he pleaded, finally finding some words. Last thing he needed was the spirit hearing about this.

I'll never hear the end of it.

'I never wish to speak of it again,' Silva replied firmly. She was about to walk away but stopped herself. 'I know it's strange, but I thought you deserved a moment of uninterrupted happiness. Both of you. I wasn't about to let anything spoil that.'

Then why didn't you stop talking before yip-bloody-ee? 'Thanks. I appreciate it.'

'Thank you,' Shift said, recovering themselves. 'That was very sweet of you.'

'Good.' The warrior nodded, looking simultaneously pleased at the acknowledgement and uncomfortable. 'Because your companionship means the world to me. All of you.'

He and Shift watched the warrior walk away with surprise. The moment was only broken when a thickly moustached man opened the door of the room next to theirs. He looked tired and grumpy, with thick bags under his red eyes. As he was leaving his room the man saw him and came to an abrupt halt. Instead of continuing with whatever business he had today, the man instead glared at Nicolas, snorted derisively then went back into his room and slammed the door. Nicolas was sure he'd heard the man mutter, *'Yippie indeed,'* under his breath.

For Deities' sake.

They made their way quickly down the stairs and found Garaz and Auron sat at the table they'd occupied the previous night. The tavern was empty, so the landlord must've relaxed his rules on the orc slightly. Not that the old man looked at all relaxed about it, mind you. He eyed Nicolas in annoyance, likely still pissed about the fight last night. Pointedly not making eye contact with the man behind the bar, he began to walk over to his companions. He suddenly became uncomfortable by the way Auron and Garaz were studying him. The spirit was making a big show of it too, pursing his lips, narrowing his eyes and tilting his head slightly.

They aren't studying me, they're studying us. They can't possibly know.

'Well, it's about time.' Auron grinned suddenly.

'Indeed.' Garaz smiled. 'Well past time for you two.'

Apparently they can.

'Was I the last to know about this?' he asked in confusion.

'Second to last.' Shift smirked. 'It took me a little time to work out what I wanted too.'

Right now, Koth, the Maestro, and an army of skeleton trolls could've marched in here, and he wouldn't have cared. His mood could not be dampened.

Lest he tempt fate and dampen it himself by saying something embarrassing, he decided to keep it all business. 'Did you and Silva learn anything last night?' he asked Auron.

'Although my night wasn't as eventful as *yours*,' the spirit replied with a mischievous grin, 'I did learn a thing or two. This city is on the edge. Everyone's talking about the murders, and their theories about who they think is doing them. The city watch have found nothing and are now talking about enforcing a curfew.'

'Why haven't they yet?' Garaz asked.

'Probably because there are vigilante squads roaming the streets at night,' Silva answered. 'They seem to be mainly patrolling the borders between the human and non-human sections of the city. I would assume they wouldn't care to be told to go home and go to bed the minute the sun goes down and would react violently if forced to. It could lead to rioting.'

'Can't they just arrest them?' Shift asked. '*Vigilante squads* don't sound lawful.'

'It will come,' Auron said. 'At the moment, everyone's on the tipping point. I assume the watch don't want to be the ones to make the situation fall over the edge. Then things will get ugly *fast*.'

'At least they've locked the guilds down in their guild-houses,' Silva said. 'Lest they go around fighting each other as they are wont to and igniting the blaze that will burn this city down.'

'It's *that* bad?' Nicolas asked. He'd hoped this nonsense with the guilds would've faded away with Ro dead, yet it had taken on a life of its own, much like the violence here could if left unchecked. 'This can't be a coincidence. *Nothing* is a coincidence anymore. A demonic presence. A place on the brink of chaos. A murder spree. This has the Maestro's stench all over it.'

Which hopefully means Koth is actually nearby.

'Maybe,' Auron said thoughtfully.

'You disagree?' Garaz asked.

'I'm not ruling it out, but I want to see the bodies first.'

'I highly doubt the Healer's Temple will simply let us in to see them,' Silva remarked.

Shift shivered. 'That means breaking into the mortuary where they're keeping the bodies.'

'Squeamish, master thief?' Nicolas asked teasingly.

They gave him a sideways glance. 'I think we've all seen enough undead creatures on our journeys together that none of us want to be in a room full of dead bodies.'

'That...is a fair point.'

Auron put his hands on his hips, almost posing. 'But I'm still your favourite undead creature.'

'Well done for being better than zombies and vampires.' Nicolas smiled.

'Hey, kid,' the spirit grinned, 'you've got to take the wins when you can.' The spirit's grin morphed into a frown as the door of the tavern opened.

Nicolas turned and saw a man of the city watch standing in the doorway.

And I highly doubt the way he's staring at us is a coincidence.

The landlord slowly lowered himself behind the bar, a malicious smile on his face.

And that *is why the tavern's empty this morning. Now I'm glad I didn't make the bed before we came downstairs.*

The officer—going by the coloured sash he wore—walked over to the table, his metal boots clomping on the ground. 'You are to come with me.' It was in no way a request.

'What's this regarding, officer?' Shift's casualness when addressing the officer suggested a long history of talking to agents of the law.

'The tavern is surrounded,' he said, as if Shift hadn't spoken. 'We have troops armed with crossbows both front and back. Fail to comply, and we will have you dragged out of here.'

Nicolas shook his head at Silva. He could hear the warrior thinking, and he'd prefer not to stay here dodging the city watch because Silva had roughed some of them up.

'Look, officer,' Garaz said levelly, 'if this is about last night, please understand my companion did not start it.' *Actually, I did.* 'There is no need to arrest—'

The officer held up his hand. 'This isn't about some bar brawl.'

Oh shit, this is about Narus.

Paling, he began to look for the exits. He even considered letting Silva loose on the watchmen. Attempted assassination undoubtedly meant a trip to the executioner's block. Or maybe the hangman's noose? He'd prefer not to know definitively either way.

'And I am not here to arrest you.'

Nicolas sighed with relief quite loudly.

'Someone wants a word with you. Now, my patience is wearing thin. Outside, the lot of you.'

'Go with him,' Auron counselled, pulling his head back through the wall. 'He's right about the crossbows. And this is kind of intriguing. Besides, I would advise against starting a fight with the law.'

Slowly, they got up and followed the officer outside. The street had been cleared, and there was quite an impressive number of armed men outside, with crossbowmen on the opposite roof and men with swords and shields by the door.

'Someone *really* wants to talk to us,' Shift muttered with raised eyebrows. 'Though threatening to shoot us if we aren't available seems a strange response.'

'Over there,' the officer said, pointing to the open prison wagon. 'Hand your weapons to the watchmen and get in.'

'Yippee.' Nicolas sighed.

CHAPTER 22

Auron's brow furrowed as he leant forward, resting his hand on his enclosed fist as he made a big show of pondering what he'd just been told. 'I understand that in certain moments we lose control of ourselves and say random things, but...*yippee?*'

Nicolas hadn't even thought about what he'd said as they were being bundled into the prison wagon. He'd just said it.

Which is what got me in such trouble in the first place.

The problem was, the usually very stoic Silva had reacted to the word, and Auron had noticed. It had taken a poor amount of badgering—probably related to the fact that they were already in an uncomfortable situation—to get her to talk. Well, for her to start talking then for Nicolas to take over and explain the situation in order to minimize his humiliation.

For all the good it did.

'I don't think this is the place to discuss it,' he remarked sourly, gesturing to their current confines.

'I disagree.' Auron grinned. 'If anything, you all need your minds taken off said confines. And what better way to do it than by having fun at Nicolas's expense?'

'I can think of several,' Garaz rumbled in annoyance.

'Garaz.' Auron laughed. 'You of all people must be curious about human responses to extreme situations, exciting or otherwise.'

The orc gave the spirit an unimpressed glance and shook his head.

Nicolas thought it the perfect opportunity to throw his own foul look at Silva, who didn't show any signs she'd noticed.

So now she's stoic and silent.

'So, kid.' *I already don't like where this is going.* 'When we arrive wherever this wagon is taking us, it might be pretty exciting. Maybe you ought to control your urge to yell anything when that happens.'

Shift leaned in close, dropping their voice low. 'As everyone else's teasing you, and I don't like to follow the crowd, well...just remember what I did to *make* you say that.'

Flushing, he decided to move away from the subject quickly. At first, he tried focusing on the scenery, but an enclosed prison wagon was less of a distraction and more of a reason for depression. The wooden walls were old and knotted. Previous occupants had carved obscenities directed at the local lawmen into the walls. One of them had even been silly enough to sign his work, which looked fresh, as did the dried bloodstain beside it. The only light came from two slitted windows with bars across them. Occasionally, as the rocking conveyance lumbered down the road, the sunlight would fire a concentrated beam through the window and right into his eyes. Just to add to his discomfort.

'Look at him,' Auron said in a soft voice. 'Gazing around the wagon in a poor attempt to move away from my new favourite topic of conversation.'

'Considering that the last woman we met who you had a romantic entanglement with, after a fashion, set demonic stone golems on us, I would think twice before making fun of other people's lives,' he found himself snapping back.

'Well,' the spirit shook his head and smiled, 'I will consider myself put in my place.' He gave Nicolas a respectful nod.

Thank the Deities. Each and every one of them.

For a moment, the claustrophobic confines of their conveyance seemed a little brighter. The creaking of the wheels as they turned almost soothing, the boot-falls of their marching escort somewhat musical.

'Considering we haven't been arrested, I find this mode of travel most undignified,' Garaz grumbled as he brushed some of the straw on the floor away from him with his foot.

'I do like to travel in more style than this, usually,' Auron remarked with a shrug.

'Says the one who doesn't actually have to be in here with us,' Shift retorted sourly.

The spirit winked at the shapeshifter. 'You'd all miss me if I jumped out.'

'Frankly, I'm surprised you haven't been in more of these,' Nicolas commented. 'You must've been arrested at least once or twice. Public indecency? Drunken behaviour? Not paying your bill at the local brothel?'

For a moment, the spirit pursed his lips thoughtfully. 'You aren't wrong there, kid,' he said, before his eyes flicked to Nicolas. 'So this one time...' Suddenly, the wagon was filled with groans that would've impressed a zombie. '...I needed to get information from a bandit who'd been imprisoned. I was young, at the time, but making a name for myself in all the right circles. I had this idea to pretend to be arrested and put into jail with him. Problem was my name was circulating in all the *wrong* circles too.

I'd underestimated my fame. Half the inmates knew me by sight, and I had to fight my way out.'

'And so began the tale of a man who'd never underestimate his own fame again.' Shift smirked.

'How difficult that must have been for you,' Garaz commented dryly.

'Not at all.' Auron smirked. 'I love being famous.'

Silva hasn't spoken in a while.

Nicolas looked at the warrior and divined the reason for her silence quite quickly. If he had to guess, she was working out the best way to neutralise their escort when the wagon door opened again.

Everyone frowned uncertainly as the momentum of the wagon shifted. They were clearly now going uphill.

'I think we're heading for the citadel,' Auron said, before sticking his head out the side of the wagon. 'We are,' he confirmed when he pulled it back in.

'The citadel? Who wants to talk to us there?' Nicolas asked. 'And why go to all this trouble? A simple invite would've sufficed.'

Silva finally decided to grace the conversation with her input. 'Invites can be ignored. Troops of armed men cannot. But if they wanted us dead, they could have done it in the street outside the inn.'

Doesn't mean they don't have something bad in store for us. He'd considered a few of the options, in great detail, already.

'Well, if they do try anything, I'm relying on you to take care of it.' Shift pointed to Silva with a half-smile.

'I will litter the courtyard with their broken bodies.'

Strangely, Nicolas found her response reassuring.

'Or...I could turn into a bear and drive them away. Maybe they'll put a bounty on my head bigger than Nick's.' The shapeshifter was strangely dreamy about the idea of a reward on their head, though it'd surely happened plenty of times in the past.

'Interesting idea of a romantic date, being jointly escorted to the hangman's noose,' he said with a frown.

'If you want conventional romance, go find some doe-eyed village maiden,' Shift remarked, side-eyeing him.

'I—' He was about to say something he hoped would come across as sweet and charming—but would most likely be ham-fisted and laughable—when a shadow crossed the window.

'We must be going through the gates to the citadel,' Garaz commented. 'At least whoever wants to speak to us will be prominent and will most likely make for very interesting conversation.'

I'd hate to be bored.

'Any conversation I'm part of is an interesting conversation,' Shift cut in quickly.

'A boast I can also make.' Auron nodded.

Any further speculation was cut off by the wagon coming to a jarring halt. The bootsteps outside were as ominous as a stomping giant's as they approached the door of the wagon. Beyond the door was an uncertain fate, but at least Nicolas didn't have to face it alone. His body tensed at the click of a lock and a chain being removed. Slowly, the door opened, flooding the enclosed room with light that made him blink repeatedly.

'Out,' a stern voice commanded. The owner of said voice was even pointing, lest they get confused about which direction was *out*.

He was sat closest to the door, but politeness dictated he give Silva the opportunity to go first.

I am just being polite. *But if she does go out there and kill a band of would-be assassins for me, I won't be sad about it.*

There were no signs of bloodshed beyond the door, so he tentatively stepped out. Nicolas had been half-hoping to see the sprawl of the city as they were at the top point of it, but in front of him was only wall and a closed gate. But what was behind him was very interesting. The domed building of the citadel rose high into the air, and proximity confirmed something Nicolas had suspected when he first laid eyes on it. The building was white.

'Where did they get all that white stone from?' Nicolas asked, scrutinising the walls.

'They didn't,' Auron answered. 'They coloured it white. It's the colour of peace, apparently. Another unsubtle piece of symbolism. They even call it the *White Citadel*.'

'They do appear to like to ram home the point,' Shift remarked. 'Even though the city below is hardly peaceful.'

'Something you can hopefully help change.'

Wheeling around, Nicolas was surprised to see a man directly behind them, hands tucked into the sleeves of his large, emerald robes. Wizened eyes creased beneath a wide-brimmed hat as the man smiled at them. He had an aura of wisdom about him.

How does a man get his beard that *straight?*

He mentally shook himself. Men's facial hair should *not* be his focus right now.

'Thank you, officer,' the man said, bowing to the watchman. 'I will take it from here.'

Maybe we aren't in danger, then. Unless this old man is a mighty warrior...or maybe a faun in disguise? Horns could easily fit under that big hat.

'Very good, sir,' the sergeant replied before directing his men back toward the city gate, the wagon following them dutifully.

'Chamberlain Basch, at your service,' the man said with a bow, sweeping his hands out to his sides.

Nicolas held out his hand and was about to speak but found himself interrupted by a wagging finger. 'No, no.' Basch smiled. 'No need to introduce yourselves. We know who you are.' With another sweep of his hand and flap of his sleeve, he indicated the door of the citadel. 'Please, follow me.'

The chamberlain didn't wait for a response; he simply began to shuffle away, expecting them to follow as the wagon that'd brought them here rolled back out of the gates.

Cautiously, he fell into step behind the old man, his companions following.

CHAPTER 23

For someone trailing a long robe behind him, which ought to have been a massive trip hazard, the chamberlain moved surprisingly fast. Nicolas found himself hustling to keep up—and wondering how dirty the bottom of that robe would get by the end of the day. Not that there seemed to be much dirt in the courtyard. Though it was bustling, it was also spotless. All around him, servants and dignitaries moved in all directions. The servants were so impeccably dressed it was occasionally difficult to tell the two apart. Generally, though, the brushes were a dead giveaway.

As he gazed at the crowd, something gleaming caught his eye. Armour. The courtyard was surrounded by soldiers in gleaming silver armour, pulled from the various races that inhabited the city. Though their sizes and skins were different, they all looked proud to wear their uniform.

'I thought Babylon wasn't allowed a standing army?' he asked Auron.

'The city isn't, young man,' Basch answered, 'but the citadel's permitted a standing force to protect the council, as long as it is drawn equally from all who dwell here, just like the council itself. No one race has dominance, to enforce our neutrality.'

'There's a boring word if ever I heard one,' Auron remarked, blowing a raspberry. 'That's why I rarely visit this place. No one ever got glory by being *neutral*.'

The ornate double doors to the citadel were open as people moved about their business. Nicolas could make out carvings on them, but not what they were. Something to do with peace, if he had to guess. This place was nothing if not on theme. It lived up to the legend.

There are a lot of legends...

'Um...' His voice broke for a second as he prepared to ask a question he wasn't sure he wanted answered. 'How do you know us exactly?'

Half turning his head, the old man smiled at him. 'Do not be coy, young man. Your legend spreads far and wide.'

Nicolas stumbled as he missed a step. 'My what now?'

'Apparently, your legend is spreading,' Shift said thoughtfully. 'And knowing you as I do, I'll head off the paranoid thought you'll have in about an hour and say it now. No, I didn't sleep with you because of your legend. And damn you for asking.'

What? My legend? How? Who's spreading it?

Nicolas coughed as the breath caught in his throat. 'I don't have a legend. I can't. It's not possible.'

'The dwarf knew you,' Auron remarked glibly.

Garaz patted him on the back. 'Any reputation you have is well earned, young Nicolas.'

'Unless it's for trying to assassinate Tobias Helstrum,' Silva said.

'Shh,' Nicolas hissed at the warrior, casting a wary eye at the guards.

'What was that?' Basch asked.

'Nothing,' he replied quickly.

But surely the only people who know about me are the villains. So…

'Auron,' he whispered out of the side of his mouth, 'he wouldn't be one of those *evil chamberlains*, would he?'

The spirit frowned as he studied the robed old man. 'My hero instincts say no.'

His instincts are usually good about this kind of thing. He was right about the High Chancellor of Sarus. And he was right about how decent King Eldric is, despite his reaction to Garaz.

The sudden change of scenery brought him back out of his own mind as they crossed the threshold into the citadel. It was…disappointing. Where he'd expected to see fine art, beautiful statues, and exquisite carpeting, everything was just so…

…bland.

'Still decorating?' Shift asked, gesturing dismissively to the white walls.

Coming to a halt, Basch turned and chuckled. 'My, no. We cannot be seen to favour any particular race's design ideals, to promote the idea that we are all equals. So we keep things plain inside the citadel.'

Auron was right. Neutrality is boring.

'Besides,' the chamberlain whispered, leaning in close. 'Some races have very specific ideas of art that would not work in the citadel. So it's better to have none.'

'I'm assuming he's referring to the fact that dwarves can't paint to save their lives, and centaurs think art is a mashing of colour hoofprints on a parchment.' Auron smirked. 'I suppose it makes sense, but by the Deities, these people must have sore asses from all this fence sitting.'

Continuing, Basch led them toward the staircase at the back of the hall, which had a large pair of double doors on the first landing it reached, before the stairs split off in opposite directions.

'This way, please,' Basch said, urging them on. 'The governor wants you to see something before you meet with her.'

Surprised glances were exchanged.

The governor wants to meet us? We're meeting the governor?

Nicolas checked his clothes. They were not meet-ing-the-leader-of-a-city wear and were indeed worse for wear due to the trip in the prison wagon. Quickly, he brushed himself down.

'Don't worry,' Shift whispered to him. 'If they've heard your legend, they know how scruffy you are.'

'Which some people find very attractive, apparently,' he retorted quickly.

Shift feigned a shiver. 'Just as I do your wit.' They grinned.

Ascending the stairs, they headed towards the doors, and his appre-hension grew. Really, he knew he was safe here. But he was also Nicolas. Slowing slightly, he created a bit of distance between himself and the chamberlain, so he couldn't overhear what he was about to ask.

'If this goes bad, somehow, we can get out quickly, right?' he muttered nervously.

'I've noticed three exits,' Shift replied.

'The guards are all on duty but have clearly not seen battle in a while,' Silva added. 'Their reaction time will be dulled because of it.'

'And that nasty beige carpet looks flammable,' Garaz said disdainfully.

'There you go, kid,' Auron shouted. 'We have an exit, poor guards, and a possible distraction. The three mainstays of a great escape plan.'

Yip...Woo.

His hand slipped to his hip, and a pang of loss struck him as the familiar hilt of the *Dawn Blade* didn't greet it. Not long ago, he'd never held a sword, and now, he felt naked without it.

It's fine. We're in a place of peace, sword or no sword.

Slowing down as he reached the top of the stairs, Basch put his fingers to his lips before gesturing to the guards beside the doors. Quietly, they pulled them open. From the moment the doors parted, Nicolas could hear raised voices ahead. The chamberlain began to move again, and they followed.

Ahead of them was a tunnel that led to some kind of auditorium. Coming out of it, he saw a large semi-circular table with various people sat at it, their body language irritable. At the back of the room, was a large raised desk behind which a banner with the symbol of Babylon hung. At the desk sat a single figure. The human woman had a severity to her that somehow made a terrible bowl haircut look appropriate. Her face was thin and her eyes fierce as she sat back in her chair, fingers steepled, listening to the ranting man who stood between the table and her desk.

Behind her, scribes scribbled furiously to keep up with the man as he spoke.

Deities, she makes Silva look emotional.

'...and it beggars belief that we're all just sitting here and allowing this city to fall into chaos.' The man was tall and thin. It was hard to tell his age beyond old. Wrinkles rose from either side of his thin lips, and his white hair whipped around as he moved, though there was none atop his head itself. His eyes were beady and cold. He stalked the floor like a predator, and everyone those eyes rested on was his prey. 'How many murders is it now? Enough to convince gangs of vigilantes to walk the streets. How long before these gangs turn to violence? How much more bloodshed must we endure? If the city watch cannot catch these killers and enforce order—'

'Honourable councillor,' the governor said with a raised hand. 'There's nothing to suggest that this is the work of more than a single killer. Unless new evidence has come to light that you have yet to share with this council?'

The man held his hands behind his back and straightened his posture. He pursed his lips, which only served to accentuate the gauntness of his cheeks. Nicolas didn't need *hero instincts* to know that this man was a hateful prick of the very highest order.

'There is no new evidence,' the man replied in his deep, cultured voice. 'Mainly because the city watch has yet to provide anything of substance about this killer, or killers. Meanwhile, the city begins to slide into anarchy. A slide that, if not checked, could bring this city to ruin.'

There were murmurs of agreement from the room.

A dignified serian rose from one of the chairs around the table. 'We must all remain calm and allow the forces of the law to do their job. Once that is done, order shall be restored. I have faith in our city watch.'

'I do think your belief in the *forces of law*, as you say, is one shared by all your people,' the man said pointedly.

'And what does the honourable Geldheart mean by that remark?' the serian asked defensively.

'Merely that if the honourable Thraish was so concerned about maintaining order, he ought to ensure the good behaviour of his own people.' The serian simmered in the loaded pause that followed. 'Correct me if I am wrong but were a gang of armed serians not arrested just last night for breaking curfew? It seems to me that your people have a less idyllic view of these *forces of law* than your good self and would prefer vigilante justice.'

'The honourable Geldheart knows very well why they were out,' boomed a proud, white-haired kascat with long fur hanging from his cheeks. 'The same reason as my people. The need to protect themselves. Shops do not burn down on their own. And we are hardly alone in having armed groups who roam the night.'

A centaur, who was not sat on a chair, bristled at the remark. 'I am not sure I understand honourable Pawgar. Is an accusation being made toward the centauran population of the city?'

'Not all of them,' the kascat growled.

Geldheart shook his head as his gaze circled the room. For a moment, it rested on Nicolas. It was brief but enough to make him wonder.

Do I know him?

'If civil disorder is becoming a problem,' the tall man began finally, 'we all know the solution. An outside military force must be allowed access to the city to restore the order we so desperately need.'

An uproar resulted. There was shouting, fist waving, pointing, the works. Maybe even the odd swear word, which seemed out of character for people who used the term *the honourable* before addressing each other.

A ringing bang resonated through the auditorium and silenced everyone instantly. The woman behind the desk stood, hands planted on the wood, as she leant forward. 'Let me be clear, *again*,' she said levelly. 'We do not require the assistance of a peacekeeping force. Allowing them into the city violates the very laws and principles that this place was built upon.'

'These laws are already being violated,' Geldheart replied, shaking his head. 'Nalbian's kind offer is only made to help us in a time of very real need.'

The uproar restarted.

'I think you've seen enough,' Basch said, before ushering them from the room.

His companions' worried glances reflected his own.

CHAPTER 24

What he had seen in the council chamber worried Nicolas. He knew it was for more than just the obvious reason, even if he couldn't articulate why, exactly, it was. Maybe it was the sense of wrongness at seeing people who governed a city shouting at each other like aggravated school children? Or maybe it was the simple fact that someone like Geldheart had a seat at the table at all, when he was clearly the worst example of his people? Either way, he found himself distracted as they followed Basch higher into the citadel. Taking the stairs without thinking, he came to a sudden halt as he realised nearly too late that the others had stopped walking. Ahead of them was an unassuming set of double doors guarded by two soldiers, who uncrossed their pikes at Basch's gesture.

'This way, please,' the chamberlain said, ushering them inside.

'Finally, a room with some personality.' Shift nodded approvingly as they took in the room.

His companion—*Lover? Girlfriend?*—had it right. This room had been decorated with some thought. A large desk dominated the far end, but around it was a casual living area, with a couple of leather sofas and an elegant rug. Crimson drapes hung from the spaces on the walls not taken up by bookshelves, which were filled with old tomes. Nicolas turned his attention to Garaz, to check if the orc was drooling. He wasn't, but looked as dreamy as Nicolas must've this morning when he'd woken up next to Shift.

Beyond the desk, Nicolas finally got to see the sprawl of Babylon. The large window laid the city out before him. And it was stunning...but odd. Almost like a patchwork quilt, with each district having clearly distinct architecture. No two were the same. And yet it somehow worked.

A creak of leather made him start slightly. He hadn't even noticed the man sat in the chair in front of the desk until he stood. *Gruff* was a good way to describe this fellow, but also proud. Standing with nearly impeccable posture, the man regarded them with a deep frown, his burnsides twitching as he pursed his lips. Judging by his uniform, he was a member of the city watch, and a very high ranking one.

'Lord Commander Greer,' Basch said with an enthusiastic bow. 'I am so glad you could make it.'

'Really?' Greer replied with a gravelly voice and raised eyebrow. 'I wasn't under the impression I had a choice when the governor's summons came.'

The chamberlain chuckled heartily. 'I suppose not.'

Despite their coolness, the pair clasped hands like old friends. 'And these people are...?'

'You could ask us yourself,' Shift suggested with a smile that underlined the sarcasm in their tone.

'I beg your pardon, young lady?' the lord commander said, his jaw set in a half scowl.

Shift maintained their smile, but Nicolas could practically see the volcanic eruption in their green eyes. The shapeshifter opened their mouth.

Uh oh.

'Nicolas Percival Carnegie,' he said warmly, stepping between himself and Shift to offer the lord commander his hand. 'A pleasure to meet you.'

Nicolas kept his hand outstretched two seconds after it had become awkward, punctuating it with a sheepish grin and chuckle.

'Lord Commander,' Basch tactfully interjected. 'These are guests of the governor. I am sure she will want to explain who they are herself.'

'Indeed, I do.'

By the Deities.

Though Nicolas controlled his urge to flinch, his heart jumped so high it nearly became stuck in his nostrils.

I get ambushed so often, you'd think I'd have developed some awareness at least accidentally by now.

Beside him, Auron slowly shook his head, tutting just to ensure Nicolas fully registered his displeasure.

The governor wore a simple beige robe as she appraised them with her hands clasped behind her back. She looked even more severe up close, as if one displeased glance would be enough to send Nicolas's testicles on holiday to a far and very isolated corner of Etherius.

Where they'd probably end up running into some kind of spider creature, knowing my luck.

With a nod to the lord commander and chamberlain, she walked to her desk and seated herself behind it, only pausing to adjust the chain of office she wore.

'Thank you for coming on such short notice, Lord Commander,' the governor said, with not an ounce of warmth in her voice. With a flick of two fingers, she gestured for them to approach. 'And thank you for coming too.' *She's very thankful to everyone she forced to be here.* 'I am Governor Ellen Morrow of Babylon. I take it you are Nick Carnage, young man?'

Give me strength. 'Not quite. It's actually Nicolas Percival Carnegie. At your service...' He wasn't sure what the proper term of address for a governor was. '...M'lady.'

Shift's sniggering suggested he was wrong.

'Governor will be sufficient, Mr Carnegie,' Governor Morrow replied. 'But please let me apologise. Usually, my intelligence is quite thorough. I am not used to getting names wrong.'

'It is kind of his name,' Shift said. 'We're working on it.'

He gave them a look that hopefully conveyed *'shut up.'*

'I am not sure what that means,' the governor said flatly. 'But I will address you by your preferred name, Mr Carnegie.'

'Nicolas will be fine.' What she was saying sounded too formal.

'But it is you I've heard tell of?' she asked. 'The saviour of Yarringsburg? Protector of King Silus of Sarus? Rescuer of Princess Janessa of the Tidal Kingdom? Slayer of Alric Tavish, a man infamous within the walls of this city?'

'Wow, she is well informed,' Auron said with an impressed nod.

Yes, but...how?

His mind raced like a charging horse, trying to discern how she knew all of this. She couldn't; it wasn't possible.

Also...why did those sound like titles when she listed off my deeds?

'*Him?*' Lord Commander Greer muttered. Nicolas doubted he could've sounded more disbelieving if a fairy had emerged from Nicolas's belly button, flew up to him, and kissed him on the nose.

'Um...yes. I was there for those things,' he muttered when he realised a response was required.

'You certainly have access to a great deal of information,' Garaz said.

The governor's mouth twitched into something that could've been construed as a smile. 'When you are in charge of a city containing numerous races, it pays to look beyond your walls to see the lay of the land around you, Garaz Galgrath.' Using the orc's last name was obviously another example of how well informed she really was. 'Your deeds are whispered by many voices lately, young man,' the governor continued, addressing Nicolas directly again. 'Your legend is on the rise.'

It is? Suddenly, the room felt quite closed in and stuffy. 'I take it Auron of Tellmark, the *Dawnblade* that was, is also here with you?'

Auron reached out and deftly flicked the handle of a nearby cup, causing a brief *tinkle* to break the silence in the room, quickly followed by a grunt of surprise from the lord commander.

'Apparently so.' Governor Morrow raised an eyebrow at the cup, which Auron was staring at smugly. 'You understand that you are here for a reason of the utmost importance?'

'The armed men stuffing us into a wagon gave that away,' Shift replied.

'You used the men of the watch to bring them here without going through me?' Greer spoke levelly, but the sudden appearance of a vein on his temple suggested he was anything but calm.

'Urgency was key,' the governor explained. 'I apologise for going around you.'

Pursed lips gave the impression that the apology was not accepted.

Not that the governor waited for a response. 'What did you make of the scene in the council chamber?'

'The term *'unrest'* comes to mind,' Garaz answered.

'That would be appropriate,' Morrow replied. 'This spate of murders has left us a city on the brink of chaos. Accusations are thrown around more freely each day. Swords are being rattled, and thus far, our efforts to find this killer have been found wanting.' Greer's face reddened. Nicolas doubted it was due to embarrassment. 'And our time is beginning to grow short. So much so that I am resorting to unorthodox tactics to solve this problem.'

'You mean for us to hunt this killer?'

At the use of the word *killer*, the governor's eyes flicked to Silva. Obviously, she knew a lot about the warrior too, though there was no sense of how she felt about what she'd learnt. But he could guess.

'If the tales are to be believed, you all have a talent for disrupting nefarious schemes, and these murders need to be disrupted immediately. If not—'

At that moment, Lord Commander Greer's rage finally boiled over. 'I shan't have it,' he roared. 'This is absolutely preposterous. I will not have a group of mercenaries...' the man cast a distasteful eye over Nicolas '...or vagabonds running around my city causing all manner of mischief.'

Nicolas had no illusions about what the group looked like. He couldn't blame Greer for his assumption. His hope was that the lord commander would at least give them the chance to prove him wrong.

And to think there was a time when I took pride in my appearance.

'Take a hold of yourself, Lord Commander,' Governor Morrow ordered. 'I do not think you understand the knife edge we are sat upon. We are on the cusp of rioting and civil disorder if these killings are allowed to go unchecked. As soon as that happens, the army not ten miles from our city will march into Babylon, whether we ask for their aid or not.' There was a loaded pause. 'If they do, the other races will take umbrage, summoning their own forces to ensure their people are not treated poorly by the occupying force, and the neutrality of this place will be forever broken. It may even lead to war. My job is to keep the peace, and I will explore every avenue to achieve that goal.'

Greer shook his head. 'No armed force will set foot here,' he protested. 'What is happening here does not affect them.'

'On the contrary,' Morrow replied. 'The Nalbians will apparently not permit a city right on their border to fall into chaos. They say that Nalbian citizens live here and would be in danger if civil disorder erupted.'

'Only a handful of them,' Greer scoffed.

'And yet the army is here. Though I suspect other forces are in play. I know Prince Razoul well.' Judging by the look on the governor's face, it wasn't an acquaintance she was all that pleased about. Or she could be. It was so hard to tell. 'All he cares about is ensuring none of his people do the slightest thing to piss off the Deities. The only reason he would make this kind of move is if someone was guiding his hand.'

Nicolas and the companions cast wary glances at each other. They could all guess who was behind this. It had all the classics: trying to start a war, something to do with demons. People dying. The floating town above them may as well have had the Maestro's name carved into it.

I would prefer it if his likeness was. Then I'd at least know who to hit when I see him.

'What do you know of this *force?*' Nicolas asked.

'Nothing,' Morrow said with evident reluctance. The fact that she was so well-informed but had no knowledge of this was equally worrying and frustrating. 'All I know is that someone has swayed the prince to action, and it is more than the rantings of Geldheart.'

'Governor, the watch can—'

'Duncan.' The sudden softness in Morrow's voice seemed very out of place, like a kascat in a bird's nest. 'I know you are trying your best. And I also know what this city means to you, because it is a love we share. We must do everything we can to protect it, even if it means calling for help from heroes. I understand your hesitancy, for various reasons, but this is the right thing to do.'

She called me a what?

The governor opened a drawer and took something out of it. Walking around the desk, she gestured for Nicolas to open his hand. When he did, a small medallion was pressed into it, made in the likeness of a shield. Shift, Silva, and Garaz got one too. Beside them, the lord commander glowered. Nicolas made sure he looked in every other direction but Greer's.

'As governor of the city of Babylon,' Morrow said as she stepped back, 'and witnessed by Chamberlain Elias Basch and Lord Commander Duncan Greer, I hereby deputise you into the city watch until this crisis has passed. Do you accept this responsibility, and will you do your utmost to uphold peace and justice in this city?'

Huh?

'Wow,' Auron exclaimed. 'This is all happening very fast.'

Lord Commander Greer obviously had strong opinions but kept them to himself. More veins appeared on his temples though.

'So?' the governor prompted.

'Um, we accept,' he answered finally, if uncertainly. He looked to his companions to check he'd said the right thing. None of them argued. He glanced at the shield again. This time, a sense of duty filled him. It wasn't just a shiny medallion; it was symbol of his responsibility to protect people. He found himself standing a little straighter. 'We will do our best to help this city and bring this killer to justice.' His face hurt from the smile of pride he was supressing.

I've gone from never wanting an adventure to being made part of a city watch to protect it from a killer.

After pinning the shield to his chest, Nicolas smoothed the clothing down around it smartly.

I am the law. I am the law.

'Looks good on you, kid,' Auron said with a nod.

'Where will you begin?' Governor Morrow asked.

Nicolas thought then remembered something Auron had been saying. 'We would like to see the bodies, please.'

'Very well.' Morrow nodded. 'Lord Commander, please escort them to the Healer's Temple and ensure they have everything they need.'

The veins had run out of room on Greer's temples, and so began to appear on his neck. Without a word, the lord commander made for the door. The governor sat at her desk and started shuffling papers, so it was clear they were dismissed. Nicolas followed the lord commander out of her office. Briefly, he glanced at the shield on his chest again.

I am the law?

CHAPTER 25

Lord Commander Greer left the governor's office at a brisk pace, Nicolas and his companions moving quickly to keep up. Not a word was said as the group traversed the staircases to the ground level of the citadel. Nicolas kept touching the medallion he'd been given. It seemed to weigh a ton, but his mind was playing tricks on him. He was adding the weight of the responsibility he'd just been given to it. That was what was so heavy.

I did come here to help this city. I just didn't know it would be like this.

At the bottom of the stairs, at a point where Nicolas assumed he considered himself well out of the governor's earshot, Greer came to a sudden halt, turning on his heel and poking Nicolas in the chest indignantly.

'Just so we are all clear,' the lord commander said through gritted teeth, 'I do *not* consider you officers of the watch, nor affiliated with us in any way, shape, or form. You are mercenaries, *at best*. Now, I will put up with this nonsense because the governor demands it. But I will be watching you lot like hawks. And when you slip up—which your kind inevitably does—I will take great personal pleasure in dragging you out of my city by the scruff of your neck. Am I clear?'

It was quite vexing that he had four other companions—though Greer couldn't see one of them—but all the lord commander's ire appeared directed at him. But he doubted that pointing that out, or saying anything at all, would be well received, so he simply nodded.

'Good.' A huff, another smart turn on his heel, and the lord commander was already striding away again. 'I had best see you to the sodding Healer's Temple like a good little tour guide then, hadn't I?'

'He's going to be a peach to work with,' Auron remarked glibly.

'He does appear to be wound a little tight.' Ironic, coming from Silva.

I'd be wound tight too if a murderer was loose in my city and I had to rely on outside help to find him...or maybe it.

Nicolas was certain this was the work of whatever demon Xedora had sensed here. He could almost sense it himself. An angry energy surrounded this beleaguered city, like the pipes that warmed it.

'Best we keep on his good side, if we wish to achieve our goal,' Garaz counselled.

Shift said nothing. Now that he thought about it, they hadn't made a smart-ass remark in a few minutes. In fact, there'd even been a couple of easy opportunities they'd missed. Glancing at his—whatever they were now—he saw the shapeshifter staring nervously at the shield in their hand.

'You okay?'

'Hmm,' Shift replied, frowning at the medallion. 'It's just strange being on this side of the law. I'm used to dodging it, not enforcing it.' The shapeshifter turned their frown on him. 'Then I met you, and now look at me. Sheriff Shift.'

'It has a cute ring to it,' he said awkwardly. 'And if it helps, it's new to me too.'

'Nooo, really?' Shift said, pursing their lips. 'Something new's happened to the out-of-place village boy?'

That's better.

'He's a hero now,' Auron interjected with a whistle. 'Apparently, he has a legend.'

'That's right.' The shapeshifter grinned evilly. 'How is it, having someone else be the centre of attention?'

The spirit mulled this over as if it were new information. Nicolas could tell the very moment the truth of it struck Auron as he suddenly became quite sullen.

'Being brought into the watch is a boon to our quest,' Silva said as the group followed Greer back out into the courtyard. 'We no longer have to break into the temple, and we are sanctioned to search the city as well. It will make our task of finding the source of the demonic energy easier, even if it is not related to these killings.'

Please be Koth. Please be Koth. Please be Koth.

A part of Nicolas's brain hoped it wasn't, because he still wasn't ready to face the creature. But he wouldn't shirk his responsibility, and this time, he wouldn't be alone in the night.

Though if we are in a fight, we need...

'Um, excuse me.' He coughed politely. 'We need our weapons back. Please.'

Greer came to a halt, not even trying to hide the huff that escaped from between his lips. 'It would be remiss of me not to arm the vigilantes running around my city, wouldn't it?' he growled, keeping his back to them. 'I'm assuming they were put in the weapons checkpoint by the gate. We will stop and get them as we pass.'

With the stakes rising dramatically, he could use the comfort of the *Dawn Blade* on his hip right now.

****

Luckily, the main Healer's Temple, the one where bodies would naturally be brought for an investigation, was at the base of the citadel itself. It made sense, really. With all those councillors shouting and screaming at each other, it was practical to have some medicine nearby, even if it was only for sore throats.

The instant the group passed beneath the archway, the cloying smell of incense assaulted Nicolas's nose. It twitched as he wafted his hand in front of his face, as if he could just swat the smell away. His nose hairs tingled, and he found himself suppressing a sneeze. In the quiet temple such a noise would make him the centre of attention, and that was against his religion.

The main area of the temple was filled with beds, many of which were thankfully unoccupied. In the centre of the room, a large statue of Ce'tal, the Deity of Healing and Wellbeing, watched over the sick and injured with an almost shepherd-like quality. Healers and acolytes moved around busily in their white robes, which was an odd choice, considering the blood and other bodily fluids they were likely to come into contact with.

'Hey, Garaz,' Shift said, nodding toward the statue. 'Remember the last time we saw a statue of a deity? An old man jumped on your back and tried to ride you around.'

'I recall,' the orc replied coolly.

'Lord Commander Greer, what can I do for you?'

Though Nicolas didn't like to judge people, if the old healer who approached them had been wearing a black robe, he could've easily passed for a necromancer with his gaunt cheeks and grey skin.

Maybe? I don't know. I've only ever met one, actually.

'High Healer Linnerman.' Greer greeted him with a formal nod. 'I've brought some *people* to look over the bodies. The victims of this damnable killer.'

Linnerman's eyes narrowed. 'This is highly irregular. I was told the bodies were to be prepared for burial. I've already begun the rites and removed the spells preserving the remains.'

Great. They're going to stink then.

Unease gripped him at the mere thought of being in a room with numerous dead bodies. Usually, the dead didn't stay that way around him.

'You are going to have to wait,' the lord commander said in a tone that brooked no argument. 'This is city watch business.'

'Very well,' Linnerman muttered sourly. He tilted his head to look at Nicolas and his companions in a way Nicolas really didn't care for. 'And these *people* of yours are...?'

I think I'll forgo my usual introduction. Besides, I'm not shaking his hand. Who knows where it's just been?

'Experts.' The word was delivered with sarcasm so thick it would've taken a master dwarven miner a week to cut through it. 'Governor's orders.'

'Ah.' Linnerman sighed. 'And who am I to deny our governor? Only High Healer of the Temple... Fine. Let us proceed to the mortuary then.'

At the back of the room, a staircase led to sub-levels beneath the building. It was wide and the steps long—Nicolas assumed because bodies were moved up and down them. Torches lined the walls, casting an eerie light.

This place reminds me of every villain's lair I've ever seen.

At the bottom of the stairs, through an unassuming door—Nicolas would've expected a skull carved on it, or at least a sign not to disturb the dead—was the morgue. Inside it lay twelve bodies, covered respectfully in thin sheets. The hairs on the back of his neck stood on end. Warily, he eyed each of the dead, looking for some sign of movement. Though fighting zombies was almost becoming boring by this point.

Though I suppose I am technically one myself now. Or not, who bloody knows?

'I suggest you are quick in your examination,' Linnerman said as he lit a few more torches in the room. 'The magic preserving the remains has not gone completely, but lingering too long may be unpleasant. Things tend to move quite fast after being held at bay by magic for so long, if you understand what I mean.'

'Let's not dally then,' Shift said dryly.

Without as much as a 'goodbye,' the High Healer left them to it.

'They've been placed in order of death,' Greer said. 'Let's see what you make of it then.'

It was a challenge. But Nicolas intended to make nothing of it at all. This wasn't his field of expertise.

'Let's have a look then, shall we, big guy?' Auron was already walking forward as Garaz followed. Pulling back the sheets of the first two victims, the pair began to study them.

Nicolas caught a glimpse of one body and decided he'd seen enough. Trying to find anything else of interest in the room, his eyes wandered to Silva. The warrior glanced at him and he gave an awkward smile.

'Alright?' he asked with a nod.

'Are you?' the warrior replied with a raised eyebrow.

'About as okay as I can get surrounded by dead bodies.' He shrugged.

'I find it quite comforting being surrounded by the dead when they are my enemies. It means they can no longer threaten me.'

My fault for starting a conversation with her.

'There will be no dead enemies in my city, mercenary.' Greer snorted angrily, his gaze the only thing in the room colder than the dead. 'Any apprehending you do will be done in accordance with our laws. Understood?'

'Of course,' the warrior replied, before adding, 'Though if they start it, I shall finish it.'

'I think they've found something,' Shift interrupted.

'*They?*' Greer asked. 'Oh yes, you have a ghost. How silly of me to forget such utter nonsense.' This was followed by a huff so drawn out it made one wonder how big the lord commander's lungs really were.

Shift seemed to be right. Auron and Garaz moved between the first four tables in the room, deep in conversation.

They have *found something.*

Auron looked past Garaz and right at him. 'Kid, come here.' The spirit beckoned him with two fingers.

'I'm fine over here, thanks.' Nicolas waved back. 'I can hear you perfectly fine. What have you found?'

I still remember King Ragus's ship. I am not getting any nearer to—

'For Deities' sake, kid.' Auron shook his head and let out a huff equal to Lord Commander Greer's. 'Come here, now.' The spirit pointed at the exact spot on the ground he expected Nicolas to occupy, like an annoyed parent when their child begins playing up at market.

He looked to Shift and Silva for support, but there was none, so he slowly walked between the bodies on the tables to where Auron and Garaz were, pressing his arms into his sides so tightly that they ached.

Please stay dead. Please stay dead. Plea—

'Time for a lesson.' Auron's sentence was lined with impatience.

'*Here?*' Nicolas looked around in surprise.

The spirit blinked a few times then rolled his pupilless eyes. 'Not a sword lesson, you saggy siren's tit. There's more to hero work than fighting. I have told you this before.'

I didn't think he meant bloody sword fighting. Does he credit me with any intelligence?

'Right...*right*, kid.' Auron repeated himself when he realised Nicolas wasn't looking at the body he was gesturing to. 'We are definitely dealing with a demon. What do you see?'

Dammit.

Closing his eyes, Nicolas took a breath to steel himself. Opening them again, he used sheer force of will to make them look at the bodies. The young woman would've been pretty, with an endearing scholarly look. But he'd had to use his imagination to work that out, as her skin was now a mess of burnt tissue. Patches of angry red welts and charred flesh covered her. Putting his hand to his mouth, he uttered a silent prayer for her soul, for all their souls. It must've been painful.

'Pay attention, kid.' Auron looked more serious than he normally did. 'One important thing about demons is that they can't exist in our realm themselves. Their bodies aren't made for it or something. So—'

'It is quite a fascinating area of study,' Garaz chimed in. 'Many scholars have posed that—'

'So...' Auron interrupted with annoyance. 'They need a host body to possess, and they generally need someone to summon them. That's why the first victim in these cases is always the most important, because it's usually the moron who summoned the thing in the first place, probably for a lark.'

'People do that?'

'It is said that demonic possession comes with an incredible high, as it were,' Garaz answered.

The stuff people do for fun...

'But even in controlled conditions, it's ridiculously dangerous,' Auron added. 'If the demon takes full possession, they walk around wearing you like a suit. But trying to contain the demon's raw energy comes with a price. Soon enough, it burns through the body, killing the host and causing...*that*.' The spirit gestured to the body of a young man two tables across.

'That is why this Koth is so intriguing,' Garaz said. 'He not only possessed a host but merged fully with him into something worse.'

Intriguing? Terrifying. 'So this isn't Koth then?'

The spirit and the orc exchanged a look. 'It could be, kid, but try not to get your hopes up,' Auron answered with sympathy. A fissure of frustration opened inside Nicolas, and he clenched his fists tight for a second. 'But the fact that this one seems to be jumping from host to host, which is how it's killing, suggests something more than just an average demon.'

'Average demon.' When did that phrase become part of my life?

Garaz put a hand on Nicolas's shoulder. 'So all is not lost.'

'Now,' Auron said, drawing his attention back to the corpses, 'tell me what you see. Compare the dead.'

'Dead people.' The spirit's narrowed eyes gave his opinion on that answer. 'Burns.' That couldn't be the answer either, so he looked closer. First, he hadn't wanted to get near the corpses and now he was studying them. He did, begrudgingly, need to learn this. It wasn't like the adventures were ever going to stop coming now. His gaze flicked between the four corpses Auron and Garaz had positioned themselves around.

'Is there difference between them?' Garaz asked. Beside the orc, Auron's white eyes were wide with expectation.

Why can't they just tell me?

Then he noticed something. There was an odd difference between the first three corpses and the fourth. It was most likely a silly answer.

But it's the only one I've got.

'The...first three bodies have charred skin around their burns,' he said tentatively.

'*Yes,*' Auron clapped his ethereal hands together before pointing at him. 'Exactly, kid, well done.'

'And what does that mean?' Garaz asked leadingly.

Again, he had an answer, but it seemed silly. Yet he had no other, so he spoke again. 'It's like the wounds occurred from the outside?'

Garaz smiled widely, showing all his fanged teeth. 'Correct, young Nicolas.'

'And that means...?' Auron said, circling his hand in the air.

'That the first three victims were burnt from the outside, whilst the fourth was burned from within. So...number four is the first actual victim of the demon, and therefore the one who summoned it. The other three are decoys.'

'Have a little more confidence in yourself, young Nicolas.' Garaz chuckled. 'You are right again.'

Oh, okay. He stood a little straighter.

'Utter nonsense,' Greer bellowed suddenly. 'The first three were the killer simply refining his technique, whatever it is. I will not stand here and listen to some crap about demons and possession.'

'You live in a city with a town floating above it, and demons is where your disbelief kicks in,' Shift said, narrowing their eyes. 'Think, man.'

As Greer's chest expanded, no doubt to unleash a verbal tirade at Shift, Nicolas got between them.

'Lord Commander,' he said, hands held up. 'We're here to help. The governor said that we may be able to provide a fresh perspective on the killings, and this could be it. Please let us help you. That's all we want.'

The lord commander furrowed his brow and ran his tongue along his teeth before huffing again.

This man does love a good huff.

'Who was the fourth victim?' he pressed.

'His name was Simon Finchly,' Greer responded with folded arms. 'He was the apprentice to Professor Shaw.'

'Professor Shaw?' Nicolas asked.

'You've seen the pipework heating the city, I take it?' Greer asked.

Yeah, seen it, burned myself on it.

'It's an absolute marvel. Professor Shaw designed it. The system runs through the whole city, heating it. No furs for us this winter, just nice temperate days ahead.'

'Where did this apprentice live?'

'Mr Finchly didn't have apartments of his own. He lived with the professor at his manor. And you can't just go knocking on his door. The professor is an important man doing important work for the city.'

'Tell him I said, 'Tough," Auron remarked, folding his own arms.

CHAPTER 26

Greer thundered out of the temple. It was getting to the point where Nicolas didn't think the man had a casual walking pace, just variations of angry striding.

'I will not have it,' the lord commander bellowed for about the fourth time. 'Professor Shaw cannot be bothered. With winter setting in, it is crucial that he fine-tunes his machine, lest the city suffer. That cannot be achieved with a bunch of badged thugs stomping around his house asking questions.'

'But if the apprentice was the first—'

'Exactly. *If*,' Greer interrupted.

'He was,' Nicolas replied, summoning his resolve. 'We need to search where he lived to find out where this demon came from.'

Coming to a halt, the lord commander pressed two fingertips to the bridge of his nose and sighed loudly. 'And I want no more nonsense about demons. It's bad enough you expect me to take investigation advice from a ghost, no matter whose it is.'

'This fellow is very tiresome,' Auron said with his own sigh.

'Indeed,' Garaz agreed.

'*Indeed* what?' Greer asked, eyeing the orc suspiciously. 'Are you agreeing with me, sir?'

Garaz was visibly thankful for the interruption as an officer of the city watch ran towards them, calling the lord commander. At first, Nicolas thought the man was quite young, but then he realised they were about the same age.

Deities, how much has adventuring aged me if I start thinking people the same age as me are young?

'Lord Commander Greer,' the man said as he came to a halt with a crisp salute. 'I have an urgent message for you.' He promptly held out a piece of paper.

'I am trying to remember a time when you *didn't* have an urgent message for me, Sergeant,' Greer replied dryly, taking the paper and reading it. 'Very well then. It seems I am needed at the Watch House.'

Lord Commander Greer glanced from Nicolas and his companions to the note several times, before letting out a low growl. 'Sergeant Tallith,' he said, addressing the young man. 'These...*folks* have been deputised by the governor to assist us with the investigation into the murders. You are to escort them as they do this *investigating*, which apparently entails running around the city chasing ghosts and ghouls.'

'Um...yes, sir,' the sergeant replied.

Greer turned to them. 'And when I say *escort* you, what I mean is that he will be watching you like a hawk. Sergeant Tallith will be my eyes and ears. For the record, in case I somehow didn't make it clear before, I think you are a bunch of charlatans and vagabonds. When the sergeant here is able to prove as much, I will have you flogged all the way out the city gates whilst whistling a jaunty tune. Do I make myself clear?'

'I think we get the gist,' Shift replied dryly. 'But maybe you could spell it out a little more? We are just simple vagabonds, after all.'

Lord Commander Greer bristled and turned to the sergeant, looming over him. '*Like. A. Hawk.*'

'Yessir,' Tallith said after a gulp.

The lord commander began to stomp away then stopped and half-turned. 'And they are *not* to go near Professor Shaw's residence,' he bellowed, pointing at Nicolas and the others.

'Yessir.'

'No goodbye then?' Shift muttered with a chuckle.

'I know I can be a bit slow on the uptake sometimes, but I don't think he likes us very much,' Nicolas said as the lord commander disappeared from view.

'I do not care for that man,' Silva said coldly.

'He is just doing his job,' Garaz soothed. 'We have been thrust upon him with no forethought and expected to achieve something he has not. A little bitterness would be natural.'

'You do know it's annoying for you to be the voice of reason when I dislike someone?' Shift asked.

'Of course.' Garaz smiled. 'But it does not make me any less right.'

A polite cough got their attention.

'I'm sorry,' Sergeant Tallith said, 'But...who are you exactly?'

Nicolas held out his hand. 'Nicolas Percival Carnegie.'

Tallith's face did something very strange. First, it dropped completely, his mouth almost hanging open before it broke into a broad grin. 'I'm sorry,' he said finally, collecting himself. 'Who did you say you were?'

'Nicolas Percival Carnegie,' he repeated hesitantly.

'*The* Nicolas Percival Carnegie?'

'Um...yes...I suppose.'

'Surely there can't be more than one?' Shift scoffed. 'Any others would've surely gotten themselves killed by now, without us around to protect them.'

Nicolas let out a small cry of surprise as Tallith suddenly grabbed his hand in both of his and shook it vehemently, broad grin returning.

'Oh gosh. It *is* you, isn't it?' the sergeant beamed. 'This is such an honour.'

'It is?' Nicolas pulled his hand back and looked at the others. They were all a variety of confused and bemused, but no actual help. 'You know me?' he asked, circling his wrist to get the feeling back in his hand.

'I sure do.' Tallith grinned. Then his face dropped again, and he frowned, as if a thought had occurred to him. 'Can I ask you something?'

No. 'Yes.'

Tallith actually bit his lip in excitement before he spoke. 'What was it like fighting pirates on the high seas? Is it true Captain Killgore had a magic hand? What was the mer-princess like? I heard they can change between fish tails and real legs, is that right?' The sergeant frowned thoughtfully. 'Well. Not *real* legs, like that. I mean, their tails are real too. But...'

Sergeant Tallith's words trailed off as Nicolas shivered. His memory of Killgore's magic hand would always be one of his most vivid. That hand had become a whip that had lashed him. He still had the scars on his back to prove it. Garaz had tended to them but said they might never fade. The orc thought it was most likely to do with the magical nature of the weapon.

I think it's just my body's way of reminding me never to get overexcited about adventuring again. Still, lesson learned.

'He had a magic hand, yes,' Nicolas muttered quietly, choosing to answer one of the tirade of questions.

Sergeant Tallith evidently wasn't skilled in reading body language, or he would've shut up there and then. 'Was it worse than fighting the minotaur? Or the vampires?'

'I'm sorry,' Shift cut in. 'But how do you know all of this?'

Tallith opened his mouth but stopped. He frowned thoughtfully. 'Um, I just heard the tales. I'm not sure where, exactly.' The grin reappeared. 'But they are coming in thick and fast now. Wait until I tell the others I got to shake your hand.'

'Others?' Garaz enquired.

'The club.' Tallith nodded. 'We get together to share what stories we've heard about the great Nicolas Percival Carnegie.' The sergeant held his hands up in a mock fighting pose. 'Or is it *Nick Carnage* today?'

'No, it bloody is not...' he snapped, not dampening Tallith's enthusiasm even slightly.

'Hold on, kid,' Auron said with a chuckle. 'Do you have a fan club?'

Wait...what?

It was Nicolas's turn to go slack jawed.

'I'm sorry,' Shift began, addressing the sergeant, 'did you say you're in a fan club?'

'No.' Tallith laughed. 'We don't call ourselves a fan club...we're a society. The Dawnblade Speakers Society. It's great to have tales of hope to spread in these dark times, so we make sure we pass on whatever stories we hear to whoever needs to hear them.'

Huh? Actually, what the f—

'Oh my gosh,' Tallith said, excitedly clicking his fingers in the air suddenly. 'That'd make you Shift, you Garaz, and you Silva. I don't believe I'm meeting all of you. Is Auron around?'

Auron walked up to the sergeant and poked him in the arm.

'*Oh my gosh,*' he exclaimed. 'I just got poked by a ghost.'

'Little shit,' Auron said dryly, taking his usual uppity stance when someone referred to him as a *ghost* and not a *spirit*.

'Nicolas Percival Carnegie, the *Dawnblade*, and the *Knights of the Rising Sun*. Such an honour.' Tallith shook his head in disbelief.

'The what now?' Shift asked, a single eyebrow raised.

Tallith repeated it. 'Well,' he said sheepishly, 'we couldn't just have you go without a name, so the group put our heads together and came up with something.'

'Unless you can come up with one that doesn't make us sound like a group of travelling fops...I suggest you don't.'

Who knew Shift would get so funny about labels? They're pretty loose about calling me that stupid name whenever they fancy.

'Companions will do,' Nicolas said with a deep sigh. This whole thing was getting very tiring.

'How odd that you are gaining fame when I do most of the fighting for you.' He didn't know if Silva was jesting or actually put out; it was always difficult to discern with her, and as mentioned, this was getting tiring.

'Be nice to get a portrait together at some point,' Tallith ventured. 'If you have time.'

Every time I think my life is as strange as it's going to get, something like this happens.

'If we have time,' he replied, shaking his head in disbelief. 'But let's get to Professor Shaw's first.'

Tallith's face dropped. 'Ah,' he said slowly. 'Lord Commander Greer said I'm to keep you away from there.'

Closing his eyes, Nicolas rubbed the bridge of his nose. This was really all becoming too much.

'This is important.' Inwardly, he cringed before he said, 'It's vital hero work. Do you not want to help us?'

'Well, of course,' the sergeant said after a pause. 'I mean, if it were anyone but you. I suppose a quick visit couldn't hurt, right? It isn't far from here.'

'*Vital hero work?*' Shift repeated, narrowing their eyes. 'What are you becoming?'

Damned if I know.

CHAPTER 27

Nicolas would've assumed he'd find the glaring differences in the architecture of Babylon, which sometimes changed from street to street, unsettling and chaotic. Instead, he liked it. The city's uniqueness was quite endearing. Mainly because of what it represented. Though the city was broken into specific districts, many bled into each other. They'd passed a random street for serians in the kascat district.

'Doesn't that cast a shadow over parts of the city?' he asked thoughtfully, gesturing to the giant floating mound in the sky.

'The township is not directly over the city itself,' Garaz replied. 'And if you look, you can see it has been moving subtly all day, ahead of the line of the sun to stay out of its path.'

'But surely there would still be a shadow,' he continued with a frown. 'I know how light works. And how is it even up in the sky? Islands don't float.'

'Magic,' Shift said.

Garaz's face took on a sour look. Chances were he'd been about to go into a long and detailed explanation of how science and magic were working as one. It didn't happen often, but when it did, he could be worse than Auron.

'Just put it all down to magic. Then get back to being an officer of the law.'

Despite Shift's hesitancy about being a representative of said *law*, Nicolas couldn't help but notice the slight swagger in their step. He'd have thought Silva would've struggled with it the most, with her past as a villain. But with her usual pragmatism, she'd just seen it as a tactical advantage.

The group, and their escort, had reached one of the main thoroughfares of the city, which was bustling. This part of the city looked odd because of the behaviour of the people. The humans did their best to give the non-humans a wide berth and vice versa. In a crowded street, some of the outcomes were nothing short of comical.

Why is it us *and* them? *Surely the other races have had issues with each other in the past. Why isn't it dwarves annoyed with serians? Or kascats pissed at minotaurs?*

The answer was quickly forthcoming when he saw a small gathering ahead. At its epicentre was a man standing on a small box, talking to the crowd with vehement gestures. Nicolas's eyes widened a little at the man's familiar red robe. This fellow was clearly one of Helstrum's followers.

Nicolas found himself looking in the opposite direction, just in case the man looked up and recognised him. Not that he wanted to get any closer anyway; he might get some of the vile crap the man was spewing on him.

'How terrible that such a noble city should be divided,' Garaz said, shaking his head sadly whilst giving the red-robed preacher the evil eye.

There was definitely a shadow over the city, and the floating town above them wasn't the one casting it. Suddenly, the patchwork nature of the city *was* unnerving. What would happen to it if the divide grew?

'How could people who are neighbours turn on each other so quickly?'

'Fear and anger are powerful tools when properly utilized.' The tone in Silva's voice made him look over at the warrior. He was sure she'd used those tools herself in her past, and equally sure she was now ashamed of it. He'd never asked Silva exactly what she'd done, and he didn't want to know.

Will her soul every truly be redeemed?

Ahead of him, a human mother hid her child behind her shawl as a dwarf passed them by.

I'm going to put this city back together.

Even if this wasn't one of the Maestro's schemes, whatever this was was going to stop. And because of him.

I will... Oh, this again...

A pair of serians walked past him, frowning as if they recognised him. His head turned to follow the pair, and they were suddenly engaged in a hushed conversation. This had happened several times so far. It was a paranoid man's worst nightmare.

Especially as my face is on a wanted poster.

'So, can I ask?' Sergeant Tallith began awkwardly as he led the group through the streets. 'What was the Underworld like? I mean—'

'How do you know that?' The only thing that had stopped Nicolas shouting it was the fact that they were in public. 'You couldn't possibly know that? How does anyone know any of the things that have happened to me?'

The young sergeant half-turned toward him and shrugged. 'I don't know. I just...heard it somewhere.'

'Good news travels as sure as bad,' Auron said. 'And some people love to hear about others' heroic deeds.'

Dying and going to the Underworld is hardly something I've been bragging about.

'Well, I'd like a word with whoever's spreading *my* deeds,' he mumbled grumpily as a kascat child stared at him as if she'd just seen a deity walking Etherius.

'It is worrying,' Shift said with a furrowed brow. 'Being a thief of some renown, I don't really like the idea of people knowing where I've been and what I've done. It makes me too easy to track.'

'Plus, I am sure we have numerous assassins on our trail,' Silva added.

That was true. The Maestro had made a concentrated effort to kill him, and while he didn't know much about the mysterious figure, he guessed he wasn't one to give up easily.

'So, what about this demon then?' he said, blatantly changing the subject. 'What are we facing? Is it Koth?'

'It could be,' Auron mused. 'But even if it isn't, it will be crazy, strong, and violent. Even stuck in a human host, it will be powerful. Demons live to kill and corrupt people. But...'

'But what?'

'It's odd,' Auron continued, frowning. 'Usually, demons pop up and kill as many people as they can before they're banished home again. There should be more bodies considering how long it's been operating. And those it kills shouldn't just be burnt-out hosts, they *should* be torn limb from limb.' The spirit scratched his chin thoughtfully. *Does he still get itches?* 'That's another thing. The hosts...I've only ever known a demon to possess a single host. This one seems capable of jumping from one to another.'

So it could literally be anyone? And it could change daily? My paranoia's certainly getting a thorough workout here.

'That lends credence to the hypothesis that it is this *Koth* creature,' Garaz said. 'And it would certainly explain the mass of demonic energy hereabouts.'

And yet the place looks normal.

'Whatever the explanation, someone's changed the game here,' Auron cautioned. 'We need to be extra careful.'

'And you believe finding who originally summoned it will provide an-swers?' Silva asked.

'Yup.' The spirit nodded. 'Demon worshippers and cults aren't the tidiest of folks. They're bound to have left a clue as to what demon we're dealing with specifically.'

Three...two...one...

'So, this one time I was hunting down this demonic cult, the Brothers of Damnation, or some equally stupid name.' The scorn was evident on Auron's face. 'Proper crazies. They were abducting folk in a town and doing blood sacrifices to some demonic god they worshipped. Thing is, that ilk does like a bit of bloodletting, and aren't big on patience.' The spirit set his jaw. 'They aren't ones for cleaning up thoroughly either. They'd rather spill the blood than mop it up. Turned out that was their downfall. I found some bloody boot prints, followed them to a door. Kicked in said door and snapped the fingers of the occupant until he gave up the rest of the cult. They were all hung in the town square the next day.'

'Not much of an investigation,' Shift noted.

'Sometimes it isn't.' Auron smiled. 'This time it is. It isn't only the lack of carnage that bothers me. It's the pattern of the killings.'

Nicolas thought back to the mortuary with a shiver. 'It went human, non-human, human, non-human.'

'Good eye, kid,' the spirit confirmed. 'But each body was also found exactly where it would cause the most chaos. Always on the border between districts, and usually around taverns, where people are already drunk and aggravated. Spots where they're likely to cause the maximum outrage and tension.'

'Spreading said chaos,' Garaz said solemnly. 'It sounds like the Maestro's hand to me.'

'I think by now we can assume every evil scheme in Etherius has him behind it.' Shift sighed.

'Do not make too many assumptions,' Silva chided. 'It may have nothing to do with him *or* Koth. There was evil before them, and there will be evil after.' *How optimistic of you.* 'Once we assume we know the enemy, we walk into his clutches.'

'For Silva, that was some Garaz-level wisdom,' Shift whispered in his ear.

'I can do some Auron-level storytelling too, if you would like,' the warrior said dryly.

'That's okay, thank you,' Shift answered quickly.

Nicolas's attention was directed to the nervous energy he could sense ahead of him, and he knew exactly who it was coming from.

'You know, this is amazing,' Tallith said, stopping and turning. 'Hunting a demon with Nick Carnage and the—'

Shift coughed pointedly.

'His companions,' the sergeant quickly corrected. 'I mean, I wasn't sure I believed the bit about the ghost, but here we are.'

'*Again* with that ghost shit,' Auron snapped indignantly. 'Someone correct him before he gets the finger poke of doom.'

'Auron is a *spirit*, not a *ghost*,' Garaz corrected.

'Is there a difference?'

'Yes, there buggering is,' Auron shouted. 'I'm not some common spectre going around wearing a sheet shouting *boo* at people or making some crazy old lady's plates float through the air or hovering in libraries reading books. So this dimwit better get the idea or he's liable to have a plate smashed over *his* head.'

'There's a difference,' Nicolas replied diplomatically.

'Okay then,' Tallith said simply.

Judging by the red in Auron's aura, it wasn't that simple, but what was he going to do about it?

Hopefully not carry out on his threat. As strange as Tallith is, he's nice enough. And useful.

Chapter 28

Once they were away from the main pedestrian areas of the city, following their guide Sergeant Tallith, the group found that Babylon had changed once again. Say what you wanted about how the city was divided by race, here, in the most affluent district of the city, it was wealth that was the great divider. It kept those with it separate from those who didn't. Each manor they passed was different to the last, created in the style of whatever race inhabited it. Though *fancy* was a common theme. This one district was like the whole of the city condensed, but with more servants and larger gardens.

One stood out clearly from all of them, so much so that even Nicolas could pick it out as their destination. The multi-level home had numerous pipes protruding from it, making it look like some kind of giant spider, or octopus. Once, Nicolas imagined, the place had looked dignified. Now it was just odd.

'Fascinating,' Garaz said with an almost childlike wonder.

'Fascinating that the neighbours put up with it,' Auron remarked, peering at the other houses.

'I would imagine that keeping the whole city warm in winter with a scientific marvel affords the professor some leeway with even the rich,' the orc muttered, his yellow eyes tracing the lines of pipework.

'Excited to meet the professor?' Shift asked leadingly.

'My love of magic is equalled by my love of science.' Garaz was doing a poor job of reining in his giddiness. 'So yes, very much so. I also wanted to consult him on this.' Garaz produced a small pouch from his cloak and held it in the air.

Nicolas recognised it instantly. It had once belonged to Oleg Hobrath, a villainous wizard in the employ of the Maestro. They'd nearly bested the wizard, hoping to capture him and learn exactly what in the Underworld was going on in Etherius. Unfortunately, Oleg had sniffed whatever was in that pouch and increased his power, before promptly exploding because of it.

'It would be good to learn more about that,' Silva said. 'I doubt this will be the last time we encounter it.'

Me neither. It's almost a depressing inevitability. Like our penchant for attracting undead creatures of all shapes and sizes.

'This is the central hub for all the pipes in the city,' Sergeant Tallith explained as they approached the thickly barred metal fence surrounding the property. 'Here, the heat is generated that will keep winter at bay.'

'To heat a whole city, you would think a larger premises would be required,' Garaz mused to himself.

It was only the mention of the heat that reminded Nicolas he should've been wearing heavy furs right now. The overcast sky of deep grey clouds supported his hypothesis. Yet here he was, nice and warm. Despite the fact they were here on urgent business, he was quite interested to find out how it all worked. Not Garaz-level interested, but curious enough.

The professor certainly values his security.

Between the bars of the formidable fence surrounding the property, Nicolas could see guards in fancy leather armour patrolling the grounds. The gate they were headed toward was manned by two more. Considering Nicolas had been accused of being a mercenary only recently—and repeatedly by a certain lord commander—he was hesitant to cast aspersions on others.

But by the Deities, they do look like mercenaries.

'Can I help you?' The guard's tone was confrontational, rather than helpful as the group reached the gate.

'City watch. We're here to see the professor.'

Despite the fact that Tallith was clearly a member of the watch, the guard's eyes slowly descended to his badge, scrutinising it before rising again. The man pursed his lips and looked to his companion. Nicolas had an odd suspicion they were contemplating telling them all to *bugger off*.

'One minute,' the man said finally, before striding toward the door of the manor.

'Helpful fellow,' Garaz remarked quietly.

'If I need to, I can have that lock open in about ten seconds,' Shift said, studying the gate.

'I can have the guard unconscious in three,' Silva added.

'Is that using your magic key?' he asked, ignoring the warrior and her penchant for violence, which wouldn't serve them well here.

Shift eyes narrowed as they held a lump in their tunic which was the magic key gifted to them by T'goth that hung around their neck. Apparently, it could open any lock. 'If you're suggesting I *need* a magic key to overcome locks quickly, *Nick*, then you are wrong. And questioning my skills this early in our relationship is not a good start.'

Relationship? 'I...uh...I...'

Shift's mouth curved into a knowing smile, and he realised yet again how good they were at getting a reaction out of him. And yet he couldn't be upset about it.

'Humble apologies.'

'Accepted,' the shapeshifter said with a wink.

'Someone's coming,' Auron said, pointing back towards the gate.

The guard was indeed returning, with another man. This one had the casual walk of someone used to being in charge, his thumbs hooked into the loops of his belt. His single eye, for the other was covered in a black patch, regarded them dispassionately.

'Judging by the number of scars on his face, I would say this fellow gets into a lot of fights,' Auron mused as he studied the man. 'And he isn't very good at fighting.'

It does make him look mean, though.

As did the scowl from beneath his thick black moustache.

'Can I help you?' the new man asked. Nicolas suspected the deep bass of his voice was just a little put on.

Why do they keep asking to help when they blatantly don't want to?

'Sergeant Tallith of the city watch,' the young man said with impressive authority that made Nicolas reassess his opinion of the young man, who must've made sergeant for a reason. 'We are here to see Professor Shaw.'

'The professor has requested not to be disturbed, and I'm inclined to grant his request,' the man replied levelly. 'He has important work to do, you see.'

'Well, if we wait for him to stop working, we'll never get to see him,' Tallith pressed.

'I'm glad we're on the same page,' came the cool reply.

The sergeant's authority began to fade. He clearly wasn't prepared to have it challenged and was unsure what to do about it. 'Well...this is city watch business,' he continued on in a faltering voice.

The man with the eyepatch didn't bother to waste words in a reply, he simply folded his arms and shrugged.

'Excuse me, Mr...' Nicolas began leadingly as stepped forwards.

'Cyrus,' Tallith offered when the man only answered with narrowing eye.

'...Cyrus. I'm not entirely sure you understand the situation. You see, this is city watch business, with regards to a spate of murders, no less. And, correct me if I'm wrong here, but this house is well within the confines of city watch jurisdiction.' Nicolas didn't wait for confirmation. 'So, I think this boils down to two options. One, you let us in, and we disturb the professor quickly with a couple of questions and then leave.

Or we could disturb the professor by kicking his gate in, humiliating his guards, and *then* asking him our questions anyway. I'll leave the choice to you. The rest of us are quite open to either.'

As Nicolas stepped back and folded his arms, Tallith gazed at him in awe. Silva took a step toward the gate, as did Garaz.

'I don't think I ever wanted you more than I do right now.' Nicolas was thankful it was Shift who'd whispered that to him and not Tallith—though judging by the look on the young man's face...

Speaking of faces, Cyrus's was working its way through a series of sneering motions.

'You can give me the evil eye all you want,' Nicolas said calmly. 'But we are coming in there, one way or another.' There were murders, a demon on the loose, and still no information on Koth. They had a lot to achieve, and Nicolas wasn't about to let some grumpy mercenary keep them away from their best lead. 'Today,' he added, letting his voice become a low growl.

'Fine,' Cyrus relented, maintaining intense eye contact as he gestured for the guards to open the gate. The eye contact continued whilst the guard fiddled with the lock.

You want a stare off, that's fine with me. I've got two eyes.

'I'm impressed,' Silva muttered.

'Don't be,' he whispered. 'If he'd chosen option two, *you* would've had to kick the gate in.'

'Don't sell yourself short, kid.' Auron smiled. 'That was very impressive. Not an ounce of out-of-his-depth-village-boy in sight.'

Just what I need, confirmation that I'm changing.

With a strained creak, the gate opened, leaving Nicolas to wonder how much science actually paid if Shaw couldn't even afford oil for his gate.

'This way,' Cyrus snarled, already walking away.

Being the polite fellow he was, Nicolas stepped aside and let his companions enter first. As Shift passed him, they slowed slightly, reaching out and stroking his arm, looking him up and down demurely. He tried not to give off pride like a lit beacon.

Walking as slowly as possible, just to be obstinate, Cyrus led them into the manor. It instantly became apparent that Shaw couldn't afford a cleaner either, as cobwebs decorated every surface. Within moments, Garaz's cape was wrapped tightly around himself.

Making a laborious show of opening every door they came to, the eye-patched mercenary guided them through the home to a set of stairs leading down. During their journey through the place, Nicolas noticed a lot more guards, but no signs that it was treated as a home.

'Reminds me of the Oracle's cottage,' Shift remarked as they stared at the dust-covered walls.

'The professor must keep to his workspace,' Garaz mused.

Cyrus strolled toward a thick wooden door and opened it. Instantly, Nicolas exhaled heavily as heat poured from the hole the door had just filled. Sweat beaded on his brow in a second, and he found himself loosening the collar of his shirt.

'This way,' the mercenary grumbled as he started down the steps he'd revealed.

At the bottom of the steps was another door. Cyrus knocked on it four times. A small metal slit slid open.

'People to see the professor. City watch.'

The metal slid shut without a word. Then the wait began. Grouped together on a narrow set of stairs only made the uncomfortable heat worse. He'd never thought there'd be a situation where he wanted to get some distance from Shift's body, but this was it. He was half-tempted to tell Silva to kick the door in when the lock clicked, and it opened.

'In you go,' Cyrus told them with distaste.

CHAPTER 29

'What is all this? Who are you people? What do you want?'

Up until now, Nicolas had thought Cyrus was the epitome of *not pleased to see you*. He was wrong. The mercenary was but an appetiser to the rotund, outraged man currently waving a dirty rag at them as if it had the power to waft them away. Nicolas wasn't sure if the redness in the man's face was due to annoyance, the damnable heat, or a lifetime of poor eating habits. But he was sure the sweat that glistened across the man's bald head was due to the heat.

'Well...answer me then, damn you,' the man, who had to be Professor Shaw, demanded.

Nicolas opened his mouth to introduce himself, but the professor cut him off. 'Cyrus, why are these people here?' Shaw bellowed. 'I gave explicit instructions that I am not to be disturbed.' He was shaking his head with such agitation that his spectacles seemed sure to fly from his nose at any second. 'And yet there are people. Here. In my workshop. At this crucial time.'

'City watch, Professor,' the eye-patched man said cooly. 'They have some questions.'

Professor Shaw's demeanour changed in an instant to one of awkwardness. 'City watch? Questions?' he repeated. 'About what?'

Shaw had to raise his voice to speak because the room was so darned loud, with odd chugging and hissing sounds, mostly coming from the thing that filled the centre of it. The thing that Garaz was gazing at dreamily.

'Nicolas Percival Carnegie,' Nicolas said, walking down the steps and extending his hand. 'Deputised by the city watch. I understand you're busy, but this is important, and we won't take up much of your time.'

Professor Shaw was clearly taken aback by the politeness and directness. Really, Nicolas wasn't sure if he wanted to shake the man's hand, judging by the visible sweat patches under his armpits.

'Time? *Time?*' Shaw scoffed defiantly. 'What *time* do you think I have, young man? I have a whole city to heat, with winter all but upon us. There is no *time*. I have no *time*.'

I thought the city was warm already, but what do I know about science and machinery?

'Still,' he said with a smile. Keeping his hand out. 'This won't take long.'

With a sigh, the professor took his hand. Nicolas had to control his reaction when the soaking wet palm clasped his. There was even a squelch as their hands connected. 'Professor Maurice Shaw,' he greeted with a forced smile. 'How can I help?'

Nicolas rubbed his hand dry on his breeches discreetly as he tried to work out how best to go about this. He *had* only been an investigator for an afternoon now.

'Kid, you need to get him to open up,' Auron counselled at his side. 'Appeal to the ego. Scientists have bigger egos than heroes.'

No one has a bigger ego than you.

'Well, before we get into that, can I just say, this machine is amazing. You say it heats the *whole* city?' Nicolas gesture to the giant brass contraption that nearly filled the room.

Within an instant, Professor Shaw's body language switched from *piss off* to *warm and welcoming*. 'It is, it is, young man.' Shaw gleefully clapped his hands. 'Are you a man of science?'

'Not as much as my companion here.' Nicolas gestured to Garaz, who stared at the machine like Tallith stared at him.

'It is a marvel, a wonder,' the awestruck orc said.

What it was, was an enormous set of metal cylinders that dominated nearly the entire room. There were dials everywhere, their hands bouncing in place as they measured...things. Pipes emerged from the machine in all sorts of random places and angles, before disappearing into the walls. Small gouts of steam erupted and vanished from various joints in the machine.

'Allow me to show you this *marvel*, as you put it,' Shaw said with pride, beginning to usher Garaz toward it.

'Are you okay?' Nicolas asked as the orc passed by. His skin appeared a paler shade of green, and his eyes were drawn.

'Just a headache.' Garaz smiled. 'It has been coming on for a while now.'

'It's most likely the heat,' Shift remarked. 'It's been kind enough to give me one too.'

It's certainly working wonders on my head.

'Pull yourself together, big guy.' Auron smiled. 'There's some amazing machinery for you to coo over.'

Garaz raised an eyebrow with a snort. 'I do not *coo*, as you put it.'

With liberal hand waving, Professor Shaw arranged them in a semi-circle in front of his contraption. 'This machine is based on a new science called *'steam energy'*,' he explained, clasping his hands together. 'This machine is a large furnace. In it, heat is produced to form steam. This steam then travels through the pipes and out across the city. For a good long while, I didn't think I'd be able to crack heating the entire city, but I had some inspiration, and now Babylon looks forward to a warm and balmy winter.'

'It looks a little small to heat an entire city...forgive me for saying,' Shift added hastily at the professor's glare.

'I understand what you mean, young lady.' Shaw didn't pick up on the glare he received back from the shapeshifter, but it was enough to send a shiver down Nicolas's spine. 'But just because something is small, doesn't mean it isn't powerful.'

'That should be your new catchphrase,' Shift said, side-eyeing Nicolas.

'Shut up,' he muttered back.

Pride emanated from the professor like light from the sun as he began to explain this dial and that mechanism. He undoubtably would've been aghast if he could've seen Auron stick his ethereal head right into his machine without a care.

'It's pretty steamy in there,' the spirit said as he pulled his head back out. 'I was hoping to see some flames or something, but I can't even make out where they're coming from. Science has always been a bit beyond me, though. If I can't slay it, I'm usually not interested.'

Or do the other thing to it.

'Fascinating,' Garaz cooed.

'Isn't it just?' Shaw beamed. 'And this is just the beginning. Steam power is something that will allow us to usher in a new age. I see limitless potential and an abundance of scientific wonders powered by steam. Imagine...wagons moving with no horse, factories capable of producing more arms in an hour than an artisan could in a year.' As he talked, the professor walked over to a desk and began to open rolls of parchment. Though he couldn't see them well, Nicolas could make out designs sketched upon them, which the professor pored over in wonder as if they were no longer even there. 'If I can just get it right.'

Nicolas wiped the sweat from his brow. It seemed right enough to him. What more did the professor want from it? Honestly, though, that was beside the point. They'd come here for an important reason.

'Amazing,' he said, speaking truly about the intricate machine. 'It must be difficult to maintain now, what with your apprentice dying.'

Shaw's face dropped, and he put the parchment back on the table sadly. 'Yes, that poor boy. A good apprentice. Terrible business. That is what you're here about?'

'We are,' Nicolas confirmed. 'He was the first victim of this killer, and there are more victims by the week.'

'The first?' the professor repeated, pushing his glasses back up his nose. 'I thought he was the fourth.'

'We believe he was actually the first,' Nicolas confirmed. 'So we just came here to learn more about him. The city's on the tipping point because of these murders.'

'I...I wasn't aware it was so bad,' Shaw replied, looking down at the floor. 'I don't get out much.'

'In the days before your apprentice died, was he acting strangely at all?' Silva asked bluntly.

'How so?'

'More aggressive. Moody. Prone to violence.' Was she describing a demon or herself?

The professor pushed his spectacles back up his nose again. 'No, nothing like that. But when he was here, it was all business. The work is constant.'

'Did he ever express any interest in demons, or the occult?' Garaz asked.

'If he had, I would've noticed,' Shaw said, his jaw setting defiantly. 'I will not tolerate that nonsense. This is a place of science.' He looked back towards his machine. 'I am trying to begin a new world here. Demons have no place in it.'

If I had to choose between science and demons, I know which I'd pick.

'Maybe we—'

'That's quite enough now,' Professor Shaw cut in, raising his hand. 'I have indulged your questions. I need to check the pressure on the pumps. As I have no assistant now, my workload has doubled. Please allow me to get on with it.'

He could tell that Shaw wouldn't answer any more questions, so he ushered the others back toward the door.

'Wait,' the professor called, just before they left the room.

Nicolas turned back and raised a questioning eyebrow.

'You are quite welcome to have a look in his room,' Shaw said, facing his machine. 'It's on the east wing of the house. Cyrus will show you.'

That's better than nothing.

'Before we take our leave,' Garaz said suddenly, 'I wonder if I could get your opinion on this?'

Approaching the professor, Garaz produced the pouch of red powder, opening it and showing it to Shaw. The scientist took a pinch of the powder and massaged it between two fingers. 'What is it?'

'This powder gives its user the ability to bolster and increase their magical potential,' the orc explained. 'It is, however, highly volatile.'

Professor Shaw brought his fingers close to his face, adjusting his spectacles on his nose with his free hand. 'Interesting,' he said slowly. 'I don't think it has the texture or composition of a natural element. I would say it is manufactured. However, I stay away from magic. I find it at odds with science much more often than I care for.' The professor rubbed his hand on his trousers. 'It's intriguing, I'll give you that, but I have no alchemical equipment here to study it—nor the time, I'm afraid.'

Garaz's shoulders visibly slumped. 'Very well. Thank you.'

'To the east wing, good sir,' Shift said with theatrical joviality to Cyrus.

Nicolas didn't need to lip read to understand what the eye-patched man mouthed back.

CHAPTER 30

When Professor Shaw had granted them leave to search his former apprentice's room, Nicolas had expected...well, a *room*. The thin, rectangular space they were all now stood in front of could be better described by the word *cupboard*.

'At least the search won't take long,' Shift said as they leant in through the doorway for a brief inspection. Given the size of it *any* inspection of the room would be brief.

'Indeed,' Garaz confirmed. 'Though how we will all fit in there to search it may require a team of mathematical scholars.'

Shift frowned then rolled their eyes and tutted. 'I wasn't talking about the size of the place. I meant that, as a master thief, I'm adept at finding people's valuable items.'

'Be careful what you do find in there,' Auron cautioned. 'I imagine it got awfully lonely with just the professor, that idiot Cyrus, and the guards for company. Who knows what he left lying around?'

At least they'd shaken Cyrus off. The mercenary had mumbled vaguely about business to attend to, before fobbing them off on the two goons who'd led them to the room, though at one point Nicolas wasn't sure they even knew where they were going. The pair had definitely taken them via the scenic route, and they were the thuggiest thugs who'd ever thugged. Why would the professor, a smart man by his very title, entrust his security to such untrustworthy looking folk?

At least these two are keeping out of the way. Though they're making no secret of the fact that their job is to watch us like hawks.

Fortunately, Silva was watching them like hawks too. And if it came to a fight, Nicolas would bet every coin he had on the warrior.

'So, you're going to search the room?' Tallith asked. 'I think it really should be me, as a, *ahem*, proper member of the watch.' The young man's face paled as he looked at Nicolas. 'Meaning no disrespect, of course.'

'Disrespect taken and given,' Shift said, entwining their fingers and stretching them outwards. 'As in, I disrespect your ability to find things. If there's something in there, I'll have it in under five minutes.'

Slipping into the room, Shift got to work, leaving the sergeant in the corridor with the others, jaw slack.

'You must've enjoyed that,' he remarked to Garaz as Shift began rummaging. 'The machine, I mean.'

'It was fascinating,' the orc replied. 'I would have appreciated it more if not for that damnable headache.'

'It's gone now?'

'Not really,' Garaz admitted. 'But being away from that blasted heat has blunted it a little.'

'The machine was a marvel though.'

Garaz stroked his chin thoughtfully. 'Indeed it was, young Nicolas. Science is a wonderous thing, as long as we never turn our back on the mysticism of the world.'

'I don't think that will be a problem whilst people walk around conjuring demons or shooting fireballs from their fingertips.' He chuckled.

Maybe a bit less magic would be nice?

Garaz raised an eyebrow. Had he insulted the orc by accidentally suggesting that demon-conjuring and his own skillset weren't that far apart? 'True,' he replied at last. 'But there has always been a balance, and it must always be maintained. I suppose that is why the Elves put down the ancient edicts.'

Ah yes, yet another thing to add to the list of things I've been ignorant about until now.

He knew Elves had existed, and that they'd once ruled a vast empire, and then they'd buggered off for...reasons. But that was about it. Well, not true. He'd heard enough about the ancient edicts to know that the *'meat and potatoes'* of them was to keep the enchanted forests of Etherius natural, untainted spaces. Though that in itself was strange, considering the Elves were said to have built the temples in the midst of each one.

'It's odd that they laid down edicts if they were leaving,' Nicolas mused. 'Why would they bother as they were...well...going?'

'Just because one leaves a place, does not mean they no longer care for it.' A sudden sad look crossed his companion's face. It had never occurred to Nicolas that Garaz might have a home, or that he was isolated from his kin...the non-murderous ones, anyway. 'The edicts were set out to protect the core of Etherius herself, maintaining the enchanted forests that nurture the life force of our world.'

'Even they can be used to serve evil,' Nicolas replied solemnly. The dwarven gangster Big Boss had turned a temple in the centre of an enchanted forest into a seedy gaming hall and arena to ensure that he was beyond the reach of the law of Sarus. He'd even gone as far as to clear a part of it to make space for carriage parking.

'Nefarious people can twist anything to their own advantage,' Garaz confirmed. 'But not enough to harm the world at large. Even in Edmoor, we saw how quickly new life regrew in place of the old. It is not just about the forest but preserving life on our world itself. That is what the Elves understood.'

'You sound well-read on this.'

'I have yet to find a topic Garaz *isn't* well read on,' Auron remarked.

'And yet science advances, sometimes in ways it very much should not.' As the orc spoke, he fingered the pouch of Oleg Hobrath's magic-boosting-slash-people-exploding powder. The idea that it had been manufactured was quite worrying. Some science was truly not worth the discovery.

The conversation was interrupted by a book being slammed against Nicolas's chest.

'False bottom in the cupboard,' Shift said with a smug grin. 'And I believe that was about three minutes.' Their face dropped slightly. 'Which you would know if you'd been paying attention, Nick.'

'Sorry,' he replied. 'Garaz was talking about Elves.'

The look they gave him said it all. Finding elvish lore more interesting than them might come back and bite him later.

'Maybe we can discern if this is useful before we heap praise upon you,' Silva said, taking the book. 'This could be a tome of crude etchings.'

The engraving of the horned creature on the front of the book certainly screamed *occult* to Nicolas.

Disdainfully, Silva flicked through it. 'I have no idea what this is,' she said finally, handing it to Garaz.

The orc's look as he studied the tome was one of disgust. 'This is it,' Garaz confirmed. 'A book of demonology and rituals to summon them.' The orc suddenly slammed the book shut. 'This type of...literature can corrupt those who study it too closely,' he cautioned. 'Even now, the malevolent forces it contains are making my fingers itch.' The orc narrowed his eyes, as if there were a bright light. On the odd occasion, Garaz had been known to react badly to nearby sources of strong magic.

'So what you're saying is that it's best not to use it?' He couldn't help the disappointment in his voice. 'Not to summon the demon to us?'

Or learn more about Koth, if it turns out he's not the one terrorizing this city.

Shift held his hand reassuringly. 'We'll find him,' they told him definitively. 'No matter how long it takes.'

Garaz looked at Nicolas then at the book in his hands. 'If I take the time to prepare myself properly, I believe I could peruse it quickly without any lasting damage.'

'No,' Nicolas said. 'I won't risk you like that.' As touching as it was, he wasn't about to let it happen. He'd done something stupid like that before, with Silva.

Any further conversation on the subject was rendered moot when the book burst into flames. With a cry, Garaz let go of the tome, but by the time it hit the floor it had turned to ash. Silva still pointed her sword at it, just in case.

'Was that you?' Auron asked. It was a daft question, really, as Garaz looked as shocked as anyone.

'No,' Garaz replied, before adding, 'And my hands are fine, thank you.'

Auron shrugged. 'You'd be screaming if they weren't.'

'The book must've been booby trapped to stop the wrong person reading it,' Shift suggested.

'Smart,' Nicolas said, looking at the pile of ash that had been his last real hope of finding Koth.

'Not all booby traps are smart.' Nicolas heard the next words in his head before the spirit said them. 'So this one time, I track this warlord to his lair—he was called something like the *Flayer*. Whatever. So I get to the gates of his fort. It was on a mountain. His lair was built beneath a rocky overhang. Flayer man sees me coming up the road, and he's all, like, '*Nyah, I don't need to defeat you, Dawnblade. I'll let the elements do it for me, nyah,*' and he triggers this booby trap and starts an avalanche from the peak above.' Quick pause for dramatic effect. 'Now, I'm a little concerned because of the tons of snow falling towards me. *Except,* when it reaches the rocky overhang above his fort, the overhang crumbles under the weight and buries him, his piddly little lair, and his minions. Poof, all gone. It was a bit disappointing, really. I'd drawn my sword and everything.' Auron glanced away thoughtfully. 'I'm not sure what he expected to achieve. The snow would've cut him and his men off anyway...'

'I'm sorry for your troubles,' Shift said faux sympathetically.

'At least we know how the demon got here.' Nicolas wanted to get back to the point before another tale reared its ugly head.

'The young apprentice was sat in his cramped room summoning demons and getting high,' Auron said, shaking his head.

Nicolas gave him the same look all his other companions were.

'I've never *tried* it,' the spirit shouted indignantly. 'Vargas Quell liked the odd snuff of demonic energy back in the day, and look how he turned out.' Auron's now-deceased nemesis was a great example of why you *shouldn't* do it.

'Any other experience you care to share?' Nicolas asked.

'Well, I don't know how it's been here so long,' the spirit replied thoughtfully. 'Even jumping from host to host, the demon should be on borrowed time simply because they aren't made to exist on our plane. No more than I could survive under the sea for long. Well, when I was alive.'

'Okay, so on the positive side, at least we're sure it's a demon now,' Shift said. 'That's a step in the right direction. Maybe this guy was part of a cult?'

'If he was, they'll have scattered to the winds the moment one of theirs was killed. It's no fun anymore when the demon you summon starts killing your mates,' Auron mused. 'Tracking them down will take an age.'

'Maybe the other victims were the rest of the cult?' Nicolas suggested.

'I don't think so,' the spirit replied after a moment's thought. 'Cults tend to be a group of like-minded folks getting together. The victims were from all races and backgrounds. Nice idea though, kid.'

'There is a way I might be able to track the demonic energy, now that we are in closer proximity,' Garaz remarked. 'There is an old ritual my shamanistic teacher taught me to protect from evil spirits. I believe I can modify it.'

'And you just remembered this now?' Silva asked.

The orc's brow furrowed. 'I always remembered it.' Garaz grunted. 'But I am no powerful seer and would prefer to exhaust all other options before opening myself to demonic energy. Besides, I am not sure it will even work.'

'You aren't opening yourself up to that,' Nicolas said firmly. 'I'm not risking you. We'll find another way. I'm sure Auron knows a demon-hunting trick or two.' The spirit bobbed his head in a way that suggested *yes and no.*

'Your concern for me is touching.' Garaz smiled. 'But the longer we dally the more people will die. I need to do this.'

'It's fascinating watching you all work. I can't believe I'm seeing this.'

Nicolas ignored Tallith. He was too busy pondering the potential effects of either path. On the one hand, he would never in a million years want to risk Garaz. But the longer they left finding the killer, the more innocent people could die.

Innocent people.

And so his mind was made up. 'Okay,' he relented. 'But not here. We'll go find the lord commander and ask him to suggest somewhere remote to do it, just in case something goes wrong. I'd rather be prepared for...' He looked up, and Auron was smiling at him. 'What?'

'Nothing, kid,' the spirit replied.

'How about saving the host when we do find it?' Shift asked.

'I'm going to stop you there,' Auron replied quickly. 'When a demon takes a host, the soul is burnt away. Even if we expel the demon, there'll only be an empty shell left.' *Well, that's just terrible.* 'And it won't go without a fight. The demon will make the host stronger, faster, and more durable. It'll be a case of causing enough damage to the host body that it can't possibly continue living.' *That's worse.* 'You okay with that, kid?'

He thought back to Koth. Whoever the man had been before the creature inhabited him, he was definitely no longer human. There was no way the host could recover from the mutations the demon had caused to his body. If it was Koth, it'd be easier. But even if not, he understood. He didn't like it, but he'd do what he needed to. There were too many bodies already to do any less.

CHAPTER 31

'Hmm.' Lord Commander Greer made a big show of shuffling the papers on his desk as Nicolas waited expectantly. He didn't know exactly what he expected; he was sure what the answer was going to be. 'No,' came the decision with finality.

'Is that your final answer?' Shift asked. 'You considered that for all of five seconds.'

Greer put his papers down and pursed his lips. 'I think my decision was clear enough.'

'Ah, he is in full bureaucratic asshole mode,' Auron noted with distaste. 'Good luck getting him out of that.'

I still have to try.

'Please, Lord Commander,' he said levelly. 'There's a demon loose in the city. We have a way of potentially tracking it—'

'Says you,' Greer interrupted.

'We just need to do this one spell and—'

'The governor asked me to indulge you. And I have,' the lord commander said with venom. 'I know your ilk well, *sir*. You and your kind charge into town believing yourselves heroes of legend and that all problems can be solved by a couple swings of the sword. You run around flouting the law because you believe you have some divine mandate to do good. Well, not here, sir. Not in my city.'

That description is about as far from me as you're likely to get.

But he had to pick his battles, and right now, he had a much more important one.

'We just want to cooperate and help you solve these murders.'

'I see.' The instant the smile crossed Greer's face, he knew he'd walked into a trap. 'And how, pray tell, do you consider yourself to be working in cooperation with me when you go and do something I explicitly told you not to do?'

Bugger.

Other than that expletive, Nicolas was lost for words. He needed something, anything, to help change Greer's mind. They were probably a minute or so away from being dragged out of the city by their ears. He needed to come up with a fantastic and compelling piece of oratory, and he had...

Bugger all.

'We were right to do it,' Silva interjected. 'We found proof that Shaw's apprentice was the one who summoned the demon. We found the book he used to summon it.'

Greer held out his hand facetiously. 'And may I see this *book* of yours?'

Nicolas bit back his retort. Tallith had been in this office before them, so Greer clearly already knew about it and what had happened.

'It burned to ash.' Shift was clearly losing patience with this at a much rapider pace than he was.

'Ah yes.' Greer smirked. 'It conveniently burned to ash in the hands of the person in your little company who uses fire magic.'

'Sir, I can assure you-'

The lord commander held up his hand, silencing Garaz mid-sentence, before looking past the group. 'Sergeant Tallith, what did you make of this book of theirs?'

In the corner of the room, the sergeant shuffled nervously, as if he were a child who'd been asked to pick a side in an argument between his parents.

The sudden lack of eye contact with me isn't a good sign.

'Um...well, sir...' Tallith gave Nicolas an apologetic glance. 'I didn't actually get a chance to examine the book myself, as they all gathered around it. But I did see there was a book, and that it burnt to ash, as everyone keeps saying.'

It isn't helpful, but at least he's being honest.

'So we have a book I cannot look at, yet am expected to take your word it existed, and is something to do with this demon, who I'm also expected to believe exists.' Greer made a show of pondering this, rubbing his moustache thoughtfully. 'And because of that, you expect me to authorise some spell that *may* work.' The lord commander fixed Nicolas with a steely gaze. 'I barely tolerate the Magic Guild here. In fact, I've had to put all the damned guilds under house arrest as they've decided to pick the most bloody perfect time to start feuding with each other. I am not about—'

'Sir, they're just trying to help.'

Though Greer looked equal parts dumbfounded and enraged by the interruption, Nicolas took the opening that Tallith had given him.

'Exactly,' he jumped in quickly. 'All we want to do is help solve these murders. I don't like the idea of this spell any more than you, but I do believe it's the best option we have right now.'

'Now you listen here, you insolent little turd.' Nicolas was stunned, until he realised the lord commander was talking to his sergeant. 'If you think—'

'Duncan, be nice to your nephew.'

In the doorway stood a bright-eyed woman with long blond hair. She had the indulgent smile of someone used to the temperament of the man they were addressing.

This'll be his wife then?

'Beba.' Greer huffed. 'You cannot just walk into my office and interrupt my meetings.' The lord commander was obviously trying to be annoyed with his wife but failing.

'If you don't want me in your office, you shouldn't go forgetting your lunch,' she said breezily as she walked around Nicolas and deposited the small basket she carried on the table. Judging by her fine crimson dress, being lord commander of the city watch paid well. 'You are under a lot of stress right now. You need to make sure you eat properly.'

'*Not* in front of the mercenaries,' Greer said through gritted teeth.

Beba turned and looked Nicolas and the others over with a chuckle. As she did, her bushy blond hair bobbed, and he was painfully reminded of his mother. 'You and I have a very different definition of *mercenary*, Duncan. I thought Nicolas and his companions were here to help?'

'You know us?' Shift asked.

'Of course she does.' Greer snarled. 'Because the men downstairs like to gossip as much as a dwarf likes digging. Bloody chatterboxes.'

Beba gave her husband a patient smile. 'People do like to talk to the lord commander's wife. One of the many perks of my station.'

'It bloody well shouldn't be,' Greer grumbled.

'So,' Beba asked, her bright blue eyes filled with curiosity, 'have you had any luck finding this killer?'

What I'm about to do may not win me any favour with the lord commander, but desperate times and all that.

'We were just discussing that,' he answered with a smile. 'We were asking the lord commander if we could conduct a spell to help find this murderer.'

Auron let out a long whistle. 'Going over his head to his wife. I'm not sure if I'm proud or disgusted.'

'Spell?' Beba said, tilting her head slightly.

'A simple enchantment that may help us narrow down—'

'*Leave*,' Greer growled, cutting off Garaz. 'Sergeant Tallith will return you to your lodgings. I want you to stay out of trouble. If that is at all possible. But most of all, you are not to set one foot outside until morning.'

'I'm going to change into something with eight feet and put them all outside,' Shift whispered.

As much as Nicolas wanted to argue, he knew he'd pushed the lord commander further than he should have already. They'd disobeyed him then argued with him. Now they needed to prove they could cooperate and hopefully win back some trust.

If that's even possible.

'A pleasure,' he said, offering his hand to Beba, trying to control the shaking caused by the frustration welling up inside him. They were here to help, and that help was being blocked at every turn.

Play nice. It'll get better.

'Likewise.' Beba shook his hand gently and mouthed *sorry* to him.

Greer said nothing as they were led from his office.

****

The tavern door swung open from the hard shove Nicolas gave it, slamming into the wall with a bang. The innkeeper opened his mouth, ready to unleash a telling off, but the man took one look at Nicolas's face and thought better of it.

'*Dammit*,' he shouted, throwing his hands in the air. 'The man is a stubborn ass.'

'You waited until we returned to the tavern to get angry?' Silva asked.

'No,' Shift answered for him. 'He's been brooding all the way back here. You couldn't *hear* him overthinking?'

'Of course I could,' the warrior replied. 'I am merely pointing out the futility of him bott—'

'Please continue talking about me like I'm not in earshot,' Nicolas interrupted dryly. 'I'm not wrong to be annoyed. Greer...' He caught Sergeant Tallith standing dutifully in his peripheral vision. '...the lord commander is making it really difficult to help.'

'True,' Auron confirmed. 'I'm sure his dislike of heroes is clouding his judgement, for whatever reason.'

'Well, his judgement needs to be unclouded,' Nicolas snapped. 'We have a killer to find.'

Not only that, but my people.

A hand squeezed his, and Nicolas stared to wonder if Shift could actually read his thoughts.

'We will talk to him in the morning, when we have all had a chance to rest,' Garaz counselled.

It made a frustrating amount of sense.

It was starting to get dark. Part of him wanted to be out hunting the demon, but if the lord commander caught them ignoring his commands again, they might be ejected from the city and then they couldn't help at all.

'I thought getting deputised would help.'

'The lord commander will come round,' Tallith offered. 'He can be stubborn, but once he sees this may be the only way, he will relent.'

'Hopefully, no one else dies before then,' Shift said.

Tallith's gaze went to the floor. He then excused himself. Something about other duties. It was hard to tell, it being mumbled and all. Ignoring the glares of the landlord, the group walked up the stairs to their rooms.

'You know what?' Nicolas sighed wearily. 'Bed sounds like a good idea.'

'*Nick*, you animal,' Shift said with a faux-coy gasp.

'I...uh... You...' Not only had his mouth stopped working, he'd flushed bright red. He could practically see the light from his face reflecting from the tavern walls.

'Not in front of us, please,' Garaz said with distaste.

Nicolas was about to respond when he found Silva's palm on his chest, bringing him to a halt. The warrior was eyeing the door of his room, hand on the hilt of her sword.

'I think there's someone in there,' Silva cautioned to the drawing of weapons.

Auron approached the door without a care and popped his head through it. When it returned, the spirit turned to the others and rolled his pupilless eyes. 'It's safe,' he said. 'Just a villain about to give us some kind of veiled threat.'

Frowning, Nicolas opened the door.

'Please, come in,' Geldheart said from the chair in the corner of the room.

'I think it's poor etiquette for an uninvited guest to invite someone into their own room,' Shift said coolly.

'Very true.' The old man chuckled. 'But my business here requires a little breach of etiquette.'

'Do you want him removed?' Silva asked.

'Maybe,' Nicolas muttered. 'Best hear his business first.' He doubted Silva roughing up a man on the city council would endear them to Greer.

The group walked into the room. As far as Nicolas could tell, Geldheart was alone.

'All he needs is some sort of familiar or minion to complete the nefarious villain image,' Auron scoffed as he walked up to the councillor and studied him.

It was true. He'd obviously gone to great lengths to sit in the corner of the room where the light would just catch his features, making him appear ominous. Then you had the lowered brow and the steepling of the fingers. Nicolas came to the firm conclusion he was a bad guy.

It is pretty obvious. Or maybe I'm just developing hero instincts of my very own.

'I will get straight to the point,' Geldheart began. 'Leave.'

That's getting to be a theme.

'But you just invited us in,' Shift said with a flourish toward the door.

'I am in no mood for games.'

Nicolas doubted Geldheart would know what a game even was. He appeared to be an entirely humourless fellow.

'Kid, you need to ask, *'Or what?'* Nicolas frowned at Auron. 'This is just how it goes,' the spirit continued with a sigh. 'They say something vaguely menacing, you ask *or what*, then they threaten you. I'm interested to see what this man has up his sleeve.'

'Or what?' he asked tentatively.

To Nicolas's surprise, Geldheart actually reached into the sleeve of his long robe and pulled out a parchment. Even more surprising was what was on it. The councilman unfurled it and held it up to the light.

'Or,' Geldheart began with the smile of someone grudgingly indulging a fool. 'This wanted poster finds its way to Greer's desk. I am sure the lord commander would find it interesting to have an assassin in his midst.' Rising in the most menacing way possible, Geldheart rolled up the parchment again and put it in Nicolas's hand. 'By tomorrow morning, you shall be gone.'

And with that, he glided out of the room. Instantly, Nicolas opened the parchment again and stared at the ridiculously good likeness of him.

'Interesting.' Auron sniffed. 'But pointless.'

'How so?' Garaz asked.

'If he was going to do it, he would've already done it,' the spirit replied. 'There's no need to come trying to scare you away.'

'Then why hasn't he?' Shift asked.

The spirit pursed his lips thoughtfully. 'If I had to guess, it's because he knows Greer would actually investigate the matter properly, which he doesn't want for some reason. Maybe because he knows something about the assassination attempt himself?'

'The Maestro likes people not to look into things too deeply,' Silva suggested, keeping one eye out in the corridor.

'Either way, something strange is going on,' Garaz said. 'My hope is that we figure it out before it comes to fruition.'

'Geldheart can waft around as many wanted posters as he likes, I'm not going anywhere,' Nicolas said, glaring at the door.

'Nor me. The rest of you can get out, though.' Shift gestured to the door to put an exclamation point on their command.

'You're...staying here tonight then?' Nicolas tried not to sound too hopeful.

Bugger it. I'm so hopeful.

'Of course,' the shapeshifter said with a confused frown. 'A man broke into your room to threaten you. You need protection. I will provide said protection. Though to really keep an eye on you, I think it best we share the bed.'

'Let's get out of here,' Auron said with a chuckle. 'Before that gormless look on the kid's face turns into something else.'

Yippee.

CHAPTER 32

No matter how much he stared up at it, the ceiling wasn't yielding any answers. By now he had spent so long staring at said ceiling that he was starting to find the lack of inspiration it was giving him quite rude. Instead, he continued to get nothing. Just once, it would be nice to have a clear path on one of these adventures. But he could usually rely on everything to just happen to him, whether he wanted it to or not. In this city, it was different. He had no idea where to go next. There wasn't even a noticeable *bad guy*, as such.

Though Geldheart has the stink of villainy oozing from every pore.

The truth of it was that the demon could be anyone in a city of who knew how many souls. But finding it was just one problem. When they did, they would have to find a way to capture it. Part of him knew it might come down to killing the creature, but he had to hope.

I'll ask Auron how to catch demons in the morning.

If they managed it, they could find his people. Unless it wasn't Koth. But surely all demons knew each other? Or maybe they'd get lucky, and it'd be Koth's cousin's fiancé or something.

This stuff has *to be connected.*

His brain began to track all the events that had brought him here. Soon his mind was a labyrinth in which he was lost, and he'd only served to confuse himself further. With a frustrated sigh, he knew he'd have to do the one thing he didn't want to do right now. Get a second opinion. He gave working all of this out by himself one last go. Nothing.

Dammit. This isn't going to be pretty.

Slowly, he turned over, trying to make as little noise as possible. Which was ironic, considering what he was about to do.

'Shift? Shift?' There was no response. Gently, he put his hand on their bare shoulder and shook it slightly. '*Shift?*'

The shapeshifter's jaw set in annoyance. 'Nick, if you wish to sleep alone, you're going exactly the right way about it,' came the bleary whisper. 'Either that, or you have a death wish.'

'Sorry,' he said, offering what he hoped was an apologetic grin.

Which means nothing, because their eyes are still shut.

'First, you cost me a bed after a long journey then when I do find one, you won't let me sleep in it.'

'I've only woken you once,' he said defensively

A single green eye opened. 'Three times,' they corrected. 'Apparently, you can't even think at night without making *hmm* and *mmm* noises. A quick tip about sharing a bed with me – if you wish to continue to do so – do not wake me for anything less than the building burning down around us. Understood?'

'It's just—'

'You feel useless because we didn't instantly find and stop the killer. You also feel like you're letting your people down because you haven't saved them yet.'

'What—'

'If they're already dead? They're not. We would've found the bodies. Besides, the Maestro wouldn't go to all the trouble of staging the wrecked slaver ship just to kill them.'

'How—'

'Do I know what you're thinking? Because I'm smart, and I can translate *hmm* and *mmm* speak.'

Despite himself, Nicolas chuckled. 'More likely, you pay too much attention to me.'

Shift's other eye opened. A second later, their pillow hit him in the face. 'You are lucky you're arguably handsome,' they warned.

'If I'm handsome...' *Ignoring the term* arguably. '...then surely *you're* the lucky one?'

Shift proceeded to batter him with the pillow, until he reached up and snatched it off them.

'We'll find something,' they said, sitting back in the bed. 'Auron's out there searching now. And if there's another murder, I can turn into a bloodhound and track the scent.'

'I'd prefer not to wait for another body.'

'Me neither. That's why we're going to let Garaz do his spell—to the Underworld with what that snotty lord commander says.'

Nicolas was about to speak, but instead he coughed and wiped some sweat from his brow.

Shaw's machine is a wonder, but maybe some way to turn it down would be...

His eyes widened as he saw smoke coming under the door.

'You know when you said I should only wake you if there's a fire?'

Shift's head swung around. 'Dammit.'

Deities-damned taverns.

Within an instant, they were both on their feet and putting their clothes on.

'Garaz, fire!' Shift cried, kicking the wall furiously.

There was a muffled curse from Garaz, which was soon followed by a louder one as he noticed the fire. Nicolas did the same to the wall between their room and Silva's—the previous tenant had checked out due to a noise complaint. By the time that was done, Shift had already ripped two strips of cloth from the bed. They gave one to Nicolas, before tying the other around their mouth. The smoke was now in the room and getting thicker. Grabbing his sword, he approached the door. Tentatively, Shift touched the handle and nodded that it was okay. Steeling themselves, Nicolas opened the door.

Logic dictated that they should've turned their bedsheets into a rope and climbed out of the window—or something like that. But other people were staying here and would need help evacuating.

Actually, they'll need help realising there's a fire.

'Fire! *Fire!*' he bellowed, cupping his hands to his mouth. 'Everybody up. There's a fire.'

Around them, he heard bleary shouts of annoyance from the surrounding rooms. Like Garaz, those soon became cries of alarm. The corridor around them was already filling with smoke. The fire hadn't reached the second floor yet, but there was an ominous orange-yellow glow coming from the stairs. It wouldn't be long.

Two doors nearest them opened and Garaz and Silva emerged.

'We need to get the people out,' he cried, pointing to random doors.

As his companions went to work, Nicolas kicked the nearest door in. A woman screamed from her bed as she used the sheet to cover her virtue.

'No time for that,' he shouted. 'Fire. Let's go.'

Quickly, he ushered the women out of the room. The corridor was filling with people now. They were confused and scared but allowed themselves to be herded. Silva strode past him holding a small child. There was an outbreak of coughing as the smoke took its toll. The heat was becoming oppressive. The fire was no longer confined to downstairs, and licks of hot flame framed the corridor as more smoke bellowed forth. The visibility was getting less with each passing moment.

'Move,' Shift said, grabbing him as they ran past.

Ahead of them, he could just about make out Silva, ready to smash the window at the end of the hall.

'Wait,' Garaz cried between coughs. 'If you do that you will let the air in and the fire will burn faster.'

'Do you see another way out?' the warrior snapped back.

She had a point, and if the orc had chosen to argue then it was lost in the smashing of glass as Silva kicked the window in. Behind them the fire instantly flared and began to progress down the corridor faster, consuming everything in it's path. Which would soon include them.

We need to get out of here. Now.

Peering out of the broken window, Nicolas could see that the fire had fully engulfed the bottom floor of the tavern.

The structure will give way soon.

'Ideas?' he asked, when he saw no convenient hay wagon to jump on.

'Shapeshifter to the rescue,' Shift said, before muttering, 'And I'd only just gotten dressed.'

Cloth tore as Shift scurried out the window. Nicolas didn't see what they'd changed into but heard a strange noise. A *thwip*.

'There,' Garaz said after a second. 'We need cloth.'

Following the orc's pointing finger, Nicolas saw a thick rope-looking strand going from the top of the window to the bottom of the building across the street, where a crowd was now beginning to gather. Some were running to the nearest well to grab water to fight the blaze.

They're going to need bigger buckets. Much bigger.

Thinking quickly, he headed into the nearest room and grabbed the bedsheet. With Garaz's help, he tore it into strips, giving one to each person. Silva showed them what to do first, looping the strip over the strand and holding both ends in one hand. The child holding on for dear life, the warrior jumped from the window and slid to the ground. One by one, the rest followed as the fire continued to make its way toward them, until it was just Nicolas and Garaz left.

'Hurry up,' he shouted to the orc.

'You go first,' Garaz replied.

'I am not arguing. *Go.*'

Staff held between his knees, the orc did as bid, sliding down the rope to safety. Which just left Nicolas. Throwing his cloth over the strand, he didn't stop to think and jumped from the window. He began to slide down, gaining speed quickly. Then the strand snapped.

Nicolas plummeted through the air. The ground awaited him. He threw his arms in front of his face, as if that'd somehow help.

Aaaarrrrrggggggghhhhh.

With a fierce jolt that shook his spine, he suddenly came to a halt. Slowly, he took his hands away and opened his eyes. He was a full metre from the ground, dangling in mid-air. Craning his neck, he turned around to see what...

'Aaahhh.' The strand attached to the back of his jacket, which had saved him from death, tracked up to a giant spider that sat on the roof of the burning building. Once he realised who it was, and that they were still sat on a burning building, he quickly cut the web and dropped to the ground with a thud.

Nicolas struggled as a hand grabbed him and hauled him to his feet.

'Thank the Deities,' Tallith said with a sigh of relief. 'I thought you were done for.'

Nicolas blinked in surprise. 'What are you doing here? I thought you'd gone home?'

The sergeant shrugged. 'I was told to make sure you stayed put.'

Nicolas looked back toward the burning building. Shift had already swung to the next one across. The inn itself was beyond saving. The fire engulfed it. Timber blackened and cracked as the blaze destroyed it. By morning, it would be a pile of ash.

'I hope Greer doesn't blame us for this.'

****

Hands clasped behind his back, Greer walked parallel to the charred ruins that had once been a building, running his tongue along his teeth, his brow furrowed. Though the fire had been quenched, with a lot of assistance from Nicolas and the others, a few trails of smoke drifted defiantly into the sky from what was left of the tavern itself, which amounted to a series of charred pieces of wood in a vague building like formation. The place would need to be torn down and rebuilt. Nicolas tried not to look at the innkeeper, who knelt before the door of his establishment, rag in hand as he stared numbly at the blackened door, which was somehow still standing when all around it was rubble.

'Apparently, demanding that you stay out of trouble was an unreasonable request.' The lord commander sighed heavily, coming to a halt. 'All you had to do was sleep.'

'I think blaming us for this is ridiculous,' Silva retorted quickly. 'We would hardly set fire to a place we were sleeping in.'

Greer's face suggested he disagreed, but he couldn't deny the logic of the warrior's argument either. 'Do you think someone did this to get to you?'

'That would only make sense if we were a threat, meaning our investigation is moving in the right direction.'

Greer's mouth set in a thin line under his moustache, his eyes practically bulging. Evidently, he didn't care much for Garaz's logic either.

'Kid, what in the Underworld happened here?' Auron cried as he rounded the corner.

'It burnt down,' he answered, rather redundantly.

'I can see that,' the spirit scoffed. 'How?'

'Fire.'

Auron shook his head in annoyance. 'Obviously. Are you all right?' he asked him pointedly.

'I don't know anymore.'

'I don't even know how you get in these scrapes,' the spirit declared, inspecting the blackened remains of the building. 'All you had to do was sleep.'

'Don't you start,' Nicolas muttered with a sigh.

'Another bed gone.' Shift looked almost as crestfallen as the innkeeper.

'It was clearly Geldheart.'

Judging by the spluttering coming from Greer, if the lord commander had been drinking when Silva said what she'd just said, Nicolas would've been wearing it.

'I beg your pardon?' Greer cried once he'd gained control of himself.

'Geldheart visited us,' Silva informed him. 'He made a threat. Then suddenly the tavern burns down. That is no coincidence.'

The lord commander's eyes narrowed suspiciously. 'What kind of threat?'

'A vague one,' Nicolas answered quickly.

'You cannot just go around accusing members of the City Council of arson,' Greer growled through gritted teeth. 'You *mercenaries* need to learn a word called *'evidence."*

'If it was him, then I'm sure...' Nicolas trailed off as the prison wagon rolling onto the street caught his attention. 'What's that for?'

'To take you back to Watch Headquarters,' Greer answered. 'Apparently, you need lodgings.'

Hopefully, it's not a room with bars.

CHAPTER 33

I can't believe we're in one of these again. Most people never ride in a prison wagon. But me...twice in two days.

Early morning light crept in between the bars on the wagon's window, serving to remind Nicolas that he hadn't slept. His tired mind had no means with which to defend itself from the negativity and worry he was getting better at keeping at bay. Instead, it swirled with scenarios of what would happen should they not catch the killer, and regrets that it had not been done already.

Sooner or later, it'll kill again. And it will be my fault.

None of his companions were any breezier, save Auron. Though, thankfully, the spirit had read the room and kept any stories to himself.

Nicolas groaned as the wagon came to a halt with one final judder. The sound of footsteps outside soon became the sound of the door unlocking. Light poured in as it opened, framing Sergeant Tallith, whose beaming smile was most unwelcome.

'Welcome to your lodgings.'

He really has no business being this chirpy at this time of the morning.

Managing the best smile he could muster, which was pretty thin, Nicolas emerged from the wagon, followed by the others. At least the morning air was refreshing.

Though the city watch had stations dotted throughout the city, the main watch headquarters was at its heart, near the citadel. The place was like a fortress itself, surrounded by a thick outer wall. Beyond it was a large and imposing stone building whose message was clear—*the people in here don't take kindly to those who break the law. Do it, and you're in trouble.*

Though the message was slightly undercut by the troop of weary watchmen trudging up to the gate. It was clearly the end of a long night for them.

'Anything to report, Sergeant?' Greer asked the leader of the patrol, a serian, as he dismounted his horse.

'Several disturbancesss,' the serian replied with a laboured salute that spoke to how tired he was. 'No murders. But...'

'But what?' the lord commander asked.

'Our patrolsss are having difficulty enforcing order,' the sergeant continued. 'Humans are openly scoffing at my authority and those of any non-humans in our units. The same applies to the human officers when they engage with non-human citizens. There is a growing undercurrent of defiance.'

'And that is why you have clubs,' Greer roared. 'A watchman is a watchman. I don't care if he's human, centaur, or bloody half-troll. They respect the badge. If they don't, they can enjoy a night in the cells.'

Giving away our rooms already?

'Are we actually going to sleep here?' Nicolas asked with a sigh.

'Problem is, kid,' Auron said with sympathy, 'tavern landlords are some of the most gossipmongering folk in Etherius. By now, every tavern in the city will know that after you checked in, there was a brawl then you were dragged out by the watch then the place got burned down.'

'We did not burn it down,' Garaz said firmly.

'I know that, but you'll be blacklisted. You being able to rent a room in this city again will be about as likely as Silva breaking into a song-and-dance routine.'

'It will never happen then,' the warrior noted.

'As long as they have some clothing in there,' Shift grumbled, pulling their blanket toga around them. They'd destroyed their last outfit by becoming a giant spider. All that had been to hand was a blanket. 'Thank the Deities for Professor Shaw's heating system, or I'd be blue by now.'

Nicolas, wanting to be chivalrous, put his arm around Shift.

'Sorry, skinny village boy, I appreciate the gesture, but your body heat won't be the difference maker here.'

'Good morning, Duncan.'

Another person who had no right being so jovial so early was Beba, the lord commander's wife, who strode toward them, waving brightly. The wave was cut short as she looked over Nicolas and his companions.

'By the Deities,' she gasped, taking them in. 'What happened to you?'

Nicolas glanced down at himself. His clothes—the couple of things he'd managed to throw on before escaping the burning building—were covered in black stains from the smoke.

'The tavern we were in burned down,' Garaz answered.

'My goodness.' Beba gasped. 'Are you all all right?'

'Besides a lack of sleep and losing all our possessions...' Shift said dryly.

Beba put down the basket she was carrying. Reaching into it, she produced a small coin purse, which she handed to Nicolas.

'Beba?' Greer asked, walking over to them.

'Duncan.' The lord commander's wife smiled. 'I was just bringing you the breakfast I assumed you'd forget to eat, when I heard about their awful turn of events. I thought I'd give them something to buy new clothes.'

'You are giving them my money,' Greer said with a slow growl.

'Don't be a grump,' Beba mock-scolded. 'They cannot assist you with your investigation in this state.'

'Considering most of them lost their badges in the fire, I don't think they—'

'*Duncan.*'

The lord commander huffed. 'Fine.'

'And where are you sleeping tonight?' Beba asked Nicolas. 'I know what tavern owners are like. You'll be blacklisted now.'

'The lord commander graciously said we could sleep here,' Shift answered with thick sarcasm, nodding towards Watch Headquarters.

Beba looked at the fortification and pursed her lips. 'Nonsense,' she said finally. 'You are not sleeping here. We have plenty of spare rooms you—'

'*Beba!*'

'*Duncan!*'

A stare-off began, the sort only a long-married couple can have, solely through a series of eye gestures. As imposing as Lord Commander Greer of the city watch was, apparently, he was no match for his wife.

'Fine,' Greer relented through gritted teeth. 'But any nonsense, at all, and Sha'then himself best be ready to receive your souls.'

I may be more welcome than last time.

'Thank you.' Shift grinned. 'I think I'll like staying at your estate.' They side eyed the lord commander to ensure their remark had achieved the desired result. The throbbing vein on his temple suggested it had.

Beba picked up the basket and put it in her husband's hands. '*You* eat something.' She then turned to Nicolas and his companions. 'And *you*, go and buy some clothes.'

'But we need to—'

'We need to buy clothes,' Shift interrupted. 'We can't investigate anything tired and in rags. That makes sense to you, right?'

'Yes.' *Doesn't mean I have to like it, though.*

But no, they couldn't do any good when they were wearing ash-covered rags, a bed sheet, and...

Silva's in full armour? How? Does she sleep in it?

If she did, it would hardly come as a shock to him, but how was it at all comfortable?

'Which first, sleep or shopping?' Nicolas asked the others.

'You missed out food,' Garaz noted.

'A conversation first,' Greer said quietly as his wife left, saying her farewells.

Here we go.

The longer it took Greer to speak, the more nervous Nicolas became. Obviously, it was something the lord commander wasn't comfortable with himself. 'Tell me about this spell of yours,' he said finally.

Oh.

Knowing he couldn't explain it properly even if he had understood it himself, Nicolas allowed Garaz to answer.

'It is an old healer's spell, designed to find negative energy in the body, a way of healing without there being a visible wound, if you will,' the orc explained. 'I believe I can modify it based on what I saw the Seer...'

'There's bloody *seers* now,' Greer muttered.

'...Xedora do. Hopefully, it will pinpoint this demon, or at least narrow our search.' Garaz shook his head slowly. 'In truth, I cannot guarantee it will work. But the theory is sound.'

'Are you reconsidering your stance?' Silva asked.

'I think taverns don't randomly burn down, especially when newly deputised folk are sleeping in them,' the lord commander said thoughtfully. 'That would be a coincidence. And I don't believe in those. It doesn't mean I'm going to give your Geldheart nonsense any credence, and ruffians like you surely have no shortage of enemies, but on the off chance someone wants you out of the way...well, that suggests you *are* on to something, and I would be foolish to ignore it.'

Today just got markedly better.

CHAPTER 34

S hift caught his gaze, and their eyes went wide.

'I said stop picturing it,' they snarled.

Quickly, Nicolas cut off his guffawing. 'I'm sorry,' he said with feeling. 'I just...can't. Your face when he held up that dress...'

The owner of the clothing shop—who was now a little richer for their custom—had been very enthusiastic about helping them pick out new clothes once he'd seen the pouch of gold they carried. Telling him that they didn't need any help had been a pointless exercise. In his excitement, the man had grabbed some pink frilly abomination of a dress and held it under Shift's neck, declaring that they would look fabulous in it. For a good few seconds, Nicolas had thought a petrification spell had been cast on Shift, forever keeping the look of sheer horror on their face.

'It *was* the latest fashion.' The corner of Garaz's lip twitched.

'I am not taking fashion advice from someone who's worn the same red cloak as long as I've known them.' Shift huffed. 'Embarrassing stuff like that is supposed to happen to Nick, not me.'

It does make a nice change.

All in all, the clothes shopping had gone well, with Nicolas and Shift now wearing things that weren't covered in black stains. And he had some new boots, finally. Breaking them in was already turning out to be a painful experience, but he knew it'd be worth it. The second part of the trip had been less successful. Garaz needed some specific herbs for his spell, but every shop they'd tried was out of stock, as people hoarded them to create homemade charms to ward off evil. With each new shop they left empty-handed, Garaz's annoyance grew, until he'd defaulted into a sullen silence—broken only by his jest at Shift's expense.

Their only recourse now was to return to their accommodation and plan their next move. The general idea was to go out on patrol tonight and hope for the best. It was not a plan Nicolas was happy with.

At least they had a good guide in Sergeant Tallith, even if he was reporting back to Greer and looking at Nicolas with an uncomfortable level of hero worship in his eyes. But the young man was sweet, and quite endearing. Every so often, he'd give them the odd fact about the city or an anecdote about a building they passed.

It still amused Nicolas how mishmash the city was. They'd only just left the main shopping district, and they were now passing some red-bricked building that looked like a temple.

'Stop!' Auron's shout was so surprising that he almost stumbled forward. The spirit was looking at the temple with an expression that was half awe, half slack jawed idiot. 'It can't be,' he whispered.

'Can't be what?' As irksome as these interruptions were, Nicolas kept his voice level. Something obviously had the spirit's attention.

'By the Deities.' And Silva's too. It was only when the warrior spoke that Tallith realised they weren't behind him anymore and turned back.

Following their eyes, Nicolas saw a circular symbol above the door of the temple. Inside that circle was what looked to be a dragon and tiger intertwined, though it was hard to tell at this distance.

And suddenly Auron was away, bounding up the pillared pathway to the door, his aura bright against the afternoon sky. When he reached the door, the spirit began to study it as if it were a portal to the Deities themselves. He was practically bouncing on the spot as the others reached him.

'What is it?' Garaz asked.

'Master Lo-Rence.' Nicolas wasn't sure if Auron was replying to Garaz, or just saying the name.

'Who?'

Auron's head wheeled around so fast he took an involuntary step back. 'You don't...no, of course you don't...but you should. Master Lo-Rence is *the* single greatest fighter in all Etherius.'

Nicolas shook his head and shrugged.

Auron put his fingers to his temples. 'Sometimes your ignorance is astounding. It's *Master Lo-Rence*. The single greatest fighter in all Etherius!'

'You said that already.' Garaz smirked.

'Master of all styles of fighting,' the spirit said, looking at his hands as if they were a pair of swords.

'Kascat Death Claw, Sslyth Serpent tail, Holfar Black Knuckle boxing. He travelled the word and learnt them *all*!' This time the excitement wasn't from Auron but Silva. Seeing her giddy was really unsettling. 'I've always dreamed of studying with him.'

'I got to.' Auron smirked at Silva's gasp. 'I mean, for a month. Apparently, I was a little arrogant. But still, a month under his tutelage is nothing to be sniffed at.'

Auron being arrogant. Shocking.

'Kid, you need to go in and ask for some lessons.'

'But I have teachers,' he said, indicating Silva and Auron.

The spirit rubbed his temples again. 'Yes, and we're both good. But a couple hours with the Master is worth *years* of training with us.'

'But...'

'Don't panic,' Auron reassured him. 'He'll accept you. One thing that people can't call you is arrogant. Just go in there, be your polite self, and ask for some tuition. And maybe don't mention my name until after.'

'We really don't have time for this.' Their quest had already been fraught with interruptions, and the killer was bound to strike again soon.

'Training with him will change your life.' Seeing Silva's eyes wide with awe was certainly odd. 'Despite our mission, this is an opportunity you cannot pass up.'

'The mission is the problem,' Nicolas said. 'We're looking for a demon. Murders. Time is of the essence.'

'And when you meet this demon, would you like to be ready to just about handle it, or would you like to be able to beat it right back to its realm?' Auron was getting testy now.

'The second one.'

'Well then.' The spirit pointed to the door, smiling broadly. 'Trust me, kid, you'll thank me for dragging you in here.'

'I think we have time for a quick introduction,' Shift suggested.

'If it benefits us in the long run, I believe the interruption to our quest is warranted,' Garaz added.

'First, Nick gets offered fancy armour, and now he gets special fighting tuition?' Shift said, shaking their head. 'Am I not worthy of this tutelage too?'

'Would you listen?' Silva had been trying to train Shift as well. Evidently, the warrior had an issue with how much hard work her second student was. And since the shapeshifter didn't respond, Nicolas guessed they knew how difficult they were to work with.

'It doesn't matter,' Auron said, waving a hand in the air. 'You can turn into a bear. The kid needs this. Go in there. Go in now.'

'Um, if you intend to go see Master Lo-rence, there might be a problem,' Sergeant Tallith put in with a cough. 'Unfortunately, he passed away last year. This fighting school is now under the supervision of Ban Dro, his number one student.' There was a slightly derisive tone in the last part of the sentence that made Nicolas curious.

Auron stumbled backwards, reaching out to the wall to steady himself, but his hand went through it instead, and he stumbled some more trying not to fall. Silva was looking around, her face contorted as if struggling to understand what she'd been told. 'But...such a talent...gone?'

'Is this *Ban Dro* good?' Shift asked.

Tallith seemed hesitant to reply. 'Well, Master Lo-Rence taught him everything he knew. And he was the *only* person to receive such knowledge.' The derisiveness became uncertainty, which piqued Nicolas's curiosity all the more.

'Good enough,' Silva remarked, grabbing Nicolas's arm and dragging him through the door like an impatient parent.

He glanced back. Behind them, Tallith shuffled awkwardly, like he had a lot more to say.

CHAPTER 35

Directly inside the door was a large, open room of soft whites against dark wooden beams and pillars. There was a shrine at the far end of the room, which Nicolas guessed was dedicated to Rel'Nar, the Deity of Warriors and Battle. The walls themselves alternated between fine art and racks of weapons. Half the area was clearly for training, with all manner of dummies that appeared to be made of wood—though Nicolas was sure they weren't, as no sane man punches wood—and training aids, the other half was an open sanded area, which had drawn quite a crowd.

Craning his neck to see over the nearest of the people lining the area, Nicolas saw a ponytailed man knelt on the ground, open hands in front of him and eyes closed as if in prayer. On the opposite side stood a smirking man and some assorted hangers-on. The man danced from one foot to the other as he punched the air as if someone who'd insulted his mother was stood in front of him.

'Oh, for Deities sake,' Tallith muttered behind Nicolas. 'Another bloody challenge.'

Combat was obviously about to take place. The whole place was an eerie reminder of Big Boss's arena, complete with excited onlookers.

'We don't have time for this.' He wanted to leave, but that damned curiosity kept him rooted to the spot.

'Shhh, I want to see how this goes,' Shift said with interest. 'Is the guy in the white robe going to fight them all, or just the smug asshole?'

We have a demon to hunt. We don't have time for a show.

'If he's Lo-Rence's best student, he could probably fight all of them and more,' Auron said with confidence.

'And yet they do not appear concerned.'

Garaz was right. If anything, they looked cocky. The group whispered to each other in excited tones. Somehow, their lack of nerves at the impending fight piqued his interest, and Nicolas found himself craning his neck so he could see what would happen.

The deep note of a gong resonated throughout the hall, silencing everyone. As the crowd hushed, an elderly, robed man shuffled into the centre of the room and bowed to the crowd then to each of the fighters.

'Today, we gather because Ban Dro, Master of the Lo-Rence School of Fighting Arts, has challenged Lingar Dux of the Black Blade Combat School...again.' The last word was delivered with exasperation. 'May this challenge be honourable and in the spirit of combat laid down by the noble lineage of warriors from whom it was passed down.'

The gong sounded again, and Ban Dro hopped to his feet, his eyes shooting open. Lingar took a few sauntering steps forward. The opponents bowed to each other as the old man shuffled to the edge of the arena and sat down. The bows were obviously forced. There was clearly a deep-seated rivalry being acted out here.

'Begin,' the old man said with a wave of his hand and, if Nicolas wasn't very much mistaken, a sigh.

Immediately, Dux got into rigid stance, putting the weight on his back leg and holding his hands before him like a couple of claws. He even put a theatrical snarl on his face to complete the picture, his eyes wide and crazed.

Ban Dro, on the other hand, adopted a neutral stance, appraising his opponent with a nod. 'I see you favour Kascat Death Claw Style today,' he remarked. 'A style focused on aggression and attack, with little in the way of true defence. The style itself was first created by Master Lion Ro over a hundred years ago.' *Apparently, we're getting a history lesson with our fight.* 'It was perfected nearly thirty years ago by Kreshanr, the White Panther Fist. It is a bold style, favouring strikes toward the upper body, the clawed palm form designed to rip and tear flesh, as well as delivering devastating palm strikes.' Dux seemed not to give a crap about the lesson. In truth, Nicolas was starting to lose interest in the fight too. 'However, this style is easily countered. You cannot tear the flesh of someone you cannot hit. Therefore, I believe Master Graga's Form of Water Style will allow me to effectively dodge your attacks, tiring you before delivering my own offence and ensuring my victory.'

For Deities' sakes. I've been in plenty of fights, and there's never this much talking.

Ban Dro went on for a bit longer, explaining the lineage of the style he was about to use, before finally adopting a loose-looking stance, almost as if he were a little drunk, his arms circling each other slowly.

'Begin,' the elderly man said, shaking his head.

With a roar, and sniggering cronies behind him, Dux charged forwards. Even Nicolas could see that he was telegraphing his strike. When he was close enough, Dux leapt into the air, swinging his arms over his head, intent on raking down on his opponent. At the last second, Ban Dro slipped to the side, with an almost exasperated look on his face.

However, as Dux landed in a crouched position, he swung his body around, lashing out with his leg to sweep Dro's legs out from under him. Nicolas could see the look of surprise on Dro's face, and he managed to jump just in time. But Dux was prepared for that too. Bringing his leg to a halt, Dux leapt up from the ground, delivering a mighty uppercut to Dro that resonated throughout the arena and made Nicolas wince. The crowd gave a sympathetic *'ooo.'* Seconds later, Dro crashed to the floor.

'Winner,' Dux said nonchalantly as he returned to his cheering hangers-on. He was puffing his chest out so much he seemed in danger of toppling over from being top heavy.

'And *that*,' Sergeant Tallith whispered to him, 'is why Ban Dro is known as *The Greatest Warrior to Never Win a Fight.* He gets beaten every single time. It's also why no one trains with him anymore. This training hall is on the verge of closure, getting a little closer with every defeat.'

Auron finally closed his mouth. 'What was that?' the spirit cried. '*This* is the man Master Lo-Rence passed all his knowledge to? What an absolute tit.'

'That was quite quick,' Garaz noted.

'The build-up wasn't.' Shift said with clear distaste for all the pre-fight talking.

'Maybe he ought to stay down until the room is clear,' Silva suggested, shaking her head.

Which wouldn't take long. Already people were filing out, exchanging chuckles at what they'd just witnessed.

'You want me to learn from *him*?' Nicolas said incredulously. 'We have a task to accomplish, and you bring me in here for *that*? How can I learn from a guy who makes such a simple mistake?'

The others stared at him in confusion.

'What do you mean?' Silva asked.

What? How can they not see it?

He opened his mouth to explain, when the others' eyes widened, just as people's do when the person you're talking about is directly behind you. Closing his eyes and sighing, Nicolas turned around.

'What did you just say?' Ban Dro said slowly, enraged. He looked dishevelled, and a large purple bruise was appearing on his jaw, yet he still looked mightily fierce. *Or would do, if I hadn't just seen that display.* 'You come into *my* school and tell *me* you know more than I do? What do you know then? Please, enlighten me.'

'I...well...I...Not much, but I know where you went wrong.' Nicolas was only stammering due to awkwardness. He doubted even he had anything to worry about if Dro attacked him.

Garaz shook his head sympathetically. 'Nicolas, do not be so foolish.'

'Kid thinks he knows fighting now,' Auron scoffed whilst Silva looked at him as if she hoped no one realised they were here together.

'I think your *fame* is going to your head a little bit,' Shift said, putting a sympathetic arm around his shoulder.

What's the matter with them? Why am I the only one who sees it?

'But it's obvious,' he protested, certain he was right.

Dro laughed aloud. 'I will tell you what,' he snapped, jabbing Nicolas painfully in the chest with a finger. 'If you think you're so amazing, tell me what I'm doing wrong. If you can, I'll bow before you and call you *Master.*'

I really don't want to do this.

However, it was clear Dro wasn't going to just walk away, and the jabbing in the chest gave Nicolas the sudden urge to take the man down a peg or two. If there was only one way to get this guy to bugger off, so be it.

'Well,' he began, choosing his words carefully. 'You talk too much. You spent more of that fight explaining how he was going to attack you than fighting. And furthermore, you told him *exactly* what you would do to counter his style. He knew you were coming. He could predict your reactions, because you told him what they'd be...at great length. There's no skill in that.'

Ban Dro's eyes moved back and forth as he thought about it then his mouth opened and closed a few times before finally settling on hanging open. He wasn't the only one; all his companions looked equally stunned.

Finally, Dro turned and walked back to the main floor of the temple. 'I challenge again,' he bellowed, stopping those who were leaving in their tracks.

'Really?' the old man asked with a raised eyebrow. 'After the embarrassment you just endured?'

'Yes, really,' Dro said firmly, pointing to the sandy floor. 'Right here and right now.'

The old man looked at Dux.

'Fine,' the cocky warrior scoffed. 'I'm more than happy to embarrass him twice in one hour.'

His cronies cheered and whooped at the idea of it.

'The only embarrassment here is you,' Dro said, pointing an accusing finger. 'You make yourself out to be a warrior but behave like a common bully. You have no honour.'

Dux shook his head. 'And you have no skill, just a desire to be put on the floor time and again.' Flexing his neck from side to side, the warrior put his fists into his hands, loudly cracking his knuckles. 'But if it's another beating you want, then another beating you shall have.' The man's face contorted into a sneer. 'Maybe this time, I'll make sure you stay down for a bit. Just long enough to realise you probably don't want to do this again.'

Dux walked to the centre of the room to meet him, getting into a stance with his two arms held at right angles to his body, his hands high and fingers together in something that almost looked like snake heads. Dro stared at him silently. After a moment of expectant waiting, Dux suddenly looked a little nervous.

'Begin,' the old man declared.

Two seconds later, Dux was on the floor. Four of his teeth decorated the sand beside him. His followers weren't laughing now.

Well, that was a flawless victory.

Dro looked at his downed opponent and scoffed. Then he looked at Nicolas. With the deep breath of a man sucking in his pride, he walked over and began to get on his knees.

'No, no, no,' Nicolas said, stopping the Master from bowing to him. 'None of that.'

'Wow,' Tallith said. 'What a *Nick Carnage* moment. Wait until the fan club hear about *this*.'

If they're really fans, they should get my bloody name right.

'I appear to have been an idiot...and an arrogant ass,' Dro said as he looked away. 'I suppose when the Master died, I was so keen to cement his legacy and showcase my knowledge that I forgot the basic principles of fighting.' That looked painful to admit. 'I appear to owe you a debt, and as you won't let me bow to you, how can I repay it?'

Nicolas thought for a moment. 'Some lessons would be nice.'

Dro seemed surprised by the boldness of the comment. In truth, Nicolas was too, but Auron was right: he needed to take his learning to the next level. Silva and Auron were good teachers, but if this Ban Dro was what they said, he couldn't let the opportunity pass him by. Besides, at the moment, he could barely hold his own in a bar brawl, and there'd been too many flukes and near-misses on his journeys thus far. At the minimum, it'd be nice to have a fight where he didn't take any punches, and maybe Ban Dro could make that a reality. And if he could learn to take down opponents as quickly as Dro had Dux, well...

'There's a question I always ask when someone joins my fighting school,' Dro began before he pursed his lips. 'Or *did* before people started avoiding me because I couldn't win a fight. Why do you want to learn to fight?'

He considered that for a moment. In his head, he went over numerous replies that he thought would pass or fail this test. In the end, though, he decided to be honest. 'I don't,' he said bitterly. 'But the world has different ideas. From the moment I left my village, I've been coming across these terrible people doing awful things for stupid reasons. A lot of people get hurt, and I can't just live my life knowing it happens. Especially not since my parents were killed. So if fate's going to shove me in front of these people, I'd best be ready for them. I'd rather stand up to them than let them hurt people because I didn't have the skill, or the balls, to stop them.'

'Kid,' Auron said, his voice full of awe.

Dro blinked a few times before he replied. 'That is one of the best answers to that question I've ever heard. Come back at dawn tomorrow, and I will begin teaching you.' His new Master turned to walk away.

'Thank you,' Nicolas said after him.

'Don't thank me yet,' Dro said with a laugh. 'Tomorrow, I'm going to throw you all over this training hall.'

Sounded painful, but if he got something out of it, so be it. When he turned back to the door, the others were smiling at him. 'What?'

'That, right there, was some *chosen one* talk,' Shift replied.

This again. 'I'm not any kind of *chosen one*.'

'You *were* chosen,' Garaz remarked with a raised eyebrow.

'By a *stick*. It doesn't count,' he snapped.

'A magic stick counts.' Auron grinned.

'It was just a twig.'

'And yet it picked a single person for a task,' Silva said thoughtfully. 'That sounds like a *chosen one* to me.'

Okay, Silva ribbing him was getting weird. He was about to correct them all at great length when something caught his attention. 'What are you doing?' he asked Sergeant Tallith.

The sergeant looked up from his notepad. 'Recording this for posterity. They will love this at the club.'

With a cry, Nicolas stormed out of the training hall. At least this interruption to their quest had yielded fruit.

Which is more than can be said for everything else I've done since I've been here.

CHAPTER 36

Babylon was a funny kind of place. It had been built to foster peace and understanding, yet right now it was the very opposite of that—it's harmony quickly being replaced by suspicious and fearful glances. It was almost as if the city was in a struggle between its better and worse natures. Nicolas didn't want to see what would happen if the worst nature won out. In fact, he wanted to be part of the solution to this crisis, and all they had right now was a spell.

And no bloody herbs to make it.

But at least the city was opening his eyes to what an amazing place Etherius could be—demonic killers aside. Here it was like the whole world had been compressed between the unseasonably warm city walls, showing him the wonders of all species who lived here. Standard human buildings looked blocky compared to smooth and circular kascat dwellings. Small homes of stone chiselled lovingly by their dwarven owners looked tiny next to the large dwellings of centaurs, several of which passed Nicolas as he tried not to stare.

'Centaurs are their own species, right? They aren't men who, well...you know...*mated* with horses?' he asked quietly.

'If I had an ale for every daft question you've asked since we've walked through the city gates, I'd have been drunk by yesterday.' It was somehow nice that sharing a bed hadn't changed Shift's penchant for teasing him.

They aren't entirely wrong, though.

'Sorry,' he said, quickly stepping aside before he walked into an aviar's large wing. The man muttered a response but was clearly not happy to be conversing with a human.

There were so many different types of people on the streets, but they all had one thing in common: they were people. Little old ladies were little old ladies. Traders were traders. City watch were city watch. How could men like Tobias Helstrum and the apes in the tavern preach that there were differences between us all, differences to be distrusted? The idea was just so blatantly wrong to him. Yet Narus had proven that people would listen to nonsense, as long as it was well-presented nonsense.

And backed up by all the trouble the Maestro and his minions are stirring up.

A human couple shielded their children behind their legs as a centaur clopped by.

Is there any hope for coexistence when people still act like that? Actually, why are they even living here, if that's their attitude?

There was something in that notion that was just frustrating. The idea that people stayed here just to be angry about staying here and who they shared a city with. Thinking about what those vocal few might do if these murders went unchecked only added to the weight he was beginning to feel on his shoulders.

I came here to save a village, and now a city's been added to my list of responsibilities.

He didn't even want to consider what else might rest on the outcome if they failed and the Nalbian army tried to enter the city.

'Excuse me,' a light voice said from beside him. 'Are you *Nick Carnage*, by any chance?'

Deities damn that name.

Nicolas turned, about to correct the person firmly, but stopped when he saw the young fairy in front of him. Other than her long blond hair, her defining feature was her innocent look. Yet there was sadness interlaced with it, so much so that he didn't have the heart to be mad.

'Nearly,' he said with a reassuring smile he conjured from nowhere. 'Nicolas Percival Carnegie, actually.'

He held out his hand, expecting it to be shaken. Instead, he was grabbed in a tight embrace. Much tighter than he would've thought the slight frame capable of. 'Thank you. Thank you so much for coming here to help.'

It took him a second to realise that the wetness on his cheek were tears.

'You're welcome,' he said awkwardly, finally prising the fairy off him.

Her eyes were red and puffy, promising many more tears to come, despite her best efforts to compose herself. As he held her arms, he noted he was touching material. There was a black band on her arm. Her translucent wings were folded inward, as if in deep sorrow.

'You lost someone?' The answer was obvious, but he hoped talking might break her out of the obvious misery that was desperate for her attention.

'My betrothed, Fallen, was one of the victims of this killer,' the fairy told him. 'One night he just *vanishes* and then four days later he's found dead by a human tavern. We've all heard the legends about you.' *Urgh.* 'So to have you here, to help us, it means everything. Thank you.'

He had no idea what to say, for many reasons. 'I'm so sorry for your loss,' he settled on finally. 'I'll do my best to bring this killer to justice.'

The fairy seemed overcome with emotion and unable to speak because of it. Instead, she patted him on the chest, before moving away, sobbing.

Nicolas went to follow her but was stopped by a merman. 'Did I hear you say that you are *Nick Carnage*?'

No, no, you bloody didn't. 'Close enough,' he answered with exasperation.

He found his hand grabbed and held by a scaley, clammy hand that shook it with enthusiasm. 'Thank you for stopping the war between Merida and the Tidal Kingdom,' the merman said. 'My brother was amongst the warriors poised for battle, and he is alive because of you.' He didn't want to take the shell he was offered, but he didn't have a choice. The merman pressed it into his hand thankfully. 'It'll bring you good luck,' he insisted. It was certainly a lovely shell, hard but with a metallic colour that reflected the light into a small rainbow of colours.

All around him now, people were murmuring, looking at him and pointing, and saying *that name.* He wasn't Auron; he didn't want people to know who he was. *How do they even know?* In fact, how did people either know nothing, or everything? He turned and looked at his companions standing in the street. A small frown crossed his face as he noticed Sergeant Tallith furiously writing in his notebook.

'If you are quite finished with the adoring fans, kid?' Auron asked with a half-smile.

'This is really surreal.' He had to admit it was shaking him a little.

Shift took his hand. 'I don't know how in the Underworld these people know what they know, but you have done a lot of good, Nick. I mean, *we* have, but it's only right that people know about you.'

And now Shift's being sincere. 'I'm going to need you to tease me,' he said. 'I can't have all this *and* you being nice to me.'

'By the Deities, you're right.' Shift said, aghast. They looked around them, eyes wide. 'If I don't stop this, I may get to my knees at any second and swear myself to your service like some kind of overly romantic knight.' They punctuated their sentence by putting a hand over their mouth as if in shock.

Nicolas had done this exact thing when he'd first met Shift. He'd hoped it'd been forgotten, but apparently not. 'That's better,' he said with a smile.

'I think he's actually ready for the next phase of his training,' Auron said, his mouth a thin line.

'With Dro, you mean?'

The spirit closed his eyes and shook his head. 'No, no, no, kid. I'm talking about learning one of the most important parts of being a hero: handling fame.'

With a sigh, Nicolas turned to Silva and Garaz. 'Anything you'd like to add?'

'I would,' the orc began, a large smile creeping across his green features. 'But I fear that we may be interrupted by one of your well-wishers before I get the chance.'

'Apologies, what was the question?' Silva asked with a raised eyebrow. 'I was trying to count the number of times I have saved your life to date.'

'Oh dammit,' Shift said suddenly, clicking their fingers.

'What?' he asked with urgency.

'I've just realised that I liked you because you were an out-of-your-depth village boy. It was ironic to like you.' They shook their head sadly. 'Now everyone seems to too, it's no longer ironic, and I'm afraid our little tryst has run its course.'

Nicolas's next sigh was much more drawn out.

CHAPTER 37

Though it was dark by the time they reached Commander Greer's manor, the lack of light did nothing to diminish the majesty of the place. Set inside large grounds with beautifully tapered hedges, the manor was an old, human-style, three-story building, with a brickwork base that gave way to thick and richly coloured wood.

Makes sense the commander of the city watch would have a home befitting his station.

Speaking of the lord commander, Greer was waiting at the steps. The folded arms and lack of greeting told them exactly how welcome they were. 'I had some pallets in the stable made up for you. Apparently, that did not make me a *good host*, so I've had some rooms prepared instead. When you leave, those rooms will be in the exact state as when you arrived. Am I making myself clear?'

Nicolas found himself actually liking Lord Commander Greer. You knew where you stood with him, and that was a rare thing in the world. Even if where they stood was near the bottom of his shit list.

'I think I'm going to enjoy sharing a bed with you tonight,' Shift whispered firmly.

There's been a time when you didn't? Oh. I suppose the fire wasn't fun.

'Any luck?' Greer asked, eyeing Garaz warily.

'Alas, no,' the orc admitted. 'The herb shops are bare. Do you have a stock?'

The lord commander pursed his lips in annoyance. 'We do,' he admitted finally. 'Give me a list, and I'll see what I can do.'

'So you'll allow us to try the spell?'

Greer bristled at Shift's directness. He was going to have to get used to that quickly if they were staying in his home. Nicolas doubted Shift would amend their behaviour. In fact, they might get worse.

Once Greer had finished simmering, he answered. 'Four times today people have been arrested for *'hate crimes'*...in a city built as a monument to peace. This place is on the brink and, loathe as I am to admit it, traditional methods are not working. Therefore, I am left with no alternative than to seek other options before there's rioting in the streets.'

That was the closest they were ever likely to get to acceptance from Greer, so Nicolas would take it.

'He's softening up,' Auron said, wrinkling his nose like he was looking at a cute cat.

'But make no mistake,' the lord commander continued, 'if you turn out to be the charlatans I'm sure you are, I will clap you in the stocks outside the city, and out of the range of our heating system, buck-ass nude until every appendage you have is frozen solid and likely to snap off if you sneeze too hard.'

Graphic and unnecessary.

'Maybe not then,' Auron noted with a half-smile.

'Once I have the ingredients, I should be able to mark the point of negative energy in this city, which will undoubtably be the demon,' Garaz explained.

'If you are keen to identify a single point of *negative energy* in this city, I think you're looking for a needle in a haystack,' Greer answered gruffly. 'How certain are you that it will work?'

'I will not lie and say I am completely sure,' the orc said neutrally. 'But I am sure it is worth the attempt.'

'Good answer,' the lord commander said. 'If you'd told me you were completely sure, I would have assumed you to be a liar.'

'I am not that,' Garaz said with a slight bow.

The lord commander unfolded his arms, looking into the distance as he stroked his moustache. 'Very well,' he said finally. 'We will try it.'

Phew.

Greer stood to the side and gestured them towards the door. With another bow, Garaz and Silva made their way up the steps and entered the house, Auron walking in with them. Nicolas was about to follow when he and Shift found their way blocked.

'Yes?' Shift asked the lord commander as he glared at them.

'After the fire, we interviewed the landlord of the tavern,' Greer began. 'He was very vocal about a certain *noise complaint* he'd had from several of his guests regarding you two. Just so we are clear...not under my roof. I will not have you turning my manor into a backstreet brothel. If you do, I'll put you both out in the stable. Understood?'

Shift tilted their head to the side and looked at Nicolas. 'What do you think, Nick? Can you manage to keep your hands off me for the duration of our stay?' Shift suddenly turned and looked at the stable. 'Mind you, if you can't, and we get *put out in the stable*, it actually looks pretty sturdy, so...'

'Please don't,' Nicolas muttered, his face reddening, but in a very different way to Greer's.

'That's not what you said last time. Last time you said—'

Quickly, he put his hand over Shift's mouth. He knew he was going to pay for that later, but he also knew Shift was one smart-ass remark away from both of them actually sleeping in the stable.

'We understand,' he said with a grin.

Greer huffed, turned on his heel and stomped toward the house. He only stopped to glare at Sergeant Tallith, who still stood at the bottom of the steps, smartly at attention.

'Still glad you volunteered for this duty?' the lord commander snapped, before continuing toward the manor. As he did, Nicolas registered a sudden pain in his hand.

Ow.

'You bit me,' he moaned, checking his finger over. The skin wasn't broken so he blew on it.

'I bite.' Shift shrugged. 'You have much to learn about me.'

'You knew you were on thin ice,' he retorted. 'I know that much. But you were bent on winding him up.'

Shift grabbed his cheek and wiggled it slightly. 'I do appreciate you saving me from myself, but no good deed goes unpunished.'

'I noticed,' he said, holding up his red finger.

Shift grabbed his head and kissed him passionately. 'Better?' They smirked when they finally pulled back.

'I hold no grudge,' he said coyly.

'Good.' They grinned. 'Because I am looking forward to having a look around this manor.'

'No stealing,' he warned.

'No promises,' they replied with a wink.

****

Nicolas let out a whistle as he entered the manor. Being lord commander definitely seemed to pay well. The manor was classically what Nicolas assumed a manor should look like. There was a grand entrance hall adorned with suits of armour and various portraits of uptight looking fellows that he guessed were the lord commander's family.

'Welcome, welcome,' Beba said, approaching him and giving him a warm hug.

A sudden burst of discomfort gripped him; there was something almost motherly about her. It reminded him of what he'd lost.

'Thank you,' he said, keeping his voice level.

'Please, have a drink,' Beba said, gesturing to a servant holding a tray of glasses. 'It's a pleasure to have you here.'

'I'm glad one of you is pleased.' Apparently, Shift's attempts to prod the lord commander weren't over yet.

Beba looked at her husband and shook her head. 'Please forgive Duncan. He's under a lot of pressure right now. He takes maintaining order in this city seriously and seeing that slipping away is taking its toll on him.'

Nicolas caught an uncomfortable glint in Shift's eye. Maybe their prodding of *Duncan* was finished now?

'Hopefully we can help,' he offered.

'Of course.' Beba smiled. 'Garaz was just telling me about this spell of his. I think we can use the drawing room. Though I suggest you go in there and hide before I break the news to Duncan. He is not a great lover of magic.'

'At least I'm not making them stay in the stable,' the lord commander said, obviously hearing their conversation. 'Which they should do, with the state of them.'

I'm in no state. *These are new clothes.*

His wife gave Nicolas's appearance a quick, appraising look. 'They look better than you did when we first met, Duncan. You were just a raggedy adventurer when I patched you up.'

If Auron had been drinking, or could, Nicolas was sure he would've spat it out right now. 'An adventurer?' the spirit cried. '*Him?*'

'That just means I know exactly what they're like,' Greer muttered quietly, but loud enough for them to all hear.

'I need to hear *that* story,' the spirit said.

Hopefully, he doesn't become obsessed with it like Sharkbait's tale. We've lost enough time on distractions.

'Maybe one day, when Duncan's out of earshot.' Beba chuckled, playing with a chain around her neck.

Something familiar caught Nicolas's eye. 'That's the symbol of Ce'tal, isn't it?'

'Hmm?' Beba held the amulet at the end of the chain in her hand. 'Good eye. I got it out of the attic recently.'

'That's a beautiful amulet,' Shift said casually. Nicolas quickly gave them an admonishing glance. Shift poked their tongue out in response.

'I thought it was new,' Greer said beside his wife.

'No.' The lady of the house tucked it back into her dress. 'With all this killing going on, I feel...safer wearing it. It's silly, I know...'

'Trust me, ma'am,' Garaz said with a smile, 'everyone is using charms right now, hence the herb shops being bare. In dark times like this, we must cling to whatever glimmer of hope there is.'

'This city needs all the help it can get.' Beba quickly shook off the grim look on her face and gave them a broad smile. 'But enough of that. Let me welcome you all to our humble abode.'

'Humble, my undead backside,' Auron scoffed.

'I assure you, my lady,' Garaz added with a polite bow, 'your abode is anything but humble.'

Beba looked pleased as she returned the bow with a small curtesy. 'We try.' She glanced at her husband before continuing. 'Maybe it'd look nicer without all the pictures of angry gentlemen along the stairway wall,' she finished with a wink.

Okay, she's good people.

'My dear,' Greer protested. 'It's expected within a certain social standing to have evidence of one's lineage on display. Besides, weren't you only just talking about remembering those who've gone before us?'

'So I was. Well, maybe we can start a tradition where we're *smiling* in our portraits,' Beba teased. 'Think of the future generations.'

Despite his frosty exterior to them, Greer warmed in the presence of his wife. 'I'll take it under advisement.'

'Now then,' Beba said. 'I have never hosted an orc before and confess myself surprised about how...' You could tell that she was trying, and failing, to come up with the politest term for it.

'*Civilised*, madam?' Garaz asked. 'I try my best, lest I never get invited back to such nice places.'

'Is he flirting?' Nicolas asked quietly.

'I hope not.' Auron smirked. 'Otherwise, he might be costing us a bed tonight.'

'It is possible to talk to a woman without flirting with her,' Silva chided. 'Several of you need to grow up.'

'There's no hope for me,' Auron retorted dryly. 'I can't age anymore since someone killed me.'

It was odd that Auron and Silva's relationship had become one of unsubtle digs from the spirit, and the warrior rolling her eyes in return. Nicolas supposed it was the best he could hope for between them.

Could I ever be so forgiving, if someone killed me?

He hoped to never find out.

CHAPTER 38

Walking into places like Lord Commander Greer's drawing room always gave Nicolas perspective. This room, with all its opulence, was something Nicolas had never strived for. He'd been comfortable in his life in Hablock. That might be gone forever, but still, he favoured the simple life.

Or life on the road.

For a moment, he daydreamed, trying to picture himself in this room, sat on one of the fine leather chairs, maybe smoking a pipe. That was what people who sat in leather chairs in drawing rooms did, wasn't it? Maybe having some highbrow conversation about economics or the government whilst he waited for the butler to bring in a drink so he could compliment its vintage and proclaim the various fruits he could taste in it.

'What are you laughing at?'

Nicolas hadn't even realised he'd chuckled until the warrior spoke up. 'Nothing,' he answered with a half-smile, looking at his companions.

Nothing highbrow about this lot. And I wouldn't trade them for a thousand fancy drawing rooms.

Shift prowled the room, making a big show of inspecting every piece of artwork, every sculpture, and every book on the shelf as Greer tracked their movements with a steely glare and a scowl. Nicolas imagined the books were all factual. He couldn't visualise the lord commander sitting down to a nice adventure, or some other mindless escapism, after a hard day enforcing the law. He caught Shift's eyes pausing briefly on the pair of animal heads mounted on the wall, giving him the idea that they would be going missing at some point in the near future, to be buried respectfully somewhere nearby.

As long as we are far away after they do it.

'Is there enough room for you in here to do your spell?' Beba asked with a sweeping gesture.

'Darling,' Greer said through gritted teeth, 'I agreed to the spell. I do not actually want it done in my house. And especially not in my drawing room.'

Beba walked over to her husband and took him by the arms. 'How many times have I heard you say lately that *time is of the essence*? And now you wish to waste time finding a better place, when they are here, now?'

'You're right,' the lord commander muttered grudgingly, before turning to the others. 'What do you need?'

'I require a map of the city,' Garaz began. 'And I mentioned some herbs to the Lord Commander?'

'Ah yes, we have quite the stock,' the lady of the house answered brightly. 'What can I get you?'

'I believe I have most of what I need,' the orc answered. 'I just require sniproot and ilivander. They are used in charms and such, though I have only a basic knowledge of their supposed properties.'

'This gets better and better,' Greer moaned. 'Now, he's barely even used the ingredients.'

'Hush, Duncan,' Beba scolded. 'We have both of those. Nathanial, would you be a dear and help me. I believe it will require some rummaging.'

Nathanial?

'Of course,' Sergeant Tallith said with a crisp, but slightly awkward, nod.

'Excellent.' The lady of the house beamed, taking the sergeant by the arm and leading him out of the room. 'Whilst we rummage, you can catch me up on how your parents are.'

'She's a force of nature,' Shift remarked, watching them leave. 'I like her.'

'That she is,' Greer said, before turning his attention to the wall of the room. 'One of you help me with this.'

With Garaz's assistance, the pair took a large, framed map of the city off the wall. Greer glowered as Silva rolled up the plush red rug in the centre of the room. Though Nicolas might have taken issue with that too, were it his rug. The warrior was none too gentle with it. Placing the map on the floor, Nicolas took an interest in learning about the districts of the city whilst Garaz removed small pouches from his cloak.

How much stuff does he manage to fit in there?

'Must admit, big guy, I'm surprised you were missing some herbs. It's not often I come across something you *don't* keep in that cloak. I was sure there was a whole civilisation living in there.' Auron smirked as he gestured to the orc's garment.

The thing must weigh a ton.

'There is,' Garaz replied with a thin smile. 'Sometimes I go and visit them for some sensible conversation.'

'Ouch,' the spirit said, feigning offence.

Sudden concern struck Nicolas as he watched the orc staring at the map. There was something in Garaz's expression, a nervousness that worried him.

'Are you okay?' he asked his companion quietly.

'Hmm.' The orc glanced at him blankly for a second, before giving him a smile that was clearly forced. 'I am, thank you. I am...just about to open myself to potentially evil forces. I must prepare myself mentally.'

'You don't have to do this,' he whispered in reply. He'd forced his friend to do a spell before, and it had had nearly disastrous results. He wasn't about to let that happen again.

Garaz held him by the shoulder. 'I know. But it is the best way. I must meditate in preparation.'

'Okay,' Nicolas relented. 'But if it looks like something's going wrong, I'll snap you out of it. I'll...throw something at your head, or...I don't know. I'll improvise.'

The orc chuckled and shook his head. 'The thought that you would throw something at my head in an hour of need is strangely comforting.'

As the orc sat cross-legged before the map, slipping into a meditative state as easily as Nicolas might slip on a shoe. A small smile tickled the corner of his mouth at how peaceful the orc looked given the situation. But he knew the orc needed to steel himself, given the risk involved. He was looking for an evil presence. Maybe it was like a window and went both ways once opened? Or maybe served to help fan the flames, just like smashing the tavern window had?

'I'm not sure this is such a good idea,' he said quietly.

'Garaz would have weighed the risks before suggesting it,' Silva replied. 'Of all of us, he is the one least likely to behave impulsively.' The warrior's eyes flicked to Shift, the suggestion that they were the most impulsive of the group was clear.

'That doesn't mean he isn't capable of it,' Shift replied tartly. 'And he hasn't exactly been himself of late. The faun on the ship, his sullenness...Shagraz.'

'This life changes you, whether it's in a direction you want or not.' There was a deep regret in Silva's tone. 'When I first left home, I had dreams of becoming a hero. Look at me now.'

'You've done some heroic things,' Nicolas offered.

'And a lot of bad between them,' the warrior said firmly. 'I... Even if there's no hope for my soul, I hope I leave the world better than I found it.'

'I personally blame Nick.'

'*What?*' he cried as he stared at Shift. 'Me?'

'When we met, I was happy going around thieving. I meet you, and suddenly, I care about things, and believe in stuff. Then you somehow manage to bloody seduce me with your damned...niceness. You're a bad influence.'

'Maybe I would've moved on long ago if I didn't have to stay and look out for you?' Auron said with a half-smile.

'Well, excuse me,' he said testily. 'And humblest bloody apologies for all the upheaval *I've* brought to *your* lives.'

'At least you give us the odd amusing interlude to make up for it.' Shift grinned.

'Oh, I'm sure he's done more than *that* to make it up to you.'

Shift swiped at the air where Auron's arm was. The ethereal limb turned into swirling cloud before reforming again. Despite himself, Nicolas sniggered. It earned him a punch on the arm.

'Fate of the city in the hands of a bunch of damned travelling fools,' Greer said as he shook his head.

'Here we are,' Sergeant Tallith said as he walked through the door, carrying two small jars. 'Are these the ones?'

Garaz opened his eyes and held out his hand. He took the jars from the sergeant and studied them. 'I believe so,' the orc said with a frown. The uncertainty in his tone was strange from someone so knowledgeable. 'As I said earlier, I have not used these often.'

'A herb Garaz doesn't use regularly,' Auron scoffed. 'That's shaken my world view to the core.'

With a glance at Auron, accompanied by a sigh, Garaz produced a small dish from his cloak, placing it on the floor before the map. With precision that seemed improbable for someone with such large hands, the orc measured out his ingredients. A pinch of this, a sprig of that. Nicolas naturally assumed Garaz knew his business, so didn't see the need to question anything. Though his admission of using slightly unfamiliar herbs was concerning. This was obviously a completely new spell to the orc, and a lot was riding on his success.

Finally, with a nod, Garaz closed his eyes and whispered under his breath. Within a minute, the hairs on Nicolas's arm rose as a subtle energy filled the room. He studied the map.

Where will the demon be? The bazaar? The citadel? The Dwarven District?

The paranoid voice in his head wanted to add *in this house* to the list, but he wouldn't give that any credibility. Instead, he gazed at the map as if he could simply stare the answer into existence.

'When we find the demon...' he began.

'We hit it hard and fast,' Silva said. 'No messing around.'

'I'll have a troop ready to go within a half hour,' Greer said. 'Like the warrior woman said. I'm not messing about with bloody demons, assuming that's what it is. It dies, quickly.'

It made all the sense in the world, yet the sentence punched Nicolas in the gut. It was what they had to do, but when they did, he wouldn't get his answers.

'It will be okay,' Shift said quietly at his side. 'Garaz knows his magic, and between us, we know ass kicking. That demon won't know what's hit it. We'll make sure we get it to talk before finishing it off.'

And the poor soul whose body it stole.

As troubling as that was, he couldn't help but smile. 'You know, since we did *that*, you've been alternating between sweet and teasing. It's strange,' he whispered.

'Well, now that we have done *that*, as you so romantically put it, things are a bit different.' The in their eye suggested teasing was on the horizon. 'Right now, you need nice. I get how much finding this demon means to you. But if you ever refer to it as *that* again, we won't be doing *that* again.' Their lips broke into a small smirk. 'I don't know why you're whispering like everyone in this room doesn't know. No one could've missed it with you shouting *yippee* at the top of your lungs.' And there it was—embarrassing yet reassuring.

He coughed and looked away so they wouldn't see him blushing, not that there was much point. As he did, he caught Silva's eye. The warrior's lip was curled into a grimace. Another awkward cough, and he looked in another direction. And there was Auron, pressing his lips together tightly as he tried not to laugh.

Nicolas returned his eyes to the map, determined not to move his gaze from it until his embarrassment had faded.

Taking a small taper from his robe, Garaz lit it with a flame from his finger and dropped it into the bowl.

Whoosh.

Nicolas stepped back, putting his hand over his mouth as black smoke burst from the small bowl. But he needn't have worried. Instead of filling the room, and their lungs, the smoke gathered above the map, hovering like the metaphorical storm cloud Nicolas already knew to be hanging over this city. It was contained neatly within the four borders of the map. Beads formed on Garaz's brow, his face twitching with exertion as he muttered under his breath. Slowly, the cloud descended onto the map, only to dissipate into nothing before it landed.

Garaz's yellow eyes widened. 'I do not understand.'

Disappointment covered Nicolas like someone dumping a bucket of water over his head. It hadn't worked. Every time they seemed to get close to anything, it slipped away. And not just here. They'd been so close to getting Tavish too...

Every hour, my people get further and further away.

'But...it should've worked,' the orc snarled in disbelief, more to himself than anyone else.

'You said that you'd never tried it before,' Silva said.

The orc quickly crouched over the map, studying it intently. 'Yes, but the theory was sound. There should be a sign here. Something.'

'Garaz, we don't—'

Shift's sentence was cut off by the orc thumping his fist on the floor. 'No,' he snapped. 'It should have worked.' The voice was almost a growl as he fixed Shift with a red-eyed glare.

Nicolas and Shift exchanged an uncertain glance. Garaz's fist was shaking. Nicolas walked over and crouched in front of the orc, who closed his eyes and lowered his head.

'It's okay,' he said, mustering all his reassurance. 'You've been drained all day. Maybe it was that? Maybe something else? Either way, it didn't work, and you need to rest.'

With an exhale, Garaz's fist became a palm, which he pressed onto the floor. Finally, he looked up, his yellow eyes meeting Nicolas's. 'You are right,' the orc said with a thin smile. 'I have not been myself since the professor's manor. Maybe if I rest and try again tomorrow when I have regained my strength, I will have more success.'

Nicolas helped his companion to his feet, forgetting how much heavier Garaz was than him until he took the weight. Either way, his shaking legs managed to get the orc up.

'Or maybe there's just no demon?' Greer suggested, rising from the chair he'd sat in to watch everything unfold. 'And you are all the charlatans I assumed you to be.'

'*Duncan!*' Nicolas hadn't even seen Beba enter the room. 'You forget your manners.'

Greer stroked his thick moustache whilst giving his wife the evil eye; it was returned in kind. Finally, the lord commander huffed and walked out of the room. Beba stroked his arm affectionately as he passed.

'You'll have to forgive him,' Beba said as she watched her husband leave. 'He had a very bad experience with magic once, in his adventuring days.' She slowly turned to them. 'He believes in this city and the people in it, and though he doesn't show it, what's happening, and his inability to find the murderer, is eating him up. I'm sorry for how he's been with you.

He's seen first-hand how bad the world can be and is passionate about that not happening within the walls of this city.'

'I understand,' Nicolas said, lowering Garaz into a chair. 'And we really don't take offence.'

'We don't?' Shift asked incredulously.

'No.' It was actually Silva who responded. 'The man is just doing his duty, and that deserves respect.'

'You'd know if Silva was upset with him. Someone would find him dead on the lavatory with a crossbow bolt in him.' Auron turned and looked at them. '*What?* I've told you all before, I put up with her being here, but I haven't for a second forgotten that she killed me.'

'There's too much death nowadays,' Beba continued. 'And like it or not, it affects everyone around it.' She visibly shook herself and smiled. 'But enough of this talk, there's supper to be eaten.'

That sounded like a great idea. Nicolas doubted they'd get any further in the state they were in. They needed their rest and some food.

Maybe then we can actually find this killer.

CHAPTER 39

The light managed to penetrate his closed eyelids, slowly switching his brain from asleep to awake. His eyes began to open slowly. They opened much faster and wider as they saw Auron standing over him.

'Morning, kid,' the spirit said breezily.

'What in the Underworld?' Shift snapped, their eyes shooting open at the sound of Auron's voice. 'If this is a dream, it isn't funny.'

'I can't exactly knock, can I?' Auron remarked testily. 'And it's dawn. The kid needs to have some food then we need to go to the temple and see to getting you trained. Once that's done, we have a killer to hunt. So it's a pretty full day for you. Hurry up.'

'Fine,' Nicolas said. 'Now get out.'

Auron set his jaw as he turned away. 'Like I haven't seen people in bedsheets before,' he muttered. Nicolas imagined he would've been stomping away if anyone could've heard his footsteps.

'Damned ghost,' Shift spat, throwing a pillow at the wall the spirit had just vanished through. 'Nobody lets me get any sleep anymore.'

Though the spirit was correct: it was dawn. Nicolas could see the first promise of a bright day through the curtains. At least it wouldn't be cold, thanks to a certain professor.

Huffing, the shapeshifter lay back down, pulling the sheet over themselves. Their eyebrow raised as they side-eyed Nicolas. 'If you're going to give me that wide-eyed look every morning, I'll be sure to wake up in my own bed.'

'Oh, sorry,' Nicolas said. 'It's just. Well, you're here. Again.'

Shift theatrically rolled their eyes before kissing him. 'Yes, I am,' they confirmed. 'Now calm down about it.'

'I will, this is just...new.'

He caught the smile from Shift before they controlled themselves. 'It is to me too, really.' They shrugged. 'But I'm here, and it's nice.' For a moment, they looked away thoughtfully. 'In truth, I didn't think we'd be sharing a bed again this quickly. I guess after you dying, I can't leave you alone.'

Hardly ideal pillow talk.

'I do get into mischief when not properly supervised.' That wasn't strictly true, though. He'd always been good on his own; it was the world around him that caused the problems, and needed a damn good talking to because of it. 'Speaking of...shouldn't you slip back to your own room? If Greer catches you here, he'll be upset.'

'No,' they replied simply, lying back down and closing their eyes.

One of Nicolas's paranoid notions popped into his mind like an un-welcome visitor knocking on the door at supper time. 'How much of you sharing my bed is because of me, and how much is to upset the lord commander?'

A knowing smile crept across Shift's face. 'You'll never know.'

Nicolas's overthinking suddenly began to work harder. The unwelcome visitor in his head was now flicking off his muddy boots, putting his feet up on the dining table and about to wolf down the bowl of porridge Nicolas had made for himself.

'Relax,' Shift said, opening a single eye and smirking at him. 'If I'd been bothered about upsetting the lord commander, he would've heard last night. But let's just say that if the animal-head-hanging asshole *did* discover I was in here, I wouldn't be upset about it.'

'If you cost me a warm bed for the night, you'll be hearing all about it, you know.'

A pillow struck Nicolas in the head. 'That'd make us even.'

Shift went to lie back down and quickly realised they'd used their last pillow as ammunition. Huffing again, they took Nicolas's.

I'm getting up anyway.

Auron was right. He needed food if he was about to start training. Hopefully, Ban was a good, and fast, teacher. Leaving Shift in bed, he proceeded downstairs to forage for breakfast. The house was eerie in the dark, the suits of armour appearing ominous and the eyes in the portraits seeming to follow his every movement.

'This would be a nice place to haunt, if I were a ghost,' Auron said as he waited at the bottom of the stairs, studying a portrait of a gruff old man whose facial expression spoke of the most severe constipation.

'Maybe it can be your retirement plan for when this is all done,' Nicolas suggested with a smile. 'Find a nice manor to haunt. Go around poking stuff and upsetting those who dwell within.'

The spirit did not look impressed. 'As soon as I'm done training you, it's off to the Eternal Forest for me. I'm hoping it has some beaches too. I plan to find one and relax on it for all eternity.'

'You've earnt it.' Nicolas wasn't sure if the next question would be welcome or not. 'So, you think I'm your unfinished business?'

'Of course you are,' Auron replied simply. 'Etherius is down one hero, and I didn't get a chance to pass the torch on.' *If you don't have at least one child knocking around Etherius, I'll be highly surprised.* 'So you're stuck with me until I do, and we defeat whoever this Maestro is. I assume there'll be some catalyst event, that's generally how these stupid, dramatic things work, but we will figure it out. Until then, we have to get you in fighting shape.'

Nicolas furrowed his brow.

'Stop it,' the spirit chided. 'You're about to kick yourself for tethering me here. Don't. It's not your fault. Besides, I'm having a great time. I never knew being dead would be such fun.'

'But...'

The spirit pointed down the hall. 'Food.'

Nicolas held up his hands and marched in the direction Auron bade. As the pair entered the kitchen, both were surprised to find Garaz hunched over the large counter that dominated the centre of the room. The orc was studying parchment by the light of a single candle. He was so intent on it, he didn't even notice them enter.

'Morning.'

The orc's hand was on his staff in an instant, the movement fast enough to make Nicolas flinch. What was more worrying was the sigh of relief when the orc finally realised it was them.

'Have you been here all night?' Nicolas asked.

'I... My mind would not allow me to sleep,' Garaz replied, sitting back down. His eyes were reddened in the way only lack of sleep could produce. 'I cannot fathom where my spell went awry. I have been writing it out, trying to discern my error...'

'I don't think you will unless you get some sleep,' Nicolas said. 'You'll certainly be in no state to try again.'

If you even should.

'How am I to find the answer when I sleep?' Garaz snapped.

'Look,' Auron said, a note of caution in his voice, 'you said the spell was new and—'

The orc's fist thumped on the counter, cutting the sentence off. 'It should have worked. There is no reason why it did not.'

Casting a sideways glance at Auron beforehand, Nicolas slowly approached Garaz. 'Look, like I said, I don't think you're in any state to do anything right now. You need to rest. You've been off since the professor's. Go sleep, and we'll look at it together when you wake. Maybe a fresh perspective will help.'

Intense yellow eyes fixed on his. The idea that he had no clue how the orc would respond was worrying.

'You are right,' Garaz finally conceded with a sigh. 'I need to rest.'

Slowly, the orc gathered up his things, rose, and left the room without another word. Nicolas wanted to say something as he passed, but some aura his companion was giving off told him not to.

'That was odd,' Auron remarked, watching Garaz leave.

That was definitely odd.

His eyes caught something out of place as he glanced at where Garaz had been sat. Getting closer to the counter, he saw shallow claw marks gouged into the thick wood, as if someone had been scratching at it. Nicolas looked again in the direction Garaz had gone.

'Morning, Garaz.'

The sound of voices made Nicolas and Auron look at each other, before going back into the entrance hall.

Shift was watching Garaz walk up the stairs, frowning. 'Not a morning person, I suppose,' they remarked sarcastically.

That's ironic.

Nicolas looked at the open door of the drawing room, which Shift had evidently just come from, and then at the two mounted heads they were carrying.

'Not a word,' Shift said sternly. 'Just go and eat your breakfast.'

Tilting his head, he gazed at the stuffed animal heads. The creatures had been posed to look threatening, but he was sure they'd been simply minding their own business when they died.

'Actually,' he said, returning his gaze to Shift, 'I was going to ask if you needed a hand.'

Shift gave him a coy smile. 'Good response, Nick.'

****

Empty city streets were unsettling, even for a boy who'd barely visited a city before. And yet, somehow, it was becoming the norm for him. Whether it was due to the city being terrorised by a vampiric horde, or the city just being a dump, this was what Nicolas was used to. Though *empty* was an over-exaggeration. They passed a couple of patrols from the city watch, and some traders en-route to set up their stalls for the day's trading. Even a spate of murders couldn't shut down the economy.

At least the city isn't waking up to a new body...that I know of.

It had to be a matter of time now. It'd been a few days since the last killing, a night or so before they'd arrived. Another could happen anytime now.

And we're no closer to stopping it.

A troop of watchmen marched past them. The officer glanced at their badges—the new ones provided by Lord Commander Greer—which Shift and Nicolas had made sure to keep on show so they wouldn't be challenged. The traders presented special permits when the watchmen began questioning some people in the street.

Staying vigilant, Nicolas warily cast his eyes along the street, checking every nook they passed, craning his neck to see down every alleyway. There was nothing.

Maybe the demon's left, fled elsewhere to do its work.

Screwing up his face, Nicolas chided himself for the pang of disappointment. The demon being gone would be a good thing for the city. It meant no more death. Right now, this wasn't about his quest to find his people, it was about saving the city. He shouldn't let grief and frustration cloud that. His parents had brought him up better than that. They wouldn't want him acting like a petulant child.

But then I doubt they wanted to be killed by a demon either.

No. He couldn't let his anguish consume him. That had nearly happened on the Ale Trail—with a little outside help. Nicolas found his gaze lingering on Auron. When Silva had first joined them, Auron's reaction had nearly gotten them all killed. Tragedy had turned him into something worse, albeit momentarily.

I won't let that happen to me. I won't let what happened to my parents make me into something I'm not. I swear it, on them.

'Kid, why are you staring at me like that?'

'Um, I was just wondering why you guys are with me?' Had he pulled that off?

The spirit's white eyes lit up, which was impressive considering they were bright white orbs. 'Are you serious? I'm not missing the opportunity to watch a master in action. If Master Lo-Rence trained this guy, showed him *everything*, then you are in for a treat.'

His mind drifted back to the easy beating his prospective new master had taken. Obviously, he'd seen the return to form moments later, but the image of his humiliation lingered.

Nicolas frowned. 'So it's nothing to do with you wanting to watch me getting beaten up?'

'That *is* always funny.' Auron smirked.

'Isn't it just?' Nicolas gave Shift an unimpressed shake of his head. They shrugged apologetically. 'It's just, well, you make these *pain faces*.'

'I do what?'

'Oh Deities.' Auron laughed. 'Those are so funny.'

'I do not make *pain faces*,' he protested angrily.

'Yes, you do,' Shift countered quickly. 'You do something like this...' They began to contort their face in an overly theatrical wincing motion.

'That's it exactly,' Auron exclaimed, pointing. 'But it's the noises he makes too. Those weird *nnnuyyyyygggghhhh* sounds.'

'Oh, by the Deities,' Shift cried. 'What *are* those? Are they pain, or bedro—'

'I'm glad me getting beaten up amuses you,' he interrupted dryly, glaring at Shift as they put their hand over their mouth to stifle laughter. 'Lovely bloody companions I've got.'

'So,' Auron switched the tone with suspicious speed. 'Speaking of *lovely companions*. What's going on with you two? Other than the obvious.'

It was like Nicolas's face had been instantly set aflame. 'I...well... We...'

Part of him was hoping Shift would answer, because it was a question he really wanted to ask himself. Yet saying it aloud might spoil things. But everything was so...uncertain right now.

'We,' Shift said, directing the answer to him with a gaze he could've lost himself in, 'are enjoying each other's company and seeing where it goes. And Nicolas gets to be the luckiest man in all Etherius. Lucky that I dropped my standards for the time being.' The sentence was punctuated with a wink.

'Like you could hold out against my charm forever.' He smiled back at them.

Shift fluttered their eyelashes in mocking fashion. 'It does appear that naïve village boys are my weakness.'

'I bet you liked him from the moment he got on his knees and offered you his sword in the vampire cave.' Auron laughed.

His step broke with surprise as he looked at Shift and found *they* were blushing.

By the Deities, Auron's right.

And here he was thinking he'd made a giant fool of himself this whole time.

Shift caught his stupefied look and shuffled awkwardly. 'Well...I... It was just...'

He knew Shift wouldn't like looking so vulnerable, so he was the one who offered the interruption. 'We're here.'

Before them sat the familiar arch and steps leading to the training hall. Ban Dro was waiting for him under said arch, arms folded. 'Are you ready?' he asked sternly.

He took a deep breath. 'Yes.'

The master raised an eyebrow. 'You aren't ready.' Turning, he abruptly entered the training hall.

Though no formal invitation had been given, Nicolas assumed he was supposed to follow, so he did, his companions trailing him.

CHAPTER 40

Is he going to say anything?

Upon entering the training hall, Ban Dro had guided Nicolas to the sandy-floored sparring area and had him sit down. The master had then sat cross-legged about four feet in front of Nicolas and proceeded to stare at him. It didn't take long for Nicolas's eyes to wander to find things less awkward to look at.

'Don't touch those.'

Quickly, Nicolas checked his hands. He wasn't touching anything. When he looked up at Ban questioningly, though, the master's eyes weren't on him. It didn't take a genius to guess who he *was* looking at.

By the wall, Shift's hands were hovering over a pair of ornate knives. Slowly, Shift took their hands away, making a production out of turning and holding them in the air to show they were empty. The actions of walking away from them and sitting down quietly were completed with equal theatricality.

'Will you behave?' Auron said with a disapproving parental pout of his undead lips.

Shift answered with a sarcastic grin and a single, rude gesture.

Allowing himself a slight chuckle, Nicolas turned to find Ban staring at him with a frankly ridiculous level of intensity.

Oh. Um...this sand looks nice.

'You need to build confidence,' Ban said out of nowhere, his voice deep and commanding. 'If you cannot keep eye contact with me for more than two minutes, how do you expect to keep your eyes on an opponent in battle?'

I'd probably pay more attention if you were trying to kill me, in all fairness.

'Gaze is important,' his new master continued. 'You can use it to connect with your inner warrior. But sometimes you can also use it to stave off a fight before it happens.'

Ban tilted his head forward slightly so his eyes were no longer visible. Slowly, the master raised his head again, until he was glaring fiercely at Nicolas from just under his brow. A shudder ran up Nicolas's spine as his courage fled his body to find some nice locality where it could live in peace. He knew the man across from him was intent on ripping him limb from limb and could do it, too. Gulping, he desperately fought the urge to start scrabbling backwards crying like a child with a skinned knee. But he couldn't help the slump forward or sigh of relief when Ban turned...whatever that was off.

Breathing heavily, Nicolas took a moment to collect himself. Then a thought occurred. 'A question, if I may?'

'Speak,' the master said with a raised eyebrow. 'But you do not need to hold your hand up as well.'

'Oh,' he said, lowering his arm. 'Okay. Please don't take this the wrong way, but...why didn't you use that on the Dux fellow?'

Now it was Ban Dro's turn to sigh. 'I suppose I thought my master would live forever,' he began, looking into some middle distance. 'Then one day, he just turns into a load of floating petals and he's gone.' *That doesn't sound like dying.* 'When he died, not only was this place and the students in it mine, but so was his legacy. I was so keen to prove my master the best, to prove myself worthy of him, that I completely forgot how to do it. I allowed my desire to honour his memory to blind me...until you came along.'

I wonder how many fights he lost in that time?

Nicolas found himself thinking of Auron. The *Dawnblade's* legacy had died with the hero. He might carry Auron's sword, but he could never carry that.

I'd never be worthy, even if I was inclined.

'A question for you,' Ban said, snapping him from his thoughts. 'How would you describe your fighting skill?'

'I...um...I've been in a few fights, and I survived.' There wasn't much more to it than that, really. He nearly said he'd given a decent account of himself, but that was only true about half of the time. If that.

Surely, I'm selling myself short? I must've learned something to get this far.

'This training hall, and this world, demands more than '*I survived.*'

Is he going to make every statement sound like he's shouting at me?

'You're looking down again.'

With a sigh, Nicolas looked up. He couldn't spend this whole session trying to pick out each dust footprint in the sand.

Why is his gaze so intense?

'Here, you will learn the confidence you need,' Ban continued. 'And the skill to go with it. I shall teach you to fight, and fight well. But first, I must see what you already know. Hit that.'

Nicolas's gaze followed his new master's pointing finger. He frowned, looked back to Ban Dro and then repeated the motion, because he wasn't sure he was looking at the right thing. Well, mostly he was hoping he was looking at the wrong thing. The item in question happened to be a thick log stood on a stand not far from them. It was sanded and varnished, with long arms at several points which he assumed were meant to represent real arms. It looked...solid.

'You want me to hit *that?*' he cried, still hoping that he was wrong.

Ban looked at him with narrowed eyes. 'I was unaware I had a speech impediment.'

Is this punishment for showing him up earlier? It has to be.

But the intense gaze never wavered once, so it looked like he was doing this.

It's fine. I know how to punch.

Nervously, he raised himself from the floor. Going from cross-legged to standing was more difficult than it should've been. Slowly, he walked over to the training aid. The closer he got to it, the more solid it appeared. Finally, he stood before it, eyeing it as if it may somehow suddenly come to life and start pummeling him.

Everyone's staring at me. I can feel it.

Taking a deep breath, he raised his fists.

If people hit it all the time, it's probably not that hard.

He picked a point on the training aid to strike.

What 'people?' There's only Ban here.

'Today,' Ban suggested irritably.

This is what I came here for, to be trained. I can't balk at my first lesson.

Before he could argue with himself, Nicolas launched his fist. At the very last second, his courage failed him, and he pulled the punch. He winced. Not from the pain to come, but from knowing the fear had won. There was a slight tapping sound as his fist grazed the dummy.

'Properly,' Ban shouted.

Deities' sake.

Crack. The second wince was pure pain as his fist connected with the wood, and lightning bolts of agony shooting up his arm was his reward. Quickly, he drew his arm back and blew on his red knuckles.

Turning, he looked at Ban for some positive affirmation. His new master raised a single eyebrow. 'I see.'

What did he see? Okay, it wasn't my best punch, but it was decent. Maybe.

'Hit it a few more times.'

His knuckles sent a throb of protest up his arm at the command. Yet he obeyed. Swinging his arms, he struck the post repeatedly. Hopefully, Garaz had a soothing balm for his abused knuckles that wouldn't affect him as badly as healing magic. Still, he gave it his best.

Well, perhaps seventy percent of my best. The post is a lot harder than a jaw.

'Enough,' Ban commanded, jumping to his feet in a fluid way Nicolas envied. 'You are flapping around like a chicken.'

I doubt Silva would be impressed to hear the sum total of her training with me being described that way.

Though Nicolas took that as a partial compliment. His life had been saved by a chicken once. Though his master would have no idea about that, so he didn't mention it.

Though he ought to know. Everyone else around here seems to know my business.

With a gesture, Ban shooed him aside and stood before the pole himself, his hands held before him, palms up. 'You waste too much energy with your motion,' he explained. 'You can generate power *and* have economy of movement.'

Slowly, his new master closed his hands into fists, a motion which created a surprising amount of finger cracking sounds. The glare at the lifeless piece of wood was so intense Nicolas thought it would splinter without a touch. Then, with a fierce exhalation, Ban Dro drove his fist into the dummy, which shook violently from the impact. The sound of the strike was so loud, Nicolas started, and his knuckles gave another throb in sympathy.

Ban followed it up with another strike, and another. Soon, his fists were flowing and moving at a speed Nicolas's eyes couldn't keep up with. All he could do was listen to the strikes: *clack, clack, clack, clack.*

It's strangely relaxing. The sound of Shift's impressed whistle was less so.

With a surprising suddenness, the onslaught Ban Dro had unleashed on the dummy stopped, and he drew his hands back.

What? How are his knuckles fine?

Slowly, controlling his breathing back into a regular rhythm, Ban turned to him. 'What did you see?'

Oh, the joy of being put on the spot. 'Well, you hit it really hard.'

'And?'

'Fast.'

'And?' Ban asked again in an insistent tone.

I don't bloody know. Closing his eyes, Nicolas replayed what he'd just seen in his mind. 'I...well...you barely moved.'

'Exactly.' *Wow, he can smile.* 'I managed to generate devastating power and hit my target without all of that *'ducking and weaving'* you were doing.' Slowly, Ban extended his arm toward the dummy. 'See how my arm doesn't fly out in an arc. My punch is a simple straight motion from point A to point B, the target. This is the economy of motion you need to learn.' Allowing his fist to hover an inch or two from the dummy, suddenly Ban hit it again, eliciting another loud *clack.* 'I maintain power generation. This is what you will learn first, structure and power. It will suit you more than that flapping around you were doing just now. I will also teach you good footwork. You are slight, but I believe you may have an agility that would be useful in any fight.'

Ban may be on to something here...

He remembered facing Silva and Grimmark on the bridge – the second time, not the first one. The first one went really badly. He'd managed to dodge between the two mercenaries until he'd made Grimmark knock...well, he'd won the fight. If he could learn to harness that he could be really good. Plus he was less likely to get hit so much.

Which is handy now I have to ration my use of healing magic.

Though Ban hadn't made the greatest first impression, Nicolas was starting to understand what he could learn here. He found himself staring at Ban's uninjured fist, his gaze soon turning to the training dummy.

I need to learn this.

It was going to be painful, but by the Deities, was it necessary. Straightening up, he looked Ban directly in the eye. 'Teach me,' he said with a bow.

CHAPTER 41

Nicolas couldn't help but feel accomplished to be leaving the training hall better than he'd entered it. It had been an intense two hours. Ban's training was rigorous, but so was the evil he was preparing to battle.

Though, hopefully, evil can wait until I'm less of a sweaty mess.

At least any lingering doubts about his new master's skill had been erased. There was still much to put right in Babylon, but he planned to make the most of Ban whilst he could.

'How you feeling, kid?' Auron asked. 'Ready to take on an army of orcs with just your bare hands?'

'Maybe a couple of drunk goblins.' He smiled back.

Auron's face became serious. 'Don't knock drunk goblins, kid. They have sharp teeth and don't care where they bite.'

'You can spare us *that* story,' Shift said, wrinkling their nose.

'I think I will.' The spirit chuckled. 'The kid's been through enough today.'

'Thank you, for taking me there,' he said to Auron.

'No problem, kid,' Auron replied. 'It will be good for you. You have an opportunity to learn here. Use it.'

'Don't worry,' he told the spirit. 'I've already decided to do that.'

'Good man.' Auron's pride was palpable.

The trio stopped by a small bridge as Silva approached with Sergeant Tallith. Her long stride suggesting she was trying to lose the sergeant, or at least ensure that any passers by assumed they weren't together.

'Morning,' the warrior greeted irritably.

'Hello, all,' Tallith said brightly

'Morning, Sergeant,' Shift said with a hearty wave. 'Nice of you to bring Silva to us.'

The warrior bristled at the suggestion, running her tongue inside her cheek whilst giving the shapeshifter a filthy look.

'Not at all.' Tallith smiled. 'She was coming this way and allowed me to follow.'

Judging by Silva's expression, *allowed* was an exaggeration.

'I take it you are ready?' the warrior asked.

Apparently evil won't *wait until I'm not a sweaty mess.*

'Yes,' he confirmed. 'You have the list?'

'Of course.' Sergeant Tallith patted a pouch on his belt. 'All the victims' immediate next of kin.'

They'd decided last night to go and question the relatives of the victims. To see if there was some kind of pattern. Sergeant Tallith insisted this had already been done, thoroughly, but they might see something someone else had missed. Lord Commander Greer had been more open to the idea, but Nicolas sensed it was only because he thought it would keep them out of his hair for the day.

'I asked for the list, but he refused to give it to me.' Silva's expression suggested that Tallith was lucky to be alive. The warrior didn't get refused often.

'Well, I am supposed to be...escorting you.'

Watching us, more like.

Nicolas didn't begrudge it. He was sure he would've done the same in Greer's boots, if some ruffians were running around Hablock.

'No trouble last night then?' Nicolas asked.

'No murders, no,' Tallith replied. 'Though we did have to raid the local hall of the Bards Guild. Apparently, a group from the Guild of Thieves marched in there and started a fight. I don't think anyone died, but quite a few were arrested.'

'That isn't going away then?'

'Apparently not,' Auron replied. 'This *Maestro* certainly knows how to stir up chaos.'

'If this *is* him,' Shift said, watching Nicolas carefully. 'I know you want it to be, and it probably is, but we can't be sure. Don't assume anything.'

I know.

'Garaz?' he asked, looking past Silva.

'I haven't seen him,' the warrior said. 'I did knock on his door, but there was no answer. I checked, and he was asleep. It must have been deep as he wasn't even snoring, so I let him be.'

He took that spell failing really badly. Hopefully, he'll feel better after some rest.

****

Nicolas put his hand on the latch to open the gate and took a deep breath. It had been a long day with nothing to show for it. So far, talking to the victims' families had yielded no useful information.

Maybe this is the one?

'Just me and Tallith this time,' he said to his companions.

Silva and Shift stared at him with equally unimpressed gazes.

'What?' he said, shrugging. 'You've both made this whole thing a chore.'

'I was under the assumption we were helping,' Silva retorted dryly.

'Oh really?' he scoffed. 'Was it helpful when you pinned that poor guy against the wall because he told me to *sod off or else*?'

'He behaved in a threatening manner. I reciprocated.'

'He was grieving.'

'He was armed.'

'It was a bloody spoon,' Nicolas cried. 'What was he going to do with that?'

'Cutting someone's heart out with a spoon is a nasty way to go,' Auron said, sucking his teeth. 'You've got to *really* want someone dead to do that. Spoons are pretty blunt, so you need some real rage behind the—'

'Please,' Nicolas said in exasperation. He caught Shift about to open their mouth and interjected before they could speak. 'And you managed to break that dwarf's entire collection of garden gnomes. Didn't exactly endear us to him.'

'Look,' Shift said, holding up their hands. 'I found it odd that a dwarf collected garden gnomes and picked one up. He asked me to put it down, and I did. Not my fault they were set up like bloody dominoes.'

'Just, please, both of you stay here,' he said, pointing to the path before the gate.

'Hopefully, the person who dwells here hasn't seen you all arguing outside.' Auron smirked. 'I highly doubt that'll create the best impression.'

His gaze flicked to the window. That was a good point.

Please let this be the one.

'Ready?' he asked Sergeant Tallith.

From the way the watchman stared at him, it was like Nicolas had offered to knight him instead of just accompany him to the door.

I swear, if he invites me to meet the fan club, I am going to lose my mind.

Steeling himself, he opened the gate and proceeded down the quaint, paved path.

'We humble followers shalt just wait here dutifully for thy next command, m'lord.'

'Thank you,' he said to Shift, ignoring the sarcasm.

The house was in the human district of the city. It was, pretty standard for a human dwelling, in all honesty. Some care had gone into the garden, yet Nicolas had to duck an overhanging branch from the tree next door before he made it to the door and knocked.

Within a minute, it opened. A frumpy woman in a dirty apron answered, eyeing them suspiciously. 'Yes?'

'Good afternoon,' he said with a bright smile, wanting to get off on the right foot this time. 'My name's Nicolas and we're with the city watch. We just wanted to ask you about your husband. My condolences on your loss. We were wondering if—'

'I'll tell you exactly what I told the other lawmen who came,' the woman cut in sternly. 'Wasn't no serial murderer that killed my Bob. It was that cow next door.'

'You bloody, lying witch.'

Nicolas jumped as a head popped over the fence. The woman's hair was as scattered as the branches of the tree she stood under.

'Oh? Lying, am I?' the lady at the door said. 'It's just a coincidence my Bob gets murdered a day before we got to talk to the magistrate about that bastard tree of yours?'

The woman reeled back as if struck. 'You think I, or my good hubby, murdered someone because you couldn't stop bitching about a branch you could easily cut down yourself?'

'Your tree, your responsibility,' the woman at the door huffed, arms folded.

'One branch, over *your* property. Just cut it.'

'Oh no. No, no, no, no, no. You don't get off that easily.' The woman wagged her finger in the air. 'It'll grow back. The whole tree goes. Don't think I'm grieving enough not to fight you on this. I'll see my poor Bob's final wishes fulfilled.'

'I'm sure your *poor Bob's* final wish had nothing to do with a stupid branch,' the neighbour bellowed. 'More like he was wishing for someone to save him so he didn't die. And if his last thoughts were about that tree, that's the saddest bloody thing I've ever heard.'

From there, the argument devolved into a series of furious curses. Nicolas made a brief attempt to calm it down, but guessed this feud had deeper roots than the aforementioned tree itself, so he instead bade them farewell and retreated down the path.

'How did that go, sir?' Shift asked with a smirk.

'Shut up.'

As the women continued to bicker, a fancy carriage made its way up the road, coming to a halt just in front of them. Judging by how well-dressed the driver was, the passenger was someone of note. A small blind on the side of the door rolled up.

Oh, for Deities' sake.

'I see you still investigate this matter,' Councillor Geldheart said in his deep monotone as he leant toward the window. 'You would have done well to heed my warning, boy.'

Somehow, Nicolas highly doubted that Geldheart often took carriage tours of the suburban districts of the city. He also doubted he often pulled up to people in the street and gave random, ominous warnings.

Don't I feel special.

'If you were going to show my poster around, you would have done so already,' he replied coolly. 'My guess is that you can't use it. Why might that be?'

Geldheart gave him a long, appraising look. 'It seems there is more to you than I thought, boy,' he said finally. 'You are not run off easily.'

Nicolas looked at the pavement he was standing on for a moment. 'Apparently not.' He pursed his lips thoughtfully. 'Even when buildings I'm sleeping in happen to burn down.'

'That was an unusual accident,' Geldheart replied quickly. 'But accidents happen. Especially when people have a tendency to put themselves in harm's way.'

'I'm sure only people who know how to handle themselves do that.'

Geldheart sat back in his seat and steepled his fingers. 'We shall see. Keep forcing my hand and see what happens next.'

'We *shall* see,' Nicolas began. 'I plan to see many things whilst I'm here.'

Try to sound brave...end up sounding like a tourist.

Geldheart's mouth became a thin line. 'Beware the things you cannot unsee.'

Before Nicolas could reply—which was probably a blessing given his poor attempt at tough talk—the blind snapped back into place and the driver urged the horse on with a crack of the reins. The carriage pulled away.

'People who are *vaguely threatening* make me sick,' Auron said, his mouth curled in disgust. 'If you're going to threaten someone, have the balls to say it plainly.'

'It seems it takes more than some menacing carriage talk to shake you,' Silva said.

'Yeah, I'm certainly growing as a person,' he said absentmindedly as he watched the carriage disappear around a corner.

'Um, excuse me,' Sergeant Tallith interrupted with a cough. 'But what was all that about? Was that Councillor Geldheart?'

CHAPTER 42

The sun was already beginning to set on the city, signalling the end of another day. A day they'd apparently wasted.

Our time is running out.

At least they'd lost Sergeant Tallith. A messenger from the lord commander had summoned him away on urgent watch business of some sort whilst the group had been grabbing some food in a tavern. Nicolas found someone looking up to him tiring. It was as if he needed to watch his every word and gesture to live up to whatever crap these people were concocting about him. And Silva was clearly not taken with the young sergeant. The reason was bugger all to do with Nicolas, and he intended to keep it that way.

The city was beginning to wind down for the night. Shops were shutting and people going to their homes. There was an unmistakeable scent of fear in the air. Everyone knew the next killing would be soon, and most likely after dark. People kept to themselves, wary of those around them. Nicolas felt the weight of it too.

We need a breakthrough. Perhaps Garaz could try his spell again?

He quickly shook the idea away. They needed something concrete to work with. Someone must know something. And there was a very obvious person to ask.

Except we can't go accusing him without evidence, or we're going to be whipped out of the city.

But the evidence wasn't just going to appear. They'd need to find it.

'Shift,' he said thoughtfully. 'How do you fancy breaking into Geldheart's residence to see if you can find any evidence linking him to the murders?' His companions all came to a halt, Nicolas stopping a second later. 'What?'

'Ballsy move, kid.' Auron smiled warmly.

Nicolas shrugged. 'We aren't coming up with anything, so I think it's time for...ballsy.' Already knowing the answer, he raised an eyebrow at Shift. 'So?'

'I fancy that very much.' The shapeshifter grinned. 'As soon as we're back, I'll find it on a map and set off. I'll be in and out before dawn.'

'We should go with you. It isn't safe.'

Shift gave Silva a playful tap on the arm. 'It's nice that you care, but I can handle myself. And if I can't, I'll die happy knowing you'll tear Geldheart limb from limb in vengeance.'

'For starters,' the warrior replied.

'I don't think we should be talking about those kinds of *what-ifs*,' Nicolas said, his voice betraying his nerves.

Shift looked at him for a moment then gave him a thankful smile.

They're about to point out the irony of me suggesting other people don't overthink various bad scenarios.

'Stand aside!'

The citizens ahead of them parted as a troop of watchmen charged down the street, their armour clanking as they ran, practically knocking aside anyone too slow to get out of their way.

'Oh no,' Nicolas whispered as he watched the troop pass. 'There's been another one.' Was it common sense or intuition? Nicolas didn't know, but he knew he was right.

Quickly, the group set off in pursuit of the watchmen.

****

I know this wasn't me...but if I'd worked harder? If I'd dragged Geldheart out of his carriage and shook him until he talked...?

Nicolas's mouth became a thin line as he stared up at the body. The blame would always be partially his for not doing better. But he was also resolute that this was the last one. Especially after the show the demon had made of this poor soul. There was no body in a convenient alleyway. This one was put where everyone could see it.

Which was the point.

Tearing his gaze from the dead dwarf, he looked around. A large crowd of horrified onlookers had gathered, held back by the city watch. Though why they wanted to get closer to *that* was anyone's guess. Carefully, he scanned the fearful faces, hoping some hero instinct would scream *'that's the demon. Him, right there'* when he locked eyes with the right person. There was nothing.

'How did it even manage this without anyone seeing?' Shift was dumbstruck, their voice having a faraway quality to it.

It was a good question. The bridge the dwarf was strung up from was in plain sight of a few houses and on a main street.

'Kid,' Auron began quietly, 'tell me what you see.'

Great.

Hesitantly, he looked back up at the body. 'It's changed its killing pattern. The dwarf has been hung. It's hard to tell from here, but I can't see any burns.' *There's that, at least.* 'Probably means he wasn't possessed. There's no blood beneath him. I...suppose he may have been killed elsewhere and brought here.'

'Why?' Auron asked.

'Because if he was hung there, I'm sure he'd have managed to at least shout something to get attention or put up a fight. Someone would've noticed that.'

I hope.

'Impressive analysis.' Silva nodded.

It was hard to take pride in his work, given the situation.

'Are we sure this *was* the demon?' Shift asked.

'Kid?'

Nicolas sighed. 'It has to be. The dwarf doesn't look light. To get him up there and flee again without being seen requires either a lot of people, who would be noticed, or supernatural speed and strength.'

Those will be fun to face when we find this thing.

Shift hung their head and let out a breath. 'Why aren't they getting him down?'

'To preserve the scene so they can check for evidence,' the spirit replied.

'But to just...leave him there, dangling...'

'I would be more worried about us right now,' Silva said, with a glance at the crowd.

The warrior was right. The crowd of onlookers were getting restless. Nicolas narrowed his eyes. Actually, there were two crowds. Humans and non-humans. He could practically hear the battle drums warming up.

'Why the change in killing pattern?' Silva asked.

'I don't know.' Auron's obvious uncertainty was unnerving, to say the least. 'It should've burned through its host well before now, which would've left a convenient body to hang. Something's changed.'

'You mean things are coming to the boil,' Shift said, their mouth a thin line. 'Now that all the ingredients have been added and left to simmer for long enough.'

'Yup,' Auron confirmed. 'So this one time, there were two rival war-lords. Hated each other, but if anything started between them, it would be mutually assured destruction. Still, they had a tendency of raiding and pillaging, so they had to go. They both had quite large forces and were very well entrenched. Getting to either of them would be suicide.' His pupilless white eyes flicked to the crowd. 'So I burned down one of their outposts and left a very clear trail suggesting the other had done it. It didn't take long for a fight to break out. As it escalated, both warlords took to the field with their armies, which annihilated each other. Then I killed them both.' Auron shook his head. 'Well, it wasn't that simple, but that's the gist.'

'And you think that's what's happening here?' Nicolas asked, eyeing the crowd nervously.

'You've seen the suspicious glances, felt the fear. All the murders, they're kindling,' the spirit said gravely. 'All it needs is a light.'

Any further conjecture was silenced as the crowd went from stunned silence to aggressive murmuring. These mutters, most likely accusations being voiced, were punctuated by venomous glances.

Here we go.

'You all need to disperse,' the sergeant of the troop shouted, sensing the change too. 'This is a crime scene, not a bloody travelling circus. Back to your homes. Now!'

His command fell on deaf ears. Nicolas understood the need to pre-serve evidence, but having the dwarf up there on display would only incite the crowd more. Besides, the dwarf was a person, with friends, family...it just wasn't right to leave him hanging. He'd been through enough. He deserved some dignity.

Drawing a knife, he held the rope with one hand then cut it. The second he did, he dropped the knife. He needed both hands as he took the dead weight of the body, gripping the rope furiously as he lowered the dead dwarf respectfully to the ground. After taking a second to blow on his sore hands, he removed the noose and said a prayer for the dwarf's soul. He doubted dwarves worshipped the same Deities as humans, but he was sure the dwarf would appreciate any well-wishing on his way to the afterlife, especially considering the way he'd been sent there.

I hope you're at peace now.

'What do you mean, *it's only a dwarf?*' The outraged shout was followed by a wave of angry noises from the assembled onlookers.

Nicolas approached the cordon and peered over the watchmen. A group of human men had pushed their way to the front of the crowd. Nicolas glowered as he recognised their leader.

Big Jaw.

'What I mean to say is,' the ruffian said to the enraged dwarf who'd just pointed an accusing finger at him, 'we ran all the way here thinking a human had been killed. Turns out I wasted my legs for nothing.'

Middle-aged and overweight. All of them. Yet despite them running *here, there isn't a drop of sweat on any of them.*

Nicolas knew what they were here for. It was all part of this great play being performed before them. The stage had been set, and here came the actors. Except these assheads were anything but entertaining.

'A life was taken here, and you bemoan having to *run*?' a kascat shouted. 'Have you no shame?'

Big Jaw scrunched his face up and shook his head. 'A *life*,' he scoffed. 'It's barely a person. And if it was, it'd be half a person.'

'Perhaps you can give your mouth a rest along with your legs.' Shift had already shoved through the cordon to confront the idiots.

Nicolas quickly followed.

'Oh,' Big Jaw said with a sneer. 'You.' Each man had a club tucked into his belt. This had all the makings of getting very ugly. 'If I don't care for the words of these *creatures,* why would I listen to a woman...except if she's letting me know what I'm having for dinner?' Big Jaw leant back and slapped one of his comrades on the chest heartily. There was a pattering of laughter from the group.

Thankfully, Nicolas knew Shift well enough to grab them just as they charged forward. They struggled a little, but let him hold them back, much to Big Jaw's amusement.

'You two get riled up so easily.' He chuckled.

'Which is exactly what they want,' Nicolas whispered urgently in Shift's ear.

Instantly, the shapeshifter calmed. Shift didn't need physical violence to defend themselves, they had their words. 'That statement only proves something I've suspected from the get-go,' they said soberly, shaking their head. 'That you've never known the touch of a woman.'

Big Jaw bit instantly. 'I've known the touch of a woman.'

'Sisters don't count,' Shift snapped back.

The man leant forward menacingly. 'My sister is chaste and dignified, not like whatever creature you are.'

'What I am,' Shift smiled, pointing to their badge, 'is the law here. So I suggest you move along. Unless you'd care to hear the dinner selection for the jail?'

'The day I give in to the authority of some female is the day I—'

Big Jaw stumbled back with a grunt as the stone hit him in the side of the head.

'Have a bloody gash on your forehead?' the dwarf who'd launched the stone suggested, body rising and falling with angry breaths.

Though Nicolas was objectively quite amused by Mr Racist McSexist taking a stone to the side of the head, he knew exactly what would come next. That single stone had whipped up a frenzy of furious shouting, curses, and threats as the two halves of the crowd began to face off.

Soon, more projectiles flew through the air—though these were the usual lettuces and tomatoes any mob of peasants seemed to have readily to hand in this sort of situation.

'We aren't *creatures!*' was the general theme of the non-humans shouting.

The humans disagreed as everything spiralled toward the inevitable finale.

'If people like that hate it here so much, why don't they just bloody well leave?' Nicolas asked through gritted teeth.

'Because if they can't live around people they can blame all their problems on, they'll finally realise that *they* are the problem,' Shift answered quickly.

This guy is definitely a problem.

'My heroic intuition tells me this isn't going to end well,' Auron said.

No shit. I need to get this under control before it gets worse.

Hopping up on a nearby crate, he drew his sword and banged the flat of the blade against his improvised step.

This won't devolve into some kind of riot. These people—save Big Jaw and his cronies—are better than this.

'*Quiet,*' he bellowed.

Surprisingly, people obeyed. Sheathing his sword, mainly to buy himself time because he had no idea what to say next, Nicolas looked out at the crowd.

The next words out of my mouth best be something bloody good.

'Look at yourselves,' he cried. 'Someone has *died* here, and you're all using it as an excuse to fight. A life was lost. That's something that should be mourned. This isn't the way to honour who this person was, or help catch his killer.' He hopped down from the crate and squeezed between the two crowds. 'You are all citizens of this city, people of Babylon. You live together, you work together. Come together now in grief, not anger. So many people have lost their lives to this murderer. Don't let his actions turn you against each other. Don't forget who you are.'

His eyes narrowed as Big Jaw stepped forward, puffing his chest out with pride—though where he found anything to be proud about was anyone's guess. All it really did was accentuate his large belly.

'You can stand there pleading for us all to *just be nice and get along* all you bleeding well like. I'll mourn when a human dies, not some subhuman half my size,' he sneered. 'Tell me when a hundred dwarfs are dead. Because that about equals one human li—'

And so history repeated itself. Before he knew what he was doing, Nicolas had hopped off of the crate and his fist was cracking the man right across his giant jaw. Luckily, he'd been punching wood all morning, so he barely registered the impact. At first, he was treated to a moment of pure pleasure as Big Jaw reeled backwards, before it turned to horror at what he'd just incited...again.

Shit.

There was a stunned silence as the man fell to the floor with an audible thud. A moment to process what had just occurred, and a moment to get angry about it. Then the two groups charged. And there he was, standing right between them.

Just as they clashed, Silva's strong hands gripped his arms and yanked him back behind the wall of watchmen. Beyond it, the city descended into violence.

'Well done,' the sergeant said with a deadpan expression.

'Sorry.'

His face softened a little. 'You only did what I wanted to do.'

That wasn't really any consolation when the streets had become a battle ground as angry people not only fought each other but began to take out their exasperation on the institutions that were failing them, such as the city watch. The crowd, which had now become a baying mob, pressed against the shield wall.

'Nicely done,' Shift told him with enthusiasm, Auron nodding in agreement. 'Someone needed to put that guy on his ass. Shame it wasn't me, but I'll take what I can get.'

'Form was poor though, kid,' the spirit added. 'You best not have wasted those hours of training.' He hadn't. He'd just gotten mad and hadn't wanted to waste a fancy punch on a middle-aged racist guy.

'All right, lads,' the sergeant shouted. 'Batons out and force them apart.'

With heaving effort, the watchmen pushed on their shields, forcing back the tide of bodies around them. When someone wouldn't budge or got too mouthy, encouragement was given via baton.

Nicolas was impressed with the efficiency with which the men of the city watch actually managed to part the crowds and take control of the area.

The real problem was that the crowds then decided to move to another part of the city to continue their fight.

CHAPTER 43

Nicolas was still dumbstruck as he walked up the last few steps toward Greer's manor. With each step, his jellified legs threatened to betray him and let him fall. His arms were like heavy logs attached to the sides of his body. The only thing that seemed to be working right was his nose, which still caught the lingering scent of burning in the air. There wasn't even a breeze. It was as if his nose had held the smell so tightly he'd never forget what he'd wrought that night.

Once the crowd had realised they weren't getting any satisfaction by the bridge with the city watch hanging around and keeping them in check, they'd moved to the adjoining streets. Before Auron could say, *'So this one time...'* a full-blown riot had broken out. Chances were taken to settle scores and push agendas. Some of the more opportunistic citizens indulged in a bit of looting to get some free stuff. Several buildings were even set alight, which he guessed was done on purpose to help spread the chaos. It was almost like a beacon to let everyone know that order was starting to crumble in their city.

But it hadn't. Nicolas had been amazed by the efficiency of the city watch. Greer had arrived with reinforcements just as the riot took hold, pausing only briefly to throw a few choice cuss words at Nicolas, before taking charge of the situation. The riot scene had been cordoned off within minutes then it had been a matter of retaking those streets where civilians had forgotten they were civilised. This required the liberal use of batons and shields. Once the streets were clear, firefighters got to work containing the blazes before they spread.

It had taken a few hours to quell the last of the rioters and fires. A few very violent hours. Nicolas had seen some things, especially about the nature of people in crisis, that he'd not cared to see. What he hadn't seen was Big Jaw and his cronies. They'd vanished as soon as the riot started.

Why would they hang around? Their work was done...once they'd set their little fires, of course.

There'd been one miracle in the night, however. No one—save the poor dwarf—had died. The nearest Healer's Temple was packed to the rafters, as was the nearest jail, but there'd been no fatalities.

Like Nicolas, his companions were numb. Even Auron and Shift were quiet. Silva had retreated into herself. Nicolas guessed setting about civilians wasn't something she ever wanted to do again. When he did catch her eye, he tried to give the warrior a reassuring smile, but Silva's eyes instantly went back to the middle distance and whatever her mind was projecting there.

Ahead of him, beside the door, the guards stood to attention. Since they'd been posted, there'd been an unspoken understanding. Greer had placed them at his manor as a warning to ensure Nicolas and his companions didn't cause any trouble.

He'd need a lot more men to keep me out of trouble.

Forcing what smile he could, he saluted the men. It wasn't returned. Word had obviously reached them about what had happened.

After opening the door to the manor with what seemed like a ridiculous amount of effort considering the elderly butler did it single-handed, the group entered, heading straight for the drawing room. Nicolas made it to the chair with just a single step of energy left before slumping into it heavily. Laying his head back, he stared up at the elegantly carved details on the ceiling.

'That was...' He had no actual words.

'It certainly was,' Auron agreed. As Nicolas turned his head, the spirit walked over to the window and looked out of it. 'I didn't realise exactly how on the edge this city was.'

'Perhaps they do need an army to come in and keep the peace,' Shift suggested.

The spirit turned and looked at them seriously. 'That army we saw isn't about keeping the peace. That force is there just to push an agenda. If they march into the city, things will become a thousand times worse, I can guarantee it.'

Nicolas stifled a yawn; it was inappropriate given the seriousness of his companion's words. He rubbed his eyes, surprised when he took his hands away from his face that they were black from the smoke he'd been wading through at several points in the night. Realising how dirty he must be, he quickly got out of Commander Greer's nice chair. His legs nearly betrayed him as he stood, but he managed it.

For a moment, he was going to go to Silva, who'd sat herself in the corner of the room with her back to the group, but Shift's hand stopped him. He translated the look the shapeshifter gave him as *'give her some time.'*

Instead, he walked to the window and looked out. A telltale glow on the horizon spoke of at least one fire still being fought.

'Was that my fault?'

'Technically, yes,' Shift said bluntly. 'But you didn't start anything that wasn't going to start anyway.'

That wasn't the answer he'd wanted to hear, and he felt himself sink into the floor. 'I'm sorry.'

Shift got up with the noise usually reserved for old men rising then walked over to him and touched their forehead to his.

Do I even deserve this?

Pulling back, they kept hold of him whilst looking him in the eye. 'That thick-jawed fool deserved his punch at the tavern, and he deserved it here. They'd blatantly come there to start the riot and weren't going anywhere until they did. You just threw the first punch.'

'Do you think they're in league with the demon?' he asked. Everything about the staged scene and them turning up to stir the pot was a little to convenient for his liking.

'Interesting theory,' Auron said as he stared into the night. 'That would suggest that this is all premediated. Which means...'

'Maestro,' Shift whispered venomously.

'I just wish there was a way to be sure.' Even Nicolas could see the pattern emerging. So far in his adventuring life, wherever trouble was, it would lead back to the same person. But he couldn't just assume that was the case here, as this could be unrelated evil. Still though, if the Maestro was behind this, then that'd make Big Jaw one of his minions, which might mean he knew something about where his people were.

'I don't fancy trying to make the demon talk when we catch it,' Shift began. 'But I'm sure Si...one of us can get Big Jaw to talk.' They cast a wary glance over at Silva, but the warrior made no sign she was even listening.

'Good luck finding him.' Auron chuckled. 'He and his cronies were there to instigate, then vanish. Now they've played their hand, they'll go to ground. Focusing on the demon would be the best plan.'

Shift suddenly laughed.

'What?' Nicolas asked. That sound really had no place here and now.

'Just the irony of it,' the shapeshifter said, shaking their head. 'You stop me from going for Big Jaw just to do it yourself.'

'Difference is, you likely would've turned into a tiger and torn him to shreds. I just punched him.'

'True enough,' Shift replied thoughtfully.

'Something else that's true is that you need to work on your self-control, kid,' Auron chided.

'I know.' Shame made him lower his head. 'I just...There are so many people I *can't* protect that...well, to hear him saying those things, I just...'

Shift put a hand under his chin and tenderly, bringing his eyes up to theirs. 'We understand, you know,' they said. 'You've lost so much. Not being able to save these people yet—even from themselves—must be driving you mad.'

True enough. Evil was weaving it's way across Etherius, and the true source of it was constantly eluding him. Having some tangible bad guy in front of him that he could actually punch...well, it'd caused him to be more than a little lax in the self-control department. He resolved to do better.

'For what it's worth, kid,' Auron said, 'You're a better man than me. I wouldn't have stopped with one punch.' Strangely, that was a small consolation.

'We do need to stop this,' Nicolas said. 'We need to find that demon.'

'It's definitely getting more urgent by the day.' Even Shift cast a wary glance out the window.

Out in the hallway, the manor door burst open.

'Where are they?' an angry voice bellowed.

Stomping feet preceded Lord Commander Greer, followed meekly by Sergeant Tallith.

'*You!*' the lord commander roared, pointing an accusing finger at Nicolas. 'You moron.' A human storm swept upon him as Greer covered the distance in a few strides, grabbing him by his shirt collar. 'You started a riot, you little *idiot.*'

'That was going to start with or without us,' Shift argued. 'Those guys came there to start trouble.'

Nice to see them leap to defend my honour occasionally too.

'Of course they did,' Greer scoffed. 'That's what they do. What you *aren't* supposed to do is throw the first bloody punch and start a shitshow like the one we've spent the night containing.' Shift went to retort but was cut off as Greer continued his rant. 'And you know what would've happened if I hadn't contained it? That so called *peacekeeping* force would be marching in here sometime this afternoon and the whole area would go straight to the Underworld.'

'But the riot was contained,' Shift replied sternly.

'Yes, it was,' Greer replied. 'Because I'm bloody good at my job, which is why I don't need you lot walking around causing trouble. I told you that if you stepped out of line, I'd have you arrested, and I'd say starting a riot certainly qualifies.' Greer clicked his fingers, and six watchmen entered the room, four of them holding shackles. 'So by the power vested in me by the city of Babylon, I hereby place you all under arrest.' A small smile broke out from beneath the moustache. 'I hope you love the hole I'm about to throw you into, because you're going to be in it for a very long time.'

'No, wait, you can't—' Nicolas began to protest.

'Yes, I can actually,' the lord commander replied. 'Resist arrest. I dare you.'

'I won't,' he said, holding up his hands. 'I did it. I started the riot. Take me in. Not them. They were just trying to help.'

Hopefully, the jail's nicer than the other ones I've visited before.

'Kid, this isn't the time to fall on your sword,' Auron cautioned as Greer grinned.

'Duncan?' the lord commander's wife glanced around in confusion as she entered the room, still wrapping her robe around her. 'What's going on? Are you arresting our guests?'

'Bloody right I am,' Greer snapped. 'Please stay out of this, Beba.'

'Sir, he didn't mean to—'

'And you can be quiet,' the lord commander snarled at Sergeant Tallith. 'You were supposed to be watching them. If I *only* put you on report, you should consider yourself lucky.'

'I...well, sir... You summoned me back to the Watch House, but when I arrived, you weren't there,' Sergeant Tallith answered nervously.

'What?' Greer scoffed. 'I did no such thing.'

'But the note came with your seal, so I thought—'

'Never mind,' the lord commander interrupted, rubbing the bridge of his nose. 'I suppose I should be thankful. Without you watching them, they went and got themselves in plenty of trouble, and now I can end this farce.' Greer looked back at Nicolas's companions.

The lord commander opened his mouth again, most likely to continue admonishing him, when the noise of the manor door being flung aside and urgent footsteps coming toward them got their attention.

'Make way for Governor Morrow.'

CHAPTER 44

Governor Morrow strode confidently into the room as if it were her own house—which Nicolas imagined was standard wherever she went. Chamberlain Basch followed dutifully in her wake, pursued by the sound of his long robe dragging along the carpet. The old chamberlain seemed grave, whereas the governor could've been happy, angry, sad...suffering from indigestion. Who knew?

Please emote, just a little.

'Lord Commander Greer,' she began as she took in the scene calmly. 'Am I to take it you intend to arrest those I deputised?'

'Yes, Governor.' Greer's tone was like an angry dog growling, ready to be challenged.

'May I ask why?'

'Because they stirred up a bloody hornets' nest,' Greer growled. 'There was another murder. A dwarf named Longshanks. A crowd had gathered and was starting to get restless. Insults were being hurled. That's when he...' Cue accusatory finger pointing at Nicolas. '...decides the best way to help the situation is to punch someone. The idiot boy went and incited a riot, one I had to put down. There was extensive property damage and injury.' The lord commander's voice rose with each passing word, to the point he had to pause, take a breath and collect himself before he was screaming. 'I knew these people were mercenaries, and now they've proven it. They will pay for the damage they've wrought.' The brief account was punctuated by many dramatic hand gestures, enough that Auron appeared impressed by the storytelling.

With the very faintest of eyebrow raises, the governor turned to Nicolas. 'Is the lord commander's account accurate?'

'Yes.'

'But omits key details,' Shift scoffed, standing between him and the governor. 'He punched the leader of a group who'd specifically been there to incite the riot. Maybe they were even linked to the killings.'

'Based on?' Morrow asked leadingly.

'They claimed to have run there when they heard about the murder,' Shift said, their tone calming. 'But there was no sign of exertion. Men that out of shape sweat walking to take a dump.'

'That logic is thin, at best.' Greer grunted.

'It's all connected,' Nicolas said, hanging his head. 'Someone's stirring up trouble in your city. Why else put the dwarf on display like that? They wanted a riot. I just...played into their hands.'

'We think Councillor Geldheart is involved.' Nicolas stared at Shift. Maybe right now wasn't the best time to go throwing accusations at city councillors. They were in enough trouble as it was.

'Reasoning?' Governor Morrow asked.

'He keeps appearing and making vaguely menacing remarks,' Shift replied, evidently less confident of their position.

'That, I believe, is his only character trait,' Chamberlain Basch said with a knowing sigh.

'He told us to leave town,' Nicolas said. 'And that very night, the tavern we slept in burnt down. That's an odd coincidence.'

'Geldheart had your tavern burnt down?' Beba asked with a frown.

Governor Morrow considered this for a moment. 'I suppose, objectively, if this city were to fall into chaos, it would serve his goal of allowing that army access.'

'Geldheart's always been a shrewd player,' Basch interjected. 'It is just as likely he's using events he isn't part of to push his agenda. That doesn't necessarily mean he tried to kill you.'

Now Nicolas was saying it aloud, it did seem ridiculous. But a cow-dragon was ridiculous, yet he'd seen one. Ridden on it, in fact.

'Maybe we ought to leave suppositions for a later date,' Morrow said, taking a seat. 'The city has more pressing matters tonight. Ones that will lead to an emergency session of the city council in the morning. I cannot stand before them with simple theories. Time is running out, more swiftly than you know.'

'What do you mean?' Shift asked.

The governor fixed Nicolas with a firm gaze. 'I refer to a key detail you didn't tell me. One that makes me think you belong in those shackles.' From behind her cape, she pulled out a rolled-up piece of parchment and handed it to Nicolas. He already knew what it was, but he still went to the trouble of unfurling it. 'I take it that *is* you on the wanted poster?'

'Yes,' he admitted quietly. 'But I didn't do it.'

Greer snatched the poster from him and stared at it in disbelief. 'I bloody knew it,' he cried. 'I knew you were trouble.' Rolling up the parchment, the lord commander looked at him with a satisfied grin. 'It's the cell for you, boy...'

'It is too late for that.' Though Morrow spoke quietly, something in her tone made Greer's face drop. 'The Nalbians already know he's here, and that I deputised him and his companions. The poster came with a letter. We have two days to surrender you and allow the *peacekeeping* force access to the city to restore order.'

'Looks like you worried Geldheart enough to carry out his threat,' Auron mused. 'I didn't think he'd have the guts.' The spirit caught Nicolas's sour expression. 'Take it as a compliment, kid. It means you're definitely on the right track.'

Oh yes. This is the day for self-congratulation.

Chamberlain Basch stared out of the window at the city beyond. Not that he could see much at night. 'If we don't agree to their terms, they will march to the gate anyway—'

'And find it closed,' the governor cut in firmly. 'I will not have the neutrality of this city tarnished. But now that we are harbouring a wanted criminal *and* have an issue with civil disorder, they won't take no for an answer. They will try to force their way in, and blood will be spilt. They will summon reinforcements. The others on the council will summon their own forces, and things will escalate to the point where the city will likely be burnt to ash.'

A justifiably tense silence descended on the room.

We didn't have much time to begin with, and I go halving it by starting a riot. Why couldn't I control my damn fist?

Though, if Geldheart was here right now, he'd likely lose control over it again.

'So tell me,' Governor Morrow began, 'what do you have so far?'

Theories.

'There's a demon loose in the city,' Shift told the governor. 'It's behind the murders. Most of the bodies are just hosts it's used up.'

'A demon?' Morrow repeated. 'Then it could be anyone.'

'We know the first victim was really Professor Shaw's apprentice, who had an interest in the occult,' Nicolas added.

'And?'

'That's about all,' he replied, his voice trailing off to a mumble.

If Nicolas could've classified the look Governor Morrow was giving him, it would've been *ice cold*.

'I deputised you in the hope you would somehow bring an end to this chaos. Thus far, the sum total of your efforts has been to start a riot and give the army outside our walls an excuse to march on us.'

'I am so sorry,' Nicolas said quickly. 'Believe me, if I could take it back, I would.'

The first part was truer than the second. He'd gotten an odd thrill from punching Big Jaw in the face. It was as if justice was being served.

Nicolas started as the governor grabbed his chin and pulled his head up so it was facing her. 'Did you do it?' she asked firmly.

'No,' he answered instantly. 'I tried to stop the assassination, and they ended up thinking I was the culprit.'

'Always in the wrong place at the wrong time.' Greer sneered.

'Enough,' Morrow told the lord commander before turning back to Nicolas. 'Let us be clear. Under other circumstances, I would be more than happy to have the lord commander arrest you. But the tales I've heard of you do not match up to this accusation, and because of what occurred during the night, I need every able body I can get. Assuming you have no intention of creating havoc again?'

'No, Governor,' he said firmly. It was a promise he hoped he could keep.

'Can you find this demon?' Basch asked gravely.

'We believe so. We have a spell—'

'That has already failed,' Lord Commander Greer added.

'It might be able to track the demon...if it works.'

Governor Morrow pondered this, holding her hands behind her back. 'Time is running out. And this creature could be anyone in the city. We don't have time to go door-to-door searching for it.'

Nicolas looked around the room and realised they were missing some-one, someone who was very important to the spell.

'Where's Garaz?' he asked. 'He can't still be asleep.'

'If he was, I'm sure we'd hear him,' Auron remarked glibly, already walking out of the room. 'I'll fetch him.'

'Lord Commander,' Morrow began, 'is there anything more we can do?'

Greer rubbed his face and sighed. 'The watch is stretched as it is keeping the peace. Our only hope is to get lucky.' He cast an annoyed glance at Nicolas. 'Or this spell.'

Nicolas blinked a few times in surprise. Was Greer possessed too?

I think that's about as supportive as he gets.

'What happens when we find this demon?' Basch asked with concern. 'I have limited knowledge on such things, but I'm given to believe they are powerful.'

'We give it steel,' Silva remarked from the corner of the room.

'A direct approach.' It was hardly surprising that Governor Morrow favoured directness.

'But there is still the issue of proof,' the chamberlain continued. 'We need a tangible killer, with evidence. If we just cry demon, there will be questions, doubts.'

'Killing it comes first. Proof second,' Silva said firmly as she rose. 'We cannot take risks with a creature like—'

'Up here, hurry.' Auron's panicked voice cut into the conversation. 'Something's wrong with Garaz.'

CHAPTER 45

The sense of wrongness hit him before he even entered Garaz's room. Inwardly, Nicolas cursed himself. He should have known something was wrong earlier when Silva mentioned that she'd checked on Garaz but that he wasn't snoring. The orc might've been wise and sophisticated to the point of snobbery, but he also snored like a thousand lumberjacks sawing...every darned night. Somehow, they'd all become accustomed to it on their travels, which was good, because Shift had threatened to suffocate the orc in his sleep more than once.

When they reached the landing, the door was already ajar. Upon Auron's call, Silva had bounded up the stairs with speed. Already, the warrior was stooped over Garaz, shaking him.

'*Get up!*' she commanded.

If I'm beating myself up about this, she must feel...

'I said *wake*,' Silva roared, striking the orc's green cheek with an impassioned smack that echoed around the room.

There was no response. The orc simply slept. Garaz appeared peaceful at a glance, laid atop the fine linen sheet of the four-poster bed. Anyone who didn't know the orc better would think everything was well.

'Come on, Garaz, wake up,' he pleaded, having his own try at rousing the orc via the liberal application of shaking.

'If Silva can't rouse him, you won't, kid,' Auron said quietly from beside the bed.

'Why won't he wake up?' Nicolas asked. 'What's wrong with him?'

'Beba,' Lord Commander Greer called from the doorway, 'please see what you can do.'

Nicolas raised a questioning eyebrow as the lady of the house ran into the room.

'I was a healer once,' she said, answering his unasked question.

As Nicolas stood back, she began to look the orc over.

'It's actually how Duncan and I met,' she continued as she worked. 'Back in his hero days.'

'Beba...' Greer said with warning.

'His star was on the rise, you know.' Apparently, his wife wasn't going to pay his warning any heed. 'Right up until some idiot misused magic.'

Is this really relevant? Should she not be concentrating on what she's doing?

Or maybe she was doing it *for* them, to take their minds from the worry he was most definitely feeling right now. He'd already lost his parents. To lose another member of his family would be too much.

Stop being so bloody self-absorbed.

This wasn't about him; this was about Garaz. The orc was clearly breathing, so he wasn't dead. Yet he wouldn't rise. Nicolas began to understand what Shift must've felt like when he'd died.

I may even kiss Garaz if we can wake him.

Staring at the orc's unnaturally calm body, Nicolas found himself willing him to rise, to suddenly sit up and go, *'Why are you all stood around my bed?'*

'Someone gets a little bit of power, and they assume they can just control it,' Beba continued as she worked. 'Never mind bothering to learn to use it properly.' Delicately, she pulled back Garaz's eyelids. Closing them again, she turned to the group. 'He's been cursed.'

'Cursed?' Nicolas cried. 'By what?'

Silva drew her sword. '*By whom* is the better question.'

Oh dammit, she's right.

Within an instant, Nicolas had drawn the *Dawn Blade*.

'Damnation,' Greer cussed, turning from the doorway and disappearing. Even though the lord commander was out of sight, his bellowed orders carried to their ears. 'Lock down the estate. We may have an intruder.' This command caused a chain of alarmed shouts to break out, followed by the sound of armoured men running to and fro.

With a frustrated growl, Silva sheathed her blade again. 'Whoever did this is long gone. I checked on Garaz hours ago, and he was just like this. I just didn't th—'

'None of us would have,' Nicolas said, putting a hand on the warrior's shoulder. 'You weren't to know.'

Silva bucked his hand away. 'I have trained myself to know better,' she snarled, before striding over to the nearest window and opening it. 'Scratches on the outside of the frame,' she told the group. 'Someone got in here.'

'Up the side of the building? With the grounds patrolled?' Shift asked thoughtfully. 'That takes some impressive speed and agility.'

'That rules out Geldheart,' Silva remarked. 'He is too old to scale the side of the manor. Unless...'

'He used *supernatural* speed and agility,' Auron said grimly, just as two watchmen appeared and took guard positions either side of the door. The spirit's brow furrowed deeply.

'What is it?' Nicolas asked.

'He...he shouldn't be alive,' the spirit said hesitantly. 'Anyone who snuck in here could've just killed him. Why go to the trouble of cursing him?'

That was a good point. As happy as he was that Garaz was still alive, bothering with a curse was a lot more effort than using a knife.

'What did Auron say?' Governor Morrow asked, clearly reading the room correctly.

'He's wondering why they just didn't kill Garaz,' Nicolas answered.

'Your companion must have been targeted because of the spell he had attempted to used to locate the demon,' Basch suggested. 'But I am at a loss to explain why they would not just kill him. Thinking on it, why bother when the spell failed? And how did they even know about it?'

The implication of that question was worrying. It meant they were being watched. Though Nicolas could easily imagine that someone like Geldheart had eyes everywhere.

'Maybe the killer is saving him...for later.' Nicolas's head snapped around, and Sergeant Tallith shrank under his glare. 'It's just an idea.'

Nicolas's body sagged. It was. And it was probably right too. But questions nagged at him, ones he couldn't answer. It didn't make sense. What worse fate was in store for their companion? Maybe it was happening already, the curse killing him slowly in his sleep.

The room became blurred for a moment. Adrenaline, uncertainty and fear were hitting him, disorienting him.

I cannot lose Garaz. I just cannot. I...will not.

Forcing his body back into line, he tightened his grip on the hilt of the *Dawn Blade*. 'We need to search the grounds for clues, tracks, anything,' he snapped, already running out of the room and towards the stairs.

****

A half hour later, he made his way back up those same stairs, despair wrapped around him like a warm cloak. There'd been nothing. No sign of any intruder, beyond the scratches on the window frame. Not a footprint, nor a slightly bent twig. His tracking skills were about as impressive as a dwarf's ability to jump high, but even Auron and Silva had found nothing. Shift had changed form to a dog but picked up no unusual scents.

How is that possible? Can the demon float from branch to branch?

For a moment, he saw the open door to Garaz's room and didn't want to approach it. Right now, for all he knew, Garaz could be up and well...

Or he could be worse. Standing here hoping will really help nothing.

With laboured steps, he approached the door, his heart sinking when he saw the orc's sleeping body lying exactly where he'd left it. Beba was in the process of lighting candles, walking around the bed to get to the ones on the other side with her taper.

A pang of pain struck him. He'd lost his parents, and that was still raw, despite his ability to push it back. Garaz like this was just a stark reminder of how fragile the people in his life were.

As if I need it, in this city.

'Any change?' he asked, more for something to say.

Beba shook her head sadly. 'I've called out to the nearest Healer's Temple, and the Magic Guild. Hopefully, someone will come soon who can help better than I can.'

A slight light behind him made him turn. 'How do you remove curses?' he asked the figure who'd entered the room.

'Quickest way, in my experience, is to kill the curser...the one who cursed...the—'

'I don't care about the terminology,' he snapped.

Auron returned his glare calmly. 'Kid, I understand. But you need to calm down. You aren't helping him like this.'

'Who *do* I help?' he spat bitterly.

The spirit folded his arms. 'Would you like me to actually list them? I'm sure Sergeant Tallith could assist with that.'

'Sorry.'

'Pfft, don't worry about it, kid.' Auron smiled. 'I'm pissed too. But I've had years of training to keep it from overcoming me...' The spirit eyed Silva as she walked through the door. 'Doesn't always work, mind you.'

He almost jumped as a hand touched his. Fighting his urge to yank it back, he stared at Beba.

'He's as comfortable as I can make him,' she said softly. 'You can do no more here.'

I really can't, can I?

Right now, there were so many potential paths he could walk, ways he could go next. It was almost as if he could see multiple doors in front of him. But which one to choose? Only one led to the end of all this, and the time he had to pick the right one was running out. He could picture the Nalbian army beginning to break camp, getting ready to march on the city.

With a single forlorn look at his stricken companion, Nicolas left the room and made his way back down the stairs. As he reached the entrance hall, he looked at all the doors around him. Which one should he take?

'Nicolas.'

Summoned by the voice, he entered the drawing room, where Governor Morrow sat with Lord Commander Greer, Chamberlain Basch, and Sergeant Tallith. Morrow watched him enter and beckoned for him to sit down. Sitting suggested resting, and he had no time for that, so he stayed standing.

'How is he?' the governor asked.

'The same.'

'To come here, to the lord commander's home' Basch said quietly. 'This creature is getting more brazen.'

'My wife was here,' Greer snarled.

'It is becoming more brazen because it believes it is winning,' Morrow said firmly. 'Whatever design it is working must be coming to fruition, and we cannot allow that.'

Can I even do anything to stop it?

'So,' Morrow said, her grey eyes firmly locked on his. 'What are you to do about it?'

'Me?'

'Yes, you.' The governor rose and walked over to him. 'The tales I've heard tell of an exceptional young man with a knack for stopping evil schemes. That is why I gave you a badge. Despite evidence to the contrary, the demon believes you can interfere. Why else burn down the tavern you slept in and subdue your companion. So, what are you going to do about it?'

'Geldheart,' he whispered.

'Cannot be touched without firm evidence,' Chamberlain Basch cautioned. 'If you do, you may as well light the city aflame yourself.'

So what then? All we know is where this began and...

There was almost an audible *click* in his head. Suddenly, all the doors merged together into one. It was the only one, their only option.

'Professor Shaw's apprentice is where this began,' Nicolas said, almost talking to himself. 'We need to go back to Shaw's and turn the place over for more evidence. Question the guards too. If they're any good at their jobs, they would notice someone sneaking out to summon demons or engaging in arcane rituals. Someone there *must* know something.' He tilted his head to look past the governor, at Lord Commander Greer. 'Is that going to be a problem?' It was a challenge, not a question.

'No,' Greer said. 'You do what you must. I need to go and prepare in case...we have an army at our gates.' The lord commander was about to leave the room when he stopped, half turning back to them. 'Thinking on it, I will write you a warrant for Shaw's. I know how difficult his guards can be. My seal will open the door like a battering ram. Tallith, with me.'

The lord commander left with his sergeant at his heels.

Governor Morrow put a hand on Nicolas's shoulder and leant in close. 'I chose you for this task, and I am rarely wrong. Go and save this city.'

Chosen again.

With a nod, he strode out into the hallway, checking that the *Dawn Blade* would unsheathe quickly when he needed it.

'You're ready for a fight?' Shift asked, tilting their head toward his blade as they entered the manor.

'We're going to Shaw's,' Nicolas told his companion. 'We're going to kick the gate in, and anyone who gets in our way be damned. We aren't leaving until we find something.'

'Suits me,' Silva said on the stairway.

'Kid, you make me so proud when you display your big adventurers balls.' Auron smiled.

'Poor choice of words,' Nicolas retorted quickly.

'Ooh, we're going to stop playing nice.' Shift grinned, rubbing their hands together. 'Sounds like fun.' It was only now he noticed the shapeshifter had a very familiar pair of knives in their belt.

Oh, for Deities' sake.

The shapeshifter caught his look and smirked. 'He shouldn't have told me not to touch them.'

'I have to go back there you know.'

All he got in response was a shrug which seemed to indicate that was very much his problem, and not theirs.

Truthfully, he had neither the time nor inclination to argue about it. Instead, he turned toward the stairs. On the landing above, Beba gazing at him with a half-smile. 'Go. I will tend to Garaz. You have my word.'

And this city has my word that the demon dies.

CHAPTER 46

With determination, the group progressed down the city's cobbled streets. Several times, the others overtook Sergeant Tallith, who was supposed to be leading them, and the young watchman had to redouble his efforts to stay ahead of those he was guiding. Other than them, the streets were quiet. After the riot, people were becoming too worried to leave their homes, even in the daytime. Whatever time of day it was. Time had sort of escaped Nicolas of late.

'One time, I would like to go somewhere with you that's just...nice,' Shift said as they walked. 'Just to visit, not to fight this or that.'

'When this is all over, we can go find one together.'

Nicolas chuckled to himself. Would this ever be over? Even when they found the demon, would it be a link to the Maestro, to Koth? In all this chaos, it was easy to lose sight of why they'd come here in the first place. To find his people. Would they be any closer when they left? Or would they now forever bounce from quest to quest, never finding the answers he needed? Part of him wished he was home, messing about with Potter. But that wasn't to be. This was his life now.

May the Oracle shove the Choosing Stick into his most uncomfortable orifice.

'We're going to have to take a slightly different route,' Sergeant Tallith said as he led the group. 'Some of the streets we went through yesterday are still potential trouble spots that Commander Greer wants kept clear.' It seemed not everyone was staying home then.

'I think the whole city's a trouble spot,' Auron remarked for their ears. 'Now's not the time to be picky.'

That was a concern. But they had Silva with them, and judging by the look on her face, it'd be best for people to stay out of her way. His too, truth be told. No more messing around; there were answers to be found at the professor's manor. He hoped.

Whoa.

Nicolas had to stop suddenly as Sergeant Tallith came to a screeching halt. 'Dammit.'

'What?' he asked the officer.

Sheepishly, Tallith turned around, patting his uniform. 'I...I must've left the warrant back at the manor.'

'You did *what*?' Silva hissed.

'I'm sorry.' Tallith flushed bright red. 'I was going to pick it up, but I was talking to Lady Greer and...forgot it.'

'You'd best go back and get it,' Nicolas suggested. It was hard to be angry at Tallith. The young sergeant already looked as if he'd just told his parents he wanted to give up a promising career in the priesthood to become a male prostitute.

I suppose he knows he's disappointed someone he...urgh...looks up to.

'Okay.' Tallith nodded, pointedly not looking Nicolas in the eye. 'I will be back as quickly as I can. If you go on ahead, then I'll meet you at the manor.'

'Which way?' Silva asked.

Though he was clearly flustered, the sergeant gave them a series of turns to take to get them where they needed to go. Nicolas got lost after the third left, but he knew Silva and Auron were great at this kind of thing, so he let them take in whatever directions he'd miss.

With that, the young man left them. To his credit, at least he was sprinting.

'Are we really going to just wait at the gate when we arrive at the manor?' Silva asked as Tallith disappeared around a corner.

'You don't think we should wait for the warrant?' Nicolas asked.

The warrior inclined her head slightly. 'Garaz is cursed. The city is on the brink. Shaw's manor may have the answers we seek and time is short.'

'C'mon, Nick,' Shift said, slapping him on the back. 'It's better to ask forgiveness than permission.'

'I doubt Greer is the forgiving type.' Nicolas stared in the direction Tallith had gone. Who knew when he'd be back? 'To the Underworld with it,' he declared finally. 'Let's go.'

'That's the stuff, kid.' Auron smiled. 'I've got all the directions, so I'll lead.'

Moving swiftly, the group made their way through the city of Babylon, Auron leading them. After a few main streets, the spirit directed them to a side alley off the main thoroughfare. It was big enough to be a street in its own right but was obviously less well travelled. Debris littered it, and thick walls obscured it from those around. It was cobbled and rough, filled with potholes, one of which appeared to have caught a victim. Along one wall, two men were hunched over the broken wheel of a straw wagon. The donkey pulling it munched a piece of straw patiently as the men went about their work. Across from them, a pair of beggars watched the men, little brown bowls sat on the street in front of them.

They haven't picked a great place to sit to beg for coin.

'You see it too then, kid?' Auron asked beside him. 'What do you think? Trap?'

'Possibly,' he replied, hand resting on the hilt of his sword. He doubted the watch was too fond of beggars on the main streets. That didn't sound like something Greer would tolerate at all. So it did make sense they would be here, where they had a smaller chance of getting arrested, even if they only made a little coin.

'Keep walking and talking,' the spirit counselled. 'But keep your eyes open and senses sharp.'

None of the others answered. If it was a trap, then it was best not to give away that they were aware of it. But Nicolas knew Shift and Silva were as prepared as he was.

'Do you think the professor knows more than he's telling?' Nicolas asked as they continued down the alleyway.

'Hard to say,' Auron answered. 'He was sweaty and a bit standoffish. But it was hot in the room, and scientists don't always make social folk.'

'If he does, he will talk,' Silva said simply.

'We'll find something,' Shift added firmly. 'We have to. There's a whole city at stake. And...'

Nicolas knew the end of that sentence. Garaz. Shift was many things, but comfortable with being vulnerable wasn't one of them. They weren't at Silva's level, thank the Deities, but close. His mind briefly wandered to Garaz, lying on his bed, looking peaceful but being anything but. They had to help him.

As the group passed the donkey, Nicolas readied himself. Adrenaline ran through his veins as his body prepared for a fight, should one come. If this *was* a trap, then their potential attackers weren't giving away anything.

Which means nothing. It'd be a pointless trap if they made it too obvious.

'We will find something,' he said casually, keeping the men kneeling by the wagon in his field of vision. 'We aren't leaving until—'

Time slowed to a crawl as he noticed the hilt of a sword sticking out from beneath the bottom of the wagon and the fingers wrapped around it to draw it from its sheath. The old Nicolas would've frozen on the spot. This Nicolas instantly kicked down on the man's elbow, driving the arm forward and forcing the sword back into its sheath.

'Ambush,' he cried, the *Dawn Blade* already half drawn.

Even with the element of surprise, four against four...three...is bad odds. Why—

Before he had a chance to finish his thought, the straw in the back of the wagon bulged upwards, before exploding in all directions to reveal three crossbowmen, who were already bringing their weapons to bear.

Again, Nicolas acted instead of reacting. Jumping forward, he slapped the flat side of his blade on the ass's...ass, with a meaty *thwack*. The donkey cried out in surprise, rearing and trying to bolt forward. The wagon shook violently, and three crossbow bolts missed their marks as aims were thrown off and the men stumbled, cursing. Silva flashed past him.

The clash of blades got his attention. Shift was breaking in their newly stolen knives, using them to fend off the second attacker, who was swinging his blade wildly. As he was moving to help his companion, he stopped suddenly. The first attacker was turning again, rising to meet him, knife in hand. His left hand being closer to the man than his right, he punched the attacker in the face.

'*Ow,*' he cried, blowing on his fist. 'Deities damn it, what the...'

His words trailed off as he looked on the face of his attacker. Except it wasn't a face. It was a mask: a leering, demonic visage of a man. He knew that mask, he'd seen it before on other warriors sent to kill him.

The Maestro's men.

With a snarl, the man thrust the knife at him. Nicolas deftly side-stepped it then swung the *Dawn Blade*. The man ducked the attack. Thinking quickly, Nicolas drove his knee into the squatting man's chin, sending him crashing to the ground. Within an instant, the man was scrabbling for another blade on his belt. Raising his sword, Nicolas intended to stop him.

Urk.

Staggering backwards, he dropped his sword, both hands flashing to his neck, fingers scrabbling and clawing at the leather strap that had just been secured around his neck.

The beggars.

Already, he was struggling to breathe. The edges of his vision blurred as he fought to alleviate the pressure on his neck. He caught a glimpse of Shift, similarly assailed, the man holding their strap shaking his companion like a rag doll.

Noooooo.

'Finger poke of doom.'

With a cry, the assassin attacking Shift stumbled backwards, clutching his eye. The spirit picked up a stone and flung it directly at the head of his attacker. There was a *ping* of stone on metal, and a curse. For a second, the strap loosened, and he curled his fingers around it, gasping in what air he could. It was momentary.

Tightening again, the strap—or its holder—dragged him backwards. Nicolas was already half conscious. What could he do?

Something I won't be very proud of and may never live down.

Struggling to breathe, he forced words from his mouth.

'That'sssss...it... Harderrrrr...yessssss...that'ssss how I like ittttttt...'

The strap slackened again. 'You what?' cried an appalled voice behind him. 'You sick little—'

Using all the energy he could muster, Nicolas thrust his elbow back into the attacker's stomach. With an *oof*, the attacker staggered backwards, and the strap loosened more. Grabbing it, Nicolas yanked the strap from the assassin's grasp and flung it to the floor. He then struck behind him again, flinging his elbow in an upward arc until it connected with his attacker's jaw.

Falling to all fours, he hacked and coughed, his lungs greedily sucking in precious air like a traveller lost in a desert sucks up water from an oasis. Reality began to reassert itself.

Shaking his head, he saw the first attacker running at him, sword in hand. With a deep breath, he pushed himself off the floor, lunging forward and driving his shoulder into the man's stomach. With a cry, he continued, forcing the man into the side of the wagon with a crash. As the attacker's sword fell to the floor, Nicolas punched him twice in the gut, before yanking the mask off and delivering two hefty right hooks across the cheek.

He froze before delivering a third punch. 'It's you.' His voice was still hoarse due to the choking.

'Blood traitor,' Big Jaw snarled at him.

With an angry roar, Big Jaw lashed out with yet another knife. Using something he'd learned from Ban Dro—surprised as he was that he'd picked something up from the master so quickly—he grabbed the knife hand, guiding it as he parried the elbow until it was turned back on his attacker. Big Jaw squealed as his own knife pierced his flesh.

'Pillock,' Nicolas spat.

Footsteps made him turn. The fake beggar was running at him, knife in hand.

I've had enough of this.

Blocking the downward swing of the blade with his forearm, Nicolas struck the attacker beneath the jaw line with the ridge of his hand. The assassin's body juddered with the impact. Nicolas followed up with a blow to the same spot with the ridge of his other hand, before grabbing the assassin's head and using it as leverage to throw him against the wagon next to Big Jaw, who was weakly pawing at the knife in his gut. Nicolas decided to be helpful. With one quick tug, he pulled the knife out of Big Jaw and used it to cut the fake beggar's throat with a single slash. Both men collapsed to the ground, dead.

Good riddance.

Turning, he flipped the knife in his hand so he gripped it by the blade. With a flick of the wrist, he threw it. The blade sailed true, striking the second fake beggar right in the side of his neck, his sword locked between Shift's crossed knives. The man's hand fell away from the ruined eye he'd been clutching as he crumpled to the ground dead, giving Shift the chance to spin round and use their knives to send his final companion to meet him.

Nicolas's intention to check on his companions was stopped as a wagon rounded the corner at speed. Quickly, he scooped up his sword from the floor.

I know that wagon.

The fancy conveyance came to a screeching halt. The driver, a well-dressed man, jumped down from the seat and ran to the door. As it opened, a body fell out onto the road.

'What in the Underworld?' Shift exclaimed.

Oh crap.

He instantly recognised the body, despite the blood that covered it. Councillor Geldheart's shocked face stared him right in the eye. There was still a glimmer of life in him then it faded to nothing. Around him, he could see the ghosts of those he'd killed, and the one he hadn't. Each had a shocked expression as their forms slowly dissipated, until they'd vanished entirely.

Have fun, Sha'then.

'Get the driver,' Nicolas cried. 'We need him alive.'

The group ran toward the driver but came to a sudden halt as the man hurled a knife in their direction. Something was off. The weapon had been thrown from the flat of the blade, not launched to kill. The knife hit the ground near his feet. It was covered in fresh blood already.

What in the Underworld?

Before he could process what had happened, an ever more unexpected event occurred. The driver drew another knife from his belt and stabbed himself in the stomach.

'For humanity,' the man sneered, blood already trailing from his lips.

What?

Nicolas frowned. What exactly was going on here?

An urgent stomping of feet drew his attention to the other end of the alleyway.

'What in the Underworld happened here?' Lord Commander Greer cried as he came to a sudden stop, a troop of watchmen on his heels.

CHAPTER 47

All Nicolas could do was watch in stunned disbelief as the driver, clutching his freely bleeding stomach for dear life—which was ironic considering he'd just stabbed himself—hobbled towards the Lord Commander.

'Please, m'lord, help me,' the man cried desperately, blood drops marking his trail with each step. 'They blocked the road...shouted accusations...then they just started killing. The councillor is dead. His bodyguards are dead.' With a forlorn face, the man looked down at his own bleeding torso. 'And I'm dead.'

Those were his last words. The man fell to his knees then to the floor. Dead. Whatever drama teacher tutored him would've been immensely proud of the performance.

What?

Lord Commander Greer's face was stuck in a confounded expression as people began to gather at both ends of the alleyway. They hid in their homes in fear of a murderer, but when a bloody fight was fought on their doorsteps, they all came out to get the gossip afterwards. People murmured and gasped in horror. Nicolas couldn't hear much of it, but he heard, *'They killed Councillor Geldheart'* enough times to work that one out.

Shaking his head, Greer snapped to attention. 'Arrest them,' he bellowed to his men. 'They've murdered the councillor.'

Huh?

Blinking, Nicolas was suddenly back in the moment. A group of watchmen charging at him was a good incentive. 'Wait, no,' he cried, dropping his sword. 'This isn't what it looks like...'

How is this happening to me again?

The officers didn't care to listen. Instead, they surrounded the group, weapons ready and shouting commands.

'Drop your weapons.'

I did.

He quickly realised who they were talking to.

'Silva, do it,' he snapped quickly, before things got worse.

As he turned to the warrior, he caught a glimpse of Big Jaw.

The driver said they were his bodyguards...

A lot of things had just happened, and none of them made sense. When he'd seen Geldheart fall from his carriage, the councillor's face had been frozen in shock. He hadn't expected to die. But his driver knew his part. Most likely a contingency plan, if the ambush didn't work. Except the trap had been so obvious that it was doomed to fail, so...

The epiphany hit him like a lightning bolt.

'The men we killed weren't a trap,' he whispered numbly, staring at the mask Big Jaw had worn, which lay on the ground near his body. 'They were a sacrifice.'

And we played right into it.

'Kid...*kid*.' Auron's urgent cry got his attention. 'Do as they say.'

He'd had no intention of doing otherwise. The Maestro had truly out-witted them this time. With a finite *click*, metal shackles were secured to his wrists.

'What did you do?' Greer whispered in disgust as the lord commander stood over him.

'We didn't—'

'I should never have let you go running off after your companion was cursed.' Greer shook his head with frustration. 'I should've known this would happen. I let myself trust you.'

'Sir?'

'Where were you?' Greer bellowed at Tallith, who'd appeared on the scene.

The sergeant's face paled as he looked around him. 'I...had to go back and get the warrant. I forgot it.'

The lord commander looked like a volcano ready to erupt. 'You *forgot* it?' He held out his hand impatiently. 'Give it to me. I'm going to tear the bloody thing up, now these charlatans have shown their true colours.'

Tallith visibly gulped. 'I couldn't find it, sir.'

'You lost it?' Greer grabbed his nephew by the collar and hauled him close. 'You idiot. If you'd watched them like I told you, this would never have happened.'

Yes, it would. We would've been ambushed anyway. Tallith would've just been on the other side of the shackles, or dead.

Before the sergeant could speak, Greer shoved him away. 'Go and summon a prison wagon,' he snarled. 'We are taking this filth to jail.'

As Greer began shouting orders to push the crowd back and cordon off the scene, Nicolas looked at the others. Each appeared as dejected as he felt.

'It'll be all right, kid,' Auron said softly.

He glanced at the shackles, the heavy metal binding his wrists. Right now, he didn't share the spirit's optimism.

****

'I suppose, were I to look at the bright side, at least we won't have to put up with him turning up to give us ominous threats anymore.'

Nicolas let out an incredulous laugh. They were in a prison wagon, going to jail, which would inevitably lead to the hangman's noose, and Shift was looking on the *bright side.*

'And we don't have to worry about encountering Big Jaw again,' he found himself saying. 'I can't say I'm sad about that.'

'Those were some impressive moves, kid,' Auron said with a nod. 'See what I mean about training with Ban Dro?'

Unfortunately, more lessons will have to wait until after I'm hung.

Tenderly, he rubbed his neck. The idea of being imminently choked again didn't appeal to him in the slightest.

'How is your neck?' Silva asked.

'I'll live.' He smiled. 'Though the dwarf is a bit late with that armour. Mind you, I doubt it'd be any use against straps around the neck,' he added as an afterthought.

Shift raised an eyebrow. 'I thought I heard you saying you liked that kind of thing.'

Despite the grave situation, Nicolas let out a laugh. 'Ah,' he said, shaking his head. 'You heard that? I suppose it'd be a shame not to embarrass myself once more before death.'

'At least we know the Maestro's definitely involved,' Shift noted. 'Though how much good that'll do us... Well, I doubt Greer's in a listening mood now.'

'This is hardly our first time being taken prisoner,' Silva said sourly. 'We survived then, and we will survive now.'

It's much easier to survive when you can fight your way out. Roughing up members of the city watch will only make matters worse, methinks.

Though Silva was right. This was hardly their first time captured. Nicolas had even been captured once before Silva joined them.

Will the straw on the jail floor be good quality?

At what point in his life had *that* became a question he would ask? When had he become some kind of prison tourist?

'Oh, look at the craftsmanship of these bars, best I've seen in the last year.'

The wagon bumping over a pothole in the road sent a jolt up his spine.

Bad wagon rides...another common problem in my life nowadays.

Not that his life would last much longer. Grimly, he looked at his companions. Theirs wouldn't either, unless they could get out of this. But what then? He was already on one wanted poster. Would they all be fugitives for the rest of their lives? How would he help his people if he was on the run himself?

Or dead.

That they were innocent felt like a moot point. It wasn't like Greer was their friend and liable to help them. The lord commander had tolerated them...at best.

'We're in trouble,' he said glumly.

'You noticed?' Shift said with a smile.

He gestured to their surroundings. 'The prison wagon was a dead giveaway.'

'We'll get you out of this,' Auron said. 'I can walk through walls. There's got to be something I can do.'

That might entirely depend on how long Greer planned to hold them. Would there be a trial? Or did them being at the scene of the murder of a prominent citizen, with the murder weapon at their feet, mean the lord commander could cut out all the usual proving of guilt and take them straight to the gallows?

Assuming they hang criminals and not cut their heads off. Or...

Nicolas drove away that chain of thought with a shudder. He found himself staring at the door to the wagon.

'We're getting out of here,' he whispered firmly. They had to.

It does not end like this.

'I'd love to know how they knew where we were going to be,' Shift said, looking at the ceiling of the wagon. 'I mean they were waiting. They *had* to be waiting. Right?'

'I highly doubt they decided to sit randomly by a wagon in an alley on the off chance someone they're interested in killing happens along,' Auron replied. 'So yeah, they were waiting.'

'So we're being watched?' That was a scary thought. They were supposed to be hunting the demon, not being hunted by it.

'It appears so,' Silva remarked.

'If their goal was to keep us out of the investigation,' Nicolas said, gesturing to their surroundings, 'they've succeeded. It may not have been the way they preferred, but...'

'To sacrifice a piece like Geldheart must mean they really want us out of the way,' Auron said.

'We won't be for long.' Shift pulled out the chain around their neck. 'I still have my magic key. When they lock us up, we can break out and...'

'Please don't,' Silva said from the corner of the wagon. 'Let's just see how this plays out.'

Nicolas was pleased his slack-jawed expression was reflected in both Auron and Shift.

'Silva?' Auron asked suspiciously. 'Is that *you*?'

'Of course it is,' the warrior replied. 'Who else would I be?'

'Well.' How could Nicolas put this diplomatically. 'It's just that you're normally more the *'let's break out of here and fight everyone we see until we make it to freedom'* type.'

Silva raised an eyebrow. 'Am I indeed?'

'In the nicest possible way,' Shift added.

The warrior let a slight smile slip past her guard. 'Between the demon, rioters, and now the Maestro's assassins, of which I'm sure there are more, I think maybe we shouldn't put ourselves in the position of being hunted by the entire city watch just yet.'

'That's quite sensible, actually,' Auron relented.

'But if it comes to it,' Silva added with a more deadly smile, 'our journey to freedom will be paved with the bodies of those who get in our way.'

That's more like it...as long as they aren't members of the city watch.

'Dire times indeed when Silva's the voice of reason.' Shift chuckled.

They all went quiet for a moment. Garaz was usually the voice of reason.

'Yeah, but we can't be imprisoned any longer than necessary,' Nicolas added. 'We need to be out there stopping all this before it gets out of control. *More* out of control.'

Shift shook their head. 'It's not like Greer's just going to let us out.'

With a jolt, the wagon came to a stop. Seconds later, the door opened. 'Right, you lot, out,' Greer commanded.

CHAPTER 48

The group exchanged wary glances. The others had worked out the same thing as Nicolas—they hadn't travelled far enough to be at the city jail. So what was going on?

'Out,' Greer repeated with a nod.

Quickly, Auron stepped out of the wagon. With the light coming through the doorway, it was hard to make out Auron's bright form, but Nicolas could just about see the spirit studying the scene.

'It looks safe,' Auron called back.

Slowly, Nicolas rose, hesitantly approaching the door, and leant outside. They were in some sort of side alley, out of view. Before him stood Greer, arms folded and face neutral. After jumping down from the wagon, he stepped aside to allow his companions to join him.

Confined space. No witnesses... Is Auron sure this is safe?

'What is this?' Shift asked, clearly as guarded as he was.

Unfolding his arms, Lord Commander Greer threw something at Nicolas. He reached up, accidentally knocked it out of the air, but managed to catch it before it hit the floor. He stared at the small key in his hand.

'What this is, is me not liking being played for a fool,' Greer said darkly. 'We get summoned just in time to see the aftermath of you murdering someone you had a reason to have a grudge against, who just happens to be taking a wagon ride down a random alleyway at this time of the day.' Greer shook his head and frowned. 'Frankly, I'm insulted someone would think me so gullible.'

'Huh, maybe he's decent enough, after all.' Auron smiled. 'I may even be starting to like the old goat.'

'It's no secret I don't want you running around my city.' Greer sighed heavily. 'But that little show suggests someone darker doesn't either, which means you're on the right path.'

'Then why arrest us?' Shift asked indignantly as the shackles Nicolas had just unlocked dropped from their wrists. Grabbing the key, they began unlocking his and their other companions' bindings.

Greer chuckled. 'I can put on a show too,' he answered. 'That whole set-up was designed to put me in a position to have to arrest you. There will have been someone watching, and as far as they know, the plan succeeded. Besides, half the bloody street saw what it was *supposed* to look like. I had to act, so I took you lot away and left Sergeant Tallith to cordon off the area. That should buy you some time.' The lord commander stroked his chin thoughtfully. 'Besides, they knew exactly where to get you. That means someone close to me let them know your route. I'm not sure who I can trust right—'

Everyone jumped at the crash back just down the street. Something had hit the ground with force, throwing up dust from the pile of boxes it'd landed on and scaring the crap out of some chickens, that were now running across the street, flapping their wings and squawking their little hearts out.

'Your weapons,' Greer said, keeping his eyes on the disturbance as he pointed to a bag resting beside the wagon door.

The lord commander ran towards the disturbance, with the two watchmen who'd accompanied him on the wagon in close pursuit. Auron was with them, though they had no idea.

'Let's go,' Nicolas said, opening the bag urgently.

Within moments, the group was armed.

'It's a body,' Auron shouted back to the others as they ran to join the spirit. 'It's—' Something caught the spirit's attention, and he looked up Whatever it was got Greer's attention too. 'There's a fight on the roof of that building. *Hurry.*'

Nicolas sped up as the lord commander and his men disappeared through the door, having promptly kicked it in. Bounding through the entrance of what might've been a butcher's shop, Nicolas chased the sound of fading footsteps to a set of stairs at the back of the room. There was a scream.

Throwing himself through the doorway, Nicolas stopped abruptly, his mind needing to take a moment to process what he was seeing. The rooftop was covered in bodies, not many of them whole. There was blood, so much blood. And it was splattered everywhere. In the centre of it all was a hooded figure, holding Lord Commander Greer in the air with a single hand. Considering how big the lord commander was, whoever was lifting him up so effortlessly was unnaturally strong.

Demonically strong.

'By the Deities,' Shift gasped at his side.

Greer let out a choking sound, bringing him back to the moment. Lunging forward, he swung the *Dawn Blade*, intent on cutting off the arm that gripped the lord commander by the throat. By the time his sword had reached it's target, the arm had vanished, and only the air was cut. Greer crashed to the floor beside the two watchmen, who were very dead. The lord commander writhed as he gasped for breath. Nicolas wanted to check on him, but there was still danger nearby.

And thank the Deities I'm not facing it alone.

Getting into a guard position, he followed the dark-robed figure as it stalked across the rooftop. The layers of clothing it wore obscured it, but what he did see scared him. Beneath the hood was a large, fanged maw from which a long, pointed tongue flicked. Its visible skin was covered in angry scar tissue. Each arm ended in a hand with sharp talons. He could see the bloody work of those talons all around him, and he really did not want to be on the receiving end of them. But worse than all that was the aura this creature gave off. It was malice, in its purest form, mixed with power. It was the demon.

And it's not Koth.

He didn't know how he knew, but he did. Fortunately, he was in a situation where he had no time to be disappointed. This creature was ridiculously dangerous. Somehow, he could tell it was fighting back its urge to kill. And, slight as it was, it would be able to kill them easily.

Slowly, his companions fanned out, readying themselves for the fight. Each one was quiet and tense, but ready. This was probably one of the most dangerous opponents they'd ever faced. The gravity of that wasn't lost on him.

Be calm. Try to discern where the creature will strike and use logic to... Oh no.

The demon's hood flicked toward Shift, and the creature hissed, lowering its stance as if to pounce. Without thinking, Nicolas charged forwards, sword already swinging.

Oh no.

With the quickest flick of its head, the demon turned to him, smiling. He'd been baited. Already, claws were slashing at him. Nicolas could only watch in horror as death made its inevitable way towards him.

Mother. Father. I'm sorry I failed you.

Nicolas's charging foot found a pool of fresh blood and slipped. Stumbling, he fell forwards, crashing to the ground. As he did, some hair slowly fell to the ground beside him. His hair.

It was that *close.*

Trying his darndest to ignore the wet substance he'd fallen into, Nicolas stared up at the demon. The surprise of missing its prey wore off, and with a snarl, it struck down at him. He rolled aside, and the talons went straight into the stone roof as if it...wasn't stone.

Deities.

The demon reared, ready to take another, literal, stab at him. Before it could, it had to fling itself backwards, out of the range of Silva's cutting blade. But if there was one thing he knew about Silva, it was that she never settled for just one attack. The warrior surged forward, slashing this way and that. The creature seemed to move effortlessly around the sword, before it struck Silva in the chest plate with a single palm. The warrior was thrown clear across the roof, the raised surround the only thing keeping her from going right over the edge.

With another hiss, the creature came at him again, only to find a net thrown over it. The demon roared as it reared upwards. Making use of his position, Nicolas kicked it in the side of the knee, and it crashed to the ground.

'I found it on the floor,' Shift shouted as they danced on their feet near the demon. They had only knives, and the creature in the net bucked and thrashed violently.

Happily, he still had his sword in hand. Nicolas scrambled to his feet, ready to finish the demon off for good—in time to see the creature tear the net to shreds as it burst from it, before jumping backwards, out of range of his blade.

'It's fast,' Shift said as they stood next to him, facing the creature.

'And strong,' Nicolas added, nervously glancing at the claw holes in the stone.

'Still, three-on-one are good odds,' Silva added as she joined them, her breathing laboured. The indent on her armour from the demon's strike made Nicolas gulp involuntarily.

'Four,' Lord Commander Greer said as he limped up to them. His own armour was rent and his head bleeding freely.

'Okay, listen up,' Auron said from the side of the roof. 'It's strong and fast, but you have the numbers. Come at it from all sides at once and hit it as one. Don't forget—' The demon turned its head towards Auron and snarled. 'It can see me,' Auron said, shock written across his ethereal features.

'The plan is still sound, though,' Nicolas said, before quietly repeating it to the lord commander.

Spreading out, the group advanced slowly as one, weapons ready. The demon bared it's talons, equally prepared for the coming fight. This was going to be tough, but Nicolas had faith in his companions, and their numbers advantage. Attacking it all at once would...

'Blasted creature,' Lord Commander Greer roared, ignoring the plan completely as he charged the demon head on. 'You dare infest my city? I'll send you straight back to whatever dark pit you crawled from.'

To everyone's surprise—which was manifested in some very bad language—the demon simply jumped from the roof.

'*No*,' Nicolas cried, running forward. But by the time he got to the edge of the roof and looked over, there was no sign of the creature. 'Dammit!' He sagged against the ledge, letting out a big sigh. 'We were so close.' He hadn't even gotten a decent look at the creature's face.

'I think we still are.'

Auron's words made him turn around. The others were looking at the rest of the bodies on the roof. Stepping over another net, he approached his companions.

'Look familiar?' Shift asked, nodding towards one of the dead.

Studying the faces of the dead men, some of whom were in pieces, he didn't recognise anyone. Then Nicolas realised Shift wasn't talking about their faces, but their uniforms.

'These are Professor Shaw's men,' he said with a gasp.

Silva picked up a third net from the floor and held it open before disdainfully discarding it. 'If I were to guess, the demon was shadowing us to ambush us when these men attempted to ambush it...poorly.'

'Shaw must know something about the demon,' Shift mused. 'Why else send his muscle to try to capture and maybe kill it?'

'Scientific curiosity?' Nicolas shrugged.

'Or trying to undo a wrong he was party to,' Silva said with a scowl.

'That makes more sense,' Nicolas agreed. 'But why would the demon attack us now? Are we somehow close to finding out it's identity?'

'Because it was the time we were most vulnerable,' the warrior replied. 'We were imprisoned and unarmed. What better time to try and remove us?'

'That would only make sense if it knew we'd be like that in advance,' Nicolas said, before clicking his fingers. 'And it could only have known if it was in league with Geldheart and his collaborators.'

Which means...

'This *is* related to the Maestro then.' Shift cast Nicolas a quick, sympathetic glance.

'A trap within a trap...' Auron frowned momentarily, '...within a trap? It certainly sounds like the Maestro's way of doing things.'

'Ambushing us when we're in shackles and unarmed isn't very fair.'

Auron let out a single loud laugh that surprised everyone who could hear it. 'That's what I love about you, kid. Only you could apply notions like *being fair* to a demon.'

'It seems I was wrong to stop you going after the professor.' Lord Commander Greer sniffed, dabbing his bloody temple with a handkerchief that would be unusable from that day forth. 'In fact, I think it's time the city watch paid him a visit. In force.'

I think I'm *starting to like the old goat.*

CHAPTER 49

Despite the frustration of the creature escaping, the fact that it had attacked them at all was a worrying portent. If the creature was getting bold enough to move in daylight, it must be getting surer of itself. Or Nicolas and his companions were just too large a pain in the ass to ignore. The urgency of the situation hadn't been lost on Lord Commander Greer, who quickly gathered a troop of his most trusted men—but even then, he hadn't given them all the details of their mission.

Doing this in the day made it riskier, as they could easily be seen coming, but there was no other option. With every lost hour, the army would get closer to the city. At least the wealthier area in which Professor Shaw resided was practically a ghost town. As out of touch as the wealthy of Babylon were, they were very aware that should public disorder break out they were likely the first ones against the wall.

From the side street, Nicolas peeked out toward the manor. Now that he knew something was very wrong there, it made it look all the more sinister. The pipework put him in mind of a giant spider creature, ready to swallow them whole.

Leaning backward, he jumped slightly as he saw Shift's new face.

'Don't worry,' they said, pinching his cheek. 'I'll be back to the form you prefer in no time.' There was a mischievous twinkle in their eye. 'Kiss for good luck?' Dry lips surrounded by stubble puckered up and moved toward him.

'I'll wait for a victory kiss after,' he replied, backing away slightly. As he did, his unfamiliar clothes pinched him slightly. 'Are you sure I'm right for this?' he asked, looking down.

'Of course, kid,' Auron confirmed. 'Shift can look like one of the professor's guards, but they can't get the way open alone. And you look the most harmless of anyone here, so you get to play the *injured comrade*.'

'Then once the gates open, we come running in.' Silva stared in the direction of the manor, and battle.

Nicolas glanced at Greer and his men, the ones who would breach the manor with them. None of them looked at all harmless. Save maybe Sergeant Tallith.

But it's my quest, not his.

Besides, it would give the sergeant a great tale for the next club meeting.

'Ready?' Shift asked, holding out their arm.

Nicolas tucked himself under their armpit, wrapped his arm around their shoulder, and let his body go faux limp. 'Let's go.'

With urgency, the pair emerged from the alley, Nicolas allowing himself to be half dragged as he made groaning sounds that wouldn't have been out of place amongst an undead horde.

'The gate,' Shift cried in their new gruff voice. 'Open the gate.'

'What happened?' a voice called back.

'What do you think happened?' Shift snarled. 'The plan went to shit. Now open the damned gate, asshole. He won't last much longer.'

The professor's plan *had* gone to shit, but at least it had left them with some handy uniforms to use as disguises. Though only two, once the demon's talons had finished their bloody work.

Urgent shouts and the sound of metal creaking suggested it was working like a charm.

'Six,' Auron said at his side. 'Three on either side of the gate.'

Six? That's a lot.

'What happened?' he heard a man say over his latest groan.

'What do you bloody think?' Shift snapped. 'The demon saw us coming.'

'The others?'

'Dead,' his companion answered. 'Take this one.'

Shift's arm left him, and Nicolas theatrically stumbled forwards. At the last second, he planted his feet and swung an uppercut at the guard who was ready to grab him. Before the man had even hit the floor, Nicolas had drawn his concealed baton and cracked the second on the side of the head. The third went to draw his sword. Checking the sword arm, Nicolas jabbed him in the throat with the baton to stop the cry of alarm his open mouth was threatening. As the man instead made a choked, rasping sound, Nicolas finished him off by introducing the baton to his jaw. By that time, Shift had already neutralised their three guards.

'Nice work, kid,' Auron said, clapping. 'I think those six will account for the patrols as well.'

Eyes darting around, Nicolas saw no other men and heard no cry of alarm. Quickly, he gestured to the alley. As he and Shift, now back in their preferred form, ran to the door, Silva, Greer, and most of his men—some had been stationed around the manor to keep out civilians and mop up anyone who might try to escape—made their way through the gate to join them. The house seemed quiet as the troop of armoured men approached the door surprisingly silently.

But that doesn't mean no one saw that.

'All right, lads,' Greer said, addressing Nicolas and the troop behind him. 'I want this quick and clean, understood? We take this place room by room. Any of Shaw's men are to be arrested. If they resist, give them a sound thrashing. We aren't messing about here.'

The men of the city watch looked back at their lord commander with a professional, grim determination.

'It's times like this I really wish I was still alive,' Auron remarked, staring at the manor door with a sorrowful look.

The group stood before it in two neat columns. Nicolas readied himself for what came next.

'Calm down.' Shift smiled. 'This is actually quite fun, if you're open to it.'

'You and I have very different ideas of fun.'

Shift's smiled broadened. 'Not all the time.'

'Noise discipline,' Greer hissed, staring at the pair with a wide-eyed gaze, under which Nicolas internally shrank.

Turning back, Greer gestured two of his men forwards. The pair carried a heavy-looking wooden cylinder, a battering ram. As they advanced, they walked right through Auron, the spirit shuddering as if violated.

He shouldn't stand right in the middle of the path then.

Carefully, the two men lined the ram up with the handles of the door then looked to their lord commander. Greer glanced at Nicolas; nods were exchanged. For a second, he dared hope he might be earning the lord commander's respect. Though why that would matter to him was anyone's guess.

As the moment for action approached, time slowed. His breathing was calm. Part of him would've been happy to just let the city watch do their duty, but he'd been deputised to stop these murders, so he wasn't about to step aside and let others finish his task for him. His grip tightened around the thick wooden baton in his hand. They needed answers, and they wouldn't get that by running in swinging swords around. The battle with Alric Tavish had taught him that. So the decision had been made to use batons instead. Besides, Greer was eager to have some people to put on trial and hang for this entire mess once the demon was finally slain, and Nicolas didn't fancy denying him.

There was no sound on the porch, nor beyond the door. It was as if the world was holding it's breath for a moment, ready to see what would happen next. Then Greer gave the command.

'Go.'

With heaving effort, the men swung the ram backwards and drove it into the door.

Crack.

Instantly, it burst open, the lock falling to the floor, surrounded by splinters.

'*City watch*,' Lord Commander Greer bellowed into the newly made opening. '*Stand down and surrender.*'

With that, they charged into the manor.

Whatever Professor Shaw was paying his men, it must've been handsome indeed, because they had showed no sign of surrendering. Before they'd even cleared the hallway, a guard ran at them, sword drawn. Two men of the watch pinned his arms to the wall whilst another clubbed him until the fight was out of him and he could be restrained.

The tip of a sword thrust towards Nicolas, but the man was slow, and he sidestepped the blow before introducing his baton to the man's thick jaw. There was a crack, and the man crumpled to the floor. He had no time to enjoy his victory, as thick arms wrapped around his waist. Digging his heels into the floor, he drove himself backwards until there was the thump of a man colliding with a wall. The grip held. Shift ran at him, swinging their baton. With a cry, he ducked his head. The grip loosened.

Once the initial surprise of the attack had faded, the professor's guards—and he seemed to have a lot—rallied, and they were forced to take the house room by room.

A tall man with a sword barred his path. With an upswing, he drove the baton up into the fellow's groin before pulling back and driving the tip into the man's throat. As he collapsed, gagging, men of the watch wrestled him down, shackling him. As he passed into the next corridor, a mercenary leapt at him, driving him face first into the wall. He couldn't afford to be dizzy or disorientated—his opponent was unlikely to just claim victory and walk off—so he drove his elbow into the attacker's stomach in an explosive burst of speed and power. A painful exhalation marked his effort. Turning, he cracked the man across the jaw.

To the tune of boots stomping up the stairs, the men of the watch went to clear the higher level of the manor. Nicolas, Shift, Silva, Auron, Greer, and a couple others made their way towards the professor's workshop.

'It's locked,' Greer said as he tried the door at the top of the stairway leading to the workshop.

'Pfft.' Kneeling, Shift had the door open in a moment.

Gazing down, Nicolas saw an alarmed face before the door at the bottom of the stairs was slammed shut. Unfortunately for the man who'd closed the door, Silva Destrone didn't care to be denied access, and was...less subtle than Shift at getting it. Following in the warrior's wake, Nicolas watched as she crashed through the door, sending it swinging into the face of the man who'd shut it, before the warrior set about him.

Upon entering the room—once he'd recovered from the sudden burst of heat—he saw a large pair of legs dangling from an open window. Professor Shaw had apparently gotten stuck attempting to make his escape, and two men were pushing feverishly on his rump to get him through. That was enough of a distraction for the guard, who punched him in the face. He stumbled backwards, trying to shake off the wooziness. Again, he doubted his opponent would just bugger off after one punch. Fortunately, Shift had his back, striking the man in the back of the knee with their baton before a watchman wrestled him to the ground.

Shift made their way to him quickly and held his head, their eyes...worried. That was odd. How hard had he been punched? 'Are you okay?'

'Yeah, I'm fine.' *It isn't like getting punched is anything new nowadays.*

'Are you sure?' Shift asked. 'Can you name five capitals of the Nine Kingdoms of Man?'

'The kid couldn't do that even before someone punched him in the face.' Auron smirked in the background.

'Yarringsburg, Sarus, Vara, Nalburg, and Valinshold,' Nicolas said quickly before petulantly adding, 'Ass.'

'He's okay.' Auron smiled.

'Are you sure?' Shift asked again.

'Yes.'

They looked at him awkwardly for a moment, before saying quietly, 'You know you died once, right?'

How could I forget? But I don't think Shift worrying about me is a bad thing. I just need to get used to it.

He wasn't sure who initiated the kiss, but they were most definitely kissing.

'Not the right place,' Silva said with a disapproving glance.

Shift pulled back and gave him a wink. 'Don't care.'

A *thud* behind them signalled the men of the watch removing Professor Shaw from his window. The two men who'd been trying to push him out had suffered Silva's wrath and were unconscious on the floor. As they approached, Shaw squirmed, desperately looking around for either help or a way to escape. He had neither.

'We need answers,' Nicolas insisted as he stood over him.

'What he said,' Greer snarled at his side. 'To questions such as, *'Why were your men trying to catch the demon?'* and *'How are you involved in this?'*

The flustered old man wrung his hands anxiously. 'It was purely scientific. I wanted to learn about this kind of fascinating creature. For...um...science.'

Nicolas looked at everyone else in the room. None of them believed it either. 'Try again,' he suggested. 'Are you responsible for the demon? Did you curse Garaz?'

The professor's mouth worked up and down, but no sounds came out.

With a grunt of frustration, Silva yanked him up and slammed him against his steam generator, which moved slightly under the impact. As in, the whole machine moved, revealing part of the floor, which had a design drawn upon it. Whatever it was, it glowed with red energy.

And it's evil.

'What is this?' Greer demanded, pointing at the design.

It looked very much like some kind of magic.

'I...I...I...' The professor's face reddened, and his eyes were wide as he looked at the design. Eventually his body went limp, and he crumpled to the floor. 'It's my folly.' He began to weep.

'I don't understand.' The urge to run from the symbol was nearly unbearable. Everyone else in the room shuffled awkwardly as if they had the same feeling.

Deities, it's hotter in here all of a sudden.

Much hotter than it had been.

'This has demonic origins.' Auron crouched and studied the symbol then disappeared into the machine completely. A few moments later, he returned. 'The floor under the machine is covered in them.'

'Are these demonic?' Shift asked, pointing to the symbols.

The professor seemed to slump even further. 'Yes,' he whispered hoarsely.

Before anyone knew what was happening, Greer had drawn his sword, and the tip of the blade was touching the professor's throat. 'What have you *done*?' the lord commander snarled.

'You don't understand,' Shaw pleaded, clutching his chest. 'Winter was coming...the pressure I was under. I was driving myself to the point of insanity trying to get it to work. I was so close. So close. But the governor was pushing for results, starting to lose faith in me. I...I just needed to buy some more time.'

'Stand up and make sense,' Greer commanded.

Shakily, the professor rose to his feet. 'The steam generator. It doesn't work. Yet.' His tone was filled with hesitance and regret. 'It will work. It *will*. I'm nearly there. It's just several months off. I was working flat out, day and night, but I couldn't make it work any faster. I just couldn't. Not on the scale to warm an entire city. But the cold wouldn't wait for me.

Nor would the governor. She threatened to pull my funding. Suggested I was a charlatan. *Me.*'

'So you...' Shift began leadingly.

'It wasn't me. I didn't do...' The professor gulped hard. 'But it was. I agreed to it. I gave it the go ahead. I know I shouldn't have, but my design was going to work. I just needed...time.'

The professor let out an *eep* as the blade pressed into his flesh. 'I said *make sense.*' From Greer's tone, it was the last time he'd ask.

'A man approached me,' the professor said. 'He said he knew of my work and my troubles. He said he could help, offer me a place-holder until I could complete my design and get it running properly.'

'What man?' Nicolas asked.

'I was too afraid to ask,' the professor admitted after a moment. 'But my pride wouldn't let me fail. So I said yes.'

'To...' Shift prompted again.

Professor Shaw gave the symbol a worried, lingering glance before he answered. 'Those symbols open a portal to Davish'mar, the demonic realm.' Shaw's voice was quivering. His chubby face was drenched in sweat. 'I needed a source of infinite heat, and what better than the realm of eternal fire? The heat is channelled through the machine and into the pipes and it...warms the city.'

The tip of the blade dropped. Greer's face showed the same horror Nicolas imagined his did.

'You...you...' Nicolas began, trying to get his head around the concept. 'You opened a portal to the demonic realm so you could fake a scientific discovery?'

'No,' Shaw scoffed petulantly. 'I did it so I could make a real one, so my life's work wouldn't be for naught. If I can heat this city, imagine the potential for the rest of the world. The marvels we could create with steam power...it would be a new age.'

'I don't think you were thinking of that.' Shift sneered. 'Just about yourself.'

'Because if you did,' Nicolas said, fighting back his disgust, which demanded that he beat the professor thoroughly, 'you'd acknowledge that doors open both ways.'

'My patron assured me it wouldn't be a problem,' Shaw cried. 'I didn't know what had happened until you came here asking your questions. Cyrus, he was the one who hid the book for you to find. He said you needed to find something or you'd just keep searching.'

'And he is...' Greer asked leadingly.

'I don't know,' Shaw whispered. 'He vanished just after you left. I...I was so wrapped up in my work here that I didn't really pay attention to what was going on outside. When you told me...the guilt began to gnaw at me. So I sent my men to catch the demon. I theorised it would come after you at some point soon.' *We were followed all this time?* 'I thought if we could put it back, all this would just go away.'

'*Put it back?*' Nicolas's grip on his baton tightened. 'And at no point did you think to just close the portal?' *The vanity of this man. The disgusting vanity that caused him to disregard life.* 'No matter how many people died. You never thought of closing the portal.'

'If I could crack this then all cities could be heated by my designs,' Shaw cried. 'No one would ever die from cold again. It'd make the world a better place. Those people died in the name of science.'

'Silva,' Auron said calmly at Nicolas's side, 'I really want to hit this guy. But I can't. And as much as the kid blatantly wants to, his better nature won't let him strike an unarmed man. Do the honours, please.'

Silva did said honours. Shaw sprawled to the floor, broken nose bleeding freely.

'Nice shot,' Greer said as he gestured for his men to shackle the professor.

'I hope it was worth it,' Nicolas said in disgust as the professor was hauled to his knees. The click as the shackles were locked into place was extremely satisfying.

'It would've been,' Shaw replied petulantly, his voice pitch changed due to his damaged nose.

Greer sneered in disgust at the professor before turning to address his men. 'I want this building cordoned off. Anyone who tries to get in is to be made *extremely* sorry for it. And I want some people from the local Guild of Magic down here to close *this*. Now.'

The watchmen ran about their business as Nicolas stared at the designs. It wasn't Koth, but they were undoing something very evil here. Something that had the Maestro's name behind it. Who else would be the professor's patron?

Hopefully, us stopping this drives him insane. If I have to take his little organisation apart one scheme at a time, so be it.

CHAPTER 50

Nicolas's brow furrowed as he watched the representative from the Guild of Magic walk the circumference of the design, now completely visible with the decoy machine above it moved. As it turned out, there was a hidden sub-basement housing the real machine that Professor Shaw had desperately been trying to get running.

The wizard stroked his beard thoughtfully as he studied the design, which glowed with red energy. Then, reaching out with a single foot, he rubbed out a random part of the chalk symbol. Instantly, the red energy faded into nothing.

'Is that it?' he asked.

'Not quite, young man,' the wizard said. 'Breaking the pattern breaks the spell, but this area will still need to be cleansed, and the entire thing taken apart more thoroughly. I suppose, to put it in layman's terms, I pushed the door to, but it still needs to be shut and locked.'

And have planks of wood nailed across it...and be guarded by some kind of terrible monster whose favourite food is demon.

'The city will become colder now.'

Professor Shaw made an *eep* as Silva's blade touched one of his chins. 'I thought you were told to be quiet?' the warrior asked venomously.

Apparently, the professor didn't know when to give up. 'I can get it to work.' Nicolas wasn't used to seeing people disobey Silva. 'There will be residual heat in the pipes for maybe a day then things will start getting cold. Give me that day. I can make it work. I can.'

'You've done enough,' Greer snarled, before turning to his men. 'Get him out of here.'

Two members of the city watch hauled the snivelling professor up and removed him from the room.

'Tallith, you go with them,' Greer said to the young sergeant. 'Make sure you throw his lying ass into the dankest cell we have.'

'Yes, sir,' Tallith said with a crisp salute, before following the others upstairs and out of the manor.

'I don't suppose we'd be lucky enough for the demon to be gone now the portal has closed?' Shift asked hopefully.

'No,' the wizard said. 'The demon will be tethered to the host, not the portal. Though...' A look of grave concern crossed the wizard's wrinkled features. '...I do not understand how only one came through. There should have been more. Demons are not known for their restraint, and the city would be a beacon to them. Also, I have never seen this kind of magic. I have heard scholars talk of portals between realms in times long past, but to see one with my own eyes is almost unbelievable.'

It seemed part of the wizard wanted to study this further. However, judging by the sigh as the old man gazed at the design, he was well aware of the saying *better safe than sorry.*

'At least we've stopped more coming through,' Auron said from the corner of the room. 'I'd call that a victory.'

'Half a victory,' Nicolas replied. 'We still have to get the one that did out of here.'

Looking at the spirit, he remembered something that had happened on the rooftop when the demon attacked them.

'Excuse me,' he said to the wizard. 'We travel with a spirit, and the demon could see and hear him. Why is that?'

The wizard gazed around the room, as if he might suddenly notice Auron. 'At best guess, I would say neither demons nor ghosts are natural to this plane of existence. Demons cannot dwell here, and the spirits of the dead shouldn't. I would suggest that means these forces can interact. See each other. Though it is just a theory.'

'Bloody charming,' Auron said sourly. 'And I'm not a ghost.'

Shift rolled their green eyes.

'What do we do now?' Greer mused aloud as he stared at the design. 'We're still no closer to finding the one that got out.'

That was the conundrum. Chances were the demon would know soon enough that the door had been shut. What would happen then? How could they find it before the worst happened? If only...

'Hey,' Nicolas cried suddenly. 'Do you have anyone who specialises in healing magic in the city?'

'Yes,' the wizard said, raising an eyebrow. 'Why do you ask?'

'My companion was going to do a spell that could pinpoint the demon, but it didn't work for some reason. Could you ask your man to try?'

'Well, it isn't as easy as that,' the wizard said with a frown. 'We'd need to know the specific spell he intended to use.'

Nicolas turned to his companions. 'Has anyone ever seen Garaz with a spell book?'

'No,' Silva answered. 'But who knows what he has in that cloak of his?'

'We need to go back to the manor, see if he'd written anything down.' Nicolas looked at the wizard again. 'Can you ask your man to come to the lord commander's manor, please?'

'Kid, this is a long shot, at best.'

Nicolas turned to Auron. 'How many stories do you have about long shots that paid off?'

The spirit's head tilted from side to side as he thought. 'At least four come straight to mind.' Auron chuckled. 'So, this one time...'

'Not now, please.'

Auron was right, though: this was a very long shot. His hope was that the other wizard could identify what had gone wrong with Garaz's spell and maybe, just maybe, it would work this time.

****

'Fortunately, Governor Morrow is a practical woman,' Greer explained as they opened the door to his manor. 'As much as she believed in the professor's work, she kept a stockpile as if winter would hit normally. The city will be all right.'

That was something, at least. Nicolas had worried Babylon might freeze to death now that they'd cut off the heat source. Thank the Deities for the governor's preparedness.

'Duncan? Are you okay?' Beba ran to her husband, staring with worry at the bandage around the lord commander's head.

'I am well,' Greer replied, hugging his wife. 'And before you say anything, I will get this seen to properly later.' Pulling back, he kissed his wife tenderly on the cheek.

With a warm smile, Beba turned to the others. 'Why are you back? I thought you'd be out hunting the demon. Did Professor Shaw's manor turn up anything?'

'Yes,' Shift said dryly. 'A giant fraud.'

'What do you mean?'

'Professor Shaw lied to us all,' Greer said with a disgusted look. 'He opened a portal to the demon realm and was siphoning heat from it to make it look like his generator worked. It's how the demon got here in the first place.'

Beba clasped her hands to her mouth. 'By the Deities. That's terrible.'

Isn't it just?

'How is Garaz?' Nicolas asked.

'Still sleeping,' Beba answered, her mouth a thin line. 'I'm sorry. No healers have come yet. I don't know why. I asked Tallith to send a message to the nearest temple.'

'Dammit.' He'd half-hoped the curse had just worn off, even though his pessimism had known better. 'Okay. Shift, can you go and rummage through Garaz's stuff and see if he wrote down that spell?'

'You're going to try it again?' Beba asked.

'A wizard from the Guild is coming. He'll try it. At the moment, it's the best we can do.'

'Hopefully, this time it works.'

A sudden banging at the door got their attention. Greer stared at it for a moment. 'Enter.'

The doors opened, and a man of the watch ran in. Whatever he needed, he'd obviously pushed himself hard to get here. That, in itself, was worrying.

'What is it?' Greer asked urgently. 'Speak, man.'

'The professor,' the watchman said once he'd caught his breath. 'He's escaped.'

What?

'How?' Greer asked with cold fury.

'We don't know,' the man admitted. 'We found the wagon abandoned and the guards dead...'

The lord commander paled. 'Sergeant Tallith? He was with them.'

The messenger shook his head. 'We couldn't find him. Sorry, sir.'

'Dammit.' Greer threw his helmet back on.

'Do you want us to—' Nicolas began.

'No,' the lord commander said. 'Wait here for the wizard and get the spell working. We need to find this demon.'

'At least take Silva with you. She's a great tracker.'

Greer looked at the warrior and nodded. Within a minute, the pair were gone, leaving them with the implications of what had happened. For the professor to be freed so quickly meant there were definitely people in the city watch who couldn't be trusted.

'Listen,' Beba said, smoothing down her dress. 'You go wait for me in the kitchen. I'll take Shift to Garaz then make you all something to eat. You look starved.'

Nicolas literally couldn't remember the last time he'd eaten.

I've definitely eaten at least once since getting to the city. I think.

'I can find my own way up the stairs.' Shift chuckled.

'I removed Garaz's cloak to make him more comfortable.' Beba smiled. 'I'll show you where it's hung.'

'In that case, lead the way,' Shift said, quickly following the lady of the house as she ascended the staircase.

After watching them leave, Nicolas made his way to the kitchen, which was empty. Maybe because it was between breakfast and lunch, and no one needed to cook anything? Finding an empty stool, he sat heavily on it, leaning on the counter and holding his head in his hands. His mind began to work furiously, trying to figure out what he was missing. Surely there was something? He always missed something.

Why did Garaz's spell fail? How did anyone organise that ambush? What...

'Kid?' Auron asked, as he slapped his hand on the tabletop.

'Sergeant Tallith,' he cried.

'What about him?'

'He's the demon.' In his mind, everything suddenly came together like a completed jigsaw. 'He's always conveniently missing. When we were attacked...when the demon appeared. Now he's missing just as Professor Shaw vanishes and...he brought Garaz the ingredients for his spell. What if he switched one of them?'

As nice as the sergeant seemed, all of that made horrible sense. How could he not have seen it? He was right there, the whole time.

Fan club, my ass. He was told all about me by the Maestro.

'I thought it was Greer for a bit, especially when he arrested you guys,' the spirit admitted. 'But now the professor's gone, and he was in charge of the troop... You know what, it makes sense. But what do we do with that information?'

'We set a trap.'

'A trap?' Beba asked as she walked into the room.

'Tallith is the demon,' he told her grimly.

For a moment, the lady of the house appeared stunned. 'No, that can't be right. Not him.'

'It has to be.'

Taking him by the shoulders, Beba gave him a warm smile. 'Look. You're tired and hungry. Maybe you aren't thinking straight. Let me make you some food. Once you've eaten and rested, you'll start to see sense.' Moving off, she grabbed some bread and a knife, beginning to cut him off slices.

'No,' he said thoughtfully. 'It has to be right. And he knows we're going to try the spell again. We set an ambush and grab him when he comes to stop it.' His eyes widened with urgency as he looked toward the door and jumped from the stool. 'We need to prepare. He could be here any moment...'

'Kid, calm down,' Auron said levelly. 'We will be ready. So this one time...' *Oh joy.* 'I was hunting this ogre that was attacking a village's livestock at night. But the attacks were random, and it was bloody good at covering its trail. The only sure thing was that at some point, the ogre would return. I ended up hiding in a bush in the field for four nights in a row before it showed up and I killed it. Sometimes, patience is the best thing.'

'Okay,' he said reluctantly. Auron's wisdom had proved valuable in the past, so it'd be silly to ignore it now.

'I tell you what, kid, you want to talk patience and discipline, try lying in a field for hours needing to take a piss but not wanting to in case you miss your target. My bladder was as engorged as a dragon's nutsack in mating season by the time I actually got to go. If you start rushing around now, you'll miss something, and the trap will be for naught.'

Miss something...

In his mind, he played out his theory again. It *had* to be Tallith. Who else could it possibly...

A sudden realisation hit him. Whatever hero instincts he was developing gave him a clear answer, as if a Deity itself had parted the clouds and screamed it at him. It made slightly less sense, maybe, but he knew he was right.

Within an instant, he'd drawn the *Dawn Blade* and levelled it at Beba Greer.

CHAPTER 51

'Put the knife down,' he demanded. 'Now.'

Slowly, Beba placed the knife on the counter and turned to him, hands raised. 'What are you doing?' There was fear in her voice. It sounded genuine.

And yet it isn't.

'You're the demon.'

'What?' the lady of the house cried. 'Me? Are you insane? I'm no demon.' Slowly, she lowered her hands. 'I think you need to calm down.'

'*You* need to keep your hands in the air,' he warned.

'Kid—' Auron began.

'If it isn't Tallith then it's her,' he interrupted. 'She said we could stay here. She went to get the ingredients for the spell. She could've used the lord commander's seal to summon Tallith away. It's her.'

'Hero instincts?' Auron asked.

'Hero instincts,' he confirmed.

'That's good enough for me.' The spirit appraised Beba.

'Please,' the lady of the house cried. 'I'm no demon. I welcomed you into my home. I was trying to help. All this time I've been supporting you.'

'Watching us, more like,' Auron scoffed. 'Sly demonic piece of shit.'

Beba's eyes flicked to Auron. Both the spirit and Nicolas noticed. With a laugh, the lady of the house dropped her hands and shook her head. 'Dammit.' She chuckled. 'I was going to play the confused innocent for a little longer. I can't believe I let a flick of the eye give me away.' She looked up at them and sighed. 'But who likes being called a piece of shit, eh? Still, to slip up because of a ghost...'

'Spirit, actually,' Auron corrected with narrowed eyes.

'Who cares?' Beba spat. 'Dead is dead.' The demon looked away thoughtfully for a second. 'I wonder what old Duncan's face will look like when I reveal myself. I was going to kill him on that roof, you know, but his wife's love for him actually managed to stay my hand for a second and made me retreat. Can you believe that?' The thing that had once been the lady of the house shook her head. 'Not that I'll let that happen again.' She tapped her fingertips on the countertop thoughtfully. 'Truthfully, he was supposed to die by that prison wagon, where he had you all nicely shackled and ready for me.'

'You were part of the whole thing?' Nicolas asked.

'Of course.' Beba grinned. 'Are you impressed with how quickly we put all of that together? I'd hoped tearing up that silly old warrant would delay you, but the ambush was set up more quickly than I expected. The Maestro is quite efficient, and quite passionate about killing you. You've cost him a few minions, you know.'

'Damn shame that,' Auron said dryly.

'Plans in plans, that's how he works,' the demon continued. 'He knew Greer would never buy that stupid assassination story but have to arrest you for appearances. The idea was for him to take you somewhere quiet, where I'd finally get to kill him, making it look like you lot did it when you escaped. I'd leave the warrior bitch's body there, just to add some credence to the story. Without good old Duncan, the chaos would spread more easily.' Beba tapped her chin with a single nail. 'And it gave us an excuse to get rid of Geldheart. Since the assassination attempt in Narus went awry, thanks again to you, the Maestro didn't want too much attention drawn to it.' *He was involved in that too?* 'But Geldheart was set on pushing his stupid agenda and started waving your wanted poster around to try and force you to leave, even though he was told not to. Well, when you stop listening to commands, you have to go.' Beba sighed. 'And the ambush would have been perfect, if those idiots of Shaw's hadn't ruined my fun.' She pouted for a moment, before her lips curled into a malicious grin. 'Well, I did have some fun on that roof, as it turned out. Nice, bloody fun.'

The roof.

All those dead men on that roof. Fighters all. Slaughtered by this creature. Even though he'd known the truth, having it confirmed made the room suddenly close around him. He was very aware that it was just him, Auron, and a murdering—and very powerful—demon. The last time he'd faced a demon one-on-one it had... Well, he needed his companions—

Oh no.

'Where's Shift?' he snapped, readying his blade.

'Unconscious upstairs,' the demon said with a broad grin. 'The *master* wants the creature for something else.'

'Like what?' he asked quickly.

'Mind your damned business,' Beba hissed, pointing her finger at him as if it were a sword.

'I don't understand,' Auron said as he eyed the woman. 'How do you look like...you?'

With a half smile, Beba tapped the amulet around her neck. 'This isn't just a trinket. It's actually a very powerful healing charm. Funny fact about demons, it's actually the host's soul we possess and burn through. We latch onto them like a parasite and consume it. Once it's gone, so is the host. The physical stuff is just a side effect of that. This thing keeps enough of the soul intact that I can ride this body as much as I want. Though it does keep me in a weaker form. And apparently gives the woman a slight chance to fight back every now and then.' With a fake snarl, Beba made one of her hands into a claw. 'But when I take the amulet off...I get to show my true nature.'

'Handy,' Auron said dryly.

'Well, what can I say?' Beba shrugged. 'The Maestro knows when to get a lady a gift. Obviously, he waited until I was in a body worthy of it. Poor woman, she didn't even know who I was when I served her at the market. But her status gave me all the access I needed to Greer, his official seal, the investigation. You lot were the wildcard. I hoped my fire would burn you all to ash, but you people have a very stubborn refusal to die. Still, I managed to get you under my roof so I could keep you close. It's been funny watching you all grope around in the dark.'

'So you do work for him?' Nicolas asked. 'The Maestro.'

A dark look crossed the demon's face. 'I do what he asks.' Her voice suggested she didn't like it. 'He wanted chaos sown in this city so Nalbina had an excuse to try to annex the place. Luckily for me, I got to have fun doing it. It's just a shame I had to take everything so slowly. But the *master* doesn't like to show his hand too quickly.' Beba pouted. 'Still, I'm nearly done here.'

'Now that we have you cornered,' Nicolas ventured. He really hoped that was the case.

The demon laughed. 'You wish, human. I was going to wait until you had a mouthful of sandwich and snap your neck. You're too troublesome to risk playing with. Ro found that out the hard way, so I heard.' With a pleasurable breath, Beba ran her hands through her hair. 'Then tonight the spree finally begins. I get to cut loose. No more of this *one body at a time* nonsense. I kill, and kill, and kill. Then the city burns as mobs roam the streets accusing each other of the attacks, so the Maestro can cackle in glee as his plans come to fruition...or whatever it is he does.'

As Beba shook her head, her hair bobbed, again reminding Nicolas of his mother. He firmly reprimanded himself. This wasn't his mother, and it wasn't Beba. It was a demon. He couldn't flinch or lose focus. Not now.

'Is Garaz still alive?' Nicolas asked warily.

'The orc,' Beba hissed. 'The arrogance at believing he could track me down. I needed him out of the way, but I wasn't about to kill him. Oh no, he gets to sleep until I'm done with my other tasks. Then I'll spend days making him understand his folly.' For a moment her eyes lit up with glee. Nicolas didn't want to know what dark things the creature was thinking of doing to Garaz to make it so excited. 'It's become increasingly difficult to rein myself in, I confess, so I had to indulge my urges elsewhere. A little instant gratification, if you will.' The demon glanced toward the pantry door, where a pool of blood was spreading beneath it. The sound of a clunk drew his attention back to the counter. Beba had removed her amulet and put it down. She lowered her head.

'Time to see the true me.' She laughed. 'Well, as true as it gets in this realm.'

Her head rose. Now her teeth were fangs and her eyes single, red orbs. Her fingers extended into talons as her skin became covered in raw-looking burns.

'You've got this, kid,' Auron whispered in his ear. 'Don't panic.'

'*Oh, you should panic, human. Panic very much.*' The sound coming from Beba's mouth was no longer human. It reminded him of Koth's voice, that overlapping whisper of many voices as one.

Panic gnawed at him.

The demon sprang forward. Not even attempting to face it head on, he flung himself to the side. The claws meant to disembowel him turned an antique cabinet to kindling instead.

Nicolas went to yell for help then remembered he'd seen no guards around the estate either. Most likely they were in the pantry too.

Just me then. Against a demon. Hope it goes better than the last time I tried this.

The demon hissed.

Was he ever going to get the bloody armour the dwarf had promised him?

'*I'll remove your flesh from your bones,*' the demon snarled.

'Remember your training,' Auron counselled him urgently. 'This thing is ugly and deadly, sure, but it's just another opponent. This is what you've been preparing for.'

With a roar, the demon came again, claws swinging. He brought the blade up to meet them, and they clashed. Withdrawing a step, he couldn't suppress his gulp. He'd hoped the *Dawn Blade* would cut the creature's talons clean off, but no.

The fanged mouth smiled. Nicolas was starting to get the impression he was being toyed with. He didn't want to glance at the door, but he was trying to map how far it was from him.

Can I make it?

The demon crouched and launched itself. Nicolas threw himself to the side, rolling across the countertop to land on the other side. From the sound of shattering wood, he guessed a stool had taken the brunt of the demon's wrath. And now he could see the door clearly, because he'd placed himself on the other side of the kitchen from it.

Idiot.

'Who is the Maestro?' If he died, the information wouldn't help him any, but he wanted to know.

Raising a single claw, the demon waved it from side to side. *'Even if I could say, I would not.'*

'Where's Koth?'

'Pointless human.' The demon chuckled, a harsh, grating sound. *'You need no knowledge when you're dead.'*

'Koth tried to kill me once and failed,' Nicolas snapped back. 'And I'm guessing he was more powerful than you.'

The demon hissed through bared teeth, scraping its claws on the counter and leaving more gouges. *'He succeeded. Your soul was supposed to be tortured for all eternity in the Underworld. That was the will of he who commands us. But no, you came back somehow.'* Its face contorted in mock sympathy. *'Just to die again.'*

Pushing off with its hands, the demon flew at him again—or would have if a flying saucepan hadn't hit it in the side of the head mid-flight, sending it spiralling over the edge of the counter.

'Kitchens are for cooking,' the spirit snarled. 'And I'm in the mood to cook up a fine plate of victory.' Auron's face dropped. 'That was awful. I can do much better. Something about recipes? Ingredients? Serving up a dish of pain maybe?'

'Are you *serious*?' Nicolas cried. 'This isn't the time. I'm fighting a demon.' *And my sword hand is shaking.*

Auron gave him a sheepish grin. 'Sorry.' Then his expression hardened. 'Speaking of...' Grabbing the knife Beba had been using, he threw it into the shoulder of the rising demon. The creature's long tongue flicked out as it gasped in pain.

Seeing an opportunity, Nicolas charged. The *Dawn Blade* swung in a beautiful downward arc until the demon grabbed Nicolas by the throat. Instantly, his vision blurred as he gasped for breath in the vicelike grip. The clattering on the floor told him the *Dawn Blade* had slipped from his grasp. Nicolas had only a second to make a very unmanly sound before he was driven back into the nearby plate rack. As the rack vibrated from the impact, just like his bones, plates dropped from the high shelf, striking him on the head. Judging by the wet feeling on his scalp, one had cut him. But he had bigger problems. The demon raised him up by his neck single-handed before slamming him to the floor. For a moment, Nicolas thought the impact had knocked the soul right out of his body as he lay on the ground, blinking away the flashing lights and groaning feebly.

Above him, the demon reared up, claws ready to slash down and end him. And just for a change, he'd dropped his sword. The last thing he'd know was being disappointed in himself. The claws flashed towards him. He covered his head with his arms and winced.

'Kid. No!'

Silence.

Am I dead?

No, I've been dead before. I'm still alive, How's that then?

When he opened his eyes, bright light stung them. Once he'd looked past Auron's ethereal buttocks, though, he saw that the spirit was holding the demon's wrists, staying the motion that would've been a fatal blow against him.

The demon gawped at Auron. Nicolas was most likely making a similar face.

What's happening?

'I can touch demons.' The spirit's voice was full of wonder. 'That means...'

Letting go of the demon's wrists, Auron cracked the creature across the jaw with vicious left and right crosses. Grabbing the demon by the hair, he brought its face to meet his oncoming knee before punching it in the stomach, once, twice, thrice. Each one drove the creature back a step. Keeping his guard up, Auron held the demon's head up and drove his fist into it's nose, before pivoting on his foot, bringing his leg around in a circle and kicking it across the jaw. The demon was thrown over the nearest table by the force of the blow.

'I'm *back*!' Auron cheered, raising his arms high. 'Auron of Tellmark's still got it, people. Demon slayer extraordinaire, even in death.'

As happy as he was for Auron, *maybe* now wasn't the best time for gloating. The demon seemed to agree as it lunged from behind the table, swinging and catching the spirit with a backhanded blow that sent him reeling back toward Nicolas. For a moment, Auron's aura seemed diminished, as if he'd faded slightly.

'Well, I don't really care for *that*,' Auron remarked, as he became whole again. Or as whole as he got, anyway. 'I was hoping that'd be a one way deal.'

Nicolas rose, grabbing his sword. The spirit looked at the *Dawn Blade* in his hand then looked at his own belt. 'I wonder,' he mused as he drew the spirit sword gifted to him by Sha'then, Lord of the Underworld. 'If fists work, so should this.'

The demon advanced carefully now, stalking slowly towards them, claws ready.

Nicolas looked at Auron, who'd taken a similar guard position to him.

The spirit winked cockily. 'Ready, kid?'

'I think so,' he answered.

As a pair, they charged. At least Nicolas's battle cry was starting to get better. The demon certainly seemed to hesitate as they ran at it. Then it was swords and claws blazing. The pair moved to either side of the creature to utilise the advantage of their numbers to its fullest, but the demon was fast enough to duel them both. Each slash of the blade was met by a flash of claw.

I can't believe I'm fighting with Auron again.

The spirit cut low, going for the creature's feet. Deftly, the demon hopped over the blade, turning as it did and catching Nicolas with the tips of its claws. He staggered back, warm blood running down his cheek. That'd been too close. Only an inch from his eye.

Suddenly, fear gripped him. He was outmatched. All his training might be good for bandits and tavern ruffians, but against something like *this*? He was out of his depth and about to drown. Well, pieces of him would be drowning anyway. There was no way the demon wouldn't cut him to shreds, at the very least. He took a step back. It was nearly many steps, at speed.

As he watched, the creature ducked under Auron's attack, thrusting in with its claws. They entered his light aura, and Auron gasped and buckled. The spirit began to fade, like he was being drained out of existence.

'*No.*' Throwing himself forwards, he tackled the demon, picking it up and driving it into the nearest heavy cupboard, which shattered as they crashed into it. Grabbing the dazed demon's head, he bounced it off the corner of the table, before he jumped back far enough that he could use his sword. The *Dawn Blade,* swung and the creature reared back with a roar, blood flowing from the wound Nicolas had inflicted.

With a hiss of rage, the creature stared down at it's wound as Nicolas prepared himself for the inevitable counter-attack. It came quickly. The demon leapt at him, it's fanged mouth contorted in a feral snarl. Nicolas was so focused on the oncoming attack that he didn't see Auron until the spirit grabbed the demon by the hair and yanked it backwards.

Again, the demon's supernatural speed saved it from defeat. The creature spun mid air, closing on Auron so he couldn't use his sword effectively. But the spirit's experience in fighting showed instantly, Auron changing tactics and cracking the demon across the jaw with the hilt instead. As it staggered from the blow, Auron quickly stepped back and slashed with his sword. The demon lost a chunk from it's side.

Yet it was nowhere near done fighting. It practically flew through the air, striking Auron with a vicious backhand that sent him sprawling nearly the length of the room. Nicolas charged forwards, *Dawn Blade* already swinging. As he closed on the demon, which had it's back to him, he saw their victory. It was going to be slain. And then it was snatched from him. Turning on it's heel, the demon spun to face him, arm already in motion. Nicolas was too committed to his attack to stop. All he could do was watch in horror as the open palm came hurtling toward him. It was like being kicked by a giant. Suddenly, he was flying in the other direction.

Another rack of fine crockery suffered as he struck it at speed, before he fell to all fours. When he coughed, specks of blood decorated the floor beneath him. He was wheezing. Something was broken.

Staggering to his feet, he stared wide-eyed at the demon right in front of him. The claws cut across his chest, tearing into his flesh. Lines that burned like a raging inferno bled freely. Only the nearby table stopped him falling altogether as he stumbled backwards.

Where is that dwarf with my armour?

A demonic hand rose for a final attack, only to be driven back by the slashing of Auron's sword. It was hard for Nicolas to focus on what he was seeing. Crashing into the cabinet had disorientated him badly, but he caught Auron striking the creature under the jaw, lifting it slightly, before it crumpled to the kitchen floor. The spirit's follow-up downward stab found nothing as the creature rolled away. But Auron hadn't gotten where he was by being slow. Swinging his boot, the spirit kicked the demon in the face, rolling it away from them as he put himself between it and Nicolas.

'Are you okay, kid?' Judging by the expression in his white eyes, Auron already knew the answer to that question.

'No,' he answered honestly. 'You?'

Auron pointed to the breaks in his form created by the demonic claws. 'This doesn't look like anything, but it absolutely kills, kid. I didn't know I could even feel pain.'

Nicolas ducked as an entire table came flying at him. The piece of furniture passed straight through Auron and over his head before crashing into the wall and dropping to the floor like a stone.

That would've really hurt.

'As much as I hate to admit it,' Auron said, 'this thing's too strong for us.'

'What do we do?' Considering the demon was stalking towards them, they had little time to decide.

'I'll hold it off whilst you get the others,' the spirit said grimly.

'But you'll die,' he protested.

'It's okay, kid.' The spirit winked at him. 'This is the heroic last stand I was due anyway.'

'No,' he snapped. 'I am not losing you. I'm not losing Garaz, or Shift, or anyone else to this creature. This ends here, in a bloody kitchen, of all places.'

In the back of his mind, disappointment swelled. They'd never have a chance to subdue the creature and get answers about where his people were. But this was the only way it could go. It had to die.

'You and me then, kid.' Auron smiled. 'Some handy advantage might be nice.'

Just then, something caught Nicolas's eye. An idea popped into his head. 'Maybe we have one.'

'What?'

In just a second, the idea became a fully formed plan. A decent one, too, even if he did say so himself. 'Keep it busy.' That was pretty much what Auron had planned to do anyway, but Nicolas was changing the endgame to keep him alive. Well, dead. Existing.

The spirit looked confused but didn't argue, jumping towards the demon, blade slashing in all directions. Nicolas sheathed his own sword and ran around the table, picking up the item he'd seen. Already, Auron and the demon were locked in furious combat. Quickly, Nicolas circled behind the demon, giving Auron a nod. The spirit came at the demon with even greater fury, forcing it backward, towards Nicolas.

As he snuck up behind the creature, there was a moment when Nicolas knew he would die. He caught the slightest turn of it's head, indicating that the demon knew he was behind it. All he could do was watch as it's body shifted, ready to swing around and slice his face clean off with those terrible claws. But as it began to turn to finish him, it hesitated. Even catching the demon's expression sideways on, Nicolas could see the surprise in it's hideous face. Someone was fighting it. Someone they couldn't see.

Thank you Beba.

Nicolas struck.

With all the force he could muster, he kicked the demon in the back of the leg, dropping it to a single knee. Before it could react, he leapt on it's back, using the chain of the amulet like the garrotte a beggar in the alley had used on him. In the second the demon let out a choked cry of rage, he secured the clasp then wrapped his arm tightly around it's neck, holding the amulet in place. Desperately, he used his free arm to try and hold the demon's at bay. The talons cut at his hands and arms as the creature bucked and thrashed, trying to remove the amulet. Nicolas held on fiercely, moving with the demon and enduring the pain. Already, he could feel it weakening. The talons began to recede. It was becoming Beba again.

'Kid, step aside,' Auron cried.

Nicolas did as bid, moving aside just as the spirit's sword stabbed right through the demonic creature. Taking no chances, Nicolas drew the *Dawn Blade* and skewered it through the back. Pulling his blade free, Nicolas cried out as he swung it again, taking the demon's head clean off it's shoulders. Blood began to spurt everywhere from the wound, like it was Etherius's grossest fountain. The amulet, nothing now to hold it in place, clinked to the floor a second before the rest of the demon's body did. As it did, it's demonic form returned, though this time it would not hurt anyone. Ever again.

Auron delivered a final blow to the demon's head, most likely just to be on the safe side, as Nicolas collapsed against the nearest solid surface. He was dazed, battered and bleeding, but he also knew he had to move, to go and find Shift and Garaz.

'Take a second kid,' Auron said in a strained voice as he rested his hands on his knees. 'You're no help to them if you pass out half way up the stairs and bash your head in rolling back down. The demon said it was keeping them alive.'

That was true. As much as he shouldn't trust any word out of a demon's mouth, he had to believe in it's desire to torture, and obey it's master.

'You're getting better, kid.' Auron smiled warmly. 'You're getting a little less injured every battle. Not so long ago you would've been on the floor half dead. Now you're just...walking wounded.'

'This doesn't feel at all positive,' he said, grabbing a nearby towel and using it to put pressure on his bleeding chest, wincing with pain as he did. 'But at least the demon's slain.'

Not just the demon.

Looking at Beba's head on the floor, he said a prayer for her soul.

At least you're free now. May your soul rest peacefully in the Eternal Forest.

'How do we explain this to Lord Commander Greer?' he cried suddenly, panic blinding him to more pressing concerns. 'His wife...the demon...' It was pretty obvious with the dead creature on the floor that Beba had been the demon. But still, for the man to lose his wife, and the way they had killed her...

'Find our friends first,' the spirit replied with a thin smile. 'Explanations later.'

CHAPTER 52

Cold air hit him the moment he walked out the doors of the training hall, making his sweat-covered body tingle. Ban Dro had put him through his paces today. Every day, in fact, since he'd recovered from the fight with the demon. Nicolas now had a lovely new set of scars to greet him in the mirror whenever he took his shirt off. Healing potions and balms, not as effective as Garaz's magic, hadn't quite done the trick, but they came with the benefit of not making him feel like he was being set on fire.

Be a shame if things were too easy for me.

Since healing, he'd thrown himself into training. It looked like they might be stuck in Babylon for the winter, so he was determined to make the most of it. He would no longer rely on others to do his fighting for him. He'd seen the face of evil. But it was only one of many. And when the next one reared it's ugly head he intended to punch it. Hard.

There's one face of evil I haven't seen yet. The Maestro's. When I do, I'm going to hit him so hard they'll feel the tremors from the blow for miles around.

Even with the chilled air, a sense of optimism was noticeable in the city as he walked back to the tavern. Unsurprisingly, they were no longer welcome at Lord Commander Greer's manor. Greer had understood that the creature had no longer been his wife, but he couldn't tolerate the person who'd killed it under his roof. Nicolas still shuddered every time he thought of the lord commander's moan of anguish when he'd forced his way into the kitchen. Luckily, other men of the watch had gotten there first. It had taken six of them to stop Greer trying to kill Nicolas and drag him from the room. Even when they'd locked him in a room so they could explain what had happened, his cries of despair had echoed around every corner of his home.

But there'd been good with the bad. Beyond the normalcy returning to the city, there was no longer an army at their gate. Said army had approached but left once Governor Morrow presented them with the demon's head. During her discussion with the Nalbians, she'd even managed to get his status as a wanted man revoked. Deities knew how she'd managed that, but she was a formidable woman.

And another of the Maestro's schemes lies in ruins.

His mouth became a thin line as he thought of his parents, and his people still in that monster's clutches. Nature was enforcing a hold on their quest. Would there be a trail to pick up once winter had receded?

There has to be something.

In his mind, he played over the events since he'd left Hablock, scrutinising every detail for something they'd missed. He was so engrossed in his pondering that he didn't realise he'd returned to the tavern until Shift accosted him outside.

'You're back just in time to leave,' they said with a knowing smile.

'Where are we going?' he asked.

Shift clicked their tongue and winced slightly. 'I can't tell you that. Sorry.'

Should I be curious or nervous? 'Why not?'

'Auron told me not to.' They shrugged.

Definitely nervous. 'When did you start doing what you were told?'

That earned him a punch on the arm, which was thankfully already numb from training. Shift's punching hand looped around his arm and pulled him towards the door. 'You're ridiculously sweaty,' they remarked, wrinkling their nose.

For the first few days, Shift had joined him in training as a spectator. But soon they'd realised it was all too serious and spent their time exploring the city instead. Their promise to return Ban's knives had yet to be fulfilled—which might be another reason they were dodging the temple.

****

Shift led him through several of the city's districts until they were in the dwarven quarter. The buildings around him had become much squatter, yet the quality workmanship of the stone used to build them was obvious even at a glance. He heard the distinct clang of metal on metal before the smithy even came into view. Auron standing outside, bouncing on the spot like an impatient child, was a dead giveaway that this was their destination.

'About time,' the spirit snapped testily. 'I wondered how long you— Deities, you're sweaty.'

'Shift collared me right from training.'

'Just like you asked,' they said flatly to Auron, lest he moan at them for his state.

'Fine,' the spirit grumbled before the exuberance took hold again. 'Anyway, come in, come in.'

The heat of the smithy was welcome for all of two seconds before it became overbearing, but the dwarves working away seemed numb to it. He was led to a large back room where Silva and Garaz waited. Even now, he was pleased to see the orc up and well. As soon as the demon had been slain, the curse lifted, just as Auron had predicted. Both smiled knowingly at him as he entered.

Okay. Now *I'm nervous.*

'Ah, you're here,' Durag said with open arms as he strode into the room. 'I can't wait to see what you think of your new armour.'

Ooh, actually, this is quite exciting.

For Nicolas, the armouring was a strange process. Auron demanded that he keep his eyes closed throughout, and having a load of people touching his body and putting things on him when he couldn't see was a disconcerting process.

'Open your eyes,' Auron said finally, punctuating the sentence with a near giggle.

Is it done? It can't be. It doesn't feel like I'm wearing anything. How good is this armour if it's so light?

Slowly, he opened his eyes. Before him was a full-length mirror—very fancy—and staring back at him from it was...him, but not like he'd ever seen himself before. Over his chest was metallic plate armour so clean it practically shone. He flexed his shoulders but could barely feel the pauldrons as they bounced. It seemed simple, yet elegant, trimmed with golden filigree and some kind of symbol in the centre of the chest.

'It's light, but tough as any of yer bulky armour,' Durag said with pride. 'Only the very best for he who restored our honour.'

On his forearms were vambraces that should've impeded his movement—same with the greaves on his shins—but didn't. Tentatively, he moved different parts of his body. There was no resistance to his movement. It was amazing workmanship.

I don't deserve this, I'm just a—

He finally focused on the symbol in the centre of the chest plate. It was a rising sun, the same rising sun that had adorned Auron's armour in life and was now visible on his grinning ethereal form.

'This...This...' he stuttered.

'It's the mark of the *Dawnblade*.' Auron nodded. 'That's you now, kid.'

'I...wait...what?'

The spirit's smile grew more fatherly. 'Really, it's been you since you first picked up the sword. You just needed to grow into it. And I think right now the world needs a new *Dawnblade*.' Auron looked like he wanted to reach out to him. 'You've got a good heart, more courage than you believe, and now the skill to back it up. Honestly, I don't think there's anyone I'd rather pass my mantle to.' The spirit coughed uncomfortably. 'Although you need to work harder on your womanising, to keep the legacy going.'

'No, he doesn't,' Shift remarked dryly.

'Oh, by the way,' Auron said, turning to Silva, his smile dropping, 'don't kill this one.'

The warrior's face didn't even twitch, but there was a hint of regret in her eyes.

Nicolas found his finger tracing the rising sun symbol. Suddenly, the armour was heavier, with the extra weight of the responsibility.

What if I can't live up to this? It's Auron, after all.

It was tough to know what to say. A slew of emotions choked off his words before they left his mouth. He was honoured. Proud. Scared.

'Maybe one day I'll be an even better *Dawnblade*.' He chuckled, opting to keep it light lest he break down in front of his companions and sully the moment.

Auron let out a disbelieving laugh. 'Wrestle a troll naked, kid, and *then* come talk to me about who's the better *Dawnblade*.'

Distaste creased Garaz's brow. 'Why were you wrestling a troll naked?'

'Do you want to hear that story?' Auron asked with a raised eyebrow.

'No,' the orc said firmly.

'That *is* arrangeable,' Shift whispered in his ear, loud enough for all to hear.

He winced in distaste. 'I'm okay. Thanks, though.'

Shift shrugged indifferently.

Thank the Deities.

'I take it you're pleased then?' Durag asked leadingly.

That's an understatement. 'I'm so pleased. Thank you. You didn't—'

Durag raised a silencing hand. 'I bloody well did, young man. Gorin stained our entire race, and you cleansed that stain. You are forever a friend to the dwarves.' Durag patted him on the arm as if they were old friends. 'By the way, those vambraces are hard enough to deflect a cutting blade, seeing as your ghost companion refused a shield. Also, I did try to sell him on the helmet, but it was a no.'

Helmets were never comfortable. But a shield...

'Shields are for people who don't know how to fight,' Auron said firmly. Then he cast a glare at Durag. 'Kid, can you do me a favour?' Auron asked. 'Please tell the dwarf that if he ever refers to me as a ghost again, he'll suffer the *finger poke of doom* in a very sensitive spot.'

He didn't relay this sentence. Thankfully, before Auron could become irked by that, a member of the city watch entered the room. The man stood to attention before Nicolas as if he were addressing a general. He even saluted. 'Governor Morrow requests your presence immediately.' The young kascat's voice was tinged with awe.

'Very well,' Nicolas said, before turning to his companions. 'You coming?'

'Not interested,' Shift said. 'Silva and I are going shopping.'

The warrior did not look keen at that prospect. But she did keep giving loving glances to her own armour, which the dwarf had repaired after the fight with the demon on the rooftop. He'd been as good as his word, and given Silva and Garaz some sturdy looking chainmail undershirts. To Shift, he had gifted a new set of elegant looking lockpicks, along with sharpening their new knives.

'I'm going to investigate Professor Shaw's residence a little more,' Auron said. 'Put my head through some walls and make sure we didn't miss anything.'

Sergeant Tallith and Professor Shaw were still missing. Meaning there were still minions of the Maestro in the city. Hunting them down could give them a vital clue about where to go next, once winter passed.

And it'll be a good use of my time between training.

'I will join you, young Nicolas,' Garaz said with a slight bow. 'After having been laid up as I was, I find myself keen to stay on my feet and explore.'

Understandable.

'Very good, sir,' the kascat watchman said. 'The carriage is waiting.'

'We'll meet you back at the tavern,' Silva said with a nod.

'Until then.' Nicolas smiled then turned to follow the watchman.

A hand grabbed his arm and spun him back around. 'Um, excuse me,' Shift said with a furious look on their face. 'Do you not kiss me before you leave a room now?'

'I...um...well...'

Shift sighed and rolled their eyes. 'You're so easy, Nick. Go rub elbows with the politicians.' Tentatively, he went to turn again. But Shift grabbed his armour and pulled him into a kiss. Allowing him to back off slightly after that, they gave him a coy grin. 'If you ever hurt me or abuse my feelings, all the fancy dwarf armour in the world won't protect you. Understood?'

Like that would ever happen.

****

'Welcome,' Governor Morrow said as she rose and inclined her head to them. 'Please, take a seat.' As usual, she looked completely indifferent to her surroundings.

Both he and Garaz seated themselves.

'I thought it best Lord Commander Greer not join us today. As much as he understands, well...' The sentence hung in the air, the sentiment too complicated to put into words.

Nicolas and Garaz nodded.

'First, I need to apologise to you both,' the governor continued.

'Because?' he asked warily.

'You and your friends have done this city an amazing service, and this is the first time we've seen each other since,' the governor replied. 'And that is a disgrace on my part. Unfortunately, there has been some delicate political manoeuvring required in the wake of this crisis to ensure that Nalbina doesn't ever think about the words *peacekeeping force* again. And of course, the inevitable clean up with regards to Professor Shaw, whose patrons have become unsurprisingly quiet of late.'

'I can imagine,' Garaz said.

'There's still a way to go to ensure the bad feelings between the various races of the city have receded, but I am quietly hopeful for our future. To aid that, and properly thank you, there will be a parade in your honour next week. You will also be presented with medals at the steps of the citadel and named Protectors of the City.' This was all delivered in a tone that could've been used to discuss sewage works or what she was having for lunch.

'I... We are honoured, Governor.'

She looked him in the eye. 'It is *we* who are honoured,' she corrected as Nicolas flushed with pride.

'But this was not the only thing you brought us here for?' Garaz asked.

'Very astute,' the governor said with a raised eyebrow. 'The reason you are here is this.' From her drawer, she produced the healing amulet worn by Beba. 'This artifact is very powerful, and I do not want it in my city any longer than necessary.'

'But it's designed to heal,' Nicolas cut in.

'And it was used for evil,' the governor replied, studying the amulet in her hand. 'And I will not risk that again. The chaos may have passed, but I fear it wouldn't take much to stoke it again. I would bid you and your companions take it to the Academy of Magic, where it can be properly secured once winter passes.'

Nicolas looked towards the door of the office. 'But you have plenty of men to do that.'

The governor pursed her lips.

Garaz spoke first. 'You fear corruption in the ranks.'

'I fear the city has been infiltrated by elements working against the principle it was built upon,' she replied. 'I believe some of these elements may work in our own security forces, yes. As much as it pains me, you are the only ones I can truly trust with this matter. That is why I'm giving it to you now instead of keeping it here, under guard, until winter passes and it can be taken from the city.'

This, annoyingly, was something he had experience with. The military of Sarus had been heavily corrupted by the malign influences of gangsters and rogue chancellors. But that meant he knew how important the request being made of them was. 'Of course we'll do it,' he said firmly.

'Thank you,' the governor replied. 'Can I just say that I approve of your new armour. Very appropriate.'

Nicolas found himself stroking the rising sun symbol on his chest plate. He hoped he could live up to it.

They left the office with the governor's thanks and the amulet safe in Nicolas's pocket. It was strange going back down the corridors, a paranoid man's nightmare.

Who can be trusted? Did that guard just look at me funny?

'Are you well?' Garaz asked with concern.

'Yes,' he replied. 'I'm just not comfortable carrying this amulet.'

The orc chuckled. 'It's a healing charm.'

'That's been on a demon.'

Garaz smiled. 'It will not be tainted. But if you are concerned, I could carry it for you?' The orc held out his clawed hand.

Nicolas looked at the hand and thought. He really wanted to give it to Garaz, but Governor Morrow had summoned him specifically, appointed him for this errand. As distasteful as he found his cargo, something in him just couldn't give it up.

If only I'd given up that bloody delivery to Potter.

Every time he thought of the people he'd lost, a stab of pain would lance his heart. Hopefully, at least Potter was still alive.

'It's okay,' he said finally. 'I'll carry it.'

'Very well.' Garaz smiled. 'You understand that it was created for good, though.'

'Of course,' Nicolas said as they continued. 'But The governor's right. Even something made for good can be misused if it falls into the wrong hands. It's best kept in a secure place so that can't happen again.'

'And you believe the Academy of Magic to be this place?'

Nicolas looked at the orc. 'I hope so. You disagree?'

Garaz sighed. 'In my experience, the place has agendas. It should not, as it should be dedicated to learning and magic. But where there are people, there are agendas. Such is the world.'

'Governor Morrow seems to trust them.'

'Hopefully that isn't her being naïve.'

The doors of the citadel were directly ahead of them when Garaz stumbled. Quickly, Nicolas grabbed him. 'Are you okay?'

'I...I think so,' the orc said, his brow furrowed. 'Maybe...an after-effect of the curse?'

'Let's get you sat down.'

Despite the guards, the citadel was quiet. Seeing a side room, Nicolas led Garaz into it and sat him down.

'Thank you,' the orc said, looking at his feet and breathing heavily. 'I think maybe the demon's curse lingers.'

Nicolas reached into his pocket and took out the amulet, removing it from the cloth it'd been wrapped in. The ruby was undeniably beautiful, almost hypnotic. 'Maybe it's because you're close to this,' he said thoughtfully. 'The demon wore it for a long time.'

Garaz stared at the amulet. 'But it can help many, if used properly.'

'Don't worry.' Nicolas smiled. 'Once we get it away safely, we can take the time to find the right people to use it. Unfortunately, there are too many who do wrong, even thinking they're doing good. Like the professor.'

The orc kept his gaze low. 'It is sad that sometimes we must all do things for the greater good. They may seem bad, but only because others cannot understand their reasons.' His tone was almost sorrowful.

'If this necklace proves anything,' he replied, tucking the amulet back into his pocket, 'it's that power, even created for purity, can be misused.'

Garaz rose, put his hand on his cheek, and smiled. 'You are everything Auron believes you to be and more. You have a good heart, young Nicolas. It is just a shame it sometimes blinds you to the necessity of life.'

That's cryptic. Maybe insulting.

In any other situation, Nicolas could've blocked what happened next, but the surprise of it stupefied him for that vital second. Garaz's staff cracked him across the jaw, his neck snapping to the side as his body spun. The room dipped and rose like a furious, stormy ocean. He couldn't even form a coherent thought.

A muscular green arm coiled around his neck like a serpent, and Nicolas was raised from the floor, choking. Desperately, he fought the grip, slapping at the hand and trying to claw his attacker's face. But Garaz had grabbed him quickly and tightly. His strength was already ebbing away. He didn't have long.

Why?

He began to feel drunk. Then sleepy. His eyes became heavy. He poured everything he had into keeping them open, but it was like trying to stop an avalanche. His limbs went limp. He had nothing left. As his eyes closed, and the light extinguished, Nicolas had one last thought.

Why?

Epilogue

Will they stop glaring at me? Don't they know who I am? I won the Academy of Science Laureate Award three years in a damned row.

Part of him wanted to return his captors' glares, to defy their opinions of him. But if Professor Nathanial Shaw was anything, it was a smart man, and he knew better. Instead, he kept his gaze on his feet as the two watchmen continued their disdainful looks.

I was celebrated. Adored. And now this.

His lips trembled as his fists closed in anger.

It was an accident. That's what it was. What are a handful of lives measured against the thousands that could be saved by my work?

He dared not voice that opinion aloud. His indignation was up, but he still knew the beating his words might earn him if they escaped his lips.

If I'd only had more time. I would have made it work.

'It's already starting to get bloody cold out,' a voice commented from beyond the wagon.

It wouldn't if I'd just been left alone. Damnable governor. Damnable city watch.

'It's going to now,' came a gruff reply. 'I bet the fur traders are smiling and rubbing their hands together. Doubtless they thought they'd have a lean year.'

The first voice scoffed. 'You watch the prices go up.'

'Yeah,' snorted the second. 'And all because of that fraud.'

Fraud? Fraud? Indignation rose from his belly anew. *Who are these common men to speak of me in such a way?* He was a man of science, a man of invention. He'd tried to help people, and all he'd gotten in return was their disrespect. Indignation became anger.

This is unfair, all of it.

He'd not murdered anyone. He hadn't known a demon would slip out, and when he discovered it, he'd tried to make it right. Well, he'd engaged his guards to do so. He was a man of science and had important work to do. His designs needed to be made whole, so the world didn't have to rely on mystical nonsense.

Yet here you are, Shaw, in a prison wagon escorted by idiots who couldn't begin to fathom your potential. Ingrates, all of them.

His patron would take care of this interruption. He knew the value of his work. Besides, when the cold really set in, they'd be begging him to return to work, and Deities, would he make sure they paid for the injustice he'd suffered.

There was a slight jolt as the wagon creaked to a halt. 'Who goes there?' he heard the sergeant—Tallith, was it?—shout from the driver's seat. There was an ominous silence. 'I said, identify yourself,' the voice demanded.

As he strained to hear, Shaw thought he caught a slight whistling sound in the air. There was a sudden gasp then a thud on the floor next to the wagon. Then everything beyond the wagon turned to chaos.

Men's shouts of alarm overlapped each other.

'Defensive formation.'

'It's a trap.'

'They're everywhere.'

Soon, those cries were joined by the clashing of metal on metal, grunts of effort, and screams of pain.

And then, the silence again. In the wagon, the two officers had their swords drawn. As if the fools could even swing them in this confined space. Yet the boys looked ready to try, in between exchanging nervous glances with one another. Shaw wasn't nervous. His patron had come.

Or had he?

What if it's some disgruntled friend or lover who incorrectly blames me for their loved one's death? If this city had one thing in abundance, it was fools.

The doors swung open, and before the guards could cry a challenge, one was dead, arrow embedded in his chest. As his wide-eyed companion watched him fall to the floor, he suffered a similar fate.

Shaw squirmed back against the wall of the wagon, away from the dead men. He was a man of science. He didn't deserve this.

There was a creak as two men boarded the wagon. He couldn't see their faces; they were covered in leering metal masks.

'Now see here—'

But his words turned into a cry of alarm as a bag was roughly thrown over his head. Unceremoniously, he was dragged from the wagon.

Do they not know who I am?

****

After being shoved into another conveyance, he'd travelled for what seemed like an eternity with nothing to see but the worn old sack. He was aware of men around him, as much as he was aware of the cold sweat of fear that drenched the bag confining his head. He could feel their presence and catch the muted whispers with which they spoke to each other.

Eventually, the wagon came to an abrupt halt. His arms were taken, and he was guided from the wagon before being escorted...somewhere.

Am I to be left to die in some back alley?

No, not possible. If they wanted to kill him, they would've done it in the wagon.

So what do they want?

Curiosity replaced fear.

They were indoors. He could tell with the change in temperature, plus the tell-tale crackling of wood in a fireplace. The bag was removed.

He was in a dwelling. Small, but homely. Toys on the floor spoke of a family, as did the portraits on the walls. Middle class, maybe. There were no extravagances here, just practical decorations.

Beside him stood the two men who'd taken him from the wagon. Another pair stood dutifully beside a door at the far side of the room, wearing the same masks as their compatriots. Shaw was sat at a dinner table and in front of him was a plate of hot food. Strange he should notice that first, rather than the man who sat directly across from him.

Unlike the rest, his face was uncovered. A neatly trimmed beard and a charming, yet roguish smile greeted him. Beyond that he wore black armour of a familiar design, save for the heart carved into the chest plate.

'Before you ask,' the man said in a thick western accent, 'it was your patron who arranged your little jail break.'

Thank the Deities. He was safe then. Yet still he was troubled. 'You're not Tavish,' Shaw probed. 'I'm used to dealing with Tavish.' Talking properly was still a struggle. That warrior bitch had broken his nose. So Shaw spoke slowly. He would not sound like some mentally deficient dolt.

The man sat back in his chair with the comfort of someone in charge of the room, putting his hands behind his head in a leisurely manner. 'Tavish is dead,' he said bluntly. 'Hazard of the job. Apparently, it comes to you no matter how many weapons you carry around with you. I'm the new Tavish.'

'And you are?'

The man smiled. 'You can call me Blackheart,' he replied. 'Old Alric Tavish going around using his real name is one of the things that got him killed, so I reckon. Henceforth, we'll be using titles, rather than names.'

The man, Blackheart, looked at him and winked. 'And Lord goes in front of the name, just so you know.'

Utter nonsense. But if that's what my patron demands, who am I to argue?

'Eat up,' the man said, gesturing to the plate. 'It'll go cold.'

He was very hungry. All the stress of the raid and the accusations. Yes, food was what he needed. Taking a leg of mutton, he bit into it, closing his eyes to savour the warmth and nourishment. Then he took a long gulp from the goblet beside the plate, some of the liquid spilling down his cheeks. 'I thought my patron may have sent...' He really didn't want to say the name.

'Koth?' the man suggested. 'Nah, mate, he's busy elsewhere. Besides, we figured you'd prefer the human touch.'

Too right. He'd only glimpsed that thing once, when the ritual to open the portal was performed, and it'd haunted his dreams ever since. He prayed he wouldn't have to deal with that creature again. Quietly, he was quite pleased not to have to deal with Tavish either—a serious, humourless fellow with no imagination. This Blackheart seemed much more personable.

'I confess myself surprised you bothered to rescue me,' Shaw admitted between mouthfuls. 'I never fully got my design to work. It was going to, mind you,' he added quickly, pointing at his new facilitator with the leg in his hand. 'Time was against me.'

'Well, we aren't done with you yet, despite your defiance.'

Shaw's mouth hung open, hovering above the mutton he'd been about to take a bite from. 'What do you mean?' he said finally, very aware that he was surrounded.

'I believe you were told to leave the demon be,' the man said casually, drawing a knife and studying it. 'Yet you had a little bout of conscience and tried to interfere, to put the demon back in the box.' With a sigh, he laid the knife on the table. 'Still, that's what we get for letting you have private security. But the master wanted as few direct ties to you as possible. He likes things neat.'

'I'm sure he does.' For some reason, Shaw couldn't take his eyes off the knife, lest it leap from the table and embed itself in his neck.

'But he does have a poor tolerance for people having their own agendas,' the man continued. 'Old Geldheart—there's one who fancied himself smarter than he was—learned that the hard way. He was told not to use something, and he tried to do it anyway. And turns out, he wasn't as indispensable as he thought.' The sentence was punctuated by a roguish wink. 'Sometimes you have to cut dead weight...'

Subtle.

Shaw jumped as the man slammed his palm on the table, dropping his food back onto the plate.

'Still,' the man grinned, 'no use crying over the dead, or losing our demon.'

Our...demon? Our?

'You won't overstep again, will you, though, mate?' Blackheart tapped one finger pointedly on the hilt of the knife.

Ignoring the implications of this new man's words, for now, Shaw gathered himself. 'So, I am not in trouble?'

'Not at all.' Blackheart tapped his knuckles on the table and pointed at him. 'The Maestro understands. You were on the cusp of getting it to work. You were so close.' He grinned. 'Besides, you didn't really *run out* of time. In truth, your time was taken from you.'

'Ignoramuses.' Shaw snorted indignantly. 'Fools who don't see the benefit of my work. If they'd just let me carry on...finish...'

'Fools are everywhere.' The man across from him chuckled. 'But your patron, he sees the benefit of your work.'

Fantastic. 'So I shall be removed from this dire city and set up elsewhere? Winter is nearly upon us and my system—'

Blackheart raised a hand. 'We'll get you out of the city, but as for your work...well, that's going to change direction slightly.'

'What do you mean?' His anger began to run away with him. 'I cannot simply *stop* when I'm this close to my breakthrough. Absolutely preposterous.'

Blackheart gave him an intense look, and Shaw suddenly realised that behind the charm was a deadly man. He wrung his hands nervously as the man reached down beside him. Surely after the theatrics with the knife, he wouldn't just kill him now?

'Here you go, have a look at this.' Blackheart put a rolled-up piece of parchment onto the table. Curiosity drove away Shaw's annoyance and fear. He'd found over the years that curiosity was good at driving away many emotions. Pushing the plate and goblet aside, he unrolled the parchment.

His eyes widened as he studied it. It was a design. An immense design. His fingers traced lines of detail, as his eyes poured over written notes. It was a thing of beauty, an impossible thing of beauty. 'You...you want me to work on *this*?' He scarcely dared to hope.

Blackheart smiled at him. 'It's nearly done, mate. We just need you to make it work.'

Shaw barely heard. His mind was full of calculations and ideas, his pudgy fingers tracing the design again. *This*, this would change the world. It took him a while to even remember that other people were in the room with him. Finally, looking up, he asked a hopeful question. 'When do we begin?'

'Soon,' the man answered, leaning forward. 'There's just one problem first.'

'What do you mean?' he asked nervously.

Blackheart pointed a finger at him. 'We need to make sure that little ember of conscience you had recently doesn't pop its ugly head up ever again. *Ever.*'

And if it does...I'm dead.

'It won't,' Shaw said with what he hoped was authority. 'I tried to help everyone, and all I got as reward was being unceremoniously thrown into a wagon. You can be assured my conscience understands that.'

Blackheart clicked his fingers in triumph. 'That's what I like to hear,' he said with a laugh. 'Be ready to leave in the morning.'

He was ready to go now. It wasn't like he had anything to pack. The intellectually weak had taken all his possessions. This would teach them his worth in the world, though. This would show everyone his value.

Acknowledgements

Firstly, let me start by asking a question...

Gemma, are you happy now? They got together.

I'd never solidly planned for that to happen when I was mapping the series, it's simply the way the writing went. Which, itself, shows you how much detail I put into planning my books in advance. I think it was around book 3 I actually made the decision and committed to it. Yes, Nicolas and Shift had the flirty banter before that, but The Odd Sea was when I finally decided that I wanted to build their relationship into something. But if it came too easily, well, where's the fun in that, which is why I teased it out and waited until now. Were any of you fooled by that *just friends* nonsense? I can't deny, a part of me will miss the inevitable message from Gemma after every book release asking me when they are getting together.

I would also like to make an apology – Beba, yes I did name a character after you and then kill them off brutally...can you forgive me?

On the subject of demonic killers, I like to make sure each book in the series has a slightly different feel to it, because it makes the series more interesting. So far we've had homages to heist movies, nautical adventures, and of course a good old fashioned origin story. Here we had a murder mystery (with all the necessary fantasy additions). Did you realise that Beba was the demon? I hoped Sergeant Tallith would throw you off the scent. I didn't want to make it too obvious, but at the same time, because the story was more complex, I was worried about plot holes aplenty.

Luckily, I have Dani to help with that. My ever amazing editor did her usual magic to the manuscript, touching things up here and there and pointing out bits I'd written that just plain didn't make sense. She continues to be an absolute legend!

As is my mum, Christine, who hunts down incorrect spelling and grammar for me with all the passion of the Babylon City Watch trying to catch demonic killers.

Speaking of legends, I can't go without mentioning my Kickstarter backers, who once again helped me fund this book for publication. Having built a following on that platform means the world to me, because it helps me live out my dream of making Nicolas's life a nightmare.

But hey, at least he has his armour now, and the official use of the name *Dawnblade*. So I am nice to him...sometimes.

You could argue that point, given how the book ended. What the hell was Garaz playing at? Should you never trust an orc? You'll find out in Book 7, very aptly titled, The Pursuit.

Until then,

Thank you for reading,

And keep adventuring,

Andrew

ABOUT THE AUTHOR

Andrew Claydon has an imagination, one full of variety.
Sometimes it's funny, sometimes it's adventurous, sometimes it's shocking, and occasionally it's outright strange...but it's never boring!
Andrew is a UK author who grew up loving fantasy movies such as Conan, Krull, Beastmaster and Willow. The epic worlds and battles of swords and sorcery therein inspired him to create his own fantasy worlds, adding to them his own brand of irreverent humour; because sometimes it's good to chuckle in between sword fights!
He wants to inspire the imagination of others, just as he's been inspired; with dashing heroes, epic quests and vile villains.
So reader beware, you aren't just opening a book, but a doorway into Andrew's imagination. It'll be a strange journey, but an entertaining one!
When he isn't writing, he loves to read sci/fi and fantasy novels. It's one of the things that inspires him to write himself. He also enjoys playing Warhammer 40,000 and is a keen wrestling fan.
He has degrees in both history and psychology, as well as black belts in several martial arts.
When he isn't creating vast fantasy worlds and populating them with good guys and bad guys to run around fighting each other, he works as a supported employment coordinator, helping others to try and achieve their aspirations.
Subscribe to my newsletter for the latest publishing news (and a FREE prequel novella) at: www.andrewclaydonauthor.com
Or follow me on social media:
Facebook: Andrewclaydonauthor
Instagram: @authorandyc
Tiktok: @authorandyc
If you enjoyed the book, then please leave a review with your preferred retailer.
Reviews are really important to indie authors to help them get their work out there.
If you do take the time to leave a review, thank you.

ALSO BY

Chronicles of the Dawnblade Series
The Simple Delivery
Strange Companions
The Odd Sea
Wrath and Wraiths
Trail of Death
Demons and Disorder
The Pursuit

Novellas and short stories
A Grudge is Born
The Gathering
Don't you know who I am?
How I learned to hate adventuring

If you are interested in any prequel and bonus chapters for the book series, then get in touch using the email address below!

andrew@andrewclaydonauthor.com

(Or if you just want to talk about the series...I'm always happy to chat to fans!)

www.ingramcontent.com/pod-product-compliance
Lightning Source LLC
Chambersburg PA
CBHW030940120726
47906CB00002B/658